SAY
GOODBYE
FOR
NOW

Also by Catherine Ryan Hyde

SAY GOODBYE FOR NOW

A Novel

CATHERINE RYAN HYDE

LAKE UNION
PUBLISHING

Published by Lake Union Publishing, Seattle

www.apub.com

Amazon, the Amazon logo, and Lake Union Publishing are trademarks of Amazon.com, Inc., or its affiliates.

ISBN-13: 9781503939448
ISBN-10: 1503939448

Cover design by Shasti O'Leary Soudant

Printed in the United States of America

PART ONE

THE HALF-WILD PRINCE

June 1959

Chapter One: Dr. Lucy

The knock propelled her out of sleep and set the dogs barking. Or maybe the knock propelled the dogs out of sleep and their barking finally broke through the nightcap, the sleeping pill, and the exhaustion.

Winston the greyhound, the only dog allowed to sleep in her room and on her bed, sat up and stared in the direction of the windows, growling softly.

She stood, cursing under her breath as a way of dismissing fear, and crossed to the windows.

She opened them out into the cool night and looked down.

Below her on the front porch stood two young men, dressed in matching uniforms of white T-shirts and jeans. Even their flattop haircuts looked identical. The only obvious difference, at least at this distance and in the dark: one was a good six inches taller than, and had forty pounds on, his companion. That and the fact that the little man's T-shirt was soaked through with a jagged map of bright blood.

"Who is it?" she called, making her voice the equivalent of a high barbed-wire fence guarded by dogs. As if to aid in the effect, the sixteen dogs in the downstairs runs continued to rage, barking and howling their fear and displeasure.

"Ma'am?" the larger man called up.

"Who is it?" she repeated.

Truthfully, she knew from experience that she would never know—or care—who they were. Only why they were here, which was clear enough already.

"Are you the doctor?"

"The question at hand is not who I am. It's who you are."

"We're supposed to say Victor sent us."

Lucy sighed and blinked a few times, grasping that fully waking up was no longer optional.

"Give me a minute to get dressed," she said, "and then I'll be down."

———

She led them through her living room, though in a more traditional sense it was no such thing. More of a zoo, really. It was lived in, all right, but never by humans.

She led the little guy by one arm, because he was beginning to go all puny and faint.

The big man stared into the cage of Archimedes the owl, who stared back. Then the man walked on, but shied suddenly like a spooked horse when Angel the golden eagle lifted and spread her wings.

"What is that?" he asked, steadying himself and pointing to an animal huddling in the shadows in a cage on the floor.

"That would be a pig."

"In the house?"

"Too much risk of infection outside."

Dr. Lucy led the men into her examining room and helped the wounded man onto the operating table.

"What're you doing with all these animals?" the big man asked.

"Fixing them," she said simply.

"Hey!" the little guy piped up. "Are you a vet?" Then, to his companion, "Did you take me to a vet—"

Dr. Lucy could tell he had almost spoken his friend's name, then censored himself.

"I'm not a veterinarian," she said. "I'm a doctor."

"A regular people doctor?"

"Yes. A doctor of human beings."

"Then why do you take in all these animals?" the big man asked.

"Because nobody else seems inclined."

"I'm not so sure about a lady doctor," the man on the table added.

"Yeah, well, beggars can't be choosers," his friend shot back, effectively shutting down the complaint.

The big guy continued to pace around the room, staring out windows into the dark and examining the medical certificates on the walls. Each time he passed by a window the dogs—outside in their runs—set up barking again.

"My name is . . . Steve," he said. "And this is Jake. Those aren't our real names, though. You know how it is."

Dr. Lucy said nothing. She was trying to figure out how best to remove the small man's bullet- and blood-damaged T-shirt, assuming he would want to wear it out into the night again. Well, he would want to wear *something*, she figured, and this seemed to be all he had.

The bullet had gone through the back of the man's left shoulder, seeming to indicate that he had been running away when shot. There was no exit wound in the front.

"What do we call you?" the big man asked.

Dr. Lucy looked up and leveled him with a gaze that stopped his pacing in its tracks.

"I respond to 'Doc,' 'lady,' and 'hey, you.' Listen. *Steve* . . ." She exaggerated the name for effect. "This is not what you might call a long-term relationship. I'm not so sure about this idea of our needing to be on a first-name basis. How about we skip the introductions and just get this done so I can get back to sleep?"

"Yeah, yeah," the man whose name was certainly not Steve said. "No need to get ticky. You got something he can bite down on? Maybe a kitchen spoon? Like a wooden spoon?"

While he spoke, Dr. Lucy filled a hypodermic with a local anesthetic and said nothing.

"Because, you know. He's my buddy, and besides, we want to keep the screaming down. Not that anyone could hear us way out here, but—"

He stopped talking suddenly when she buried the needle into "Jake's" back near the entrance wound, right through his T-shirt.

"Ow!" the stuck man yelled.

The dogs set up barking again, briefly.

"You've been watching too many motion pictures, *Steve*," she said. Then, to her patient, "We'll give that a few minutes to work."

She stepped over to one of her counters to fetch a pack of cigarettes. She leaned on the counter and lit one with the silver lighter that had been tucked under the pack's cellophane.

"Hey," the wounded man said. "That's starting to feel a little better."

"Yeah, well, that's my job," she said, blowing a cloud of smoke toward the examining room's ceiling. "Which leads me to a point. It's my job, not my hobby. In other words, I do it for money. A hundred."

"A hundred?" both men echoed.

"That's a little steep, don't you think?" the big man said. "We could go to the emergency room and get out for maybe thirty, tops."

Dr. Lucy pulled another deep drag. She had no patience for games and no innate ability to hide her impatience.

"If you could go to the emergency room," she said, "that's where you'd be."

"Yeah, yeah. All right. A hundred."

"In advance."

"Why in advance?"

"Because one guy walked out of here without paying. You can thank him for the new policies."

"The money's out in the car," the big man said. Sheepishly enough that she knew he would go get it.

"Well, don't just stand there."

He sighed and walked out.

The small wounded man stared into her eyes the way one might expect a hamstrung deer to regard a hovering wolf or coyote.

"You've done this kinda thing before, right?" he asked.

"Oh yes."

"Does it hurt?"

"Some. You'll feel it. But with that lidocaine I just shot into your shoulder, I expect it'll hurt less than it did to get out of the car and walk up to my front door."

"That's good to hear, ma'am. Can I trouble you for one of those cigarettes?"

She took the pack off the counter and shook it in his direction until three cigarettes popped up to be grabbed. He took one, and she lit it for him.

"I appreciate your not asking how I got myself into this bind," he said.

"At the emergency room they ask questions. And, more to the point, they file reports. That's why I charge more."

"Yes, ma'am."

"Steve" returned and pushed a hundred-dollar bill in her direction. She took it without comment and tucked it deep down into the pocket of her skirt.

Then he glared at his friend on the table. "That's coming out of your half," he said.

"What? Why? It's not my fault I caught that bullet, not you. Dumb luck is all."

"Yeah, well, dumb luck just cost you a hundred bucks."

"You ready, Jake?" Dr. Lucy asked, wanting an end to the squabbling. No reply.

"Or whatever your name is?"

"Oh, me. Right. Yeah. Let's get this done."

"I'm going to leave this T-shirt mostly where it is. Just pull it up enough to get to the problem. It would hurt a lot to take it off and put it back on, and I don't want to cut it off. Because I expect you won't want to walk out of here without it."

She almost gave him a piece of advice. She almost said, "Make your next stop someplace where your friend here can buy you a clean shirt. Maybe something you can put on right over this. Nothing like red on white to attract attention."

She didn't.

She was being paid for basic wound care. Not to help him get away, beyond that, with whatever he'd done.

"Yes, ma'am. What're you going to do now?"

"What you paid me to do. Try to relax."

She stubbed her cigarette out in the ashtray on the counter. The patient continued to smoke his. If anything, he smoked faster.

She chose fine forceps from a jar of alcohol on the counter, wiped the instrument off with sterile gauze, and entered the wound with its long tips. She made it fast. It's better to make it fast, she had learned. To get beyond the idea of gentleness and caution. Because the patient is suffering every minute those forceps are exploring the wound. Psychologically if nothing else. The patient wants you to be done.

She grasped the mangled bullet, pulled steadily until it was free, and tossed it in the direction of the metal trash bin. It hit the inside of the bin with a clang that made both men jump.

Dr. Lucy placed two sutures in the flesh of the entry wound, dressed it with a sterile gauze pad, and pulled the shirt back down into place.

"There," she said. "You're as good as you ever were. However good that was."

The men ignored the slight and moved toward the door.

"Wait," she said. "I need to give you some tetracycline. So that doesn't get infected."

She counted him out thirty of the pills into a paper envelope.

"Three a day until they're gone."

It might or might not be enough, she knew. But Dr. Lucy was happy to let the patient's care be somebody else's problem after that.

"And you probably need a tetanus booster. But I don't happen to have one."

And she knew he likely wouldn't get one. But anyway, she had done her duty. She had advised the patient.

———

"On your way to Mexico?" she asked as she walked them to the door.

The big guy turned back, blinking.

"Mexico?"

"Yeah. Mexico. You know it? It's a country near here. I figured that's why you were on that highway. Most people who come by here are headed south."

"No, ma'am. Not us. We live around here."

"Uh-huh," she said. "Good to know."

They left without further comment, and she was blissfully alone again. At least, alone in human terms.

—

On the way back through the living room, Archimedes stared deeply into her face. Truth be told, he always did. There was nothing special to be read into his gaze and—at some level—she knew it.

"Don't you give me that look," she said. "You think I do this for myself? Well, I don't. I do it for you and your friends."

Then she put herself back to bed.

Chapter Two: Pete

"Hey, Petey," Jack said. "Whose dog is that?"

Pete shaded his eyes from the sun with one hand and looked up and down the deserted stretch of two-lane highway.

"Don't see a dog."

"There. Lying down."

Then Pete saw the dog—lying flat out on his side on the highway shoulder—but figured he was dead.

"Got hit, most likely," Jack said.

"We should go see if he's okay."

They set off down the highway shoulder together, even though it led them in the wrong direction, away from the lake. It was early morning, the first day of summer vacation from school, and the goal had been fishing. Not looking at a perfectly good dog someone had killed on the highway, which Pete figured would likely ruin his whole day. Or, if it was gruesome, maybe even his whole summer.

Pete liked dogs, provided they were healthy and alive.

"I don't know that dog," Pete said to Jack as they drew closer. "You'd think we'd know all the dogs around here."

"Maybe he's not from around here. Maybe somebody didn't want him and they put him out of the car."

"Maybe he's not hit then. Maybe he's just taking a nap while he's waiting and hoping they'll come back for him."

"That would be nice," Jack said.

He was a big dog, Pete couldn't help noticing. It brought a slight jump to his stomach. He liked dogs but he could be afraid of them, too. It depended on the dog. This one looked grayish-tan with a heavy coat like one of those sled dogs up in Alaska, where Pete had never been and didn't figure he'd ever go. Which was about as far away from south Texas as Pete figured you could get.

"He's not moving," Jack said when they were less than ten steps away.

Just at that moment the dog lifted his head and looked right into Pete's face, causing Pete's blood to run cold and making him wonder why the dog couldn't have given Jack that scary look instead.

The dog struggled up onto three paws—one of his back legs seemed to hang limp from the hip—and tried to move away from the boys. Instead he quickly collapsed to his side again with a pained grunt. But at least it got him a couple of steps farther from the traffic lane of the highway.

"Oh yeah," Pete said. "He's hit all right. Poor guy."

"What're we gonna do?"

"We gotta take him to the vet, I guess."

"Why us?"

"You see anybody else around?"

"Damn," Jack said. "There goes fishing."

Pete eased a little closer to the dog, one hand out as a peace offering.

"It's okay, boy. We're not going to hurt you. We want to help. That's okay, boy."

The dog's upper lip peeled back. It was a silent but terrifying gesture, displaying a shockingly long and pointy set of canine teeth on either side.

Pete stepped back, feeling the blood drain from his face.

"I ain't going near that dog," Jack said. "No chance, no way. I'm going fishing. You coming or not, Petey?"

"We can't just leave him here."

"I can."

"Well, I can't."

"Damn. I hate fishing alone. Well, okay, Petey, if that's the way you want it. But gimme your hook and line at least, so I can have two hooks in the water. I'll catch more that way."

One eye on the dog for safety, Pete pulled his "poor man's fishing pole" out of his pocket. At least that was what Jack's daddy called it. It was really just an old empty beer can with the line wrapped around it, so you could reel back in by rewrapping line around the metal can.

"Yeah, okay," Pete said, "but you have to give it back to me when you're done. My dad doesn't drink beer."

"I know you always say that, but everybody's dad drinks beer," Jack said.

"Not mine."

"What does yours drink?"

"Bourbon. In those heavy bottles with the square sides. Not the same at all."

Jack took the makeshift fishing gear and stuck it in his shorts pocket, so that he bulged comically on both sides instead of just one.

"I can't believe you're missing out on fishing over this dog. It's not even your dog. It's not even friendly. First day of summer, too. How much of it you gonna waste?"

Pete shrugged, beginning to feel uncomfortable. Like maybe Jack was right.

"Not sure. Long as it takes, I guess."

"Well, if you get done, come out to the lake."

"Yeah. Okay."

Jack shook his head and walked away. Then he stopped after just a few paces. Turned back and scrunched up his face at Pete.

"You're gonna get bit. You know that."

"I'll be careful," Pete said. Because he didn't know what else to say.

———

He stuck his head into his father's bedroom, relieved to see that his dad was still fast asleep.

He tiptoed out to the garage.

Pete found his old Radio Flyer wagon immediately. Finding it was not the problem. Laying his eyes on it was not hard. It was laying his hands on it that would prove challenging.

On top of the wagon his dad had stacked two big bundles of *National Geographic* magazines tied up with twine, a taped-up carton of the good china, which they had not been allowed to use since Mom left, two old lamps with no bulbs or shades, some of those milk cartons you can stack, and a coiled hose that—Pete knew from memory—leaked.

He quietly pulled the items down one by one and arranged them in the opposite corner of the garage. When he finally reached the rusty wagon he lifted it up and lugged it through the house, knowing that any movement of the garage door would wake his dad.

He set it down in the front entryway and opened the door, slowing his actions at the point where he knew the hinges squeaked. Then he carried the wagon to the concrete front walkway.

He pulled the door closed behind him and he was gone.

The sun was high by that time, the day already warm. It was a good three-mile walk between the spot where the dog lay waiting and the only vet in the area. Unless it was farther. And that was only the one-way trip. He'd still have to get home.

But Pete couldn't take the time to think about that. He had gotten himself into this thing, and it seemed to have no exit.

He'd once overheard his mom telling her best friend, Judy, "Almost everything is easier to get into than it is to get out of."

He hadn't understood her words at the time.

The wagon followed along behind him with a distinctive squeak on each revolution of the wheels. It became a monotonous focus for Pete. Something in which to submerge any thoughts and lose himself, if only for the moment.

—

When he got to the spot where the dog had been hit, Pete was sweating heavily, and he could feel his own face radiating heat.

There was no dog.

At first he looked up and down the highway, feeling the shocking and sudden wind of cars racing by his back at intervals, flapping his shirt around. He assumed for a moment that he was in the wrong place. But he'd paced it off carefully from the mileage sign, and he didn't want to do it again. It was hot and he was tired.

He looked down at the empty highway shoulder and saw what looked like a trail of disturbed dirt. It looked the way dirt looks when you drag a burlap sack of something along because you don't feel like spending your back to lift it.

Pete followed the trail to a spot under a scraggly tree, towing the wagon along behind.

"Oh, there you are," he said when he saw the dog. "Good."

The dog growled at Pete from deep in his chest.

Pete sat down in the dirt and sighed.

He looked at the dog and the dog looked at him. For whatever reason—maybe because Pete was sitting down—the dog did not threaten him again. They stared at each other for an extended time.

The dog's small eyes were a golden color. Almost yellow. He had a mask of markings on his face like a sled dog, and a massive ruff of fur at his neck.

"I got no idea what to do," Pete said.

The dog seemed to listen. To follow the words almost as though they had meaning to him. He seemed to be carefully gathering signals from Pete. Probably because his life depended on the boy's intentions.

"I'm scared of you. I'll just say it straight out. I got no idea how to get you on this wagon. If I can get you on it I can get you to the vet. But I don't figure you can get on it by yourself, things being what they are with your hip. And I can't imagine how to get it through to you to try on your own anyway. And if I pick you up and put you on it, I figure you'll bite the hell out of me, sorry for the cuss. Or maybe you don't care about stuff like that. Well, of course you don't. You're a dog. You don't understand English. I guess I'm just used to apologizing for any little cuss. My daddy cusses all the time, and he doesn't have to apologize. Grown-ups can get away with that. If I tried to do it like they do I'd probably get my mouth washed out with soap. That happened to my friend Jack. Our teacher did it. Washed his mouth out with soap. He went home and told his parents, thinking maybe he could get the teacher in trouble, but they were all for it. 'We applaud her.' That's what they said. They applauded her for it. I didn't know what that word meant but it turns out it means clapping. Like when you enjoyed a show."

Pete fell into silence. He looked into the dog's face again. Again their eyes locked.

"I'm gonna move just one step closer," he said.

And he did. He settled in the dirt on his left elbow and hip. The dog rose into a sit and tried to move away.

"No, it's okay. Don't hurt yourself. I swear you got nothing to worry about from me. Wish I knew how to tell you that so's you'd understand."

Pete stayed still as he spoke, and the dog stopped short of any painful evasive action. He just sat, staring at Pete, prepared. For what, Pete hated to think.

"I'm mad at my friend Jack," Pete said. "So mad I'm not sure I want to be his friend anymore. I guess I always had some things about him I didn't like so much. But, I don't know. He's my friend. I guess I figured that's just the way things are when you have a friend. But I'm not so sure now. Looking at a poor hurt dog by the side of the road and then saying you just want to go fishing. And complaining how he hates to fish alone. Like his problems are worse than anybody else he met this morning. I bet he never gave you another thought after he left here."

He looked at the dog again. The dog looked back. Then, slowly, almost daintily, the dog settled all the way back down to the dirt with a sigh.

"See, that's good. You trust me more already. I swear I only want to get you somewhere. I couldn't bear to just leave you here all hurt and scared. Now that I seen that look in your eyes, if I didn't do what I could to help you, I'd never stop seeing that look as long as I lived. I'd be lying in bed at night trying to get some sleep and when I closed my eyes all I'd see was that look. I bet you defend yourself real good when you're not hurt. I bet this must be real different for you, feeling like you can't defend yourself hardly at all."

The dog's face seemed to soften. He blinked his eyes once, which Pete couldn't remember seeing him do before. Maybe he had, but Pete didn't remember. Maybe he just blinked them differently this time. Left them closed for a fraction of a second longer. As if he trusted he could do so without paying a price.

Pete thought the dog might be more comfortable if Pete stopped staring at him as though just about to make a sudden move. So he rolled over onto his back, laced his hands behind his head, and stared up through the leaves of the scraggly tree. Pete liked to look up through full, leafy trees on windblown days. It was one of his favorite pastimes. But there was not so much as a whisper of a breeze on that hot summer day, and this tree was not so abundantly leafy as trees go. Pete figured you just have to work with what you're given.

"I'd get somebody to help put you on the wagon if I could. I got to say . . . I hate to let on when I'm scared, but I'm telling it now. Even if I am only telling it to a dog. I think you're gonna bite the hell out of me when I try to pick you up. But I don't know who to get. Jacky's a big coward and I don't think he rightly cares. And his dad works at the plant days. Hell, everybody's dad works at the plant. Except mine. Mine used to. But then there was the accident. So now he's home, but he can't help. Because of the accident. Not that I think he would have anyway."

He glanced over in his peripheral vision. The dog had set his chin down on the dirt, eyes still wide open.

"Well, that's some progress," he said. "You're getting to know me some."

———

Pete had no idea how much time had gone by. Only that the sun was more or less overhead, and he had a good start on a sunburn on his face and his bare arms and legs. The tree was too scraggly to provide much shade.

He stood up and dusted off his shorts.

The dog followed him with wide eyes, but did not lift his head or otherwise try to move.

"This is stupid," he said. "I been here for hours, telling you practically my whole life story. If you don't know me by now, I guess you never will. I'm just putting it off 'cause I'm scared. I'm tired of being scared. I'm just gonna get it over with. But before I do, I'm gonna tell you something important. So listen real good, okay? I promise you . . . if you go with me, you're gonna be okay. And that's a cross-my-heart-and-hope-to-die promise. I know you don't really know the words I just said but I hope you can tell something by the way I said 'em. You're in trouble out here. Come sundown if you're still here the wild animals'll come and get you. Don't know if you're smart enough to know that or not."

Pete looked deeply into the dog's eyes again. He was smart, that dog. Pete couldn't tell what he knew about wild animals. But the dog knew he was in trouble. Life-or-death trouble. That came through.

Pete took hold of the handle of the wagon and pulled it around close to where the dog lay sprawled in the dirt. Moving with exaggerated slowness, he lifted out the wagon's wooden railing on one side and set it on the ground. The dog watched his movements with what looked like curiosity more than anything else.

"I guess the trick is gonna be to lift up that back end of yours. You can lift the front on your own. If you couldn't, you'd still be up on that highway." He stalled, both in his speech and his movements. "Yeah. That's the part I'm scared about right there."

Pete took off his belt, which almost caused his shorts to fall down. He instinctively looked behind him to see if anybody on the highway was about to get a glimpse of his underwear, which would have been mortifying. But he could see only the roof of the two cars he watched speeding by.

He hitched up his shorts until he could use his elbow to clamp the waistband in place.

He began to contemplate how to get the belt under the back of the dog's body. Without losing his life.

"Hmm," he said.

He located a stick, or at least the opportunity for one. It was actually a complex network of dead, bare branches in the dirt on the other side of the tree. He broke off one that struck him as the right size. Then he carried it back to the wagon and the dog, pulling his penknife out of his shorts pocket.

"I'm going to get this real nice and smooth," he said to the dog. "You know, so's I don't poke you. I cross-my-heart promised I wasn't gonna hurt you and I'm not about to go and make a mistake with that right outa the gate."

He sat cross-legged in the dirt and worked the stick with his knife until it had no side branches, no sharp edges—nothing that could hurt as he slid it under the dog's body. He whittled down the end of the stick until it was narrow enough to wedge into the last hole of his belt.

"Okay, here goes," he said to the dog. "Remember that promise I made. I stand by that promise."

He walked around behind the dog, who followed Pete with wary eyes. Pete crouched down and began to slowly, gently, slide the belt under the dog, just in front of his hips, with the help of the stick. He kept the belt on top, the stick underneath, to further ensure the dog's comfort.

The dog struggled to his feet. Three of them, anyway.

"Okay, now," Pete said. "We'd best do it now."

He took one end of the belt in each hand and lifted until he was supporting the dog's hind end. Now all he had to do was lift the back end onto the wagon. And hope the front end would somehow take care of itself.

"Please don't bite me, please don't bite me," he chanted.

He lifted.

Truthfully, despite his pleas, he expected to be bitten. In a flash of images and intention in his brain, he geared up to finish the movement with teeth sunk into his flesh. Maybe right down to the bone. He would heal later. He had all summer to heal. But he would finish the action regardless.

A sharp cry of pain seared through Pete's insides, but it was not his own.

Then the dog's back end was resting on the wagon. And Pete was unharmed.

"Good dog," he said, gently pulling his belt out from under the dog's body.

The dog was bigger than the wagon. His hips sat inside, but with almost all of both back legs sticking out. Pete figured the weight of the unsupported leg must be painful to the dog, but he had no idea how to fix that.

And another thing that would be a good trick to fix: the dog's front paws were still firmly planted in the dirt beside the wagon. On the same end as the teeth.

Pete looked at the size of the wagon and the size of the dog, then pulled the wooden rail section up and out of the front, above where the handle attached. He wedged the end of the stick into the last hole of his belt buckle again, and slid it under the dog's chest, which was easy and unthreatening with the dog more or less in a standing position.

As he moved in to grasp both ends of the belt, his new mental image was far more disturbing. Now it was his face he was presenting to those flashing teeth. His throat.

He froze a moment, and felt like it was all too much. Too much of a risk to take for anybody or anything. But then he imagined what it would mean to abandon the plan now. He would have to tip the poor dog off his wagon and walk away. And leave him out here, helpless. After everything they'd shared. After his solemn promise.

"Please don't kill me," Pete said, and lifted.

Then the dog was on the wagon, at least the main body of the dog, and Pete had his belt back, and he was alive and unharmed. And his shorts were down around his ankles.

Red-faced, he pulled them back into place and secured them with the belt.

"Well, come on," he said. "We got a lot of walking to do."

He hauled the wagon up the steep incline, puffing and sweating, and going slowly. Painfully slowly. Because he knew any bumps would jostle the dog's injured leg. Then he set off along the smooth tarmac of the highway, just outside the traffic lane.

As he walked toward the vet's, pulling the wagon, Pete could feel a shakiness at the cores of his thighs that almost made it hard to stay on his feet.

———

"The vet is with a client," the woman said.

She was one of two women assistants, and she was the younger one, the one Pete didn't like. Pete hated to think thoughts like that about anybody, but it was a hard feeling to get around. Her eyes were cold and her voice was brusque. The whole woman was like a wall made out of bricks and spikes and razor wire. How could you like her when she was clearly asking you not to?

The older lady looked nice, but she was putting a label on a tube of ointment, and so was too busy to talk to Pete at the counter.

Pete wanted to ask if he could have a glass of water. He'd intended to ask first thing. It was all he'd been able to think about for the whole last mile. But somehow this young woman had knocked those words out of his mouth unsaid.

"We can wait, I guess," Pete said. "But it's kind of an emergency."

"What kind of emergency?" she asked, as though she'd already decided it couldn't be much of one.

Pete wanted to know how people got to be like that, and why, but he didn't have time to ponder. And he sure didn't dare ask.

"He got hit on the highway."

"Let me talk to Dr. Morton," she said.

She walked a few steps and opened the door to the examining room—Pete knew it was the examining room because it said so right on the door—and called in to the vet.

"There's a boy here with his dog and he says it got hit on the highway."

The vet came to the door and then stepped out into the waiting room and stood a few steps from Pete and his wagon and the dog. He was a huge man, both tall and wide, and Pete thought being underneath him felt like standing in the shadow of a small mountain or a fully grown tree. The vet had a look in his eyes similar to the woman Pete didn't like—a look that said he wasn't buying any of it, whatever he thought Pete was selling.

Pete figured the vet and his mean assistant would like him even less when he told them he had no money and couldn't pay for the dog's care.

"I didn't say he was *my* dog," Pete said. "Just that he was a dog."

"Well, it's not," the vet said. Words like walls. Like big wind gusts, blowing him over.

"Not what, sir?"

"That's not a dog."

Pete's head swam slightly, and he began to wonder if this was all a strange dream.

"I don't get it, sir. What is he if he's not a dog?"

"It's either a wolf or a wolf hybrid. Probably a hybrid. I don't treat wild animals and I want you to get him out of my waiting room right now. People are here with their pets. It's not safe."

Pete looked around. There was a skinny woman with a cat carrier, waiting, and a man with a wiener dog on a bench along the far wall. They both drew their pets closer to themselves.

"Oh, he can't get down off this wagon, sir. He's too broken up to go after anybody or anything. Honest."

"I want that animal out of my waiting room."

"Yes, sir. Any idea where I could take him?"

"Call the state wildlife department. They'll come out and shoot it."

"Oh, no, sir," Pete said, talking through his shock as best he could. "I couldn't do that. I made him a promise."

The vet shook his head as if Pete were simply too much of a burden for a man of his stature to tolerate.

"I don't have time for this," he said. "I'm with a client."

He turned crisply on his heel and walked back into the examining room, slamming the door harder than necessary.

Pete looked up into the eyes of the young woman assistant.

"Yeah," he said. "I get it. I'm going."

—

Pete sat outside for a long time, baking in the sun. Not really sure where to go. He sat on a high curb that separated the walkway to the vet's office from its parking lot. He stared down at his own sunburned legs, streaked vertically where rivulets of sweat had tracked down through the dust and dirt.

Now and then he glanced over his shoulder at the dog—or whatever he was—still dangling half off the wagon under a nearby tree. The dog stared back with a look that seemed to say, "Well?"

Pete had left the wagon in the shade on purpose, because he had no water for the dog either. Still the animal panted.

Pete heard the door of the vet's office squeak open, and he whipped his head around, fully expecting to be told he was still too close, still a burden in his need.

It was the older woman assistant. She had pretty red hair in a bob, and she met his eyes and smiled at him. And didn't tell him to scram.

Instead she leaned her back against the shingled siding of the office and lit a cigarette.

"Ma'am?" he asked her.

"Yes?"

"I can see it's your break and all. But maybe I could trouble you for a glass of water for me and this dog? Or whatever he is. What did the vet say he was?"

"He thinks probably a hybrid."

"I don't know what that is."

"It's just a fancy way to say 'cross.' A cross between a wolf and a dog."

"Well, then, why don't people just say what they mean in a simple way and skip all the fancy?"

She laughed lightly, and smoke came out with the sound.

"No idea," she said.

Then she disappeared back inside. Pete couldn't tell if she intended to bring him water or not.

He looked down at his sneakers again, trying to force his brain to work. He had to have a plan. He had to move on from this place. And he had to bring the dog—or hybrid, or cross—along, because he'd promised. But where? He could not make his mind wrap around the challenge.

A minute or two later the woman plunked down onto the curb beside him with a sigh. Pete looked over at her, and she smiled. She handed him a bottle of orange soda with the cap already popped off. It was wonderfully cold against Pete's hand as he took it from her.

"Thank you!" he said, clearly relishing the surprise gift.

"You're welcome," she said, and puffed on her cigarette.

He took a long drink. He could feel the icy soda trace its path down into his belly, changing everything. It felt like being lifted out of hell and plunged into luxury.

"This is the best thing I ever had in my life," he said. "I swear."

"Never had an orange soda before?"

"Yes, ma'am. Couple times. But never when I was this thirsty."

She smiled. Almost sadly, Pete thought.

"I brought some water for him, too," she said. She pointed to a jumbo paper cup sitting on the curb near her hip. "But I figured I'd let you give it to him."

"That was nice of you, ma'am."

"Is he tame?"

"I have no idea."

"Was it hard to get him on the wagon?"

"Yes and no, ma'am. It was hard to get up the courage to go at it. But then once I did, he didn't try anything. He didn't do me no harm. Sorry. Any harm. Just because I'm out of school for the summer doesn't mean I get to be all sloppy. Anyway. He did growl and bare his teeth a couple times. But that was before we talked and got to know each other. I think if he wasn't tame, though, I'd probably be in a dozen pieces right about now."

"Yeah. He might have known some people sometime."

"The vet said he was wild."

"I think he meant he wouldn't treat a wolf cross under any circumstances because he thinks they're too wild. He doesn't believe in them."

"How can he not believe in them?" he asked, pointing to the animal. "There's one sitting right over there."

"No, that's not what I meant," the woman said. "He believes they exist. He just doesn't believe people should own them. People get them who don't know how to handle them. You can't always train them by hitting them on the nose with a rolled-up newspaper, if you know what I mean. It's more complicated with something that's half-wild. Sometimes people get them and then end up being afraid of them or having problems. He could have belonged to somebody, and that's why he trusted you. Or it's possible he could be completely wild. Maybe he let you put him on the wagon because he knew he didn't have any better choices."

"Are they smart like that when they're wild?"

"Sometimes. Yeah. Everything and everybody wants to live. So it's not unheard of for an animal to go against its nature if it really comes right down to surviving or not surviving. These people came into the office once. They had this watchdog. He was really vicious. They meant for him to be. His job was to guard an auto parts yard. One night he was choking to death on a bone and a total stranger walking down the street stuck his arm through the fence and put his hand down the dog's throat and pulled out the bone. And the dog let him. Which makes sense when you think about it. What did he have to lose?"

Pete gulped the soda as she spoke. It was only half gone, but he already missed it. Already mourned its loss in advance.

"I wish I knew where he came from and stuff," he said. "But I guess the big question is, what am I gonna do with him now? I can't call the wildlife people to come shoot him. I can't. I made him a promise that if he came with me nothing bad would happen to him. I swore on my honor, you know?"

"I do know one thing you might try."

"Where they won't shoot him?"

"Yeah. Maybe. There's a lady doctor who lives way out in the boonies. Close to six miles from here as the crow flies. She's a doctor, not a vet. But she takes in animals when no one else will. I went to her once with a sick cat when the owner wouldn't pay to save her and the vet wouldn't save her without pay. She wasn't very nice to me but she did take the cat. I have no idea what she'd say if you showed up at her door with a wolf."

"Or maybe just a cross," he said, hoping that helped his case.

"She doesn't seem to like people. She's not very nice. She just wants everybody to leave her alone, I guess. She's not such a young woman. Not old, either. Maybe late thirties or even forty. You'd think she'd be raising teenagers, but instead she's looking after animals. Not that it's any of my business. I guess she likes them better than people. On a bad day I probably see her point. Anyway, I can't see what you've got to lose by trying."

And with that she slid something that looked like a prescription pad or a message pad out of her skirt pocket. She made a stubby pencil appear from behind her ear.

While Pete watched, draining the rest of his orange soda, she drew him a map.

As she worked, he brought the cup of water to the . . . animal. If anything, Pete felt more afraid now, having been told he had a maybe-wild thing in his wagon. But the beast didn't growl, or roll back his lip. He just reached out his muzzle and drained the cup of water, gratefully from the look of it.

"Now don't you tell anybody I told you about her," the woman said, pressing the paper into Pete's hand.

"Why not, ma'am? I mean, right. No. I won't. Anyway, who would I tell? And even if I had somebody I wanted to tell, I wouldn't if you said not to. 'Cause you been real nice to me. I just wondered. Is it a secret?"

"I'm just not sure if it's something I'm supposed to be telling people. I'm one of the few people I know who've met her. People talk about her, but most people haven't talked *to* her. But you have to try something."

"That's the plain truth, ma'am."

"Good luck."

Pete watched her walk back inside the office.

He looked at the dog again, and wished he'd never made that promise, because now he felt it was beyond his control to say whether things would be okay or not. But regardless, it was too late now. He'd promised, and there was no getting out of it. He just had to head for okay and hope for the best.

He steeled himself for another very long walk.

—

Pete was in the third or so mile of his walk, just reaching the far edge of the built-up part of town. He was walking in the street, near the curb, to avoid sidewalk cracks that might cause his passenger pain.

He heard a small voice from behind him.

"What's wrong with your dog?"

Pete stopped and turned around.

Behind him on the sidewalk stood a dark-skinned boy. An older boy than his voice had made him sound. He was small in stature, much smaller than Pete, but he wore thick glasses that made him look smart and mature. His wiry hair was cropped short, so much so that Pete could see his scalp. Pete wondered if your scalp got sunburned when the sun could find it like that. But maybe people like this boy—*colored* was the word Pete used in his head, because he didn't like a lot of the words he'd heard—didn't get sunburned as easily as Pete did.

"He's really not my dog," Pete said. "In fact, I just had him to the vet and the vet's not even sure he's a dog."

Pete watched the boy relax. He could see it in the boy's shoulders, and the way he carried his head. The very fact that Pete had spoken to him—not even especially kindly but certainly not unkindly, just matter-of-fact—had put him at ease. He moved several steps closer, his eyes wide with what looked like a cross between confusion and awe.

"That seems strange," he said. "What is he if he's not a dog?"

"That's exactly what *I* said!"

Pete hadn't meant to shout, but it was exciting to hear someone think thoughts that were such a good match for his own. It made him feel less alone and confused. But his enthusiasm made the boy jump. Just a little, though. You'd have to be watching to see. Pete had been watching, trying to think why he'd never seen this boy around before.

"The vet thinks he's a wolf or maybe a wolf cross," Pete said.

The boy regarded the animal with a renewed look of respect. But he didn't back away at all. Which earned him Pete's respect.

"What happened to him?"

"Got hit on the highway."

"How'd you get a wolf onto your wagon?"

"Not really sure. I sat with him a long time. And then he pretty much let me. We think either he lived with people once upon a time or maybe he just knew he didn't have any other good choices."

"Where're you taking him?"

"Oh," Pete said, realizing how easy it would be to break a promise without even thinking. "I can't say. No offense to you or anything. But somebody told me where I might be able to take him. But they made me promise I wouldn't tell anybody."

"Oh. Well, you wouldn't want to break a promise. I can see that."

"Good. Thanks. I'm glad you get it. I don't like people who break promises. I take a promise real serious. And I made two already today, so that's a hard day, because I have to make sure I don't break either one."

"That *is* a hard day," the boy said. He pushed his glasses higher onto the bridge of his nose with the tip of one thumb.

"Well. Goodbye, I guess," Pete said.

"'Bye. I hope that wolf feels better."

"Thanks."

Pete walked a few steps, the silence broken only by the rhythmic squeaking of the one unoiled wagon wheel. He thought about Jack, out at the lake having a good time without him. Not even supporting him enough to help him with the dog. Wolf. Cross. It made him feel alone, like he had no friends in the world at all.

He stopped and turned to see if the boy had walked away. He hadn't. He was just standing there on the sidewalk, hands limp at his sides, watching Pete go.

"It's a long walk," Pete called to him. "You want to walk with me a mile?"

"Sure," the boy called back.

He ran to catch up.

"Why are we walking in the street?" he asked Pete.

"The sidewalk's too bumpy. I'm afraid the bumps'll hurt him."

"Oh. Right." A brief silence. "Thanks for inviting. I don't know anybody around here. It's hard. You know. Not knowing anybody."

"How long you been here?"

"Two days."

"That would explain it, then."

"It would have been better if school was still in session. Then I would've met some of the other guys. But it was the second-to-last day of school when we got here, and my dad said it was silly to sign me up for two days. He said I should help unpack all our stuff and he'll sign me up in the fall."

"What did your mom say?" Pete asked.

"I don't have one."

Pete stopped dead and tried to look into the boy's face, but the boy only looked down at the sidewalk.

"That's something we got in common," Pete said.

Then the boy's eyes came up to meet his, with a renewed look of confidence. "Oh. Your mom died, too?"

"No. She didn't die. But I still don't have one."

"Where'd she go?"

"I don't know."

They stood for a moment, Pete feeling confused and unsure how to proceed. Then he set off walking and towing the wagon again.

"I'm sorry your mom died," Pete said.

"Thanks."

"You miss her?"

"I didn't really know her. She died while I was being born. But I kind of miss her anyway. I don't know if that makes sense or not. You miss your mom?"

"I do," Pete said, hoping not to have to go into the matter at any greater depth.

"What am I supposed to do all summer if I don't know a solitary soul? That's what I've been wondering all day."

"You know me," Pete said.

"Except I don't even know your name."

"Pete Solomon."

"Justin Bell," the boy said, pointing to his own chest with a hooked thumb.

"There. See? We know each other some."

They walked in silence for a few steps, listening to the wagon wheel squeak. Or at least Pete was listening to that.

"I can show you how to oil that squeaky wheel," Justin said.

"Well, thanks all the same, but I know how. Just that the wagon's been sitting in the garage since I was about ten. And the dog was waiting for me and all, and my dad was asleep and I didn't want to take the time and take a chance on waking him up."

"He doesn't work, your dad?"

"He worked at the plant. But then he had an accident."

"Oh. I'm sorry. My dad works at the plant. Today's his first day. That's why we moved here, because he heard they were hiring. Well, that and because his dad—my grandpa—grew up around here. Used to work at that exact same plant. So he always wanted to come here, I think. My dad, not my grandpa. I hope he didn't take your dad's job or anything."

"Nah. He's only on a leave. Workman's . . . something. I forget the second word. Besides, the plant's always hiring. Men come and go like crazy."

"You know, you can just say if you don't want to be friends."

Pete stopped. Justin stopped. The silence of no squeaking wheel resonated.

"Why wouldn't I?" Pete asked. But he thought he might know.

"Well, you know."

"I don't care about that. I'm kind of picky about friends. I think maybe more than I used to be. But not about stuff like that."

"What're you picky about?"

"Well, say for example . . . if you were with me and you saw this dog—or whatever he is—by the side of the road, all hit and in trouble . . . would you go on to the lake fishing and leave me alone, or would you stay and help with the dog?"

Justin was silent a moment, and Pete could tell he was thinking. He felt as though he could see wheels turning in the smaller boy's brain. Pete was glad Justin was taking the question seriously, not just rushing an answer off the top of his head. Not just telling Pete what he figured Pete would want to hear. Justin looked deeply into the eyes of the wolf-dog, and the wolf-dog looked back.

"I think it was brave what you did, getting him on that wagon. I think I'd probably wish I didn't have to do anything so brave. You know. If I could help it. But I think if he was hit and by the side of the road and he had nobody . . . I don't figure I could just go on down to the lake and fish and not give his situation another thought. I think I wouldn't be able to sleep if I did that."

"Good," Pete said.

And they walked again.

"That's the kind of thing I'm picky about," Pete added.

—

About two miles later, when the road had turned into a tunnel of leafy trees with not a single car in sight, Pete began to worry that he was leading someone besides himself too close to the lady doctor's place.

"I think maybe I better go on from here on my own," Pete said. "No offense. Just that . . ."

"Yeah, I know," Justin said. "So as not to break a promise."

"Right."

"Maybe I'll see you around."

"Oh, I expect you will," Pete said. "I'll be around all summer."

Justin peeled away for home with a wave that looked a little despondent.

Pete stood and watched him go.

It hit him then, for the first time, that he was scared of what lay ahead. He was scared to go see a lady doctor who didn't like anyone but animals and only wanted to be left alone. He regretted not having a friend along on this next part. Even a very new one.

Still, a promise was a promise.

Chapter Three: Dr. Lucy

She cursed all the way to the door—this being broad daylight and all, and just one time of many when she preferred not to be bothered. She could barely hear the curses over the baying of the dogs in their outdoor runs.

She collected herself for a long moment, then swung the door wide.

Standing on her doorstep was a boy who looked to be a very big, husky twelve years old, or maybe thirteen or fourteen with a baby face and a too-childlike demeanor. His thick, dark hair was cut short, with clippers from the look of it. His eyes remained on his feet, never looking up at hers, as if he'd already decided she must be a biter.

He also seemed intimidated by the barking dogs, as if a forced meeting with them could happen at any moment. Each jump in their volume brought a wince.

"I don't want any," she said.

"Of what, ma'am?"

"Whatever you're selling."

"I'm not selling anything."

"Then you must have the wrong house. Because there's no way I could have any business with you."

The boy stepped sideways two paces.

Behind him on her walkway sat an old rusted Radio Flyer wagon with two of the wooden rails missing. On the wagon was what appeared to be a wolf-dog. If she'd had to make a quick guess, she'd have said a hybrid of wolf and Alaskan husky or malamute. A good seventy-five or eighty pounds. Its left hind leg rested on the right one at an unnatural angle.

She looked into the animal's eyes, and he looked back.

She had seen that look before. Many times.

The wolf-dog was plainly out of options. And even though it wasn't right for an animal to know so much, he knew this was his last chance. He would get help here—from her—or there was no help to be had for him in this world.

Dr. Lucy averted her eyes and sighed.

"How did you find out about me?" she asked the boy.

"I can't say, ma'am."

"You can't say because you don't know? Or you can't say because you know but you can't tell me?"

"That second thing, ma'am."

The moment stretched out. The silence seemed to put pressure on the boy, like a foot on a toothpaste tube. Words squirted out.

"I found him on the highway. He'd got hit. I tried to take him to the vet. But the vet wouldn't touch him. I think he's not a very nice man. Well, I guess from what I heard, you're not, either. Well, not that you're not a nice man. Of course. 'Cause you're not a man at all. Not a nice woman, is what I heard. Oh crud. What am I saying? Sometimes when I get nervous I don't notice that just the wrong thing's about to come out of my mouth. Anyhow, if it helps to know it, what I heard about you was part good. I heard you're nice to animals, which is really all our situation needs. Anyway, the vet said he was wild, and that he won't treat wild things, and that it was dangerous to even have him in the waiting room. But he's so broke up, he wasn't coming off that wagon to do no harm to nobody. Sorry. Any harm to anybody. That's what I meant to say."

Then he stopped, as if desperate for breath.

"He's not wild," she said.

The boy looked at her face for the first time. Then at the wolf-dog. Then back to her face.

"How can you tell, ma'am?"

"First of all, you'd be more likely to come dragging up here towing a purple kangaroo than a wild wolf. They've been bounty hunted near to extinction."

"I didn't know that," the boy said.

"And there's another obvious clue. One that the idiot Dr. Morton would have noticed if he'd been using his head. He's not a nice man. You were right about that. He's also not a very good vet. He moved out here from two of the bigger cities because he couldn't sustain a practice where there's competition."

"Not sure I follow, ma'am."

"If there's more than one vet in an area, the best ones get the business."

"That makes sense," the boy said. "But you still didn't say—"

"He's had his rear dewclaws removed."

The boy ran his eyes over the animal, seeming not to know where to rest them.

"Look at his front legs," she said. "Just above the paws. See how he has that extra claw on the inside? Higher up?"

"Yes, ma'am. I thought all dogs had that."

"They do. But they're also born with dewclaws on the back as well. But most breeders take them off when the pups are very young. If he'd been born in the wild he'd still have them. Plus there's an even easier way to tell. You put him on that wagon, right? And you're standing on your feet talking to me. And I can't help but notice you're not bleeding out."

"Well, that could've gone more than one way, ma'am. He did growl and bare his teeth at me a couple times. I had to sit with him for hours before I dared try."

She tried to look into the boy's eyes, to take a better measure of him, but he turned his face away.

"That was an awfully brave thing to do," she said.

"I just figured I wouldn't be able to sleep if I up and left him there after looking into his eyes. You know how it is."

"Oh yes," she said. "I know all too well."

Another long silence.

"Well," she continued, "I can't say for a fact that he hasn't been living on his own for a time. How long a time, we'll probably never know. But he knew people at some point in his life. So, fine. We're in this now, aren't we? Okay. Just leave him here. I'll take some X-rays and then do whatever bone repair seems indicated."

The boy looked up into her face, his eyes wide. He seemed more surprised than necessary by her simple instructions.

"Oh, I can't do that, ma'am."

"Then how am I supposed to fix him?"

"He'll be here for you to fix, all right. That's not the worry. But I can't leave him. I can't leave him until I know for a fact he'll be okay. See, I made him a promise. I promised him if he came along with me he'd be okay. I kind of half wish now I hadn't. I learned a lesson from that promise. Because sometimes it's outa my hands whether somebody else is okay or not. But for this promise it's too late. I made it. And now I'm with him and he's with me until we know he's okay."

Dr. Lucy stared at him for a long, discouraged moment. Then she sighed deeply.

"You don't have parents who'll be looking for you?"

"Yes, ma'am. I'll likely take a whipping from my dad when I do finally get home. But I can't think of that just yet. I promised, and here I'll stay."

"Well," she said, and loosed another deep sigh. "I guess you two had better come in."

———

"How old are you?" she asked him, while she prepared a handkerchief soaked in ether.

"I'm twelve, ma'am."

"Hmm," she said. Not purposely out loud.

"Hmm what, ma'am?"

He stood near the wagon, which he'd towed into her examining room, one hand on the wolf-dog's head. She wondered if this was the first time the boy had dared touch him.

She dropped the soaked handkerchief onto the wagon in front of the animal's chest, then used her hands on the boy's shoulders to guide him through the living room and out the door.

"Where're we going, ma'am?"

"We're going to wait outside for a minute."

They stepped out together into the scorching afternoon sun. Dr. Lucy pulled a cigarette from her shirt pocket and lit it, drawing deeply. She looked up through the leaves of the nearby trees, which stood utterly still in the windless heat.

"It's just that . . . ," the boy said, and then seemed to fade for a time. "I figure when people say 'hmm' they tend to be thinking something. So I guess I just wondered what you were thinking."

Dr. Lucy blew a cloud of smoke out into the hot air.

"I suppose I was thinking you look older."

"Yes, ma'am. I'm real big for my age. Biggest in my class."

"And also that maybe in some ways, when you talk . . . maybe you seem younger."

"Oh. Well. I'm not the smartest kid in class, if that's what you mean. Kind of sorry you brought it up, though. I try not to think about that if I can help it."

"Why not? It's not an insult, you know."

"Of course it is. Not being smart? That's a bad thing in anybody's book."

"Let me tell you something, kid—"

"Pete."

"Fine. Pete. Let me tell you something, Pete. Smart is overrated. Most of the harm done in this world is done by people who fancy themselves smart. And they are—book smart. But most really smart people have no sense. They value their brains too highly. I'd rather have someone with sense. And a little heart. Now come on. We're going back in."

"Yes, ma'am."

He followed her through the living room, stopping briefly to stare into the open faces of Archimedes and Angel. As though this was the first he'd noticed them. And maybe it was. Maybe he had been able to entertain only thoughts of the wolf-dog on the first trips through.

"Those are some beautiful big birds," he said.

"Yes, they are."

"What happened to them?"

"The owl had a badly broken wing. He tried to swoop down and fly through the headlight beams of a moving car. The eagle was shot."

"Oh. That's too bad."

Lagging behind, he followed her back into the examining room, which smelled strongly of ether. She opened all the windows and turned on the two fans.

"Oh no!" he shouted when he saw the wolf-dog slumped unconscious on the wagon, head trailing toward the linoleum floor. "What happened to him? What did you do?"

"Well, you certainly didn't expect me to operate on that leg while he was wide awake and feeling pain, did you? That would be cruel. Not to mention dangerous."

"Oh. He's just asleep, then. Phew. Scared me."

"Help me get him up on the table."

She lifted the animal's front end, and Pete lifted the back. The wolf-dog's head lolled. With a grunt or two from each of them, they managed to slide him onto the table.

—

Dr. Lucy examined the developed X-ray film—clipped to a light box on her wall—for an extended time. Partly just getting her thoughts together. It was better than she had feared. A greenstick break in a long bone. It would require screws to repair, because it was up high toward his hip. But so much better than shattered bones in or around that hip socket. It made his prognosis seem reasonably good.

She left the X-ray hanging, the light on behind it, and moved back to the wolf-dog, who lay stretched out flat on the table. She had placed a cone around his muzzle so he could keep breathing gas throughout the procedure.

She plugged in her clippers and began to shave the area over the injury.

Pete jumped as the clippers came to life.

She looked up at the boy. He was sitting on a stool near the operating table. He looked white, as if he'd seen a ghost. His eyes looked too unfocused.

"You okay?" she asked him.

"Feeling punk, ma'am."

"What variety of punk?"

"Woozy."

"Probably the ether. Go stand by the window."

He did as he was told, but she couldn't help noticing that his hands instinctively reached out for something he could use to steady his balance. He stood at the window and breathed deeply.

She scrubbed her hands and pulled on her sterile surgical gloves. Then she painted the wolf-dog's leg area with a skin disinfectant and made her incision.

"Why were you nice to me, ma'am?" Pete asked. He was staring out the window as if enjoying the view. He looked a bit steadier.

"Was I?"

"More than I was set to expect."

"Hmm. Didn't know I was."

The boy turned his attention back into the room. And saw that she had the wolf-dog's leg open. She watched it register on his face.

"Oh, holy cow," he said, and waved like a stalk of wheat in a stiff wind.

"Better sit down again before you pass out."

"Yes, ma'am."

He dove for his stool.

"Wasn't the ether this time," she said, "was it?"

"No, ma'am. I didn't quite expect to look over and see the inside of that poor guy's leg."

"You knew I had to open the leg up to fix it, didn't you?"

"No, ma'am. I broke my leg when I was nine, and the doctor just put a cast on it."

"This is broken too far up near his hip for that. It's not an area I can stabilize with a cast. I have to put screws in it."

"*Screws?* In his *bones?*" He had his eyes pressed tightly shut.

"That's right. That's his best bet for getting back up on it again anytime soon."

"If I pass out, don't pay any attention to me. Just keep fixing."

"Put your head between your knees."

And he did.

"I'll tell you why I was nicer to you than most," she said, gloved hands still working. Gently moving the bone back into alignment.

"Thought you didn't know you even were, ma'am," he mumbled from between his knees.

"Well, I thought about it. About you promising an animal who might be dangerous that you'd take care of him when you knew full well that taking care of him involved taking a big risk. When he'd already growled and bared his teeth at you. Most people would have just walked on. Maybe called the authorities to come out and put him down. But you sat there gaining his trust for hours. And then not being willing to go back on that promise . . . even after somebody put it in your head that he might be a wild animal. Well, he's not. I'll tell you another way we know for sure he's not. He's been neutered."

"Neutered, ma'am?" Pete asked from between his knees.

"Fixed."

"Fixed how?"

"Fixed so he can't sire any puppies."

"Oh. That kind of fixed."

"A lot of people will do that to make a dog more tame. But once you do it, once you neuter a wolf-dog, it's kind of a shame to put him back in the wild to fend for himself. Wolves are pack animals. They mate, and they raise pups. But if he can't mate and he can't raise pups, what's he supposed to do? He's pretty much destined to live his life alone. Not that he was likely to find a wolf pack around here. A dog pack, maybe."

First, silence.

"That breaks my heart, ma'am," Pete said weakly. After a while.

"It should. It breaks my heart all the time, seeing what people do to animals."

"Is that why you don't like people?"

"Part of it. That and what people do to each other. But I'd best concentrate on what I'm doing here when I go to set these screws."

For a good forty minutes or more, though she wasn't watching the clock, the boy sat on the stool clutching his own head with his knees.

Right up until the moment she said, "You can look up now. I have him all sutured back up."

Then he lifted his head and blinked into the light as if waking up from a disastrous dream.

———

"How far away from here do you live?" she asked him.

Pete had his front end draped over the kennel cage where the wolf-dog lay, still unconscious. The boy was staring straight down. As if the animal were just about to do something interesting.

"It's a real long walk," he said. "I hate to even think about it."

"Want me to give you a lift home?"

"That'd be much appreciated, ma'am. But not till after he wakes up."

"That could take a while."

"Well, it don't matter. Doesn't matter. Sorry. I have to be here when he wakes up. Otherwise he's just here, and in pain. And where am I? How's he supposed to know I even helped him like I said? He'll just know he's in a cage and hurting like the dickens."

"I've got some painkiller going into that IV drip."

"Oh, well, that's good to know, ma'am. At least he'll feel better. But I need to stay. I need to look in his eyes and say, 'There. I took care of you, just like I said I would.'"

"No idea how long that'll be."

"Oh heck, I got nothing but time."

"But you said you'd get a whipping when you got home."

"Oh, we're way past whipping time, ma'am. So long as I'm going to get it, I might as well make it good."

Dr. Lucy sighed.

"I guess if you want to lean on that cage for the rest of the day, go ahead. But I can't just sit here with you and keep you company. I have to feed the dogs and the horses."

The boy's eyes grew wide.

"Horses? You got horses here?"

"Oh yes. Eleven, in fact."

"I'd like to meet the horses, ma'am. If that's okay. So long as my wolf-dog is sleeping anyway. But I sure don't want to meet those dogs I heard."

"They're in kennel runs," she said.

She did not say that referring to the wolf-dog as *his* might have been the beginning of a tactical error. At least, not out loud.

—

The sun was on a long slant as they stood outdoors, leaning on the top rail of a white board fence surrounding the horse pasture.

"They're eating grass," Pete said.

"Yes," she said. "A pastured horse will do that."

"But then why do you need to feed them?"

"They're not easy keepers. They need a little hay and grain to keep their weight."

"What's an easy keeper?"

"A horse that can just eat grass or hay and keep its weight. One that doesn't need grain."

"So I bet these guys cost more money to feed."

"You can say that again."

The boy looked into her face as they spoke, then back at the eleven Thoroughbreds—all lanky and tall, mostly bays, but with one sorrel and two grays mixed in.

"They don't look like any horses I've ever seen around here. I've seen some cattle horses in my life before. They're short and stout. They don't have such long legs as these guys."

"These are Thoroughbreds."

"Yeah, okay, but thoroughbred what?"

"No. Not purebred. Thoroughbred. It's a breed of its own. They're racehorses."

"Oh, *racehorses*," he said, as though she should have just said so in the first place. "Are they fast? Are they any good?"

"Obviously they're not good *enough*," she said. "Or they wouldn't be here."

———

She handed Pete a bucket of oats with a scoop. And then, because she had only one bucket and scoop, she stood in the withering late-afternoon sun and watched him move down the line of feed buckets, each tied to the fence. Watched him scoop the grain into the feeders, seeming unafraid and unaffected by the horses nipping and half-heartedly kicking at each other as they jockeyed for position.

Each time he scooped grain into one—as a horse picked his way through the crowd and claimed the feeder—Dr. Lucy heard Pete say something to the horse. But she couldn't hear the words from where she stood. It appeared to be the same length and number of sentences each time, but the only word she ever made out was "sorry."

She faintly heard Smokey, the gray gelding, nicker in his throat to the boy as he took the last feeder.

Pete came back and joined her at the gate.

"I like those horses," he said. "I like them real good."

"You like them *very well*," she said. Then she immediately wished she hadn't corrected him.

"Right. Real *well*. Sorry. My favorite is that gray guy. The bigger gray. Because I talked to all of them, but he's the only one who answered me back."

"Yes, I heard that. What did you say to them?"

"I told them I was real sorry somebody ever thought they weren't good enough. And that I think they're plenty good. And then I told them I bet they run really fast. Like the wind."

"And what did the gray say to you in return?"

"Just 'Thank you,' I think."

———

"Hey," Pete said, drawing out the word into a long and modulated sound. "You're back."

He lay on his side on the linoleum floor of her examining room, his face about three inches from the wolf-dog's cage.

The animal's eyes flickered, but he did not try to lift his head. His nose lay inches from the boy's face, and Dr. Lucy saw it twitch as the animal took in the boy's scent.

"Sure am glad to see you back," Pete said. "Now, I know you probably don't feel all that good right now. But I'm telling you, you will. Now you will. Before this nice lady doctor did what she did, things weren't looking so good for you. But now you'll be okay. You just need some time to rest up is all. Rest up and heal."

A long silence.

Dr. Lucy waited for the boy to get up. For his visit to be over. But the longer she waited, the less he seemed inclined to move.

"The sun is nearly down," she said quietly, flipping her head in the direction of one of the open windows.

Pete looked up, as if he'd forgotten all about time, about days and nights, about the cycles of the sun. As if he'd never intended to move.

"So it is, ma'am."

"I'll drive you home."

"Can't tell you how much I appreciate that, ma'am. It's a long walk." Then, to the wolf-dog, "I'll see you tomorrow, Prince. Don't try to move. And don't be scared. Just get some rest. I'll be back when you wake up again. Or not too long after that, anyway."

The boy lumbered to his feet, as though sleepy and sore, and she took him by the shoulders and guided him to the front door.

"I was thinking that you were turning him over into my care," she said as they passed the pig's cage.

She succeeded only partially at hiding her irritation.

"Not sure I follow, ma'am."

"I thought you were going to leave him and go. And trust me to do the rest."

"Oh, I can't do that, ma'am. I just promised him I'd be back in the morning."

Dr. Lucy sighed. She opened her mouth to say something—some exhausted complaint—but then thought better of it and closed her mouth again.

———

As she was backing out of her driveway she looked over at the boy's slack face. His head was back against the seat, his eyes closed. He might even have been asleep.

"Prince?" she asked him.

"Yes, ma'am," he said without ever opening his eyes. "I thought that was a good name. I think it suits him."

"I'm not sure it's such a good idea to name him at all, though. I always feel you name an animal only if you're planning to keep him."

"I *am* planning to keep him."

"I don't think that's a good plan, though. That's the point I'm hoping to make here. He's been living in the wild. He can be aggressive. He's not anybody's puppy dog."

"Oh, he wouldn't hurt me, ma'am. Not now. Not after everything we been through."

"Maybe not. But even if you're right about that, he could hurt somebody else. He could hurt a neighbor. He could kill a neighbor's dog or cat. Or start going after somebody's chickens. Why wouldn't he? It's how he's been surviving."

The boy's eyes were open now, and full of turmoil. She looked away from him briefly to pull out onto the road.

"Couldn't I train him?"

"Yes and no. You can't change an animal's basic nature with training."

"But we can't just let him go again. He's all alone out there. He's living this lonely life. You said so yourself. What if he doesn't want to go back out there by his poor self again?"

"I suppose he could stay with me, but he'd have to live in a kennel run. That might not be a very welcome option for a wolf-dog who's lived in the wild."

"How do we know what he wants?"

"I would say when the time comes that he's healthy enough to go, we give him the option to go. If he doesn't want to, he won't. If he does and he wants to come back, I suppose he will."

Pete never answered, and she looked over at his ruined face.

"You have to be willing to do what's best for him," she said.

"Yes, ma'am, I know that." But he looked and sounded as if about to cry. "You need to make a right at that stop sign up ahead. We're on Lacey Road about four miles up."

Silence.

"Thank you again for the ride, ma'am."

"It's no problem."

"And thank you for fixing Prince."

"Maybe it's best if we go back to calling him the wolf-dog."

"With all due respect, ma'am, you can call that dog, or wolf, or wolf-dog, or whatever he is . . . you can call him whatever you want. But to me he'll always be Prince. Wherever he ends up, wild or tame, he'll always be Prince."

Chapter Four: Pete

———————

Pete eased the front door open with his fingers crossed on both hands. Maybe his dad was already asleep. Since the accident he tended to go to bed early, and get up late. And snore in his chair in front of the black-and-white TV.

He always said the painkillers and the muscle relaxants—the ones the doctor gave him for his back—made him feel "nappish."

Pete stepped into the living room to see his dad wide awake and staring back at him.

He froze, his stomach icing over, waiting to see what would be said. Or done.

His father's face looked dark, but also calm. He didn't speak. He only nodded in the direction of the hook behind the door.

Pete's heart sank. He could feel it all the way down into his belly.

The hook was where they hung jackets, which they hadn't needed for a month or two. And it was where the razor strop lived.

Nursing a tight feeling in the pit of his throat, Pete took down the strop and carried it over to his dad, who sat quietly—almost impassively—in his chair, waiting. It was a ritual that had its own special flavor, literally and otherwise. Right at the moment it tasted like ashes and metal in Pete's mouth.

His dad took the strop with his right hand and nodded again in the direction of his lap.

Pete squeezed his eyes closed and leaned over his father's huge thighs, presenting his tender behind.

Pete hated the sound as much as anything. Maybe because the sound and the pain could no longer be separated in his mind.

Thwack. Thwack. Thwack.

Three fierce hits. Each lash sent its own shock wave through every cell of Pete's body. It didn't matter how much you were expecting it, or for how long. It was always an unimaginable jolt.

Pete straightened up, feeling the stinging numbness of the welts rising. He noted a spot on one buttock that felt wet against his shorts, which probably meant the strop had drawn blood. He didn't dare investigate.

"Got an explanation?" his dad asked in that booming bass of a voice.

"Yes, sir. There was a dog hit in the road and I was trying to get him some help."

"All day, until nearly nine o'clock at night?"

"Yes, sir. Vet was no help at all. And I haven't eaten all day, so if you don't mind . . ."

"Too bad supper's long past."

"You didn't save me anything?"

"I threw yours out fifteen minutes past suppertime. This is a civilized household. We eat at mealtime. You want to eat, you show up at mealtime. You got that?"

"Yes, sir."

Pete's stomach groaned, as if in direct response. He could hear it, and he wondered if his father could hear it as well. He could feel the sickening pains of its contractions.

The lady doctor had tolerated his presence, but she had offered him nothing. In essence, she had treated him like a stray cat, being careful not to make it any easier or more desirable for him to stay. At one point he had asked permission to use her bathroom and had drunk his fill with his mouth greedily attached to the sink faucet. But his stomach had remained empty.

"I'll just go on to bed, then, sir."

"Reach over and get me that pack of cigarettes," his dad said. "And hand them to me."

Pete looked into his father's face for the first time since arriving home.

It was fully dark outside now, but the reading light was on over his father's chair. His dad's growing belly strained at the buttons on his checkered shirt, and Pete could see the comb marks in his dad's wet-looking, slicked-back hair.

The cigarettes were sitting just a matter of inches from his dad's hand. So it was a strange and potentially dangerous request. Quite possibly a trick request.

"Ain't got all night, Petey boy."

Pete leaned over his father's lap. Before he could grasp the pack, he felt his upper arm grabbed too tightly and his shoulder pulled down. Wrenched down, in fact.

He loosed a little cry of pain. Unexpected pain. But that was nothing compared to what followed.

Thwack. Thwack. Thwack.

The strop hit him more ferociously this time, and right on the fresh and tender welts of his last thrashing. Pete had never been strapped twice in a row before, and was stunned—literally stunned into immobility—by the pain of it. It was generally hard even to sit down on the once-smacked bleeding welts after a good strapping. It was hard to touch them gently with his palm or fingertip.

This pain was hard even to register. It was a sensation he honestly hadn't known existed.

Pete pulled away, wrenching his arm free, and stood spraddle-legged and defiant in his surprise.

"Hey! What was that for?"

"Boomer Leggett come by today. Said he saw you walking down the road with some Negro boy."

"What about it?"

"You said you was going fishing with Jack."

"Well, I tried to. But then I found that dog, like I said. And Jacky wouldn't help me with him. He went on out to the lake without me."

"So where's the Negro come in?"

"He just started talking to me on the street. And we walked together a ways."

"Next time he wants to talk, tell him to make himself scarce."

"Why?"

"Because he's not your kind, that's why. You stick with Jack. We know his parents. He's one of us. Choose your friends wisely, boy."

"I don't want to play with Jacky anymore. He's a rat fink."

"Fine. Then spend the whole summer by yourself. But I best not hear about you spending any of it with that colored boy. It's unseemly."

"I don't know what that means," Pete said, still reeling from the pain. His voice sounded stressed, even to his own ears.

"It explains itself, Petey. It's easy. Unseemly. If it don't seem right, it's unseemly."

Pete opened his mouth, fully prepared to say it seemed right to him. But he didn't. Because his dad still had the strop in one hand, and Pete feared it now more than ever. Now when he knew that, in his father's grip, it unexpectedly could be applied to the painful welts of previous applications.

A third time would be impossible to bear.

"Yes, sir," he said. Then he closed his mouth.

"Tell me you understand what I just said to you."

"I understand."

And he did. He just didn't agree. Or feel particularly inclined to obey.

He felt inwardly relieved that his father had not extracted an express promise to obey.

—

Pete lay on his belly in bed, desperate for sleep, but knowing his hunger would continue to keep him awake. His father had gone to bed about an hour before. Or, anyway, it seemed like an hour to Pete.

He gingerly lifted up on his arms and listened. As if the utter silence of the house might hold clues for him. As if the lack of any stirrings might still provide a litmus test of potential dangers.

He slipped soundlessly out of bed and padded barefoot into the kitchen.

A loaf of white bread sat by itself on the counter. For some reason his father had not bothered to put it back in the breadbox. He slid two slices out of the wrapper and hid them in his pajama pockets.

He opened the cupboard that held the cereal. The hinges squeaked. Not much. Not loudly. But still Pete froze for second upon second, bracing himself.

Nothing happened.

He took down a box of cornflakes.

The top of the box opened silently, but the waxed-paper inner bag rustled lightly as he unrolled it.

The silence was shattered by his father's deep voice.

"If I hear one flake hit a bowl," he shouted from his bedroom, "you can bring me that strap again."

"Yes, sir!" Pete shouted, all but flinging the box back onto the shelf. "Sorry, sir. No need for that. I'll just be going back to bed."

He ran back to his room and leaped onto the bed, causing the springs to groan under his sudden weight and hurting his welts. He pulled the covers up to his chin and waited.

No sound. Nothing moved.

A good fifteen minutes later, when he could clearly hear his father's snoring through the wall, Pete pulled the slices of bread out of his pockets and ate them quickly.

A few minutes later, he slept.

—

"Pete! Hey! Pete!"

Pete stopped walking and stood on the sidewalk of his street, shielding his eyes against a strong slant of morning sun. He recognized the voice as Justin's, and it made his stomach fall. And it was too bad, too, because if not for the three extra lashes the night before, he knew he'd be pleased to run into Justin again. It seemed a shame for anything so fine and harmless as a new friend to be spoiled like that, and for no good reason to boot. Like getting a shiny new toy for Christmas and then watching somebody break it before your eyes just to be mean. Just because they don't want you to have nice things.

"Where are you?" Pete called, looking around.

He even tried looking up, but he realized as he did so that it was silly. There were no tall trees on this block of his street, and Justin couldn't fly.

"I'm here. In my house."

This time Pete was able to follow the voice.

Pete was passing by a row of brown brick houses on his way back to the doctor's house. Or at least he had been, before the voice brought his feet to a halt. They were tiny, those houses. More the size of shacks, though shacks aren't often made from bricks, he figured. And old. But they were neat, and tended, with flower beds out front, and white shutters that looked as though they might have been painted within the previous week.

Behind the screen of an open window Pete saw Justin's beaming face.

He walked closer. As close as he could go without stepping on the flowers, which were too pretty to trample. Pete wondered how you keep flowers going in the heat of a southern Texas summer. You must have to water them with the hose every day.

"Oh, there you are," Pete said, though he'd actually spotted Justin some time earlier.

"How's that dog? Or whatever he is?"

"He'll be okay. His leg was broke but the lady doctor operated on it." A silence fell, and Pete realized he'd said too much. "Oh," he said quickly. "Just pretend I never said that, okay? I took him to a place, and he got an operation. I think he'll be okay, but maybe not for a time. I broke my leg when I was younger and it was weeks before I felt much like walking on it. But in time I think he'll get back on his feet just fine."

"Are you gonna keep him?"

"I'm not sure," Pete said, feeling his eyebrows scrunch down and his forehead wrinkle with the unpleasant weight of the subject.

"You going out to see him now?"

"Yeah."

"I'll walk with you."

Justin's face disappeared from the window.

The two bowls of cereal Pete had eaten for breakfast suddenly refused to sit still in his belly. His face felt hot, and a cloud of what felt like certain doom formed over his head, pressing down on his morning. On his very being.

He gently touched the worst of the welts on his buttocks, the one that had bled. He couldn't imagine doing anything to get a whipping again until he was fully healed. But at the same time he knew he would not—could not—tell Justin not to walk with him. Or not to call out for a talk when he saw Pete come by his house. Or not to be Pete's friend. It wasn't Justin's fault, and Pete was not in the habit of hurting feelings and breaking hearts, or even spirits. Never had been. Didn't figure he ever would be.

The next thing he knew, Justin was walking next to him down the sidewalk, eating what appeared to be a peanut butter and jam sandwich. Pete was paying close attention to that sandwich, because he was still hungry, and it looked and smelled good.

Every step caused Pete's undershorts to rub against his welts, but he resisted the urge to express his pain out loud.

"Want half my peanut butter sandwich?" Justin asked, apparently seeing Pete eyeing it.

"I'd love it, if you really think you could do without."

"It's okay. It's my second one."

Justin tore the sandwich in half carefully, using the tips of his fingers to break it along a fairly straight line.

Pete took the half from him and scarfed it down in three bites.

"Mmm," he said. "That raspberry jam is good."

"I know, huh?" Justin replied.

They walked in silence for a moment or two. Pete glanced over his shoulder to see if they were being observed.

"You didn't eat breakfast?" Justin asked.

"No, I did. I ate twice as much as I usually do. But I didn't hardly eat yesterday, except breakfast before the sun came up, and now I just can't seem to get enough."

"Because of that dog?"

"Right."

"What did the lady doctor say he was? Oh. Sorry. I probably shouldn't have mentioned that. After you told me to forget it and all."

"It's okay. I know you can't really forget. It's my own fault for saying it out loud. I wasn't thinking and it just slipped out. I guess I meant . . . don't say anything about it to anybody else."

"No," Justin said, a bit solemnly. "I won't."

"She thinks he's a wolf-dog."

"Part of each?"

"Right. And she says he knew people at some point in his life because he had some kind of claws removed. And because he's fixed."

"How long did you stay with him?"

"Till the sun went down."

"She didn't give you anything to eat?"

"No. And then when I got home, my dad'd thrown my dinner away. Fifteen minutes. That's what he gives me after suppertime and after that it's my own fault for being late."

"Wow. He's strict."

"Plus I got a whipping."

"For what?"

"Being gone so long," Pete said, carefully withholding the second part of the whipping story.

They walked in silence for a time. The sun was just getting a good fire going, and it gleamed out from between the leaves of the big trees that grew farther down the long blocks of their seemingly endless street. Justin glanced over at Pete. More or less at his lower half, Pete couldn't help noticing.

"I wondered why you were taking such little bitty steps," he said.

Pete never answered. He glanced over his shoulder again. Justin seemed to be watching Pete watch the street behind them. But when the smaller boy opened his mouth to speak, he took the conversation in a whole different direction.

"Your dad sounds tough."

"Does he?"

"Yeah. Really tough."

"Huh. I don't think so. I think he's just like anybody else's dad."

"He's not like my dad."

"You never get a whipping?"

"Never. Well. Once he swatted me on the butt with his hand. But then he couldn't stop apologizing for it."

"So what does he do if you make him mad? You know. Break the rules or something."

"Just sits me down and gives me a good talking-to. He doesn't believe in hitting kids. He says if you hit kids then they just grow up to hit."

Pete stopped walking for a moment to consider that idea, deeply relieved because his undershorts were no longer rubbing his painful welts. It took Justin a moment to notice he'd stopped. When he did, he walked back to where Pete stood thinking.

"I don't think that's altogether true," Pete said. "Because I never hit anything or anybody, and I never will." He paused a minute, chewing over his own thoughts. "Then again, my grampa strapped my dad when he was growing up. So I guess it's not altogether false, either."

Pete looked up.

A filthy white tow truck had pulled up level with them and slowed. Pete looked through the passenger window. His heart fell when he locked eyes with Boomer Leggett.

"Aw, crap," Pete said under his breath.

"What's wrong?" Justin asked.

Boomer tipped his head forward and to the side the way he tended to do when stressing something important, usually without words. It made a section of his stringy blond hair fall over his eyes. He smiled that smile Pete had never liked. There was something mean about it.

And when he smiled it, nothing good ever followed. Then he looked forward, through his windshield again, and gunned the engine, his tires squealing on the warm asphalt.

"What's wrong?" Justin asked again. Sounding as though he'd caught the fear like a cold.

"Oh. Nothing, I guess. I just don't like that man."

They began walking slowly along the sidewalk again.

Pete briefly considered making an excuse regarding why he had to go on alone. But he couldn't bring himself to hurt Justin's feelings.

And besides, the damage was already done.

———

"Where's your wagon?" Justin asked as they turned onto the lady doctor's street.

But Pete was a hundred miles away in his head, running over his fears like those white rats run on exercise wheels, and he hadn't registered the fact that he'd led Justin too close to Dr. Lucy's house.

Instead his brain just pulled away from razor strops and his daddy and Boomer Leggett and chewed on the fact that it seemed like a strange question about the wagon. Because there would be no earthly reason for him to drag it along on this walk. Then his busy brain went on to note that he really didn't know where the wagon had gone off to. He had lost track of it sometime deep into the previous day. Which seemed like weeks ago when he tried to mentally access it.

Let's see, he thought. *The lady drove me home. And she didn't bring it. So it must still be—*

Pete looked up to see the lady doctor's house. They were only a few dozen steps away from her door. The house was set back from the street, and the windows were blocked from a few angles by overgrown bushes and trees. But, as Pete's luck would have it, the lady was not inside. She was standing in her front yard, grass and weeds up to her knees. On her right hand she wore a long and heavy leather glove. Like a work glove, but extending higher up on her arm.

On the glove perched that beautiful golden eagle. The one she'd said had been shot.

Pete stopped in his tracks, and looked over at Justin.

"Right," Justin said. "I know. I get it. I'm going. And I didn't see a thing."

Then Justin hurried down the street, back the way they'd come. He swung around the corner at an efficient trot.

Pete looked up to see the lady still staring at the bird perched on her gloved hand. She didn't seem to have noticed either one of the boys.

Pete breathed a sigh of relief.

Chapter Five: Dr. Lucy

It wasn't so much that a movement caught her eye. Her eyes remained fixed on Angel—in case she never saw the bird again, which was likely—until something caught Angel's eye.

Then she looked over to see that boy approach her.

She knew she shouldn't have been surprised. He'd said he would come back in the morning. And, little though she knew of him, she knew he took his commitments seriously. To understate a case.

"Morning, ma'am," he said, looking as though he would tip his cap to her if he had one.

She nodded, rather than speaking.

"Mind if I go in and see Prince?"

She aimed him in the direction of the house with a flip of her head.

Pete walked a few steps, then stopped. Looked back at her.

"What're you doing out here with that pretty eagle?" he asked. "Do they need to get out in the fresh air sometimes?"

"Angel needs to be out in the fresh air all the time. I'm letting her go."

He walked back to where she was standing, his eyes wide.

"Is she fixed enough for that?"

"Unfortunately, yes."

Angel flapped her huge, patterned wings, leaving them spread for a moment as if for balance. As she did, Dr. Lucy could see the spot where the bullet had torn through her left wing.

"Hey, wait," Pete said. But then he didn't tell her what she was waiting for.

"Yes?"

"You named that bird Angel."

"So?"

"You said you should never name an animal unless you're planning to keep it."

"Well, if it helps any to know," she said, "I'm paying for it now."

"Not sure I follow, ma'am."

"It means I'm better at giving advice than taking it."

"Still don't quite get it. But anyway, now I'm kind of torn. I want to go in and see Prince, but I also want to see you let that bird go. I don't suppose you'd hold off? Just long enough for me to say a quick hello to Prince."

Dr. Lucy felt something small happen on her face, almost akin to a smile. It brought a wave of relief to be given a good excuse to keep the bird a few minutes longer, and to be able to pretend sentimentality played no role in the decision.

"Sure," she said.

She expected him to run into the house. Instead he walked toward the door in tiny steps, as if his hips were too tightly attached and only partially mobile.

She looked back at Angel.

"Here comes your pep talk," she said. "The world out there is no nicer a place than it was last time you were in it. So keep a low profile, okay? Never trust a man with a gun. Actually, never trust a man. Period. Stay away from power lines and don't swoop too low over highways. It's not that I would mind putting you back together again. It's that once you fly away from here the chances of anybody bringing you back to me if something goes wrong are pretty much nonexistent. So just find yourself a decent mate and build a sturdy nest and pay good attention to the eggs. Because the world could use more eagles. More eagles and fewer people, though I'm not making that last part your problem. That would be nice, though, wouldn't it? A world full of eagles who shoot at people regularly to keep their numbers down?"

She looked into the clear, intense eyes of the bird, who looked up into the trees.

"And . . . you know . . . ," she said, her voice just at the edge of cracking, ". . . have a good life."

Pete's voice startled her.

"Does she understand all that?"

"No," Dr. Lucy said. "She doesn't understand any of it. That was awfully fast. I thought you wanted to say hi to Prince."

"I didn't want to miss seeing that bird go."

"I told you I'd wait."

"I didn't want to keep you waiting too long, though. Prince seems better today."

"I think so, too. I gave him some solid food this morning and he ate it."

"He wagged his tail at me."

"Well, that's not too surprising. He's canine."

"I didn't mean it was surprising, really. Just nice."

She smiled the tiniest bit. Maybe it hadn't even been enough to show on her face at all. They stood in silence for a moment. She did not release the bird, and Pete did not ask why not.

Though, actually, Angel was not tethered in any way. Her huge talons wrapped around and inside Dr. Lucy's gloved fist, but if the bird had chosen to fly away, she would have.

"I guess it's time," she said.

"Seems sad," Pete replied.

"Sad or not, she's a wild animal. And it's time."

"Is it like Prince?"

"Is what like Prince?"

"What you said last night about letting him go. How if he wants to go, he will. And then later if he wants to come back, he can."

"I suppose," she said. "Except an eagle isn't half-wild. She's one hundred percent wild. It's all she knows."

Dr. Lucy opened her hand. And, as she did, she extended the gesture even farther. She lifted the hand and the bird, a kind of universal signal for a bird to take flight. A little help to start them on their way.

Angel flapped her wings. For a moment, for two or three flaps, she gained little altitude. If any. It seemed as though she was testing that once-wounded wing, rather than just assuming it would perform.

Then she put more effort behind the lift, and soared up onto the branch of a tree, nearly directly overhead.

"She's not leaving!" Pete nearly shouted in his excitement, craning his neck back and shielding his eyes from the sun.

"Give her time."

"Maybe she wants to stay!"

"Don't get your hopes up, Pete. Wild birds fly. It's what makes their lives special."

"But maybe she just wants to fly around *here*."

"We'll see," she said.

They waited. They watched.

When Dr. Lucy's neck grew a bit stiff, she turned her gaze down to see that Pete had his first two fingers tightly crossed on both hands.

She wondered if—through some type of superstition—the boy felt a bird who wanted to stay would be a good omen of a wolf-dog who wanted to stay.

"Oh, damn," Pete said suddenly.

She looked up to see Angel soar away, gliding to a speck in the distance, then out of view.

"Sorry I cussed," Pete said.

"Don't worry about it."

"Aren't you sad to see her go?"

"I don't like to talk about how I feel."

"Sorry," Pete said.

They turned and walked toward the house together.

"What about the owl?" he asked. "Are you going to have to let him go pretty soon, too?"

"No. He was too badly hurt for that. He can't fly, and he never will again—at least not well—so he'll always be with me."

"What about the horses?"

"The horses are not wild. They're domestic horses. Born and bred in captivity. They'll stay."

"Good. 'Cause I like those horses. Could I ever ride one of those guys, do you think?"

"I don't guarantee they wouldn't buck you off."

"You wouldn't need to. I'd be willing to take my chances. Not today, though. Definitely not today."

———

He lay on his belly on the hard linoleum of her examining room floor. Nearly nose to nose with the wolf-dog. She leaned on a counter and watched the boy. Wondering when, if ever, he planned to leave.

"Give you a ride home?" she asked.

He turned his head to her, and his face looked positively emotionally scorched. In fact, he looked as though he was just about to cry, or had been crying quietly. But there had to be more to his mood than what she'd just asked. This seemed to be a preexisting condition.

"What's wrong, Pete?"

"Everything."

"Can you be more specific?"

"I can't go home."

"Why not?"

"Yesterday I got whipped. Twice. My daddy never whipped me twice. Not before yesterday, I mean. I could try to say how it feels to get whipped on the places where you just got whipped a minute ago, but I swear there just aren't the words, ma'am. Or if there are, I don't know them. And now it hurts like the devil just to walk. I can't even sit down. And if I go back there again, he's going to whip me again. And I swear, ma'am, I just can't take it." On the words "take it," his tears gained ground. He swiped at them violently with the back of his hand and turned his face away. "Not a third time."

"Would it help if I went back with you and asked him to take it easy?"

"No, ma'am. Might make it worse. He doesn't like to talk about family stuff outside the family and he doesn't like people telling him what to do."

"You have to go home, though," she said.

She told herself she would have said the same had it not been her house, her privacy, he was invading. But, truthfully, she did indeed want him to go away now, ignoble though that might have been.

"I just can't bring myself to do it, ma'am."

"Well, you can't stay here," she said, and then immediately regretted it.

"I understand, ma'am," he said, pulling gingerly to his feet. "I'll just be going."

"Wait," she said. "Where will you go?"

"No idea, ma'am."

She sighed.

"No. Don't go yet. You can stay a little longer. I'll fix us something to eat."

—

"How bad are those spots where he whipped you?" she asked him.

She sat at her kitchen table. He stood. He had to raise his soup bowl to his face to spoon it up, because it apparently hurt him too much to bend over.

"Pretty bad, ma'am," he said.

"Want me to have a look?"

His eyes went wide. He dropped his spoon into his bowl with a clank.

"At my . . . *behind*? Are you kidding? I'd be humiliated!"

"But I'm a doctor."

"But you're a *lady*!"

"Okay. Fine. It was just a suggestion. Forget I ever brought it up."

In time he picked up his spoon again and they ate in silence.

"Wait," she said. "Why would he whip you a third time if you went home now? What have you done *this time* that's so bad? You've only been here less than two hours."

At first he averted his eyes and said nothing.

"I guess it's your own business," she said, "and none of mine."

"Last night he told me not to do something. But then today I went and did it. Anyway."

"But if you were so afraid of another whipping . . ."

He shifted uncomfortably on his feet.

"I guess you can't really understand it, ma'am, unless you know what the thing was."

She waited. But they fell back into eating their food, and the silence took root and grew. And stayed.

And he never told her what the thing was.

—

"This is stupid," Pete said. "I'm just going to go home."

He'd been lying on his belly in her examining room again, his face close to the wolf-dog's through the wire mesh, offering his fingers, which Prince tentatively sniffed. As he spoke he began the clearly painful process of standing.

Archimedes the owl had been making a lot of noise for as long as Dr. Lucy could remember. All morning. She'd been trying to pretend she didn't know why.

She wanted to argue with Pete about going home. She also wanted to move on with her day. Get back to the way it was before: with no overly conscientious kid hanging around, being so constantly . . . *there*.

"I think you should call me if things get bad," she said.

He leveled her with a look she couldn't quite interpret.

"That's mighty kind of you, ma'am."

"Don't sound so surprised."

"I didn't mean to say you can't be nice. Just that I didn't think you cared."

Funny, she thought. *I didn't think I did, either.* She never answered out loud.

Archimedes continued to hoot and fuss.

"My dad and I don't have a phone, though. Is the thing."

She dug some loose change out of her skirt pocket and singled out a dime. Held it out in Pete's direction. It was shiny and new looking.

"Then go find a pay phone if things get bad."

"Thank you, ma'am. That's very neighborly of you to do." He accepted the coin and pressed it deep into the pocket of his shorts. "I don't know your number, though."

"If I told it to you now, could you remember it?"

"Probably not, ma'am. No."

"Well. I'm listed."

A long silence.

Then Pete said, "I don't know your name, ma'am."

"I didn't tell you my name?"

"No, ma'am."

"It's Lucille Armstrong. It's listed under L. K. Armstrong."

"What's the *K* for?"

She rocked her head back a little and found his eyes, not attempting to hide her curiosity.

"Why do you want to know my middle name?"

"It'll help me remember those letters you just said."

"There's no other Armstrong listed with just initials. But anyway, the *K* is for Kay."

The boy looked confused. For a long, silent moment.

"How can it be . . . ?"

"Not the letter *K*. The name Kay. K-A-Y."

"Oh, right. Got it. Okay. Now I think I'll remember." He turned toward the door. Stopped. Turned back. Seemed to wrestle with a thought in his own head. "Thing is, I'm not going to take the whipping this time. I'm just going to say no."

"Didn't know you had the option."

"Once upon a time, maybe not. But since he hurt his back in that accident at the plant . . . I honestly don't expect he could catch me if I didn't want to get caught. It's risky, but . . . He tells me to take the strap down and bring it to him. This time I'm going to say no. It'll make him mad as hell. Sorry. Heck. And I'll pay for it once his back is feeling better. Except . . . I don't know. I'm almost as big as he is now. But I'm not sure I think it's a good idea to point that out. Maybe I'll just tell him I'll take the whipping, but not until I'm healed up from the last two. And—what's wrong with that owl, ma'am? He sounds upset."

She reached for a cigarette. "He misses his next-door neighbor," she said.

"Oh. Right."

He'd obviously forgotten about Angel's new status as a free bird. It obviously pained him to remember.

She lit the cigarette and puffed at it.

"Okay," he said. "Well. If it gets real bad, you just might see me again. But I still think it's time to buck up and face what's ahead of me."

"Good luck," she said, drawing deeply on the cigarette. And she meant it sincerely.

He moved toward the door.

"Take your wagon," she called after him.

"Oh. My wagon. Right. Where is it?"

"On the front porch."

Silence. Pete didn't respond. She couldn't hear him moving toward the door. She looked down at the wolf-dog. Prince, as Pete was determined to call him. He held his head high, following the sounds in the living room with his vigilant upright ears. Except there were currently no sounds to follow.

Pete stuck his head back into the room.

"I have this friend," he said.

Then he stalled. As if this hadn't been such a good idea after all.

"Go on."

"He's new. He just moved here. I've only known him since yesterday. But I only had one really good old friend and he was never very good. If you know what I mean."

A pause.

"I think I do," she said to fill it.

"Anyway, my dad said I can't see him."

"This new friend."

"Right."

"Why not?"

"Different race."

"I see."

"But that didn't feel right to me at all, ma'am. I mean . . . how am I supposed to say that to my friend? He didn't do nothing wrong. Sorry.

Anything wrong. So this morning he walked me part of the way here again."

"Maybe your dad will never know."

"Oh, I wish, ma'am. But he'll know. We got seen. By the same guy who ratted me out in the first place."

Another long silence. This one she did not fill. The boy was clearly surrounded with the rottenness of others. Hardly surprising. The world was full of it. And she couldn't fix that for him. She couldn't even fix that for herself, and not for lack of trying.

"Well," he said, "wish me luck."

"I did, actually. But I will again if you like. Have you always had so much trouble with your dad?"

Pete leaned his shoulder on the doorframe, and his gaze moved up and away. As though going for a trip in his head.

"I been thinking about that lately," he said. "And I swear he used to be a whole bunch easier to get along with."

"Before the accident?"

"No, ma'am. It started earlier than that. It's like I was little, and he was this pretty good dad. Not perfect, but good enough. I was a little harder to handle back then, too. I did a lot of stuff wrong."

"That's hard to imagine," she said, laughing out a puff of smoke.

"It's true, though. But then I got bigger and he got madder and I kept getting more and more polite and trying to cooperate. You know? I figured if I was good enough he wouldn't be so mad. But it just seems like the bigger I get the madder he gets. But I don't suppose it's got much to do with my size."

"It might," she said.

He screwed up his face in an outward mask of his own inability to understand.

"That's interesting," he said, "and maybe you'll explain it to me, but next time. Right now I'd best get this done."

With that, he disappeared from the doorway.

"Pete," she called after him.

"Yes, ma'am?" he asked without reappearing.

"I think you did the right thing."

"About my new friend, you mean?"

"Yes. That."

"Thank you, ma'am. That's what I thought, too. Nice to have somebody back me up on that."

This time she heard the front door close behind him.

She stubbed out her cigarette in the ashtray and walked out the back door. Into the blazing morning sun. The horses crowded near the fence, nickering to her, but she paid them no mind.

She leaned on one post of their pasture fence and stared off into the woods on the other side. Scanned the trees one by one, hoping to see Angel hanging close by. Keeping an eye on the house, and her. Expressing some kind of loyalty or affection for the place.

She never saw Angel.

In time the sun became too much and she had to take herself back indoors.

Chapter Six: Pete

————————

Squeak. Squeak. Squeak. One irritating note on each revolution of the wagon's wheels.

Pete continued to register the sound. Because he didn't know how not to. He would have stopped listening if he could have. He found it almost unbearably irritating. Since he couldn't, he just winced once on each squeak and continued to scan the sky.

"I know you're up there somewhere, Angel," he said.

But even as he said it, he knew "somewhere" could be twenty miles away or more. After all, it was a big sky.

Pete caught the toe of his sneaker in a sidewalk crack and pitched forward, landing hard on the concrete on his chest and the heels of his hands.

"Ow!" he bellowed, mostly from the jostling of his previous wounds.

He lay facedown on the hot pavement for a moment, cursing quietly to himself.

Then he heard the sound. What kind of sound, though, he couldn't quite sort out. It definitely sounded human. But a human trying to communicate what? That was the question he couldn't answer.

He lay still a moment longer, waiting to hear it again.

The second sound was much clearer. Much easier to identify. It was a sob. A wet, helpless sob.

Pete pushed carefully to his feet.

"Hello?" he called.

Under a shade tree in a vacant lot, half obscured by tall weeds, hunched a small figure that looked a lot like Justin. Little dapples of sunlight that filtered between the leaves shone alarmingly on the bright red blood that covered his closely cropped scalp.

Pete broke into a run in the weeds, in spite of his own pain.

"Justin?"

The figure raised his bloody head. And he was indeed Justin.

"Justin, what happened?" Pete reached his new friend and dropped to his knees in the weeds. "Justin! Talk to me!"

Justin raised his eyes to Pete, but there was none of the familiar sharpness or clarity there. Instead he gazed almost foggily at Pete's face, as if recently jostled from sleep.

Pete looked down to see Justin clutching his thick glasses in one hand. They were covered with blood and smashed beyond repair.

"Pete?"

Justin reached one bloody hand in Pete's direction. He missed. His hand touched a spot half a foot left of Pete's left shoulder.

"We have to get you to a doctor," Pete said. "Or the hospital."

Justin offered no response. He seemed to have drifted back into his sleep state again, despite his eyes remaining open wide. Too wide, Pete thought.

"Come on. I'll help you up."

But Justin had ceased responding now. It wasn't a matter of helping. It was a matter of doing it for him.

Pete hooked one arm under each of Justin's armpits and pulled the smaller boy to his feet. Justin fell limply forward onto him, and Pete was aware of the blood. The fact that Justin's blood was all over him. He changed nothing as a result of it, but he couldn't help finding it alarming.

Pete lifted straight up again, wrapping his arms around Justin's waist. He was able to lift Justin's feet a few inches off the ground.

Pete carried him—in a desperate series of tiny steps—to his wagon.

The only doctor in town was a good four miles away. The hospital was over the line into the neighboring county. But Pete figured he was less than two miles from the lady doctor's house. She might be mad if he brought someone there. But he would do it anyway. He would have to do it, regardless.

Some things were simply more important than others, and everybody with half a brain knew it.

—

"Ma'am?" he screamed from the end of her road. Even though he knew he was too far away to be heard. "Ma'am?" he screamed, even louder.

He looked around at Justin as he jogged. Pete was pulling the wagon right down the tarmac in the middle of the road, because there was no sidewalk out here in the sticks, and the dirt beside the road was too broken up and bumpy. Justin had loosed a muffled shout of pain on every bump, and that was something Pete simply could not abide. He'd have rolled the wagon over his own body to spare his friend that pain. That is, if such a thing had been possible.

Justin slumped in the wagon with his back resting at the intersection of the two remaining wooden rails. His neck was purposely craned in the direction of their travel. His eyes looked more focused to Pete, and he seemed to be taking in the fact that they were headed for the lady doctor's house, which filled Pete with a tremendous sense of relief.

Justin had blood in one of his eyes. And he didn't seem to notice. At least, he wasn't trying to fix it.

"Ma'am?" Pete screamed again.

She hurried out onto her front porch.

Just for a split second she was looking down at her apron. Apparently her hands had been wet when he'd screamed for her, and she was hurrying outside and drying them on her apron at the same time. She looked perturbed. As if he shouldn't have bothered her again. As if she'd really counted on spending the rest of the day with no troublesome young boy to pester her.

Then she looked up.

"Holy mother of God," she said. "What in hell happened to him?"

"I'm not sure, ma'am," he called, jogging up her bumpy walkway, towing the wagon. Trying to ignore his friend's grunts of pain. "He was woozy and I couldn't get him to tell me much."

She ran to meet them halfway.

She bent over Justin in the wagon. Examined his broken scalp. Opened his eyes wide with gentle fingers and peered inside. She held up two fingers in front of Justin's face.

"How many fingers am I holding up?" she asked him.

"Two, ma'am," Justin said, his voice frighteningly small.

"Good." Dr. Lucy straightened up and addressed Pete. "We need to get him to a hospital," she said.

"No hospital!" Justin said, his voice higher and stronger.

"But you're a doctor," Pete said.

"But I'm not a hospital."

"No hospital!" Justin piped again.

Dr. Lucy leaned over him a second time. "Why would you not want to go to a hospital when you're this badly hurt?" she asked him.

Justin's answer was small and hard to hear. Pete moved in closer, but by then he seemed to have missed it. Whatever it was.

"How would a hospital make it worse?" Dr. Lucy asked Justin. "That doesn't make sense. Hospitals make it better."

Another mumbled reply that didn't make it all the way to Pete's ears.

"Who's 'they'?" Dr. Lucy asked.

Justin looked down at his lap and offered no reply.

"Did the person who did this to you tell you not to go to the hospital?"

At first, nothing. Then a movement of Justin's head that might have been a nod, or his head might just have teetered slightly in his difficulty holding it up.

"Or the police," Justin said. A little stronger this time.

Dr. Lucy stood up straight and sighed. For a time, nothing moved. It seemed like a long time to Pete but he knew in the back of his brain that it probably wasn't. It was probably only seconds. But they were long seconds.

"I don't have permission to treat this boy," she said, apparently to no one in particular.

"Justin!" Pete said, still caught and twisted in his panic. "Tell her she has your permission!"

"That's not what I meant," she said.

Another long second. She seemed calm in some ways. Troubled, but not excited. She seemed lost in her own brain. Pete could tell she wanted to help, that her impulse was to help. And yet she stood still another second or two.

"This is a minor child," she said. "And he's not my child. I could get in a lot of trouble treating him without his parents' permission. Especially if something goes wrong and it turns out I should have taken him to a hospital."

Another excruciating second. Or two.

"His mother died," Pete said.

"Where's his father?"

"Working at the plant."

The doctor's attention disappeared again, into her own head. Pete waited, thinking he might burst. As if everything he was feeling could not fit inside his skin another moment.

"Bring him inside," Dr. Lucy said.

—

"Okay, here's what I want you to do," she said to Pete. "We're going to scrub you up, and then I want you to come here and hold pressure on this scalp wound. Be gentle, so as not to hurt him. But firm enough to stop the bleeding."

She had Justin on her metal examining table, with a towel to catch the blood. She had flushed out the long, open wound in Justin's scalp and squeezed something from a bottle onto the area. Now she stood beside the table holding a wad of sterile gauze against the boy's scalp.

Justin's eyes were open, staring up into the doctor's bright fluorescent lamp. But Pete couldn't tell how much he was taking in.

"Okay, ma'am, but . . ."

Then Pete hardly knew how to go on.

He could think of a million endings to that sentence. Mostly, though, he was lost in an unfocused feeling of dread. The doctor was supposed to hold pressure to stop the bleeding. Not Pete. Pete might hurt his friend. He might do it wrong. He might make everything worse.

Meanwhile he was keeping the doctor waiting. And, more to the point, keeping the emergency situation waiting.

"Pete, I need you here. We have to move this along."

"Where are you going to be?"

"I'm going to go call the plant and see if I can reach his dad. You know his dad's first name?"

"No, ma'am."

"You know Justin's last name?"

"Yes, ma'am. It's Bell. Justin, what's your dad's first name?"

But Justin seemed to be gone again. Faded out into a land Pete couldn't understand. Gone where Pete couldn't follow. He'd gone there before, Pete reminded himself. As Pete was helping him into the wagon. And he'd come back.

He'll come back again, Pete told himself. *He'll come back.*

But he also knew there were no guarantees.

"Pete!" the doctor snapped, breaking him out of his trance. "I need you here now."

Pete did as he was told. He moved to the table and cautiously placed his hand on the gauze pad.

Then the doctor was gone. She hurried out of the room, and it was just Pete and his grievously injured friend. And if something went wrong now, Pete was on his own. At least for the minute it would take him to find her and get her back in the room.

He looked down at Justin, who returned Pete's gaze with eyes that seemed reasonably focused.

"Oh good," he said. "You're back."

Justin said nothing. Just looked up into Pete's face. Pete could see lines on Justin's face, track marks made by his tears sliding through the blood.

"Who did this to you?" Pete asked.

Justin didn't answer.

"Did you know them?"

"No," Justin said.

"Am I hurting you the way I'm pressing on your head?"

"No," Justin said again. "I mean, it's okay."

"Did they say why?"

Justin turned his eyes away.

Pete looked up, only to be reminded that he and Justin were not alone in the room after all. Prince was lying in his kennel cage with his head held high, watching the two of them with great interest. In his small golden eyes Pete saw concern.

Prince was smart enough to know trouble when he saw it.

"What's your dad's first name?" Pete asked, still looking Prince in the eye. Still sharing concern in that visual line of communication.

He mostly asked as a way of checking whether Justin was still with him.

"Calvin," Justin said.

But by then it was too late to go tell Dr. Lucy anyway.

Chapter Seven: Dr. Lucy

"Falco Manufacturing," said a gruff male voice on the line.

The man sounded as though Dr. Lucy were already troubling him. Already wasting his time. And she hadn't even said hello yet.

"I need to talk to one of your workers. A Mr. Bell."

Silence. And what might have been a sigh.

"We don't pull men off the line for phone calls," the voice said.

"This is an emergency."

"What kind of emergency?"

"His son has been seriously injured."

Another belligerent pause. Or maybe she was reading too much into the silence. But probably not.

"Last name again?"

"Bell."

"First name?"

"I'm sorry. I don't know it."

"We have more than one Bell here."

"I'm looking for the one who's new in town."

Silence.

"The one with a young son."

Silence.

"With dark skin."

"Oh," the man said. "Why didn't you say so?" Then, obviously not to her—but without covering the phone in any way—he said, "Frank. Go pull Calvin Bell off the line. Tell him there's been an emergency with his son."

He never came back on the phone with her. Just set the receiver down.

She could hear what sounded like a cigarette lighter firing up, which made her want to light one of her own. But she'd left them back in the examining room.

She pulled back the curtain and looked out onto her own front porch.

The wagon sat abandoned there, puddled with blood. Small drips of blood marked her front porch in a path to the door.

She wondered if the boy would need a transfusion. She should have taken his blood pressure. Part of her felt she should hang up and go do that right now. But Calvin Bell was about to pick up the phone, having been told there was an emergency.

Besides, barring a stroke of luck, it was unlikely they would have a match for a blood donor until the father arrived.

She let the curtain fall closed again and wondered how long the boy had sat bleeding before Pete happened along and found him.

And she also wondered *why* he'd sat bleeding.

"Hello?"

A new voice came on the line, and she knew it was the right one because it was laced with the panic only a parent can display.

"Calvin Bell?"

"Yes."

"You have a son named Justin?"

"Yes. Tell me what happened. Is he okay?"

"He's injured."

"But he's alive."

"Yes. He's alive."

A brief moment while the man breathed. Swallowed down, or shrugged off, the worst of what he had been feeling.

"What happened to him?"

"We're not quite sure yet."

"He had some kind of accident?"

"No. It doesn't seem like it was an accident." She paused, but then went off in the necessary direction. He needed to digest that information, but he could do it in a moment. First things first. "Listen. Mr. Bell. I need your permission to treat him."

"Of course. Whatever he needs."

"I'm a licensed doctor but I don't have an actual practice in this area. Or anywhere else anymore. He was brought to my home. I'm not sure he doesn't need to go to the hospital. But apparently the men who hurt him told him not to go to the hospital or the police. So of course he doesn't want to do that."

She waited for his reaction. It took a few seconds.

"But he may need to," was all Calvin Bell said.

But it was clear there was more. She could almost hear what he didn't say, too. Or at the very least she could feel the weight, the pull, of his not saying the balance of what was on his mind.

"He may be right that they'll only make it worse if he does," she said.

"Can you do what a hospital can do?"

"No. Well. Yes and no. I have all the training the doctors there have. Maybe more, in this neighborhood. But I don't have access to all the equipment they have. Here's what I can do: I can stitch him up to stop the bleeding. I can x-ray anything I think might be broken. My biggest concern is the head wound, because I'm sure he has a concussion. Which could be dangerous. Potentially, at least. There could be complications. But I can monitor his condition. And if I think he needs to be hospitalized I can get him there fast. And if not, we can avoid . . . well, that different set of complications."

"You honestly think they're watching the hospital?" he asked. His voice sounded full of a dread wonder, as if poking the world to see how horrible it might prove itself to be.

"I have no idea," she said.

A silence fell.

"Tell me where you are," he said. "I have to get out there."

"Do you have a car?"

"No. But I could take the bus. How far are you from a bus route?"

"A good four and a half miles."

Another silence. In this one, Dr. Lucy thought she heard defeat. The dull thud of options dropping away.

———

She hurried back into the examining room.

Pete seemed ecstatic to see her. Inordinately relieved. Even under the circumstances.

"How's he doing?" she asked.

"Aw, heck, I don't know. You're the doctor. Did you get his dad?"

"Yes. Any changes?"

"Not as I can see, ma'am."

"Okay, here's how it's going to go, Pete. I'm going to stitch up his head and bandage it. I'm going to give him a simple neurological exam—"

"I don't know what that is."

"Doesn't matter. Just keep listening."

"Yes, ma'am."

She moved closer and relieved Pete of his job holding the gauze. She pulled it gently away from the injured scalp. The wound had stopped bleeding.

She hurried to the sink to scrub up again.

"I'm going to clean him up some. Wash off all this blood so we'll see more about where he's injured. I'm going to take his blood pressure to make sure he didn't lose too much. Then I'm going to x-ray him to see if anything's broken. And then comes the part you won't like."

She waited for a reaction from him, but he didn't have one. Or, more likely, he kept it to himself. He said nothing. Just waited for her to go on.

"Then if I'm satisfied his condition will likely hold for twenty minutes or so, I'm going to leave him here with you and go get his dad."

Dr. Lucy could actually see Pete swallow, but he said nothing.

"But . . . ma'am . . ."

"I'm sorry, Pete. I know this is a little scary for you. And I'm only going to do it when I'm pretty sure he'll be okay for twenty minutes."

"*Pretty* sure," he repeated.

"Look, I'm sorry, honey, but I have to get his dad back here." She paused in her hand-washing motions briefly, wondering where the "honey" had come from. But she didn't have time to wonder. She had a wound to close, and it wasn't going to suture itself. "Pete. Go sit down and put your head between your knees and don't watch this. It'll make you faint."

"Yes, ma'am," he said.

But he didn't sit down. Just moved to the window and stared out in the direction of the horse pasture.

"Pete. Sit down."

Silence. No motion. At least not on Pete's end of the room. She moved back to the table. She was ready to begin suturing. She looked down into the face of Justin, who looked back with clear eyes.

"You okay, son?" she asked him.

"Yes, ma'am."

"You ready to get that stitched up?"

"Ready as I expect I'll get, ma'am."

She looked up at Pete again, who stared back.

"With all due respect, ma'am," Pete said, "I'm not much on the idea of sitting today."

"Oh. Right," she said. "Sorry. I forgot."

—

"I didn't realize until I got off the phone," Calvin Bell said, "that this meant you'd be leaving him at your house all alone."

He'd barely sat down on the bench seat of her station wagon when he said it.

"He's not exactly alone," she said.

She glanced over at him as she pulled away. Because she was afraid of him.

Not because of anything he had said or done, or anything he was. Except that he was a man, and a stranger. And a parent. And he was upset. Though hopefully not at her. But upset is a funny thing. It looks for places to direct itself. It's an emotion given to action, and it needs somewhere to go. Even if it has to make something up as it goes along.

He was a compact man, not very big. But strong looking. In many ways, he was a dead ringer for his son. Small stature. Dark skinned. Hair cropped close. Glasses.

Taking him in with her eyes made her feel better. There was something . . . for a second she couldn't quite find the word. Civilized. There was something civil about him. Compared to most of the men she had met.

He returned her stare and she looked away.

"I'm glad to hear that," he said. "Who's with him?"

"Well. It's not ideal. It's not anyone with medical training. It's not even an adult. It's just his friend. But I want you to know I gave him a very thorough exam before I left him. I'm not convinced that nothing could possibly go wrong in the medium run. I'm a little worried about swelling on his brain. Not that I think he has any at this time. But it could still happen. In that case we rush him to the hospital. But after my exam I was confident that nothing life-or-death was going to happen in the space of twenty minutes. And I knew it was important to get you to him."

She waited. She winced inwardly.

It's a very delicate space, she knew, between a parent and a child. Not a good place to thrust yourself. And she knew that leaving Justin with Pete was not one hundred percent without risk.

Nothing in life really is, she thought.

She waited for some reaction from him. Watched him from the corner of her eye, but there were no outward tells.

"Justin has a friend?" he asked, his voice heavy with wonder and almost at the point of cracking.

"He does."

"I didn't know that."

They passed a state police vehicle on the highway, going the opposite direction. The trooper stared into their vehicle until his patrol car shot past. She looked in her rearview mirror to see him crane his neck to stare after them.

She wondered when the trooper was going to watch where he was going again.

"What color friend?" Calvin asked.

"White," she said.

A long silence.

She cranked her window down for more air. Calvin did the same. He was wearing a blue work shirt soaked through with sweat on its back and underarms. She wondered if the plant was air conditioned. Probably not.

"Think that's why this happened?" he asked.

"It crossed my mind."

A moment passed in silence.

Then he balled up a fist and brought it down hard on his own thigh. He dropped his face into his hands and sighed.

"If anything happens to him," he said through his hands, "I swear . . ."

"Something already did happen to him."

"I meant . . ."

"I know what you meant. And look. I'll be honest. I don't know if I did the right thing at any point today. I don't know if I should have driven him straight to the hospital. I don't know if I should have stayed home with him and let you make your way to us. All I can say is that I was trying to do it right. I knew how you must feel."

He dropped his hands into his lap again. Turned his face to her. It looked blank of emotion, and she had no idea what was going on inside him, or what words were about to burst out. And she felt afraid again.

"You have kids?" he asked.

"Yes," she said. "A boy. I mean, I had a boy."

She wondered when, in the course of the day ahead, he would ask her where the boy was, or what the word "had" meant in this case.

"Mind if I smoke?" she asked.

He only shrugged.

She offered him one by holding the pack in his direction, but he shook his head and turned away.

—

"Wait a minute," he said as they hurried through her living room. "Wait just one minute."

Against odds, his feet stopped moving.

"What?" she asked.

"You're a veterinarian? My son is being seen to by a *veterinarian*?"

"No. I'm a licensed physician."

"So what are the pig and the owl doing in your waiting room?"

"I crossed outside my training to take care of *them*. Not your son."

Pete stuck his head out of the examining room. "Oh, thank goodness you're here!" he said on a rush of breath that seemed to have been held in too long.

Then he disappeared again.

"Everything okay?" Dr. Lucy asked him.

Her feet moved again, as did Calvin's.

"Yeah," Pete called back, "but it's too much responsibility for me."

Justin was sitting up on the edge of the metal table, looking about halfway steady. His eyes were open, but they looked droopy. Pete had raced back to his side to be sure he didn't teeter.

"You said to keep him awake no matter what," Pete said. "So that's why he's sitting up."

"You did fine," Dr. Lucy said.

Justin's eyes came up to his dad's.

Calvin Bell closed the space between himself and his son in one impossible step. It was a step Dr. Lucy would have sworn—bet money—he was too small a man to take. He grabbed the boy up into his arms and lifted him into the air, holding him tightly to his chest.

For a moment, father and son remained silent.

Then Calvin asked, "Am I hurting you?"

"Yeah," Justin said.

"Should I put you down?"

"No."

So the embrace continued.

Chapter Eight: Pete

Dr. Lucy leveled Pete with a stare he didn't like. It made him feel anxious.

"I should give you a ride home," she said.

It was late afternoon. Pete didn't know how late, but the sun was on a long slant, heading lazily toward dusk.

"Please don't do that, ma'am," he said.

He felt a little shaky. Mostly in his hands, and in the pit of his throat. He worried that the shakiness had come through in the words.

Justin was settled in his father's lap in a chair at the corner of the room. His bandaged head was laid back on his dad's shoulder, his eyes closed. But now and then Calvin Bell jostled him gently to be sure he was awake.

Dr. Lucy was leaning back on one of her counters smoking a cigarette.

"I thought you were all fired up to go home and stand up for yourself," she said.

"Yes, ma'am. I thought so, too. But it's been a bad day. Upsetting, you know? And I just sort of . . . well, there's really only one way to say it, I guess. I just up and lost my nerve."

"You have to go home sometime."

"I was thinking maybe when I don't hurt anymore."

A silence fell. Pete thought Calvin Bell was listening to them. It would be hard not to. He was sitting just a handful of feet away. But if so he was quite purposely staying behind the invisible boundaries of their privacy. Staying out of the way.

And Pete knew he could only avoid going home if the doctor said he could stay with her.

"Course that's up to you," he added.

"You're talking days now."

"Yes, ma'am."

More silence.

Prince lay in his cage with his head high, his ears tuned forward, and looked from face to face. He'd been doing so as long as they'd been in the room. Almost as though he could read something helpful there. Almost as though each face held a different piece to the puzzle of the wolf-dog's understanding, if only he could put them in perfect order.

"You'd have to call your dad and tell him you're okay," she said.

"We don't have a phone, ma'am."

"Oh, that's right. Write him a note, then. I'll drive it over later and leave it on your door."

Pete was pretty sure she had just said yes to his staying, but he wasn't positive, and he didn't intend to ask. Just in case he was wrong.

A comfortable silence fell. Within it, Pete noticed Mr. Bell looking at the doctor while her attention was elsewhere.

The doctor is pretty, Pete thought. And it was a surprising thought, because he'd seen her so many times. But he'd never bothered to notice. He just hadn't looked at her as pretty or not pretty, because why would he? He wondered if he was suddenly seeing her through Mr. Bell's eyes. More the way a grown man would look at her.

The only thing not pretty about her was that hardness in her face and eyes. That indefinable something that warned you to keep away. That part was a little scary, and not appealing in any way.

"I haven't fed the horses yet," she said, knocking him out of his thoughts. "Will you do that for me, Pete?"

"Yes, ma'am."

"You remember how much they get?"

"Yes, ma'am. The scoop makes it easy."

"Will you feed the dogs for me, too?"

"Do they bite?"

"Not the hand that feeds them, they don't."

"I don't know how much they get."

"Give them as much kibble as their bowls will hold, then. Some will stop on their own when they're full. The rest won't get fat from overeating this one time. It's their lucky day."

—

As Pete was scooping out grain into the last horse's feed bucket, a movement caught his eye. He looked up to see Calvin Bell leaning on the top rail of the fence. Watching him.

Pete didn't know whether to feel flattered by the attention or afraid.

He walked to where the man stood at the fence and gingerly ducked through.

Mr. Bell said nothing. Just leaned on the fence and watched the horses eat. So Pete did the same. Nearly elbow to elbow with the man.

"How's Justin?" Pete asked. Because he didn't know what else to say. "Still okay?"

"Seems so. The doctor is taking his vital signs. So you're Justin's friend."

"Yes, sir."

"I didn't know he'd made any friends. He didn't tell me."

"I'm sure he would've told you by and by. I've only known him a couple days. Maybe he thought it was too soon to say we were friends. But *I* thought we were."

He waited a moment, in case Mr. Bell wanted to fill the silence. He didn't.

"Is it okay with you that Justin and I are friends?"

"Yes, I think so. If you really like him."

"I do."

"What do you like about him?" As he spoke, Mr. Bell took a white handkerchief out of his pocket and carefully wiped the sweat off his neck and brow. "Sure gets hot around here," he said.

"Yes, sir, it sure does. I found this wolf-dog. Like a cross between a wolf and a dog. He'd got himself hit on the highway."

"The one that's in a cage in the doctor's examining room."

"Yes, sir. I had this friend. Jack is his name. So we found this dog . . . at least we thought he was a dog at the time, and anyway he halfway is . . . and Jacky just left me and went on to the lake to go fishing. Made me figure out the whole thing about how to help the dog by myself. That made me kind of mad."

"I assume you're telling me this for a reason."

"Yes, sir. When I met Justin I asked him what he would do. If he would go on to the lake without me. He thought about it for a minute, which was good, because sometimes questions like that are harder than you think. He said no, once he'd seen the dog was in trouble he didn't think he could just walk away and forget about it."

"So that's why you like him."

"Yes, sir. That's a pretty good reason to like somebody, isn't it?"

"Very good, I'd say."

They leaned a moment in silence, watching one of the horses. The sorrel. He'd finished his own grain and was trying to horn in on one of the other feeders. But he was getting nowhere. None of the other horses were afraid to bite or kick if necessary to protect what was theirs.

"Those are fine-looking horses," Mr. Bell said.

"They're racehorses. Only they didn't race fast enough, I guess. Dr. Lucy's going to let me ride them sometime. Just not now. I'm not feeling like I want to do it right now."

"What needs to stop hurting?" Mr. Bell asked. "You told the doctor you wanted to stay till you stopped hurting. Not that it's any of my business. I just wondered if it had anything to do with what happened today."

"Oh. That. No. I just got a whipping from my dad last night. Well. Two, actually."

"So you don't know anything about what happened to Justin?"

"No, sir. I wasn't there. I was walking home with my wagon and I heard him. I just found him that way. I asked him what happened but he was kind of groggy. And after that all he told me was that it wasn't anybody he knew. Then again, who would he know around here? He only just got here. I'm sorry I can't help more. I feel real bad about what happened."

"Let me ask you a question, Pete. You asked me if I was okay with you and Justin being friends. And I said I was. But now I'm going to ask you if *your* parents are okay with it."

"I just have a dad. I think that's another reason why Justin and I get along."

"How would your dad feel about you and Justin being friends?"

Pete felt the sudden presence of what felt like an anvil in his gut. His face tingled, so it might be getting red, and Mr. Bell might be noticing.

"Do I have to say?"

"I wouldn't ask if it wasn't important."

"He wasn't too happy about it."

So, there. He had done it. Because he'd had no choice. But he'd hated having to do it. He looked away from the horses and down at his own sunburned hands. He'd just told a perfectly nice man that someone thought his son wasn't good enough to walk down the street with Pete.

Who does a thing like that? he thought. *Hurts somebody with their words that way? And how, of all people, could it have just been me?*

"So could that be why?" Mr. Bell said.

"Why what, sir?"

But then he knew. It hit him like an unexpected slap in the face.

"Holy cow," Pete said. "I sure wish you hadn't gone and put *that* idea in my head."

He stood blinking a moment, then decided to take his brain in an entirely different direction. It felt like an act of self-defense.

"I have to feed those dogs," he said to Mr. Bell. "But there's just one thing. I'm afraid of those guys."

"Want me to work with you on that?"

"That would be very nice, sir."

Pete figured he shouldn't be too surprised. Any dad who gives talkings instead of whippings might also be the kind of dad who would offer to help when he didn't even need to. Still, a day ago Pete hadn't known either variety existed. So it came as a pleasant shock all the same.

———

"Hey," Pete said. "A lot of these guys are little. They sure sounded big to me when I first showed up at the door."

He dragged the heavy bag of dry kibble up to the nearest kennel run gate. Inside were two friendly-looking little guys, just the kind of dogs Pete would be thrilled to meet at almost any point in his life. One was a brown-and-white beagle, the other a smaller tan terrier-type dog. But what type, Pete wasn't sure. He only knew it was some wire-haired variety.

They barked excitedly at Pete and Mr. Bell, but their tails wagged frantically at the same time.

"I like these guys," Pete said. "What kind of dog do you think that little tan one is?"

"Probably a mix, I'd guess," Mr. Bell said.

"Oh. Well, that's okay. Mutts are good, too. Prince is half wolf and half dog, so even that's sort of a mutt. Except somehow with him it comes out looking kind of important and regal. That's why I call him Prince."

Pete filled a scoop with kibble and opened the kennel gate, quickly filling both food bowls before the dogs could get out. But he needn't have bothered, because they weren't trying. They were more interested in food than time outside the gate.

Pete dragged the kibble sack on to the next run.

In it sat a huge German shepherd. What his dad called a police dog. The dog simply looked at Pete. He didn't bark or growl, but he also didn't wag his tail. He just stared deeply into Pete's eyes.

It made his blood run cold.

"Holy cow," Pete said to Mr. Bell. "I'm not so sure about this guy."

"Would you like me to feed this one?"

"I sure would, sir. Thanks."

Pete stepped back a good five steps to watch Mr. Bell work.

"Sir?" he asked as Mr. Bell scooped up a helping of kibble. "I was thinking. If somebody hurt Justin because of me . . . which is hard for me to even say out loud, because that would be the worst thing in the whole world if it was true . . . If it was because they wanted to teach him not to hang around with me, wouldn't they have to've told him that's why they were doing it? Otherwise what good would it do?"

Mr. Bell's hands stopped moving. Stopped reaching for the big dog's gate. But he didn't turn back to face Pete as he spoke.

"Anybody ask Justin if they said why?"

"I think *I* did, sir. At least, I asked him something like that. But he never answered."

"Well, later, when he's feeling better, we'll see what's what. You want me to finish up here by myself?"

The words hit Pete in the form of a sharp lump in his throat. Because he took them to mean he was no longer welcome in Mr. Bell's presence. That he was not wanted here.

"Okay, sir," he said.

He found his way back into the house without crying. But only just barely.

———

Pete lay with his front end draped over Prince's cage, his face pressed straight down. Even though that meant the thin metal bars of the cage pushed deeply into the skin of his face. He didn't care about that.

Prince raised his head as high as he could and snuffled, and for a moment their noses were only a couple of inches apart.

Pete reached a few fingers in through the bars, as deep into the cage as he could, and Prince licked them.

It made Pete laugh, but it loosed the tears at the same time. They fell on the wolf-dog's face, and Pete watched Prince's eyes register concern. Prince reached up again, but couldn't quite touch Pete's face with his nose or tongue.

"No one is talking to me at all," Pete said, more or less to Prince. "I think they think it's all my fault."

They had the examining room to themselves, which seemed strange. Dr. Lucy was elsewhere, and so was Justin. Mr. Bell might still have been out feeding the dogs, or he might have joined the doctor and his son, wherever they were.

Wherever that was, Pete felt sure he would be unwelcome there.

He nursed a terrible feeling in his gut that he recognized, but he could not remember why it felt familiar. Some great sense of dread about the near future, and how it would reveal itself when the trouble at hand crystallized into a clearer form.

Then he remembered.

He remembered listening to his mother and father scream at each other, and getting up and peering through the keyhole of their bedroom door to see that his mother was packing suitcases. And then going back to bed and having to wait to see what that would mean for his life going forward.

Sometimes you don't know exactly what it is but you know in your heart it's not good.

—

A hand on the small of his back made Pete jump the proverbial mile. Even Prince jumped in solidarity.

Pete straightened up suddenly, which hurt. It hurt his welts, and it hurt his back because he'd been bent over the cage for so long. Hours, by the feel of it. It was dark outside the open examining room windows, and the breeze that came through felt almost vaguely cool.

He turned to see Dr. Lucy holding a small pad of writing paper and a ballpoint pen in his direction.

"Write a note to your dad."

"Okay," he said, his voice sounding limp to his own ears.

He took the pad and wandered slowly and stiffly to one of her counters.

"You okay?" she asked him.

"No, ma'am. Where's Justin?"

"He's upstairs in the spare bedroom. He's going to sleep up there tonight with his dad. That way he'll be close by if I'm needed."

"Where do *I* sleep?" he asked, turning his eyes up to her with a gaze that felt burning. Which he hadn't intended. He didn't like the slight whine in his voice, either. But the truth was simply that he'd begun to believe no one wanted him around, and that there was not one corner of the earth in which he was welcome.

"I'll make you a bed on the couch. Is that okay?"

"That would be fine, ma'am. Thank you."

He turned his attention back to the note.

Dear Dad, he wrote in his best school-quality penmanship, *I'm okay. I'm just going to be gone for a little while. But I'm okay.*

Then he paused for a long time, thinking there must be more to say. But—if indeed he was right and there was—he had no idea what it might be.

So he went ahead and signed it: *Your son, Pete Solomon.*

He folded it up and handed it to the doctor, who looked deeply into his face. It made him uncomfortable.

"Thanks for driving this over there," he said.

"You're welcome. If I slide it under the door, will he get it? Can he get up and move to the door with his back injury?"

"Yes, ma'am. He goes from his bed to his chair and back. And to get the mail when the mailman drops it in the little box by the door. But he's not very fast. So you should have plenty of time to drive away before he sees you."

She did not reply. Just continued to study his face.

"Did Justin tell you anything more?" he asked her. "Like whether those men who hurt him said why?"

She remained silent a moment, and Pete could hear her breathing. Which seemed odd. Maybe every one of her breaths was coming out as something like a sigh.

"He said they told him to keep to his own kind."

"So it *was* my fault."

"No. It was the fault of the people who hurt him."

"But if I'd just stayed away from him . . ."

"But you had no idea anything like this would happen."

"No, ma'am."

"So you can't blame yourself."

Pete looked down at his sneakers and said nothing.

"But you will anyway," she said.

"Yes, ma'am."

———

Pete lay awake on the couch bed for a long time. Hours. The light of a strong moon bathed the room in a spooky glow, and that owl wouldn't stop staring at him. And there was a dog downstairs with him. A big greyhound. Pete was a little bit afraid of him but he kept to himself.

In time Pete got up and picked up the pillow and blanket the doctor had given him. He hauled it all into the examining room and made a bed on the floor, right up against Prince's cage.

"I was wrong," he told the wolf-dog, who blinked steadily at him in the dim light. "*Somebody* still wants me around."

Within a few minutes he was able to sleep.

Chapter Nine: Dr. Lucy

She wound her way through the living room by moonlight, a bottle in one hand, a pack of cigarettes in the other, allowing her eyes to gradually adjust to the dimness.

There was no one sleeping on her couch. No Pete. Even the bedding she'd given him was gone.

She looked into the face of Archimedes the owl, who predictably stared back.

"Where did he go?" she asked the bird.

The bird, of course, offered no suggestions.

Dr. Lucy made her way to the door of the examining room.

A spill of moonlight poured through one of the open windows and fell across Pete, sleeping mostly on his belly on the hard linoleum, his face pressed close to the wolf-dog's cage.

Prince raised his head to regard her. Pete kept sleeping, snoring lightly.

—

She sat outside on a rickety wooden lawn chair, watching the full moon begin to set over the backs of the sleeping Thoroughbreds.

She put a fresh cigarette to her lips.

A nearby sound made her jump.

"Sorry," the deep male voice said. "Didn't mean to startle you."

Calvin Bell stood over her chair in his jeans and a sleeveless undershirt, his feet bare. The shirt was so white it glowed in the moonlight.

Now there's a man who understands how to do his own laundry, she thought.

He was pulling the other rickety chair up beside hers.

"Is this okay?" he asked. "Or are you out here trying to think your own thoughts in peace?"

"It's fine," she said. "Sit with me."

He did.

She held the pack of cigarettes in his direction, but he only shook his head silently.

"You don't smoke, do you?" she asked him.

"I don't, no."

"Did you ever?"

"Oh, yes."

"So you quit. You're a better man than I am. Well, that came out wrong, but you know what I mean. When did you quit?"

She looked over at his face. He had a trace of jet-black beard showing. He'd apparently left his glasses inside.

"June 12, 1957. Recognize the date?"

She didn't, at least not for a moment.

"You should," he added. "Being a doctor and all."

"Oh, right," she said when it hit her. That was the day the U.S. Public Health Service had taken its official position on smoking. "All that cancer stuff."

"You don't believe it?"

"Oh, I believe it." She could have said more. Probably should have. Instead she just held up her bottle. "What about this?" she asked. "Can I interest you? Given a year or two they'll probably find out this stuff is killing us, too. All the good stuff is bad, if you know what I mean."

He laughed, but just a little. Just low and almost private. "What is it exactly I'm being offered?"

"It's a decent Scotch. I only brought one glass. But you can have the glass. I'll be uncouth and take a drink right out of the bottle."

She held the glass out in his direction and he took it from her. Their fingers bumped briefly.

"Now *that* I'll take you up on," he said. "Owing to the fact that it's been such a miserable day. But just two fingers. Just enough to take the edge off this horrible time. I won't stay."

"Don't leave on my account."

"I'm not. I just don't want Justin to be alone long."

"Oh. Right."

She was too embarrassed to admit that she had briefly forgotten about the boy's need for close care. Her mind had been drifting a million miles away from such concerns.

"I mostly just came out here to thank you for stepping in where you were needed. And also . . . well, sooner or later I have to ask . . . I've been doing some worrying about what I'm going to owe you when all this is over."

"Oh, that," she said. "Nothing. Or, I don't know . . . whatever you can. Just pay me what you can when you can. I really don't practice for money anymore. If it wasn't for how much it costs to feed the animals and buy their medical supplies I'd say it's on me. But as it stands, I'd say pay what you can, down to and including nothing if you can't manage it."

She heard something wordless come out of him. A rush of air. Fear exiting.

"That's a big relief," he said. "I've only been on the job since yester-day. And then I went and missed hours today. I haven't even been paid yet. I guess I owe you more than one thank-you."

"You'd better tear yourself away from him and go in tomorrow."

"Tomorrow is Saturday."

"Oh, right. So it is. You lose track of the days of the week when you don't have to obey them anymore."

They sipped in silence for a minute or more. Dr. Lucy was aware of the cicadas, their special sound, in a way she usually wasn't. Because normally she was so used to it. On this night everything felt vivid and almost new. If called upon to say why, she likely would have been unable to pin the feeling down. Probably just the startling experience of "not alone."

"Let me ask you a question," Calvin Bell said.

"All right. I'll answer it if I can."

"What the hell is wrong with people?"

A pause as she allowed the enormity of the question to settle in. It matched so well with the enormous wondering that filled her own days.

"Calvin, I'll be damned if I know. And it's not for lack of trying to figure it out, let me tell you. My personal theory? They're scared. Crazy world full of a bunch of people who are scared out of their wits over everything and playing a bunch of stupid games to fool you into think-ing they're not. Maybe even to fool themselves. But, I don't know. I'm a doctor, not a psychiatrist. I could be full of it."

Another long silence.

"It's none of my business," he said, "but . . ."

Dr. Lucy figured her time was up on his asking about her children.

". . . how do you manage out here if you don't work?"

"Oh. That. I get alimony from my ex-husband. It would be enough for just me, but the animals strain the system. I have to get a bit creative sometimes to cover their costs."

A brief pause. Then Calvin said, "Please feel free to tell me to shut up and go away if you like."

But she didn't want him to shut up and go away. Another comfortable silence filled only by cicadas would have been nice. But she didn't want him to go away. Which was an unusual feeling. To say the least.

——

"I'd like very much to hurt somebody," Calvin said after a time.

His voice was constrained into something like an artificial calm. She could tell it wasn't easy for him to constrain it.

"I hope you won't."

"No. I won't."

"Good. Won't help your son much to have you in jail."

"True. But there's an even better reason. I refuse to let them pull me down to their level. I won't let them turn me into *them*. I decided that a long time ago. But still. An eleven-year-old boy. The temptation is almost too much to tame. I hope I never find out who did this. It'll be a lot easier to keep talking myself down from violence if I never know. But . . ."

He never went on to say but what. Dr. Lucy didn't think the end of the sentence was hard to figure out, though.

"Pete told me a man saw them walking together today," she said, "and it was the same man who'd told on them to Pete's father last time he saw them together. So I'm thinking it's not a hard trail to follow. Can't literally be Pete's father, though, because he has a work-related injury that keeps him down."

"Recent injury?"

"I think so. I'm not sure."

"What's his name?"

"Pete never told me his last name. But I was over there earlier this evening and the mailbox says Bernard Solomon."

Calvin did not reply. Not for quite a while.

In time he held his glass out to her and she poured him another two fingers.

"I've only been at the plant not quite two days," he said, startling her. She'd begun to think he never planned to speak again. "And already you hear things."

"What kind of things?"

"Like if a man goes out with an injury. Goes out on worker's compensation, so the industrial accident board has to pay him to stay home. Some men, nobody questions it. If they say they're hurt, they are. Other men I guess don't get the same full measure of faith."

"You think he's faking?"

"I don't think anything about it. I've never met the man. I'm just passing along what I've heard." He threw back the glass and downed the balance of the Scotch. "I'd best be getting back to my son," he said, handing her the empty glass. "Thank you for this. Thank you for everything."

"Sleep well."

Calvin laughed. There was a bitterness to the sound.

"I won't sleep a wink," he said.

"Can't sleep when you're worried?"

"Can't sleep when I'm angry."

He carefully returned his chair to the brick patio outside the back door of the house. Then he was gone.

———

A knock on her bedroom door blasted her out of sleep. Winston the upstairs dog had opted to sleep downstairs to better keep an eye on the wolf-dog, as he had done since Prince's arrival. So there was no one to bark. No one to protect her. And for a panicky moment she couldn't remember why anyone would be in her house.

"Doctor?"

It was a deep male voice calling through the door, and she recognized it. She pulled a deep breath and sighed out her fear. Of course. It was only Calvin.

"Everything okay?" she called back.

"I'm not sure. I'm sorry to bother you, but—"

Before he could even finish the sentence she had made her way to the bedroom door and thrown it wide.

"I hated to wake you—"

"What's going on? What's wrong?"

"Justin got up to go to the bathroom just now and he got scared because there was blood in his urine."

She hurried into the spare bedroom. The bedside lamp was on, casting a warm glow in one corner of the room. Justin was lying awake with the covers pulled up to his chin. He met her gaze with wide eyes.

She sat on the edge of the bed and instinctively held a hand to his forehead. Even though it really wasn't a question of whether he had a fever. In that instant she came fully awake. Her first awareness was that of a sense of familiarity to the moment. Waking in the night to look in on a sick child—that often-repeated scene every mother holds etched deeply into her cells.

Except in her personal memory there had been no father present. He had lived in the home, but had rolled over and gone back to sleep while she dealt with nighttime issues.

Her second revelation was the fact that she had not bothered to put on a robe. She was sitting on the edge of the twin bed wearing only a short nightgown. Calvin stood over her wearing only his boxer shorts and sleeveless undershirt.

She looked down at her own exposed legs.

Calvin reached over to the other twin bed and grabbed the thin blanket, pulling it toward them. He half draped it over her lap, half handed it to her to do the same.

"Thank you," she said.

She reached over to the bedside table for her blood pressure cuff.

"It's really not so very unusual, what happened just now," she said to Justin in her best calming voice. "Usually when someone is hit hard in the soft parts of their belly, or kicked like you were, it's pretty common for their organs to bleed a little. It's like a bruise, except in this case the blood ends up in your kidneys instead of just sitting under the skin like a bruise on your arm or leg. So if it's only a little blood I'm not too worried. Did the urine look bright red like it was almost all blood? Or just pink?"

"More pink," Justin said, relaxing some.

"No cause to panic just yet, then," she said, wrapping the cuff around Justin's skinny upper arm.

He had been sleeping in his underwear. One strap of his sleeveless undershirt was stained with dried blood.

"That's good," he said.

"I'll take your blood pressure to make sure you've still got plenty moving around in your veins. And I'm going to feel very gently around your stomach if you'll let me. It'll hurt some but I'll be as careful as I can."

"It's okay," he said. "You can do that."

"Let me do the blood pressure first."

As she squeezed air into the cuff in short bursts she glanced over at Calvin, then quickly looked away. He was climbing into his Levi's to cover himself.

She focused on the dial and turned the valve, deflating the cuff.

"His blood pressure is fine," she said to Calvin, who stood over them again. "It hasn't changed at all. If he had serious internal bleeding it would be dropping. Maybe I don't even need to feel around that poor injured belly."

"It's okay," Justin said. "You can."

He sounded so brave and cooperative that Dr. Lucy had to give him the exam. Even if she did know it wasn't entirely necessary.

She pulled the covers down to his hips and gently pressed his midsection.

"What are you looking for?" he asked, clearly working hard to manage his wince reactions.

"With serious internal bleeding there might be a soft swelling where the liquid pooled. Well, there would be. Internal bleeding has to go somewhere. But it might be where I could feel it. I think you're doing okay. Tell you what I'd like to do. I'm going to go downstairs and get you a specimen cup. And next time you have to urinate, you can go in the cup and save it for me to see in the morning. And then I'll know how much blood. Does that sound okay?"

Justin nodded. And smiled at her unguardedly.

A thin outer layer of the ice around her heart melted.

She hated it when that happened.

—

Calvin joined her in the kitchen at a few minutes after six a.m. She was standing up, peering into cupboards, trying to figure out what she could serve four people for breakfast.

She'd been smoking a cigarette, but she ran it under the kitchen faucet and dropped it in the trash when she saw him.

He was wearing yesterday's shirt—what choice did he have—but it looked noticeably wet at the seams, leading her to believe he had washed it out in the sink. He smiled in a way that looked . . . she couldn't find the word for it. Not at first.

Sheepish?

"You don't have to do that," he said. "It's your house, remember?"

"I don't mind. I should cut down anyway. You know. All that cancer stuff. How's the patient?"

"He seems fine. He's upstairs trying to figure out how to brush his teeth without a toothbrush. Right now he's using his finger and a little table salt. I hope you don't mind. He came down here and got some salt out of that shaker on your stove. He's fastidious about his teeth."

"I think I'll manage without it," she said. "So here's what I'm thinking. I don't have enough eggs for four people. I wasn't expecting anyone. But I have enough eggs to make French toast for four people. How does that sound?"

"It sounds wonderful, but it's more than you owe us. Wouldn't you rather we just get out of your hair?"

His words hit her in unexpected ways and places. She had not considered the possibility that he might be about to go. And so, without warning, she had to admit—to herself, anyway—the fact that she didn't want him to. It was a thing that had floated just beneath the surface of her consciousness for most of a day and yet it startled her when it broke out into the light.

"It might be better if I observed him for a little longer," she said.

"I hate to impose on you."

Did he want to go? she wondered. Or did he merely assume she wanted him to? And that statement she'd just made, that Justin would benefit from observation. Had that been a full truth?

"Did he fill that specimen cup?"

"He did. It doesn't seem like much blood."

"It's probably fine. But you're more than welcome to stay until we're a hundred percent sure."

"You're so generous with your time," he said. Then he sat at her kitchen table. "Will you come sit with me a minute? I need to get something off my chest."

She joined him at the table and sat not a foot from his side, something almost akin to a tremble roiling in her insides from waiting to hear the something. To learn what kind of something it would prove to be.

"I want to apologize for last night," he said, his voice deep and serious.

"What about?"

"Here you are a woman, and living on your own, and you're good enough to offer us lodging right by your bedroom door. And then to come over and knock without even thinking to dress first, and in my panic drawing you out without even giving you time to wake up enough to think whether you're decent. I feel like I stepped over a line of your privacy, and I want to be sure you know that was never my intention. But I'm apologizing for it all the same. Because I put you in an awkward position, whether I intended to or not."

Dr. Lucy shook her head. A few more times than necessary.

"Calvin, don't be silly. You have nothing to apologize for. You were just worried about your son. We both were."

She placed one hand gently on his arm.

He had his sleeves rolled back, and her hand touched his bare skin, and they both looked at the hand and the arm as if they'd never seen anything of the sort before. She wanted to pull the hand back again but she didn't. Or at least *it* didn't. She felt as though no routine signals to her extremities were being received.

She looked up to see Pete standing in the kitchen doorway, staring at them with wide eyes.

She quickly pulled her hand away.

Chapter Ten: Pete

When he got to the kitchen, Dr. Lucy and Justin's dad were there. They were sitting at the table leaning in together, their heads close, the way people do when they know each other well. Not all people, though. His dad would never do that with his man friends, for example.

She had her hand on his arm, touching him.

It seemed a little confusing to Pete, because he thought of Dr. Lucy and Mr. Bell as hardly knowing each other at all.

Then she looked up and saw Pete standing there. She took the hand back too suddenly, as though Pete had caught her doing something embarrassing. Or just plain wrong. But it had been a friendly and kind-looking gesture, that touch. Maybe she didn't want anybody to see her being so nice. Any time he'd observed her being nice she'd always treated the moment like something she wouldn't want to see catch on.

She looked away from Pete's face and rose from the table and bustled around the kitchen, taking plates down from the cupboard and bread from the breadbox and milk and eggs from the fridge.

Pete was hungry, so he was happy to see this action toward breakfast.

"I'm making French toast for everybody," she said, her voice strangely fast and light. "Are you hungry?"

"I'm starving, ma'am. Thanks. How's Justin?"

"He seems okay, but he might have a touch of internal bleeding, so he and his dad are going to stay here a while longer, until we're sure it's no problem."

"Where is he?"

"Upstairs," she said. "Brushing his teeth as best he can. Calvin? Coffee?"

"I would love some. Thank you."

"I'm going to give you a job this morning, Pete," she said. "It's not a very pleasant one. But I know you think of that wolf-dog as more or less yours, so I expect you'll agree to take it on."

"Oh, yes, ma'am. I'd do anything for him. I don't know that he's mine but he's more mine than anybody else's. What should I do?"

"If you go back in and look at his cage you'll see he's lying on a wire mesh. And under that there's some space for . . . things to drop down. And there's a tray under that. It slides out and I lined it with old newspaper. It's so he can relieve himself without having to get up and out of the cage. I'd like you to slide that tray out and clean up after him and line the tray with nice fresh paper. And put the soiled paper in the outside trash."

"I'll do that for him. I don't mind."

"Good. And rinse out his water dish and give him some clean water."

"Yes, ma'am."

"And . . ." She paused, and reached down into a cupboard under the kitchen counter. "Give him this can of dog food. He'll like that. There's a can opener in that drawer under the sink."

"Yes, ma'am."

He found the can opener and carried it and the can of dog food out of the kitchen. But he didn't get far. He stopped in his tracks just a few steps into the living room. Because he heard his name spoken. But quietly, in conversation. Not as if he were being called back.

"Pete seems like a nice boy," Mr. Bell said.

"He's actually . . . amazing," Dr. Lucy replied.

Pete moved a step or two closer to the kitchen. That owl was staring at him. And the pig, too, which was more unusual. Pete put a finger to his lips, as though they might understand that gesture. As if they'd been just about to blow his cover but a shushing motion could change their thinking.

"I worry about him, though," Dr. Lucy said. "I don't think he comes from a very good home. And somehow he's managed to convince himself that everything bad that happens in the world is his fault. He takes on too much."

"Better than taking on too little," Mr. Bell said.

"Yes, I suppose that's true."

"I think that's why I like him."

"I like him, too," Dr. Lucy said. "Which comes as a bit of a surprise."

Then silence. Pete waited, nursing a warm feeling in his belly, but nothing more was being said.

When he was pretty sure that was all he was going to hear, he trudged off to the examining room to take care of Prince.

Just as he did, he heard Mr. Bell say, "And he calls me 'sir.' I don't get that a lot."

———

He was coming back from carrying the old papers to the outside trash. When he stepped back into the examining room, he saw Justin. Justin was standing at the far end of the room, in the doorway closest to the kitchen. He was dressed in yesterday's clothes, but the blood was mostly gone. But they looked partly wet, those clothes. One side of his head was swathed in bandages, which Pete was more or less used to seeing. But an angry bruise protruded from under the bandages now, spreading out along Justin's temple.

Justin smiled but it was a weak little thing. Weak and unsure of itself.

"Hi," he said.

"Hi," Pete said back.

Then no words. Just awkwardness.

"How're you feeling?" Pete asked when he couldn't stand the silence another minute.

"Better."

"Must hurt like the devil, though."

"The doctor gave me a pill. It helped."

Another murderous silence, much longer and deeper and more intractable than the one it followed.

"You're awful quiet," Justin said.

The short sentence felt freighted with worry. As if he might be about to find out the "why" of Pete's silence. As if the why might hurt him.

"I thought you'd be mad at me," Pete said.

With that, Pete broke his feet loose and walked back to Prince's kennel cage. He was pleased to see that the wolf-dog had finished the whole can of dog food and licked the bowl clean. He wanted to call to Dr. Lucy and ask her where the fresh papers were kept, but then he saw them stacked on top of the cage where it touched the wall at the back.

"Why would I be mad at you?" Justin asked.

The worry was gone. Possibly replaced with something else equally unfortunate. Maybe some brand of sadness.

"I figured it'd be pretty obvious."

"Well, it's not."

Justin stepped in close to Pete and squatted down, gingerly, bracing his hands on the linoleum for balance. He watched Pete line the gigantic metal tray with papers and slide the whole thing back into place.

"Hi, boy," Justin said directly to the wolf-dog, who looked back with calm eyes.

"His name is Prince."

"Hi, Prince." A pause. "He doesn't answer to that much better than 'boy.'"

"I didn't say he *knows* it's his name. Just that it is."

"Why would I be mad at you?"

Pete hadn't realized, until that moment, that he had been battling to hold back tears. The minute he acknowledged that battle, he lost it.

"Because I got you in all this trouble," he said, swiping tears away with the back of his hand. As if he could hide them. As if Justin weren't crouching right there, wouldn't see, and so would never have to know.

"That wasn't your fault, though."

"It kind of was, though."

"How do you figure? I mean, I know they were mad we were walking down the street together like regular friends. But it's not like you told them to think that way."

"But I knew it would be a problem."

He dropped to his knees because it still hurt too much to sit. Justin settled cross-legged on the floor. Their heads hovered close together, like Dr. Lucy and Mr. Bell. But different, too. There was that connection, that sense of leaning into a greater trust. But it was simpler when Pete and Justin did it. More of an everyday thing. Less shocking than Pete had found the scene in the kitchen.

Justin wasn't talking. Just waiting for Pete to go on.

"Night before last my dad gave me a whipping because somebody told him they'd seen me walking with you."

"So when you said he whipped you for being out so long, that wasn't true."

"No! It was. I didn't lie. I never lied to you. He gave me a whipping for being late. And then another one for being with you instead of the guy I told him I'd be with. And he told me not to hang around with you. And I just didn't tell you that second part, because . . . well, I hope you know the because. What a terrible thing to have to tell somebody. So I left it out. But I swear I never in a million years thought it would get *you* in trouble. I thought it would get *me* another whipping. I never thought anybody would go and take it out on *you*."

They sat in silence for a moment. Pete braced himself for blame. For all friendship and caring withdrawn. In other words, for the very worst life could deliver. He had only one friend left. He felt himself poised on the brink of none.

"You let me come out and walk with you, and you'd just had two whippings the night before, and you thought it would get you another one, and you did it anyway?"

"Well . . . yeah . . . ," Pete said, as if there were more to the thought. But there wasn't.

"Why?"

"Because you're my friend."

"Huh. Wow. So we really are friends, then, aren't we?"

"*I* thought so."

But in the silence that followed, Pete was engulfed in a terrible thought. And Justin's silence seemed to lead in the same direction. Granted, you can never know what somebody else is thinking. Pete understood that well enough. But the cloud over Pete's brain was so obvious and unavoidable that he couldn't imagine Justin's head being anyplace different.

What did it mean to be friends in a world where just walking down the street together could get someone viciously beaten? In what ways could that friendship be expressed? Or even exist? Though inside Pete it was a thought with no words. More a clutch of fear.

"That doesn't make it your fault," Justin said after a time.

"Feels like it does."

But Pete breathed deeply and realized it felt less like his fault now that he knew Justin didn't blame him.

Dr. Lucy called in from the kitchen.

"Pete?"

"Yes, ma'am?"

Justin winced at Pete's volume so near his ear.

"Sorry," Pete said quietly.

"Will you feed the horses and the dogs before breakfast?"

"Yes, ma'am."

Justin's eyes grew wide.

"There are *horses*?" he asked Pete.

"You didn't see them?"

"No. When would I have seen them?"

"I figured you'd see them out the window."

"I've been mostly lying down."

"Oh. Well, there are eleven of them. And they're *racehorses*."

"I'll come with you. I want to see the racehorses."

"You sure you feel good enough for that?"

"I think so. I can try, anyway. I want to see the racehorses."

———

They stood leaning on the pasture fence together, elbow to elbow. Except Justin had to reach up so high to get his elbows on the rail it was almost funny. That is, if anything could have been funny right about then.

"Dr. Lucy says I can ride them," Pete said. "You know. Later. When I get to the point where I can sit down again."

"Think I could ride one, too?"

"I don't know. Maybe. When you're feeling better. Only one thing, though. She says she can't guarantee they won't buck me right off again. Would you ride a horse that might buck you off?"

"Not sure," Justin said. "I'd have to think about that."

While he thought, Pete stared at the bandage on the side of his friend's head. It was so huge. Justin seemed lost in the vastness of the injury and its treatment.

"How did you end up with that big old deep gash on your head?" Pete asked, almost without knowing he was about to do so. "Unless you don't want to talk about that," he added quickly.

"Bottle," Justin said.

He pantomimed the act of bringing a bottle crashing down on some invisible head.

"Ouch," Pete said. "Sorry I asked."

"And now my dad and I are going to stay longer because there's a little bit of blood when I pee, from getting kicked in the stomach. Are you going to be here, too, Pete?"

"Yeah. I'm staying a while."

"Good. I was hoping you'd be here, too." Then, just as Pete was basking in the warm bath of being wanted by someone—by everyone, now that he'd overheard Dr. Lucy and Mr. Bell speaking well of him when they thought he couldn't hear—Justin added, "Won't your dad be mad?"

"Oh, hell yeah," he said, trying not to think it out much beyond that.

"Won't he come get you and do something terrible?"

"He doesn't know where I am. He knows I'm going to be gone, but not where."

"Oh," Justin said.

He didn't say, *But you have to go back there eventually.* He didn't need to.

"Well, I better get to feeding these horses."

But just then he heard Dr. Lucy call to him again.

"Pete! Justin! Come in for breakfast."

Pete turned to see her standing in the back doorway, looking . . . Pete wasn't exactly sure how to describe her expression. Looking a way he had not seen her look before. Lighter somehow. Almost . . . happy.

"I still need to feed the horses and the dogs," he called. "I'm sorry. I was slow. Justin and I got to talking and I didn't do what you said I should do. I mean, not fast enough."

"Come eat your French toast while it's hot. You can feed them right after breakfast."

"Okay."

She stood in the doorway and reached an arm out to each of them as they approached, and touched them each on the shoulder. Physically ushered them through the door. Which seemed odd to Pete, because normally she seemed to brace silently—or sometimes vocally—against anyone entering her private space.

He wanted to say, "You sure are in a good mood today." But he thought it might be better left unsaid. A lot of things were, he'd found.

"I'm sorry I was slow."

"Pete, you don't have to be sorry about everything."

"I don't?"

"No. You don't."

"Oh. Well. Okay. Thanks. That'll be a hard habit to break, though."

———

"Jam or syrup?" Dr. Lucy asked, seemingly to no one of them in particular.

"Jam, please," Pete said.

"Jam for me, please, ma'am," Justin said.

"I'm a syrup man," Mr. Bell said. "If you don't mind putting out both."

She set a bottle of syrup on the table near Mr. Bell's right hand. She set the jam in front of Justin—which Pete found mildly disappointing, but also more than reasonable, because Justin was hurt, and she couldn't give it to both of them at once.

"What kind of jam is that?" Pete asked Justin, leaning closer to try to take in the smell.

"I don't know. I'll taste it and tell you."

"It says right on the jar," Pete said, because he couldn't read the label at that angle.

"I don't have my glasses."

"Oh, that's right."

They both looked up into the face of Mr. Bell, as if on cue. It was a face quickly falling.

"Your glasses," Mr. Bell said. "Of course. I was so worried about everything else I never thought to notice. Any idea where they are?"

"We could look in the side yard," Justin said.

"That's where this happened? The side yard of our house?"

Justin nodded and handed the jam to Pete, then took his first bite of the French toast and sighed with pleasure.

"This is real good, ma'am," he said. "Thanks for making this for us."

"Wait," Pete said. Before she could even reply. "You got beat up in the side yard of your house?"

Justin nodded, apparently not wanting to talk with his mouth full.

"Then how did you get not two miles from *here*?"

"Didn't know I did," he said, swallowing quickly. "Is that where you found me?"

"Yeah. It was under a tree in a vacant lot less than two miles from here. You walked all that way? Hurt as you were?"

Justin set down his fork. As though the utensil prevented clear thinking.

"I guess I must have," he said. "But I don't remember. I just remember I didn't have money for a phone to call my dad. And I didn't know where there was a phone, anyway. I remember thinking there was a doctor where you were. But then I thought I shouldn't go there because I wasn't even supposed to know about her. That's really all I remember."

"I know where his glasses are," Pete said to the table at large. "But they're ruined. If they hadn't been smashed to bits I'd have put them in my pocket and brought them along. But they're no good to anybody now."

Mr. Bell only nodded blankly. Dr. Lucy sat down with her own plate.

"Wait," Pete added in Justin's direction. "You walked that whole way down our street and then along that highway a spell, and you were all bleeding, and not one person stopped their car to help you?"

Justin had gone back to eating, which seemed amazing to Pete, because this was appetite-killing stuff.

"Heck, there were cars going by our house while we were out in the side yard and while they were kicking me in the stomach and nobody stopped or did anything or said a word."

A long, ringing silence. Pete did not spoon jam onto his French toast or in any other way move to eat it. Which said a lot about the content of the talk, because Pete was hungry. The doctor had made sandwiches the night before, but it hadn't felt like enough.

"Let's talk about better things while we eat," Dr. Lucy said.

"I'm all for that," Mr. Bell added.

But they talked about nothing. Until the moment that, out of nowhere, Mr. Bell startled Pete with a sudden comment.

"Maybe we should go back to Philadelphia," he said, seemingly to no one.

And that's who answered him. No one.

"Hey, Pete," Dr. Lucy said after a long silence. "You're sitting."

"Yes, ma'am."

"Does it feel okay?"

"No, ma'am," Pete said.

Chapter Eleven: Dr. Lucy

"Were you serious about going back to Philadelphia?" she asked.

They were in her car, on the way back to Calvin's house, so he could fetch a toothbrush and change of clothing for himself and his son. The windows had been rolled down for air, and the wind blew her hair around. It made the world seem fresh somehow.

Dr. Lucy had been nursing an odd but pleasant sensation in her chest all morning. A kind of buoyancy. It made it harder to breathe, but she wouldn't have traded it away for anything. It felt like a brand of enthusiasm for the simple fact of being alive. It had been too long missing from her world.

"I'm not sure yet," he said.

"Is it really so much better there?"

"It's far from perfect. But nothing like this ever happened."

"Could Justin have a white friend in Philadelphia and no one would care?"

"Well, that's a good question," he said. "I'm not sure. We never happened to put that to the test. There's the house. Right there."

She pulled over to the curb in front of one of many tiny, carefully tended brick homes.

A woman in her housecoat was walking a white poodle, curlers in her hair. She glared at them as Calvin got out of the car. She watched after Calvin as he walked to the house and disappeared inside. Then she glanced back at Dr. Lucy in the driver's seat.

As the woman stepped level with the passenger-side window she paused and stared directly into Dr. Lucy's face. Disapprovingly.

"Go away," Dr. Lucy said, in a voice that left little margin for misunderstanding.

The woman raised her eyebrows in an overly dramatic fashion and hurried down the street, dragging her uncooperative little dog behind her.

———

Calvin came out after a time, carrying a paper grocery sack in his arms. He started down the walkway toward her car. Then he stopped. Turned back.

He walked around to the side yard of their little home.

He stood for several seconds, staring down at the dry dirt.

Then he walked again, this time all the way to where she sat parked.

"Give me just a minute, please," he said through the open car window. He placed the grocery sack on the passenger seat. "I have to get something I can use to clean this up."

He disappeared back into the house.

She stepped out of the car and walked to the side yard.

In the dirt was a heavy bottle, smashed. She touched the unbroken neck of it. Picked it up and turned it in her fingers. It was made of thick glass, and tapered out to square sides with rounded corners. She dropped it back into the dirt and, with the toe of her shoe, kicked over the piece that still held most of the label. It said "Jim Beam Kentucky Straight Bourbon Whiskey."

So it comes down to who drinks bourbon, she thought. *But around here that won't narrow it down much.*

The dirt around the broken bottle was pocked with dark miniature puddles of dried blood.

Calvin came back with a broom and dustpan, startling her. She had been lost in thought.

"I think I'd like to hurt somebody, too," she said as he swept up the glass.

"If I can resist the temptation," he said, "so can you."

———

"You don't have to answer this if you don't want," she said to him on the drive home, "but has it been hard raising Justin by yourself?"

At first he just studied the side of her face, as if considering her. She could see his gaze in her peripheral vision.

After a time he said, "So you know I lost my wife."

"It's none of my business if you don't care to talk about it."

"Everything is hard without Rebecca."

A long silence.

Then she said, "Tell me about her." And immediately wished she hadn't. She was gathering words to withdraw the statement when he spoke.

"Make a deal with you," he said. "I'll tell you about her if you'll tell me about your ex-husband."

"That seems fair enough."

"Feel free to go first," he said.

"Oh. Me. All right. Well. His name was Darren. He was handsome. Maybe too much so. Handsome can get in the way. It can become that thing you seek after, and then other failings seem to get justified away.

And he was smart. College educated and smart. We met at the university, in fact." She didn't tell him which one because it was a prestigious university and she didn't wish to appear to be bragging. "He gravitated toward the law and I went off toward medicine. He seemed fine with that. I wonder now if he assumed I wouldn't succeed. Or if he just thought I was filling my time until motherhood came along to fulfill me in a whole different way. A more permanent way. Because when I graduated from medical school and started my internship, things started to go sour between us."

"He didn't like the feeling of being surpassed."

"That's the conclusion I've drawn after the fact, yes."

"Then he didn't deserve you."

That sat in the air between them in utter, awkward silence. Dr. Lucy felt strangely aware of her hands on the steering wheel. And that sensation of being abnormally alive.

He broke the silence, causing her to jump.

"Rebecca was something of a force of nature," he said. "Which was amusing in a way, because she was so tiny. I swear she weighed all of ninety-five pounds. But you would *not* want to cross that woman. I'm not suggesting she was mean. She was nothing of the sort. But she had this finely sharpened sense of justice. And when she saw anything she perceived as injustice it fairly made her see red. I could almost picture steam coming out of those wonderful, tiny little ears."

He paused for a time, as if remembering.

"And she had no truck with any kind of killing. She wouldn't even kill a spider. She would catch it in a cup and put it outside. She'd put it on the roses so it could eat the aphids. She said everything in this world had a purpose."

A long silence. About a mile of it.

"You miss her a lot," Dr. Lucy said. It was a statement, not a question.

"I do."

"How long has she been gone?"

"She died in childbirth. So more than eleven years. But I still miss her. I'm used to living without her, but the missing never goes away. You think you'll get over the loss of someone. Eventually. Because it seems we get over everything, given enough time. And I guess in a lot of ways I've partially gotten over the traumatic event of her passing. But what you don't realize, until you have to live it, is that it's the absence of the person that's the trouble. The ongoing absence. And when you're missing someone, a longer time without them doesn't solve the problem. The longer you don't see someone, the more you miss them."

He went silent for a time. Dr. Lucy added nothing to the conversation, because she couldn't imagine what to add.

"She was well-educated, too," he said. "We both went to college. We were both the first and only person in our family to graduate from college. And now here I am on the assembly line with all the men who dropped out of high school."

More silence.

"Do you miss your husband?" he asked as they pulled into her driveway.

"No. I thought I would. But I don't."

"I'm not sure which one of us is luckier, then."

"No," she said. "I'm not sure, either."

He did not ask her if she missed her son. She was grateful for that.

"Maybe I should have left that bottle alone," he said. "Think it would accomplish anything to report this to the police?"

"Honestly? Aside from the fact that it could make things worse, I'd say no. I'd say the police around here are more dedicated to protecting and serving the bourbon drinkers."

"Right. That was a surprisingly naive question, wasn't it? You would think I would know the answer to that question and you wouldn't."

———

They sat on their respective patio chairs in the late afternoon, hidden from the sun by the back porch awning, drinking iced tea and watching the boys. Which was a peculiar way to pass time, because the boys were doing exactly nothing. They were lying on their bellies in the grass outside the horse corral, their heads leaned together as if talking.

"Penny for their thoughts," she said to Calvin after a time.

His left hand was dangling off the arm of his chair, just relaxing there in the air, and her right hand dangled just a few inches away. In that split second before he answered, she almost slid her hand inside his and held it. And the strangest aspect of that idea was the fact that it seemed quite natural. When she came to her senses and did no such thing, she was startled most by the fact that it hadn't struck her as a startling thing to do. There was really no sense of thought behind it at all. It just would have been easy.

"I expect they're talking about the horses," he said.

She had to take a moment to remind herself what they'd been discussing.

"Could be," she said, her voice calm. Or it sounded so, anyway. Inside she was surprisingly rattled at what could have happened, and how benign it had seemed at the time. How could such a big idea have disguised itself as harmless, everyday, and small?

"If I were a boy their age," he said, "I'd be devising a strategy to get on one. Trying to figure out which was the most docile and where to ride first with the best chance of my own survival. Do the horses ever get ridden?"

"There are two or three I used to ride regularly. But it's been a while."

They fell silent again.

Dr. Lucy felt herself preparing to go out on a limb. Surely it would be a much lower and stronger limb than the one she'd just avoided.

Wouldn't it? She found herself less sure than usual of what she could expect from herself next.

"This may sound odd," she heard herself say, "because we've only been here together for . . . what? A little over twenty-four hours? But already it feels familiar in a strange way. It feels . . ."

She stalled there, knowing that her sentence had no acceptable ending. She had almost wanted to say it feels a little bit like a family. Like spending time with your family. But she couldn't say a thing like that.

"Go on," he said after a time.

"I'm not sure," she said. "I'm not sure what I was meaning to say."

"Happy?"

She looked over at him, and felt her breath ease, her lungs fill more naturally.

"Yes. I guess that does sound right. Does that seem like a crazy thing to say?" But of course it helped that he had been the one to say it.

"Not sure why happiness should ever seem crazy."

"Although I don't know why it should be a familiar feeling," she added, wanting to fill the world with words. "Because I haven't had much experience being happy. Not in the family I came from originally and not the family I created. So here I am looking at this scene and feeling this feeling, and I seem to know somehow in some deep place that a family can be happy. Not that I'm calling us a family. Of course. I just . . . I hope you don't think I'm sounding insane." But she quickly talked over any chance he might have had to say. "But now I look at those two boys and I think, how can there be anything happy in this? They've both been recently beaten. One by the parent who's entrusted to love him and keep him safe and the other by total strangers. So clearly this can't be happiness."

"But it's happy from the inside," he said.

She waited to see if he would go on. He didn't for a time. She felt the urge to light a cigarette, but she resisted it.

"When I grew up," he said, "we were a happy family. Except there were all these problems. But it was from outside of us. My father sometimes had trouble getting work. Food wasn't absolutely guaranteed. We had to wear our pants until our ankles showed and our shoes until they pinched." He paused, and she felt the weight of something deeper in his mood. Something of more gravity than too-short pants. "My uncle was killed because he was accused of stealing something we knew for a fact he didn't steal. So there was no shortage of bad times. But they came from the outside. From the inside we were strong. I almost think that's better. In some ways, anyway. I mean, as opposed to living a fairly uneventful life with no great tragedies but not being particularly loving or happy within the home. That seems almost sadder to me in the long run."

"You know, it's funny," she said. "My father used to always say we were a happy family. Over and over he said that. And I always assumed it must be true, and that there must be something wrong with me for not feeling happy, but now I look back on that and it just sounds like whistling past the graveyard. It suddenly occurs to me that happy families probably don't repeatedly say out loud how happy they are. They probably think it goes without saying. They probably figure they all already know."

"Protesting too much," he said. A brief silence fell. "Should Justin and I stay another night? Or should we go home and sleep in our own beds?"

"Give it the weekend," she said. "A little extra patient care never hurts."

She didn't even make up an excuse why it was required. And he never asked questions nor objected in any way.

Chapter Twelve: Pete

————

Justin came down to the living room at bedtime to get him.

"My dad said to come down and tell you you're sleeping upstairs in the twin bed next to me," he said to Pete.

"I am?"

"Yeah. My dad's going to take the couch."

"Why?"

"Because of the lady."

"What about her?"

"Well. You know. Because she sleeps upstairs. And she's a lady."

"Oh," Pete said. "Okay."

But he still wasn't sure he understood.

———

It might only have been nine o'clock or it could have been midnight. Pete might have slept briefly, but he wasn't sleeping now.

He lay on his belly—in his underwear, with just a sheet pulled up to his waist—feeling the barely cool breeze that blew through the window. Watching the way it lifted up the gauzy curtain and curled it out and around, then allowed it to drift back into place again.

Now and then when it blew aside he could see the moon low in the sky over the horse pasture, and the horses sleeping together in a huddle, their heads resting on each other's backs. It looked peaceful.

Just for a moment Pete wished he could be a horse. Maybe an old unwanted racehorse with nowhere else to go, so Dr. Lucy would take him in. Then he could stay here forever. Then he could be peaceful, too.

"Pete," Justin whispered. "Are you sleeping?"

"No," Pete said. "Just lying here thinking."

"What were you thinking about?"

"Oh. That might be kind of hard to say. I guess my mind was just wandering more than anything. And I was watching the horses sleep. I wish I could sleep standing up. That would solve a lot of problems right now. I sure am tired of sleeping on my belly."

Justin sat up. Gingerly. Pete still couldn't quite do that without an immense penalty of pain. Not even gingerly. So he just sprawled there on his belly. It made him feel as though he had given up on something somehow. Given up on everything.

"But where was your mind wandering?"

"Oh," Pete said. "I'll have to think about that."

He didn't *think*, exactly. More made a space inside himself for a thought or feeling to come up.

Justin waited patiently and didn't speak.

"I guess I was wondering why it can't always be like this."

"Like what? You mean always at the doctor's house?"

"Maybe. I don't know. More like always okay where we are. And never needing to go home and be in trouble."

Justin knocked the covers aside and swung into a sitting position on the edge of his bed facing Pete.

"I'm scared to go home, too," he said, overly loudly.

They both waited and listened to see if they'd wakened the doctor. But nothing moved.

"What are you afraid of?" Pete asked. "Your home is great."

"It used to be. But now they know where I live."

"You think they'll come back?"

"I don't know. I think maybe I'll just keep thinking they will. And then I'll be scared to death whether they do or they don't. But they might. What if they find out we were here together?"

"How could they find that out?"

"I don't know. I don't even know how they found out we were together in the first place."

"Oh, that's easy," Pete said. "I know that. Boomer Leggett."

"What's a Boomer Leggett?"

"Remember that guy who pulled over in the tow truck while we were walking? That was Boomer Leggett. He's a friend of my dad."

"The guy you said you didn't like."

"Right."

A long silence. Pete had gone back to watching the curtain blow, because he found it calming. But now and then it moved aside and offered him the view of the moon, with that man-face the moon wears when it's close to full. And it felt to Pete like the moon was watching him be a coward. And noticing. And judging. Even though Pete knew in some part of himself that such a thing couldn't be true. But it kept feeling that way. Maybe because Pete was watching himself be a coward.

"So, listen," he said. "I keep wanting to ask you this but then not asking it. Maybe because I don't want to know. But anyway, here goes. Was Boomer one of the guys who did this?"

"I don't know," Justin said. "I didn't get a good look at him."

"You didn't see the guys who did it?"

"Oh, no. I saw *them* all right. I'll never forget *their* faces as long as I live. But I didn't really see the guy in the tow truck. By the time I realized there was anything to look at he'd started to drive away again."

"Oh."

"The more I can't forget their faces the more I'm afraid to go home," Justin said.

It felt as though Justin was edging his way toward something, but Pete wasn't sure what.

Pete said nothing. He was thinking about his own home situation. About the punishment he was postponing, and how unmanageably huge it was likely getting as he kept pushing it ahead of him down the road.

"I mean, not if my dad and I go home tomorrow," Justin said. "That would be okay. But then it'll be Monday and he'll have to go in and work at the plant, and then I'll be scared."

"Yeah. I guess I see what you mean. I guess I would be, too. Maybe Dr. Lucy would let you stay here while your dad is at work. So nobody can find you."

"You think she would?"

He asked it eagerly. As if he'd struck gold in Pete's simple idea.

"I don't know. Maybe."

"Will you ask her for me?"

The last thing in the world Pete wanted was to ask any more of the doctor than he already had. His sense of imposing on the better side of her nature seemed to have pushed their relationship to the edge of a treacherous cliff. The next push could be the end of everything.

Every cell in his body wanted to say no. That he was sorry, but that he couldn't bring himself to do that. He could do many things. Almost anything, really. But not that.

"Yeah," he said. "Sure."

They fell into silence.

Justin gathered the covers around himself and lay down again, as if he might be able to get back to sleep.

"Wish I could see the horses from my bed," he said after a time.

"Want to trade?"

"No, that's okay. You can have them. Say. Pete. Do you think it's just me? Or just us? Or is this really scary?"

"You mean having some guys after you?"

"No. Not just that. All of it."

"Not sure I follow," Pete said. "All of what?"

"I guess I can't say it right."

"Well, try. I'm interested."

"Just . . . I don't know. Being a person, I guess. Is it just me, or is it really scary?"

"That's a good question," Pete said. "I'll have to think about that."

But once again, he didn't exactly think. More left simple openings for thoughts or feelings to volunteer.

Pete figured if someone had asked him just a few days ago he'd have said no. That being a person was not particularly scary. But now he was afraid to go home. And it was the same damned home.

"Think it's possible to be scared and not know it?" he asked Justin.

"Not sure. I usually know it."

"I'm scared a lot of the time."

"Maybe it's just being a kid. Maybe it's okay to be a grown-up but it's scary to be a kid."

Pete thought about Dr. Lucy making her face into a high wall to keep everybody away from her except the animals.

He thought about the look on Mr. Bell's face the first time Pete had ever seen him. The sheer terror in his eyes because his son had been hurt, and he didn't yet know how or how badly but he knew he was about to find out. And the way Pete watched that terror melt away as they held each other.

"No," he said. "I don't think it's better for grown-ups. I think you were right the first time. Being a person is just hard."

"Why doesn't anybody say so, then?"

"That's a good question."

Justin asked a lot of good questions, Pete thought. It was too bad Pete didn't feel smart enough to answer any of them.

Chapter Thirteen: Dr. Lucy

It was long after midnight, and she couldn't sleep. And she didn't know why. Except for the parts of her that did.

She had developed a trace of indigestion, and she decided she had to fix that situation because it was keeping her awake. Even though she knew on some level that the indigestion probably wasn't the heart of the issue.

Still, she felt as though she had to do something. Move in some direction. So she pulled on her summer robe and wandered downstairs in search of some sort of antacid.

She was standing in the kitchen in the dark, because the moon had gone down and she didn't want to wake Pete by flooding his couch bed with light.

She was looking at her life.

It was the same array of property and belongings she looked at every day. Except you don't look at your life every day. You don't stand a step or two outside it and say to yourself, *This is my life*. You just walk through it the way she assumed a fish swims through water, never registering it as water. It's just what is.

Now she looked out the window at her backyard, and its horse pasture, and its dog kennels, and its shed, and its trees. And she looked around at her kitchen, and the teapots and knickknacks she kept there.

And she thought, *This is my life. This is the totality of it.*

The strange part of the feeling lay in the fact that just a few days ago it had felt like enough. Just the animals and the otherwise empty house. But she knew when it reverted to that status quo, when the company was gone, it would never be enough again.

All had been revealed. The jig was up.

"Don't let me startle you," a voice said.

It was not Pete. It was Calvin.

But before she could register that it was Calvin, it startled her deeply. It knocked the breath out of her for a moment, and left her standing with one hand on her heart. As if to restart it.

"Oh," she said. "Calvin. You frightened me."

"Exactly what I was trying not to do."

He was sitting up on the couch, a thin blanket pulled up to his waist. She could see just well enough to make out that much. Now that her eyes had adjusted.

She quickly, thoughtlessly ran her hands through her hair to tame it. Then it struck her after the fact that it was probably too dark to bother.

She walked into the living room and flopped onto the couch beside him.

"What are you doing down here?" she asked. "Where's Pete?"

"I asked him to sleep in one of the twin beds upstairs."

"Why?"

"Just seemed righter that way. I'm not sure that's a word. Righter. But just then, in that sentence, it felt like the one that wanted to fit."

They sat in the dark in perfect silence for a time. Maybe a minute.

"My reaction to having this company," she said, "is not at all what I was expecting." She regretted the confession immediately, because she knew she would have to elaborate. But he didn't directly ask her to. He just waited. "I guess I thought I liked being alone," she said at last.

"And now you find you don't?"

"Maybe I just didn't have much to compare it to."

"Nothing wrong with learning new things about yourself," he said.

"I wish I could agree. But it makes me feel like a phony."

"Oh, I doubt that. Phony and you are two things that don't go together in my head at all. But go ahead and tell me what you mean."

She didn't, at first. She was wondering whether she could. Or even should. She had to keep reminding herself that she didn't know this man well. That her feeling of easy familiarity in his presence was not supported by any facts.

When she opened her mouth, the easy familiarity won the day.

"I guess I feel like I've been putting up this big front to the world like I don't need anybody or anything. Like I'm happier by myself. I don't like being alone any better than anybody else does. I just got confused because it was better than being with most of the people I've known."

"There's a difference between confused and being a phony."

"Yes," she said. "Self-deception is the difference."

Another long silence followed. It grew problematically long. It wasn't a comfortable silence. In fact, it began to make her edgy. Especially when their eyes met. Her vision had adjusted to the dim light from the kitchen. She assumed his had, too. And their gaze snagged, and stuck there a moment, and it felt like an admission of something they had been tiptoeing around for a long time. Which was impossible, since they hadn't known each other a long time. But that's how it felt.

The silence broke, and it was Calvin who broke it.

"Maybe I'm mistaken about the undercurrent here."

"Maybe," she said. "But probably not."

"In that case, I feel I have to say it . . ."

"That you don't feel the same."

"No," he said.

Just in that moment, in the reverberation of that one word, she heard him saying, "No, I don't feel the same." He may not have meant that, but she heard it. All her gates slammed shut, and she felt herself surrounded by a sturdy shell. Something to stand guard over her retreat. Something that would pretend to keep her safe. Pretending was the best that could be done with the situation, as was so often the case in her life, and she knew it.

"No, that's not the problem at all," he continued. "Our problem is not that you feel one way and I feel another. Our problem is coming to us from outside this house."

She tried to digest his words for a moment. To reverse her brief misperception. But the gates that had slammed shut resisted slamming open again. So she just sat, feeling numb and more than a little bit stunned. It reminded her of the time a few weeks earlier when she'd accidentally reached into the socket of a plugged-in lamp while changing the bulb. Or, more accurately, the aftermath of that moment. The adjustment back to something like normal.

"You're not saying anything," he added. "But I know you know what I mean."

"Why does anyone have to know our business?"

"I wish I knew," he said. "I don't know why people feel they have to know each other's business. I just know they do. This is a town of only a few thousand. People take stock of each other. They know their neighbors' comings and goings. You think nobody's made note of us driving around together?"

"No. I don't think that. I know they have."

Her shock was melting away now. Morphing into a sense of utter defeat. Limp, enervating defeat.

He reached over and placed his left hand on her right. His hand was warm, and surprisingly uncalloused. And determined. As if it had one opportunity only, and would not be cowed.

"When an eleven-year-old boy can be beaten within an inch of his life for walking down the street with the wrong friend . . . ," he said, ". . . well, I just don't see what chance we have, Lucy. We'll get somebody killed."

She couldn't help noticing he said "we'll." "We will." Not "we would." She wanted to think it meant something, that it was a signal of his intentions. But that didn't match with his words.

"Maybe I don't care," she said.

"Maybe you can say you don't care whether something happens to you. But how will you feel if something happens to me? And vice versa. What if I say they can all go to hell, I don't care, and then it's you who gets hurt? Then how will we feel? And I have a son. A vulnerable son. I'm sorry."

He gave her hand a gentle squeeze and then took his own away. The warm area where it had rested reverted to cold. Quickly and completely cold. Maybe even colder than it had been in the first place.

"I'm sorry, too," she said.

And with that she rose and moved off toward the stairs.

"What did you come down here to get?" he asked her.

"I don't even remember."

Then she climbed the staircase and went back to bed. And did not sleep.

—

He joined her at the breakfast table in the morning before the boys were awake. She was sitting with her elbows on the table, her face in her hands. She had not brushed her hair or her teeth, or put on makeup, and she regretted that now.

He put a hand on her shoulder, but only briefly.

"May I pour myself a cup of coffee?" he asked.

"Of course," she said.

He sat down close to her side a moment later. She left her face in her hands and did not look at him. And did not allow him to look at the wreck that was her face after such a sleepless night.

"I hope nothing I said last night came out sounding hurtful." His voice sounded deep and calm. And so familiar. As though he'd been at this breakfast table for a hundred morning coffees instead of two.

"No. It's not you, Calvin. It wasn't your fault. I was being stupid. Everything you said was absolutely right. I don't know what I was thinking."

"I don't suppose we got into trouble by thinking. I'd say this is more of a feeling proposition."

"No wonder I hate it," she said.

"Nothing wrong with feeling."

"On a morning like this I find it hard to agree."

"Look. There's nothing unusual about what we're going through. All over the world people are meeting and getting to know each other and discovering that there's a little spark between them."

"Answer me this, then. Why are they all excited and happy and optimistic about the future while I'm sitting here with my head in my hands?"

She heard him take a long drink, but she still didn't look.

"They're not all," he said. "Some might have feelings for someone who doesn't return them. Others might already be committed to someone else. Or about to be separated by physical distance. Some are too young for their parents to approve."

"I suppose you're right. I haven't cornered the market on problems."

She took her hands away from her face. It was hard to do. She knew she looked a wreck. But if you can't trust a man to look at your real face and not run screaming, what good is it to have him around in the first place?

He looked into her eyes and smiled. He was freshly shaven and looked as though he'd just stepped out of the shower. But his eyes seemed tired, as though he'd aged over the weekend.

"Maybe . . . ," she said, and then weighed whether to go on. "Maybe for just one day . . . one lovely, harmless Sunday . . . we could live out one day of our lives pretending there was no world out there. What could it possibly hurt?"

He shifted uncomfortably in his chair and took another long gulp of the hot coffee.

He did not immediately reply.

"Something tells me you can think of what it would hurt," she said.

Another brief silence.

"My mother told me a story when I was little," he said. "I don't think it's a true story. I think it's more of a fable. It was about a boy who takes in these orphaned baby birds. But he doesn't have a cage or a box to keep them in. So he keeps them in a bottle. A big, round bottle with a wide base and a narrow neck. And he feeds them well, and gives them plenty of water. And they grow. Comes a day they still fit in the bottom of the bottle but they've grown too big to fit through the neck. Sooner or later they'll outgrow their living space in the bottom. Then the challenge is how you get the birds out of the bottle without harming the birds and without harming the bottle."

Silence while she digested that scenario.

She lit a cigarette even though she worried that he would mind. She was simply too despondent to scrape through the moment without one.

"I suppose you couldn't," she said. "Something would have to give."

"Right."

"So you're saying you don't feed something in a situation where it would be a big disaster for it to grow."

"Exactly."

She pulled a long draft of smoke and exhaled it toward the ceiling. Then, at the end of the stream, she blew three perfect rings.

"But how much can something grow in one day?" she asked.

A movement caught her eye and she looked over to see that Pete and Justin had walked into the kitchen. Calvin sat back in his chair, moving his upper body farther away from hers.

"You okay, ma'am?" Pete asked. "You don't look very happy."

"I just didn't get a lot of sleep," she said.

"Us neither. I sure am hungry. Is there anything for breakfast?"

"I think I'm going to have to make a run to the market," she said.

—

She already had two cartons of eggs in her cart and was trying to decide on a brand of bacon when she first noticed it. Or, at least, noticed the first instance of it.

She glanced up to see two young housewives, their hair looking nearly beauty-parlor fancy and fresh, one with rhinestones in the frames of her eyeglasses. They had their heads together, whispering. And they were looking directly at her.

The moment she returned their attention they broke off their stares and hurried in opposite directions.

She chose the bacon that happened to be in her hand without knowing much about it, then moved on to the produce section in search of a few nice-looking grapefruit.

The produce man looked up as she approached and did not look away again.

A moment later he grabbed his cart and moved it around to the other side of the potato and onion island.

That last one could have been my imagination, she thought.

But then, as she felt her way through the grapefruit, he kept stealing glances.

She found herself trying to remember if it had always been this way. Granted, she'd always been something of an enigma in this area, being a woman living alone, and so far away from everyone else. There seemed to prevail an attitude that she must be up to something.

But it couldn't have been as bad as all this, she decided, or she wouldn't be so suddenly aware of it.

She wheeled her cart up to the checkout and placed her purchases in front of the checker, a young man who could not have been more than twenty years old. He looked up at her briefly as he punched in the prices of her groceries. He smiled, but the smile did not look natural at all. It looked like something you'd serve straight from a can.

"Oh," he said, and paused in his ringing things up. "I have to ask you a question."

She felt a burning along the tops of her ears.

"No," she said.

"Excuse me, ma'am?"

"No, you may not ask me anything. There is no part of my life that is even remotely any of you people's business. So you can just get that through your head right now."

Silence.

The checker's mouth hung open. The bag boy's eyes grew wide.

A woman had moved her cart into the line behind Dr. Lucy. That woman's mouth fell open as well.

"I was just going to ask you if this was the bacon in the special section with the 'Sale' sign over it."

"Oh," she said. And looked away. "Right, of course. I'm sorry. Um. I didn't notice. I'm sorry."

"Well, we'll just go ahead and give you the discount on that all the same," he said.

She gave him a five-dollar bill and did not wait for her considerable change. She hurried out of the store without looking back.

—

Calvin was in the kitchen when she got home, standing at the sink doing the dishes from the previous night's dinner. His gaze was fixed out the window into the backyard, and he wore something like a faint smile at one corner of his mouth.

All the tension and humiliation of her brief foray into the world fell away. She could literally feel it go, like water pouring off her when she stepped out of the Gulf of Mexico and walked to her towel on the sand.

She thought, *Right. Of course. None of that exists. Today and today only, there's no world out there. I'd just for a moment forgotten.*

He turned his head and looked into her eyes, and smiled at her. Their eyes froze that way. Locked into a gaze. She was immensely relieved to see that he couldn't prevent such moments, either. It would have been tragically disappointing if he could find it within himself to be rational and wise.

"Give me all those groceries," he said, "and then go out back and sit and relax. And have a cigarette. You know you want to, and you shouldn't be shaking up your routine just for me."

"But I have cooking to do. You don't know Pete as well as I do. He's quite the bottomless pit. I'm sure he's been champing at the bit this whole time."

"I'll do the cooking. It's the least I can do. You've been taking care of our every need for days."

She hung motionless for another moment, then moved in and handed him the bag.

"You know how to cook?"

"Of course I do. How on earth would Justin and I have survived all these years if I hadn't learned? Now how do you like your eggs?"

"And I can have them any way I want! This is an awful lot of luxury. I'm afraid I'll be spoiled."

"You deserve to be spoiled. You take care of everybody and everything, all the time, and nobody ever takes care of you."

To her surprise, she felt the presence of potential tears somewhere behind her eyes. She did not allow them to have their way.

"You're very sweet," she said.

She moved in a step closer and kissed him on the cheek.

She closed her eyes at the moment of contact. His skin was warm and clean. And fragrant. It smelled of a pleasing aftershave and the natural skin scent of a real living human man. It flitted through her mind without actual words that skin is an odd thing for the world to make a fuss about, especially when, with your eyes closed, it all feels more or less the same.

"Over easy," she said. "Thank you. You're an angel."

Chapter Fourteen: Pete

"Are you bored?" Justin asked Pete. "Or is it just me?"

It was an hour or so after breakfast. They were lying on the linoleum floor near Prince's cage. Staring at the wolf-dog. Watching him stare back. Watching the soft way his eyes blinked as he gazed into Pete's eyes. Pete wanted to feel it was a measure of affection, that softness. But in truth he wasn't sure.

"Yeah. Kind of," Pete said. "I mean, I love spending time with Prince and all. But he can't really do much. Not that it's his fault. But he has a broken leg and everything. And he can't do anything but pretty much just lie there."

"And mostly neither can we," Justin said.

"There are things we can do."

"Like what?"

"Not sure. How do you feel?"

"Pretty good," Justin said. "Last time I peed there was practically no blood in it. It was almost all pee."

"That's good. Still, we don't want to push our luck. But we could do something easy like checkers or card games."

"But it's hard for you to sit up," Justin said.

"The game could be on the floor right here between us. Let me go see what Dr. Lucy has."

He pulled carefully to his feet and began to search the house for the doctor and Mr. Bell.

He found them sitting next to each other on the living room couch, their heads tilted close together. This time neither one jumped away from the other when they noticed Pete watching.

"Ma'am? Do you have a checkers set? Or a board game, like Monopoly or something?"

"I'm sorry," she said. "I don't."

"Deck of cards?"

"No. Sorry. I know you boys must be bored to death."

"I thought everybody had checkers and cards," Pete said.

"Nobody to play with," she said.

Her hands swept wide, as if inviting Pete to see the reality of her world for himself. She sounded strangely calm and satisfied in the statement, as though that wasn't the saddest thing in the world to have to say.

"Now you do," Pete said, and flipped his head in the direction of Mr. Bell.

That brought a long silence.

"Justin is a fan of hide-and-seek," Mr. Bell said. "Or anyway, he always used to be. Maybe he feels he's too grown up for that now."

"Aw, heck, nobody's too grown up for hide-and-seek," Pete said.

He went off to share the idea with Justin.

———

While Justin covered his eyes and counted, Pete scoured the backyard with his gaze. There was no place very promising to hide. There was a shed, but that's the first place anyone in his right mind would think to look. And he sure wasn't going anywhere near those dog runs.

He circled the house via the side yard and noticed a good climbing tree in the front yard of the house. He'd be so close he could watch Justin roaming around looking. But with any luck Justin would never think to look up. Besides, it was leafy, and would provide great cover.

He took a running start and grabbed for the lowest limb. Got it on the first try. Then he swung himself up and braced the bottom of his sneakers on the rough bark.

"Ow!" he said out loud as the skin on his backside stretched.

He scaled the tree fairly easily from that point on, as high as he could before the branches seemed maybe not strong enough to support him. And that was pretty high. He was just about level with the second-story roof when he stopped.

Then he wondered if he'd made a tactical blunder. Because now he'd committed to sitting until he was found. But he swung one leg over a strong branch and discovered he could straddle it quite comfortably. The branch only made contact with the insides of his thighs.

He set his chin down on a higher branch and sighed.

A police cruiser was moving down the street. Which Pete thought nothing about until it pulled level with the doctor's house and slowed considerably.

Pete's heart hammered in his chest as he watched, though he wasn't fully clear on why.

Then the black-and-white car pulled away again, and Pete breathed more deeply.

Faintly in the distance he heard Justin call out, "Ready or not, here I come!"

Pete found it impossible to suppress a smile, because he was delighted by his hiding spot.

But just then the police cruiser came back, rolling slowly in the other direction this time. Again it paused in front of the doctor's house.

Pete's smile vanished.

"Don't come out," he whispered out loud, talking to Justin in his head. "Don't come out front. Don't even let him know you're here."

Or maybe it was Pete the cop was looking for. The idea hit him as a jolt to his belly. That made so much more sense. After all, Pete was the runaway. Justin had his father's permission to be here.

Pete still wished with all his might that Justin would not come around to the front yard. Pete wouldn't want his friend to be forced to answer questions. Wouldn't want him to have to decide whether to lie to the law on Pete's behalf.

And now the cop car wasn't moving at all.

A single uniformed officer stepped out of the cruiser. He was lanky and tall, and Pete thought the man looked intimidating even from above. Something about his size and the determined way he walked.

Pete watched, his heart pounding, a high lump in his throat. He expected the cop to march up to the front door, but he didn't. Instead he moved to the front windows, first on one side of the house, then the other. He looked in, shielding his eyes from the midmorning sun.

Then he walked back to his cruiser and drove away.

A moment later Justin came around to the front yard and searched in the bushes on either side of the front door.

He did not look up.

—

It might have been ten minutes later, or it might have been fifteen, when Justin finally, finally gave up. He was a determined player, Pete had to give him that.

"Olly, olly, oxen free-ee," Justin called out.

Pete was just making his first move to down-climb the tree when he saw the police cruiser coming back.

He froze, and waited.

This time the cop, the same single cop, walked right to the front door and pounded out a strong knock that made Pete's blood feel frozen.

A long, heart-hammering pause, and then Dr. Lucy came and opened the door.

"Yes?" she said.

Pete could hear her well from his perch in the tree. They looked far away to him, the two figures, but their voices carried.

"You know a Calvin Bell?" the policeman asked.

Which surprised Pete, who had been strangely sure this was all about him. What would the police want with Mr. Bell? He hadn't run away from anything.

"What if I do?" Dr. Lucy asked.

Pete could hear the stiffening in her voice.

"Seems a woman called down to the plant for him. Something about his son. We thought that might be you."

"What do you want with Calvin Bell?" she asked.

"Nothing, really," the cop said. "He's not in any trouble. We just thought it was strange. You know."

"No," she said, her voice turning to steel wrapped in sandpaper. "I don't know. Why don't you explain it to me?"

"What's your connection to Bell and his son?"

"No connection. I barely know them."

"You weren't driving around town with the man?"

"You can drive around town with a man you barely know."

"Why would you, though?" the cop asked.

He shifted his cap aside with one hand and scratched his head with that same hand. As if it were literally a head-scratcher of a question he'd just posed.

"His son was injured in an accident. I put in some sutures. That's it. That was the end of the thing. And none of that is illegal, so I'm really questioning this use of police time."

"You know it's illegal to practice medicine without a license, right?"

Pete watched the doctor shift from foot to foot. But it wasn't a nervous gesture. Not at all. She was getting fed up. Pete knew her plenty well enough to tell.

"It's a pretty good bet," she said, "that anyone who's well trained enough to practice medicine has learned somewhere along the way that there's licensing involved. Yes, I know that. I'm licensed to practice medicine in this state. I just usually don't. So now that we know for a fact there's no illegality going on anywhere around here . . ."

She swung the door closed. Or, anyway, she tried to. She swung it *toward* closed.

The cop raised one beefy hand and stopped it with a whump.

"There happens to be a law against miscegenation," he said.

This time it was his voice that sounded formidable and hard. But Pete had never heard the word before and had no idea what it meant. So he didn't know if the doctor was guilty of it or not. He knew only that her face turned frighteningly dark.

"I met the man on Friday," she said, sounding not the least bit cowed. "We didn't get married in the forty-eight hours since then."

Pete wished he could see the look on the cop's face, but mostly what he saw was the flat top of his uniform cap.

"Miscegenation is more than just mixed marriage, ma'am. It's any kind of . . . you know . . ."

"I'm sure I don't."

"Relations."

"Meaning?"

"Don't make me say it, ma'am."

"You're going to have to."

"Sex relations."

A brief pause. Pete's brain crowded with sudden thoughts. Was that true about Dr. Lucy and Mr. Bell? He couldn't imagine it would be. They had met so recently. They were not married. That mattered. Didn't it?

"How dare you," Dr. Lucy said. Quietly. Her voice was just above a whisper, but it made cold shivers run down Pete's back. He could picture icicles dangling from each word.

The gravity of the moment almost knocked Pete off his branch.

"Just calm down, ma'am."

"How dare you come stand at my door and accuse me of cohabitating with a man I've known only a couple of days? Who the hell do you think I am? For that matter, who the hell do you think *you* are? You can't possibly prove what you just accused me of, and I know you can't, because I know it never happened. So here's what we're going to do now, officer. In the next thirty seconds or so you're either going to arrest me for a crime, something you actually have evidence to charge me with, or you're going to get the hell off my land. This was still the United States of America last time I checked."

A long, freighted silence fell. Pete felt as though it might prove fatal, that silence. Maybe not to either one of them, but to him.

Then the cop touched the brim of his cap, but did not lift it.

"You have a good day, ma'am," he said.

He turned on his heel and walked back to his car.

Pete could hear Dr. Lucy mumbling to herself, but he couldn't make out every word. She seemed to be wishing the officer something in return. But, from the sound of it, it was not a wish for a good day.

Then she slammed the door, closing herself back into the house.

Pete waited for the cop to drive away, then carefully—very carefully—climbed down toward the yard. The cores of his arms and legs were shaking, and he couldn't afford to make a mistake. He hung from the lowest branch by his arms, then dropped lightly onto the grass. Or as lightly as he could, anyway.

"Ow," he said out loud.

He walked around to the backyard, where he found Justin standing, looking confused.

"Oh, there you are," Justin said. "Why didn't you come out when I called 'Olly, olly, oxen free'?"

"I was up in a tree," Pete said. "Took me some time to get down."

"Oh, a tree. I never thought of that. What's wrong with you? You look like you just saw a ghost."

"No, I'm okay."

"You want to be it now?"

"Not really," Pete said. "I don't really feel like playing anything. I need to just go and lie down or something."

Chapter Fifteen: Dr. Lucy

She stood with her forehead pressed to the door. For how long, she wasn't sure. And she was shaking. But it was only due in slight measure to fear. For the most part it was rage causing the shaking. Abject, bottled rage.

Calvin's voice made her jump the proverbial mile.

"You okay?" he asked.

"Yes," she said.

She wasn't. But she also wasn't keen on sharing her reactions to such a moment. So she shook it off as best she could, right in front of him, almost on command.

"I hope I did the right thing by not coming to the door when I heard what it was about."

"Yes! Definitely. That would only have made things worse."

"That's what I was thinking," he said.

He stepped in closer and held out his hand as if offering it for her to take.

For a moment she stood back, away from the idea of touch. As though she didn't know what it was, or why he would offer it. But she was shaken, and off-balance, and almost robotically she accepted the gift. She reached out and squeezed the hand, and they stood that way for a time with a bizarre amount of space between them.

She could feel her hand still shaking and she assumed he felt it, too.

"I'd offer you a hug," he said, "but I'm figuring it's just that sort of thing that got us into this mess to begin with."

His voice was gentle, and it softened everything up inside her, but not in a good way. Especially in the part of her that was trying to shake off the upset. It made that job harder—shone a light on the fact that she could only force it back behind a partition. She couldn't literally make it disappear.

She offered no reply.

"You're shaking," he said.

She stepped away from him almost defensively, and dropped the hand.

"No, I'm not." Then she collected herself and began again. "Oh, I'm sorry. What a foolish thing to say. Old habit. It's mostly anger. I shake when I'm really fed-up mad. I've been alive nearly forty years and I've never once had a policeman speak to me that way, or treat me like that."

"I have," he said.

"Well, it's quite a shock to *me*," she said.

"And I hope it never happens to you again as long as you live, Lucy," he said, gently holding her by both upper arms as if for literal support. "But I worry you may have stepped into a time where you'll keep running into it, now that you've associated yourself with me in people's minds. I'm sorry if that's the case. I don't wish it on anybody, least of all you. I'm only forewarning you for your own safety."

Silence.

She just stood. Not speaking. Not thinking. She would need time to untangle every thread of her mood before a process like thinking or speaking could find a clear path through.

If the officer had been standing in front of her in that moment she would have struck him with her fists.

"I'll say one thing," Calvin said. "You're a force to reckon with. A brave woman. You really stood right up to that man."

She pulled a long, cleansing breath and blew it out again. Audibly.

"Sometimes you have to let people know you won't be intimidated," she said.

"Still think we can pretend the world isn't out there? Even for just one day?"

Oddly, she laughed. She wasn't sure why. Maybe because she refused to cry.

"It would help if the world would stop banging on the door," she said.

———

A few moments later, after Calvin had gone to the kitchen to make her a cup of tea, Justin came wandering through the living room looking tired and dispirited. And without Pete.

"Where's your friend?" she asked him. "Is he counting while you hide? You'd better hurry if that's the case."

"He doesn't want to play anymore. He seems upset. But I don't know why."

"Did you ask him?"

"Yes, ma'am. He says he's fine. But it doesn't seem like he is."

"Where is he now?"

"Talking to Prince."

Dr. Lucy rose from the couch and made her way into the examining room, where Pete lay on his belly on the floor, nearly nose to nose with the wolf-dog.

She sat cross-legged near his side. She put one hand on his back, then removed it again, deciding they didn't know each other that well. Or at least that they didn't have that kind of touch-driven bond.

"You okay?" she asked him.

"Yes, ma'am."

"You seem down."

He didn't say anything for a time. Just pressed his fingers through the bars of the cage. The wolf-dog sniffed the fingers, then gave them one lick.

"I heard that policeman," Pete said. "I heard everything. I'm sorry. I wasn't meaning to snoop. But Justin and I were playing hide-and-seek, and I was hiding, and then it was too late, and I couldn't help it. I had to hear."

She drew a deep breath and blew it out. She pulled a pack of cigarettes from her skirt pocket and lit one.

"I'm sorry you had to hear that," she said.

"Why did he even come here?"

"I really don't know."

"It's not true what he said about you and Mr. Bell. Right?"

"No. Of course not. I'm not involved with Calvin that way. We barely know each other."

"So isn't it . . . like . . . isn't it pretty mean and terrible of that cop to act like you were? Wasn't he saying something kind of nasty and bad about you?"

"Because Calvin is black or because we just met?"

"Mostly that second one."

"Yes. It was rude and unpleasant and I'm certainly not used to being treated that way."

But Calvin is, she thought. But she pushed the thought away again because she couldn't fix the world, and she had enough to be upset about in the moment.

"I need to go home," Pete said.

"Why now all of a sudden?"

"Because I don't want to get you in trouble."

"You didn't, Pete. It wasn't about you at all."

"I know I didn't get you in trouble *this* time. But I need to make sure I don't. What if my dad called the cops because I ran away?"

"I'm not worried about it."

"Well, I am," Pete said. "And I need to go home. I'm just being a big coward. I need to go home and face my dad now."

"You want a ride?"

"No. I'll walk. Thanks. I don't want people to see us driving together. Then they'll know I was with you. I don't want to get you in trouble."

"You still have that dime I gave you?"

"Yes, ma'am. I don't know how long it'll be before I can get back here to see Prince. But please promise me you won't let him go until I can see him again. I wouldn't want to get back here and find out he was gone and I never even got to say goodbye."

She thought she saw him blink back tears, but she couldn't be sure. And besides, she quickly looked away to give him his emotional privacy. They were alike in that way—neither of them anxious to share their pain with the world.

"Don't worry about that. It'll be weeks before he's healed enough to go."

"Good. Well, not good. Sorry, boy," he said directly to the wolf-dog. "It's not good at all that you have to sit here so long. Just good that I'll be around to see you again."

He climbed to his feet.

"Oh, hi, Mr. Bell," Pete said.

Dr. Lucy whipped her head around.

Calvin and Justin stood in the doorway, Calvin's hand on his son's shoulder. In his other hand he held the grocery sack he'd used to bring clothing and personal items from home.

"Don't tell me you're leaving, too," she said.

"I'm afraid so. There's a cup of tea on the kitchen table for you."

"I'll drive you," she said, trying to keep the disappointment from her voice.

"Absolutely not," Calvin said. "We've brought enough problems into your life. We'll walk. Justin says he's up to walking and if he changes his mind halfway home he can ride on my shoulders."

"But there's just one thing," Justin said. His voice sounded high and tight.

Silence while everyone waited. It took close to a minute for Dr. Lucy to realize he wasn't about to say what thing it was.

"What's on your mind, son?" Calvin asked.

"Pete knows," Justin said.

"I do?" Pete asked, sounding as though he'd just been dropped into the conversation from a sound sleep.

"Yeah. You do. We talked about it. Remember? You were going to ask Dr. Lucy something for me."

"Oh," Pete said. "Right. That." He stopped a moment. Wiggled uncomfortably. "Justin is afraid to be home alone while his dad goes to the plant tomorrow. Well . . . you know. Most days. But I guess since this is Sunday he's mostly worried about tomorrow."

"He should be *here*," Dr. Lucy said.

She couldn't help noticing that Pete looked inordinately relieved. As if someone had just lifted a hundred-pound brick wall off his chest.

"It's not like nobody would think to look for him here," Calvin said.

"But at least he wouldn't be alone."

"What would you do, though? If somebody came here?"

"I'd sic the dogs on them. I'd let the dogs out and then call the police while the dogs held them at bay. And if absolute worst comes to absolute worst," she said, remembering that she could no longer assume the police were on her side, "I have a pistol."

"I guess anything's better than just leaving him to fend for himself," Calvin said. "Not sure how he'd get here, though. Seems like it would be even worse for him to be out walking alone."

"It doesn't matter," she said. "We'll find a way. We'll figure it out. Nobody's laying their hands on that boy again. I know what we can do. Tomorrow morning just before it gets light I'll drive to the end of your block and park. Justin can walk down the street. You can watch him from one end and I'll watch from the other. And when we're sure no one is looking he can jump into the backseat and ride with his head down."

Justin nodded enthusiastically.

"That sounds wonderful," Calvin said.

"I'll walk you to the door."

Then she regretted the offer. She should have just said goodbye. Not drawn this out. She should have just left things right there.

It's the long goodbyes that get you every time.

———

"I'm gathering up a million ways to tell you what I appreciate about all you've done," he said as they walked down the hall.

"Nonsense, Calvin. Don't you dare say a word."

Pete was walking ahead and had almost made it to the front door.

"Do me a favor," she added. "Obviously you can't walk with Pete, but maybe walk half a block behind and keep an eye on him."

"Of course."

When they reached the door he turned to her, as if to offer some sort of farewell. She stopped him with one raised hand. Like a crossing guard.

"Don't," she said. "Please don't, Calvin. Don't even say goodbye. The birds are just barely small enough to fit through the neck of the bottle. Just get out while you still can."

Much to her disappointment, he did as he'd been asked.

———

She sat at the kitchen table for a time, drinking her tea. And telling herself over and over that it was better this way. That she liked the peace and quiet. That all those people had been an unwelcome intrusion.

Her intention was to keep saying it to herself until it became a thing she could believe again.

In time she gave up, washed her cup in the sink, and walked out back to let the dogs out of their runs for exercise.

They whined and howled and wagged when they saw her. They knew. They always knew when it was time for the gates to open wide. And she never knew how they could tell the difference between those times and any other times she might come out.

She let the greyhounds out first, and they took off running, stretching their impossibly long legs, chasing each other around the horse pasture and beyond. All except Winston, of course, who hadn't even bothered to come out with her, and who was too mature and refined for such foolishness.

The horses pranced and ran, catching the dogs' enthusiasm as if by contagion.

She let the German shepherd, the beagle, and the terrier mutt out, and they hung close to her, jumping into the air and inviting her to play.

"I'm sorry it's been too long," she said.

She picked up a ball from the dirt and threw it as hard and as far as she could.

The terrier got it. The terrier always got it.

"I'm sorry it's been too long," she said again when they came running back.

But dogs don't regret what they didn't do soon enough, or didn't do enough of. Or what you didn't do enough of. Dogs are where they are right now, in this moment, and nowhere else.

Which is why I generally keep the company of dogs, she thought.

Chapter Sixteen: Pete

Pete eased the front door of his house open and then froze, allowing his eyes to adjust to the dim living room.

His father's chair sat empty.

He pulled a deep, fortifying breath and took a step inside, quietly closing the door behind him. He walked through the room the way he'd seen actors walk through a haunted house in scary movies. As though his father might be just about to jump out from behind the furniture and scare him half to death, and catch him before he could run.

He eased down the hall and peered into his father's bedroom, thinking his dad might be in pain and lying down. But the bed was empty as well.

That was when Pete registered the lovely smells. They had been there all along, making him feel hungry, but he'd been too preoccupied and afraid to give them any conscious thought. Something like a seasoned tomato sauce was tempting him from the kitchen.

Pete ever so cautiously stuck his head through the kitchen doorway.

His father was sitting on the high stool in front of the stove, stirring the sauce. Something was boiling hard and free in the big pasta pot, steaming up the windows. Pete had no idea if his dad even knew he was there. Pete took one step into the room and opened his mouth to announce himself, to get this over with once and for all. But he only found that his words didn't work anymore. His coward of a voice had abandoned him.

So he just stood, paralyzed in his fear.

His father had gained even more weight, he thought, if such a thing were possible in just a few days. And all in his belly. His belly walked the world ahead of him these days, weighing him down from the front. Leading the way into rooms. Pete wondered if that was even harder on his dad's back, but only in that disconnected way one wonders things within a brain muddled by fear.

"It's ironic," Pete's dad said.

Pete jumped as though high voltage had jolted through his body. He knew he was supposed to ask what was ironic, or what the word *ironic* even meant, but his voice was still out of order.

"Here you show up just in time for dinner," his dad continued, "but the ironic thing is, you're at least two dinners late. So is that late, or is it on time?"

He never turned to look at Pete as he spoke, which felt like a bad sign. And still Pete could not speak.

"Answer the question, Petey boy."

His dad's voice sounded deadly calm. Maybe too much so.

Pete cleared his throat and pushed hard at some words.

"I'm not sure, sir. That seems like a hard question."

The voice he managed sounded croaky and weak, as if Pete had been so sick as to be hovering near death.

Pete's dad looked around at him. Drilled through Pete's heart with his eyes. Then he looked back at his sauce.

"Your turn to talk, Petey boy."

"And say what, sir?"

"I think you know what you owe me."

"Not really."

"What're the first questions I'm going to ask you?"

"Oh. You mean like where was I and why was I gone so long?"

"Bingo."

A long silence. Pete realized he should have been prepared for this moment. He should have rehearsed what he was going to say. But he hadn't. Because it hadn't occurred to him that his dad would be in a listening mood.

"I was afraid to come home," Pete said.

A long silence fell. It felt dangerous.

"That's it?" his dad asked after a time.

"Pretty much, sir."

"Nope. Sorry, Petey. You're going to have to do better than that."

"That last whipping. It was too much."

"I think I'm the one that gets to say if it's enough or too much."

"I couldn't even sit down. I still barely can. I'd scream if somebody just touched some of those spots. And the idea of you strapping on them again . . . I just couldn't face it, sir. It was just too much. I'm sorry. I couldn't do it."

"Well, here's a question, then," his dad said, setting down his spoon and fixing Pete with a look that made him squirm. "Why'd you turn around and do just what I said not to, then? You're in control of your own fate here."

"Well, that's just it, sir. I don't feel like I am. I feel like my whole life I've been trying to guess what'll make you mad so I can steer clear of it. But it never works. I just try to be so good you couldn't possibly get mad, but then you do anyway. Yeah, I knew that second time. That thing with my friend. But I did it because I don't think it's wrong. He's my friend and we're not hurting anybody. I know you think it's wrong, but I don't. I was just trying to have a friend and save the life of this dog I found on the road. I can see if I was lying and stealing and breaking people's windows with rocks just to be mean. But I'm just trying to be good and be okay. And that last whipping was too much. I couldn't face another one. So I didn't come home."

"But you're home now."

"Yes, sir. I decided I was being a coward and I needed to come face you."

Pete's dad slid off the stool and stood. Pete reacted as though someone had thrown a heavy skillet or taken a shot at him. He bolted backward and accidentally slammed his back into the wall. He could feel his eyes stretched too wide, and he couldn't calm his heart.

Meanwhile his dad was coming no closer.

He forced himself to look into the older man's eyes. He saw no rage there. Nothing to run from for the moment. His father looked almost curious and strained, as though trying to do math in his head. And he looked a little hurt.

The moment stretched out.

"I didn't know you were that scared of me," his dad said after a time.

"Yes, sir. I am."

"That wasn't ever the idea. Just to get you to do right is all."

"That never seems to work, sir. I never know what you'll want."

His dad sat on the stool again with a deep sigh. He reminded Pete of a slashed tire. Just going flat nearly all at once.

"Under the circumstances," his dad said, "I'm going to allow for the possibility that I might have overdone it that last time. So here's what I'm going to do. I'm giving you a pass."

Pete felt himself begin to breathe again. Even though he wasn't sure what a pass would mean in this context.

"A pass, sir?"

"I'm going to let it go by."

Silence. Pete figured he should be saying thank you, but he was too stunned to say anything.

"You know how many passes you get, Petey boy?"

"No, sir."

"Guess."

"Before just now I would've said zero."

"Well, now you know it's more than zero. So what's our magic number?"

"One?"

"Good guess. One is correct. And you've had your one. So you'll want to tread carefully. Now go wash up for dinner. And then come back and serve us both up here. I'm going to go take another one of those pain pills. My back is all in an uproar from cooking us dinner."

"Thank you for cooking us dinner," Pete said.

"We're still strong, right, boy?"

"Strong, sir?"

"We're still a team, you and me."

"Yes, sir."

But it was an open lie. Bald-faced. They didn't feel like a team to Pete. They hadn't felt strong for as long as Pete could remember.

———

Pete's mouth was filled with an outrageous amount of spaghetti when his dad next spoke.

"You only answered one of my questions."

Pete chewed as fast as he could, then swallowed before he was really done. He was wiping sauce off his chin when his dad spoke again, beating him to it.

"You told me why you were away when I asked. But you didn't tell me where you were."

"No, sir. I didn't."

"So tell me now."

"I can't do that, sir."

A silence radiated. Pete thought he could hear it bounce off the walls in waves, like an actual thing he could listen to.

This was the moment, Pete knew. He would have to follow through on his plan, just the way he'd outlined it to the doctor. He'd have to flat-out refuse to bring the strap. He might even have to outrun his dad, relying on the fact that the older man was injured. It would infuriate his father, and dig Pete in deep. But it just might have to be done.

Pete felt his appetite abandon him, and the food he'd already eaten began to sit uneasily in his stomach.

"Pass me that salt and pepper, boy," his father said.

Pete didn't move. Because it felt like another trick.

"You gone deaf, boy?"

"No, sir."

"Then pass me the damned salt and pepper."

"Yes, sir."

He grabbed both shakers in one hand, then slid them across the table toward his father, pulling his hand back fast.

A trace of that hurt look passed through the older man's eyes again. But he said nothing. Just picked up the salt and pepper and shook far too much of both on his food.

It struck Pete, in a dizzying realization, that the moment was over. But he had no idea how. He'd never seen his father set an argument down, or retreat from anything. So he almost couldn't believe it now, when it was right in front of his face.

Pete forced himself to take another bite, even though his stomach felt dicey. He shifted uncomfortably on his still-sore welts. He had to use his legs to keep his full weight off his backside, and the muscles were growing hot and sore.

It struck him that he hadn't asked his father if Boomer Leggett had been one of the ones who beat Justin. And if his dad had known—had given his blessing, or even not gone out of his way to stop it.

He didn't ask.

He hated himself for not asking. And he knew it was a deep shame that would not leave him anytime soon. If it ever left him.

But he had survived coming home. He was not screaming in pain again. He was being fed, and he could live here. Since he had no place else he could live, he shoveled spaghetti into his mouth and said nothing at all.

—

"I'm going out for a walk," Pete said to his dad.

His father was in the living room, reading an outdated news magazine, with those funny half-sized reading glasses on. Squinting to see in the dim, golden light from the chair-side lamp.

"Not until you do those dishes, you're not."

"I did them."

His father looked up into his face as if listening for the first time.

"What do you mean, you're going for a walk?"

"Just what I said, I guess."

"You never go out for a walk for no reason."

"I just feel too full, kind of. I thought it might help me settle my dinner."

"How long you plan to be gone?"

"Not long. Ten minutes. Twenty, tops."

"All right, well, go then."

Pete slipped through the front door and out into the world.

It was dusky now, the air still warm and humid, but not so oppressive without the glare of direct sun.

He turned toward town. Toward the liquor store.

As he walked, he fingered the dime in his pocket. And thought about his weekend up until now. Being at the doctor's instead of home.

It felt something like the time his parents had taken him on a vacation to Washington, DC. Pete had loved every minute of it. He'd loved seeing the government buildings, and staying in a hotel, and being Not Home. Then the vacation had ended and Pete had been forced to come back to his dreaded routine and go right back to school.

What does that mean, he wondered, *when where you are is exactly where you don't want to be, and you know it?*

He crossed the street toward the liquor store against the light, because there was no one to see him and no cars coming. Then he padded across the parking lot, his sneakers making flapping noises on the hot tar.

He tucked himself into the phone booth and pulled up the telephone directory.

"Armstrong," he said out loud, running his finger down the *A* names.

He found it right away. "L. K. Armstrong."

He dropped his precious dime into the slot and dialed, allowing the rotary dial to pull his finger back into place after each number.

She picked up on the fourth ring.

"I hope I didn't get you away from something," Pete said.

"Pete?"

"Yes, ma'am. It's me. But it's not an emergency. I'm okay."

"Did you go home?"

"Yes, ma'am."

"What happened?"

"I'm not really sure. It didn't go like I thought it would at all. I really don't understand it. And maybe that's part of why I called. 'Cause you're good at figuring out stuff like that. Much better than I am. But that's not the main reason I called. Mostly I called because I thought you might be worried about me. Even though I know maybe that's not true. I mean, why should you worry? I'm not your kid. I'm not really yours to worry about. I guess what I'm saying is that I was *hoping* you were worried about me."

A brief pause, during which Pete realized he was talking over any chance of finding out.

He kept going.

"It would be nice to have somebody who actually cared enough to think about me after I went home and wonder if I was okay. But it's not your job or anything. So if you didn't, that's okay. I don't blame you or anything."

"You're not really letting me get a word in edgewise, Pete."

"Sorry, ma'am."

It was nearly dark out now, and Pete watched the headlights of a car go by, lighting up his strange new world and then plunging him into the dim again.

"Of course I was worried about you, Pete. What happened?"

"It was weird."

"I was hoping for more detail."

"He asked me some questions. And I tried to tell him how scared I was to come home. At first he seemed the way he always does. Kind of too calm but like he was just ready to blow. And then it's like he got it, how I'm so scared of him now. And then he said he'd let it go by. And what was really weird . . . he tried to get me to say we were a team, me and him. Strong, you know?"

"That doesn't seem so strange. You're his son. He doesn't want to lose you."

Another set of headlights lit up his face.

"How could he lose me?"

"I don't understand the question," she said. "People lose each other all the time."

"But I can't just move out and get my own place or anything. I'm twelve."

"I didn't necessarily mean lose you in a literal sense. I meant he doesn't want to lose your love."

"Oh," Pete said. But he could not force his brain to decode that idea. How does one remove love from one's only parent? It was a concept—an option—Pete had never considered. "I lied to him. I said we're strong. But we're not."

Silence on both ends of the line.

"Was that wrong to lie?" he asked.

"I don't know, Pete. I really don't. Things like that are hard. But I know you were trying to do what you thought was best, and that's the main thing."

"Thank you, ma'am."

He wanted to tell her how he hadn't asked his father about a possible role in Justin's beating, but it was too terrible. He was too ashamed. And maybe she already knew. Maybe everybody knew Pete should be finding that out from his dad. And maybe nobody would want to be anywhere near him if they could see he wasn't brave enough to do it.

When they could see.

All he said was, "So I guess I can come see Prince again tomorrow. I was wondering if you'd wait for me. You know. When you come to pick up Justin. I'll be up and ready while it's still dark. I promise. I won't keep you waiting."

"Of course," she said.

"Thank you, ma'am."

"I'm glad you called, Pete."

"You are?"

"Yes. Very. I *was* worried. I *do* care what happens to you when you go home."

Pete wanted to thank her again but he was just on the edge of crying, and knew she would hear it in his voice if he did.

"See you tomorrow," he said as fast as he could.

Then he hung up before she caught on to his emotion. Or at least, he hoped so.

—

When he arrived home, he slipped through the door to find his father dozing on the pain pills. Snoring in his chair.

Pete slipped past him and into his bedroom.

He had an early morning. He was exhausted, purely drained from fear and emotion. It was time to get some sleep.

Chapter Seventeen: Dr. Lucy

She sat parked in her car at the curb, in a space as far from a streetlight as she could possibly have found. The whole moment felt unsettled inside her, leaving her vaguely guilty and afraid, as if she were about to be caught and punished for some serious transgression. And familiar. It felt so familiar.

At first she couldn't remember why.

Then she connected it to the fear in her belly when someone pounded on her door in the middle of the night, and she knew—before even crossing to the window—that against her best judgment she'd feel compelled to allow them into her home.

She looked up at the rearview mirror to see Calvin standing in the glow of a streetlight halfway down the block, his arms aimlessly at his sides, as if wanting to do a number of things he could not. She might have seen some small movement of Justin in that same mirror image, but if so she did not register it. Her eyes remained glued on the motionless form of Calvin, and she raised one hand as if to wave, not even sure if he would see in the darkness and at the distance. She didn't wave, exactly, just raised the hand and held it very still.

A moment later he mirrored the gesture perfectly.

They froze that way a moment, staring at each other in a setting that allowed them to see almost nothing.

A thought filled Lucy's head, more or less uninvited.

Look at that, it said. *I'm a tragic figure in a love story, and I don't even remember how I got myself into the thing.*

And it all happened so damned fast.

Then the sound and feel of her car door being opened knocked such thoughts out of her head.

"Good morning," Justin said, a small mouselike voice from her backseat, pulling the door closed behind him.

"Good morning, Justin."

"Thanks for coming to get me."

"Of course."

A silence and pause. She looked up into the glass of the rearview mirror again. The street was empty. Calvin was gone.

"Why aren't we driving away?" Justin asked.

"We have to wait for Pete."

"Oh, Pete. Good! Pete's coming, I didn't know. I thought he might be in so much trouble with his dad that we wouldn't see him for a long time."

"We got lucky on that score," she said. "Well, mostly he got lucky. But yes, it's lucky for us, too."

———

A minute—or two minutes, or five minutes—later Pete jumped into the backseat, and Dr. Lucy fired up the engine and eased the car down the block toward home.

"I'm sorry I made you wait," Pete said.

"You were fine, Pete. The timing was fine."

They drove in near silence for a mile or two, marked only by a quiet whispering between the boys. It was too quiet for Dr. Lucy to make out any words. Which seemed regrettable. Their tone, their body language, the very energy that surrounded them like a cloud and followed them through the world, smacked of genuine trust and friendship. It was an animal so foreign to her that she was anxious to study the phenomenon to see how such a thing was done. But in its quietness it evaded her grasp, as usual.

She looked up to see some kind of law enforcement vehicle in her rearview mirror. It jolted into her stomach as a big, undisguised fear. More fear than she had openly felt for some time. If he pulled her over he'd find two boys hidden in her backseat, neither of whom belonged to her. How would she go about explaining a thing like that?

She couldn't tell what branch of law enforcement the car represented. It could have been police, or sheriff, or state highway patrol. She couldn't even make out the color of the car in the dark. But one thing was very clear: The car had a red light on its roof which, blessedly, remained dark.

She watched it from the corner of her eye as she drove, praying it would not light up.

Then she wondered what she was doing praying. Praying to what, or to whom? She'd long ago given up on any sort of God—probably while she was still a child—particularly the one forced on her by her parents. It seemed wrong to drag that relationship back into play now simply because she was afraid. It felt two-faced and selfish.

She made a left onto the two-lane highway.

So did the car with the light.

Strangled by a rising fear, she attempted to rehearse what she would say when he pulled her over. If he pulled her over. But there was nothing to rehearse. It was a story she did not intend to tell, and one that would not help her case even if she did choose to share it.

She decided, in a panicky moment in her brain, that she couldn't do this every morning. The idea that she could keeping picking up the boys unnoticed simply because it was dark was naive. It wasn't going to work. But what suitable arrangement would replace the plan? Her desperate brain could not imagine, could not even organize itself to try.

She glanced again without moving her head. He was still back there. The light was still dark.

She saw her street up ahead, the place where she would make a left off the highway for home, and knew she was headed for a moment of truth. What felt like her stomach and her heart—the whole of her frightened insides—seemed to sit in her throat, refusing to be swallowed back down.

She slowed. The police car behind her slowed. But how could it not? There was only one lane in each direction, and it had to accommodate her speed.

She turned left.

The cop car kept going straight.

The moment it was out of sight she pulled over and rested her head on the steering wheel and tried to calm her heart and normalize her breathing.

"You okay?" Pete asked from somewhere behind her.

"Yeah. Fine."

"Are we there?" Justin asked.

"Not quite. We'll go in a minute."

She pulled a few more deep breaths, then drove the rest of the way home.

"I'm going to pull around behind the house," she said to both of them at once. "I want you to get in the habit of staying out of sight from the road. Not that there seems to be anybody on the road right now, and normally there isn't, but you never know. So every morning when I pick you up, just try to remember that you never want to get out of the car when anyone else can see."

"How do we know if they can see?" Pete asked. "We're back here with our heads down."

"Right. Well, every morning I'll tell you when the coast is clear."

But as she pulled into her driveway the question of whether she dared do this again the following morning remained.

———

"I'm beginning to think it's time to put Prince into one of the indoor-outdoor runs," she said a couple of hours into the morning. "It's so small, that little cage where he's been confined. It must be hard for him. It's starting to seem cruel."

"Sure," Pete said. "It'd be nice if he could move around a little."

They stood in the examining room staring at the wolf-dog. All three of them. He looked back with a pleasant anticipation, seeming to know they were talking about him, seeming to gather that there was nothing to dread in their conversation.

"How do we do it, though?" Pete asked.

"Not sure I've figured that out yet," Dr. Lucy said.

"Can he walk on that back leg now?"

"Not really. But it should be easy enough for him to move around on three legs now that the bone is stable. It shouldn't hurt much to hold it up and hop around. And the incision is mostly healed. I'm not worried about him popping those stitches."

She looked into the animal's deep eyes and he returned her gaze.

"It's amazing that he hasn't tried to take out those stitches himself," she said. "I thought when the anesthetic wore off I'd have to put some kind of cone around his neck. But he's just leaving them alone."

"He knows," Pete said. "He knows it's all to help him."

A brief silence.

Then Pete said, "I could put a leash on him and lead him out there."

"No. I wouldn't suggest that. We have no idea if he's ever been trained to walk on a leash. If not, he might object to being held by his neck. If he broke away from you, that would be very bad. The last thing we want is for him to run away now, when he can barely hobble. The coyotes or some other wild animals would have him in no time. That would be it for him by sundown."

"Hmm," Justin said, as if wanting into the conversation but not quite knowing where he fit.

"I sure wouldn't want that," Pete said.

"I know!" Justin said. "We could carry the cage outside and into one of the kennels. And then open the door."

"We could?" Dr. Lucy asked. "He's heavy."

"All three of us could."

"Yes," she said. "Maybe so. Maybe all three of us could."

———

"It won't fit through the gate," she said. Or rather, she huffed it. She set down her end of the cage in the dirt, leaned on it, and tried to catch her breath.

They had walked the cage right up to the chain link of an open kennel run, but it had hung up on both sides, too wide to fit through.

"It was a good idea, Justin," she added. "But I think this is as far as it goes."

"I could climb over the cage and into the run," Pete said. "And then I can open the door of his cage. And if we keep the cage real tight up against the opening of the kennel run, he'd have no place to go but in."

"But if you can climb over it," she said, indicating the space above the top of the cage, "he could jump up onto the cage and get away through that same space."

Pete's eyebrows scrunched down, as if thinking pained him.

"Think he could do that with his bum leg?"

"I don't know. Probably not. But if he goes into a moment of panic . . . well, I hate to take the chance."

"Okay, leave it to me," Pete said.

He carefully climbed up onto the cage and moved along it on hands and knees to the fence of the run. Prince lifted his head and watched his every move. Pete leaned through the opening, over the top of the cage, and dangled his upper body downward until he was able to flip the latch on Prince's cage and swing the door open.

Then Pete pulled up to his knees and used his body to block the only space the wolf-dog might have utilized to escape.

Prince reached his muzzle out and explored the empty space where the door had been. Almost as though he couldn't believe such an unfamiliar thing as all that space. He crawled forward a few inches and stuck his head out. Looked around.

Then he rose onto three legs and hobbled out into the run, where he stood, bad leg held slightly off the ground, and sniffed his new surroundings.

"Oops," Pete said. "Just one problem. Now we have to figure out how to close the door."

Pete jumped down into the run, startling the wolf-dog. They both stood frozen a moment, Prince with his head down in a surprisingly defensive position.

It occurred to Dr. Lucy that this might be the first time boy and wolf-dog had stood face to face, both fully able to move closer together, or to evade. Pete seemed to be realizing it, too.

"It's okay, boy. It's only me. Pete. You know, the guy who saved you. I'm just going to close the door so you can't get out. Not like we're trying to keep you captive or anything, but just until you can run fast like before. We don't want the coyotes to get you."

Pete reached back and closed the gate of the kennel run as far as it would go before hanging up on the cage. But it left far too small a space to allow a wolf-dog to escape. Dr. Lucy and Justin lifted the cage and pulled it away and Pete closed and latched the gate with himself still inside.

"Be careful coming out," Dr. Lucy said. "Don't let him squeeze through with you."

"I think I'm going to stay and keep him company for a while," Pete said.

"Okay. Watch yourself, though. He's feeling a little defensive."

"I'll just sit in the corner and let him come to me. If he even wants to."

Before she could answer, she heard the phone ring inside the house.

"Okay, out of there for now," she said to Pete.

"Why?"

"Because I have to go get the phone. Sit with him just outside the fence."

His shoulders sagged more dramatically than necessary, but he did as he was told. And still the phone was ringing.

She muttered to herself as she walked inside to answer it. She had gone months at a time, maybe even a year at a stretch, without her phone ringing. And here Pete had called last night. And now . . . who this was and what they wanted from her she could not imagine.

As she let herself back into the house, irritated by the continued ringing, she noticed that Justin was following closely at her heels.

She stormed into the kitchen and grabbed up the phone.

"Yes?" she said, barely attempting to hide her inconvenience.

"It's me. Calvin."

She hadn't needed to be told. She had recognized Calvin's voice immediately. And she knew, from his tone, from the very situation of his calling, that he had nothing casual or happy to say.

"Calvin, what's wrong?"

"I have to talk fast," he said, "because I have no idea how long they'll let me use the phone. I have to ask you a huge favor. I wish I didn't have to ask, but I need you to do it. I have no other plan. Nothing to fall back on. It's so important."

"Calvin, what is it? What's happened?"

"I need you to take care of Justin. I need to ask you to keep him for a time."

"Well, of course. We already agreed to that."

"No," he said, and the gravity of the message began to settle. "A longer time."

"Oh. How long?"

"I don't know yet. I have an arraignment this morning. I suppose a judge will settle that. Thirty days, maybe. I'd hate to think they could saddle me with more than that."

"You've been arrested?"

"I'm afraid so."

"On what charge?"

"Aggravated assault."

Dr. Lucy became suddenly aware of Justin's stare. He was standing not two feet from her left hip, gazing up into her face. He knew this was his father on the phone. He knew all was not well.

"Did you . . . ?"

She never finished the sentence. She had intended to say, "Did you assault anyone?" But she chose not to ask that in front of his son.

"No," Calvin said. "I absolutely did not. I was assaulted by two men at the plant. All I did was try to defend myself. But they told a different story and, well, here I am."

"Are you all right? Were you hurt?"

"A little bruised up, but I'll be fine."

"I could—" she began.

"Wait," he said. "Let me speak. This is very important. What you can do for me is to hold on to Justin and keep him safe. I know you'll want to help in other ways. I know you'll want to come down here. Bring me things I need, or get me a lawyer. And it's really important that you know this now." His voice dropped to a near whisper. "If you make it clear that there's a connection between us, any clearer than it already is, our situation has nowhere to go but down."

"I understand," she said.

She did understand. Mentally. But her inability to move forward into any kind of helpful action on his behalf tangled up in her gut, winding back on itself and causing a jam of emotion that felt something like heartburn.

Still, he had said what she could do to help him. Best to stay calm and move in that direction.

"Justin can be here as long as he needs to be. We'll be fine."

In a strange, disconnected thought, it occurred to her that having the boy here for thirty days or more would solve the problem of picking him up in the morning. They would stay home together. Stay off the streets. No comings and goings. No one would need to know.

Calvin's voice knocked her back into the moment.

"Thank you," he said. "I can't tell you how much that means to me. If I didn't know he was safe with you . . . well, I can't imagine it. I don't even want to try. May I speak to him?"

"Of course. He's right here."

She handed the phone to the wide-eyed boy. He regarded it with some caution, as if it were a snake. Or a half-wild wolf-dog. But after a brief hesitation he did reach out and take the receiver from her.

She could hear nothing of Calvin's end of the conversation. In fact, she could hear nothing. Justin didn't speak for the longest time. Just listened, and nodded. And began to cry quietly.

"Sorry, Dad," he said at last. "I nodded, but I know you can't hear that. I just wasn't thinking. Yeah, I know she will. Do you need to talk to the doctor again?"

She reached out for the phone, but Justin did not hand it to her.

"Love you, too, Dad," he said quickly. "'Bye."

He looked up into her face with wide, wet eyes and handed her back the receiver.

"Sorry, Dr. Lucy," he said. "He couldn't talk anymore. That was all the time they let him have."

She hung up the phone and they stood a moment, not quite looking at each other, neither moving. Dr. Lucy could feel the weight of their emotions, and she suspected their emotions were a good match. But it was all so sudden and unprocessed inside her that it was hard even to pin down what she was feeling. She only knew it wasn't good.

"Well," she said, putting one hand on Justin's shoulder, "I guess it's just you and me for a while."

"And Pete," Justin added quickly.

"Right," she said. "And Pete."

Then, unsure of what else she could do, she walked around the kitchen for a few minutes, putting away breakfast dishes and thinking about all the days she would not see Calvin, not even a faraway image of him standing under a streetlight waving. It was so unexpected, both his sudden absence and the fact that his sudden absence should matter so much to her and feel so entirely impossible to digest.

She wondered if he had minimized the report of his injuries so as not to upset her.

She busied herself finding spots in the cupboard for the spoon rest and the salt and pepper shakers—items she generally allowed to live out on the counters. It felt good to put herself to some use. In fact, she found it hard to stop.

Until she looked over at Justin.

He was standing in the middle of the kitchen, his torso wrapped in his own arms. He wasn't crying anymore. He just looked completely disconnected from himself and his surroundings and more than a little bit lost.

She rushed to him, fell to her knees, and wrapped him in an embrace, which he returned. She could feel the clean gauze of the fresh dressing she had applied to his head wound that morning. It brushed against her cheek.

"I wish I could explain the world to you," she said. "I wish I could tell you why things like this happen when we all know they're not supposed to. But the truth of the matter is, frankly . . . I don't understand it myself."

A light silence. Yes, it had a lightness to it, which seemed unexpected.

"It's okay," he said. "I mostly just needed the hug."

So they stayed with the hug for a while.

Chapter Eighteen: Pete

Pete ran into the house, already shouting out his question.

"Dr. Lucy, do you have a bed for Prince? Because he doesn't want to lie down on that . . ."

Before he could even finish the second sentence he picked up the change in mood. Something must have happened while he was sitting near Prince's kennel run. It couldn't have been more than ten or fifteen minutes, but everything felt different.

Both the doctor and Justin looked as though they had been crying. And nobody so much as glanced up at Pete or even tried to answer his question. The three of them just stood in the middle of this dark cloud that hung around the inside of the house, feeling the weight of it. Or at least Pete was feeling the weight.

"What happened?" Pete asked when he couldn't bear the silence.

Dr. Lucy pulled her back up poker-straight and hurried out of the room, as if she couldn't bring herself to hear what would come next.

"My dad got arrested," Justin said without meeting Pete's eyes.

"That's terrible."

"Yeah, it is."

"For what?"

"For nothing. It was a bad deal."

Silence. A lot of it. A big, long, painful stretch.

"When's he coming back?" Pete asked.

"We don't know yet."

"Did the doctor say you could stay here?"

"Yeah."

A big feeling welled up inside Pete. Big and annoying. He would almost have been tempted to call it jealousy, but he didn't really begrudge Justin staying here. He just desperately wanted the same thing for himself.

Envy might have been a better word.

Dr. Lucy stuck her head back through the doorway.

"There's a whole stack of dog beds in boxes in the garage," she said. "Some are older than others, so try to find one that's in better shape. They're all clean."

—

Pete was standing in the garage—just standing and looking and noting the differences between the doctor's garage and his own—when Justin stuck his head in.

"Oh, hi," Pete said.

"Can't find the dog beds?"

"I sort of haven't started trying yet. I was just looking at all this and thinking it looked weird to me. And between that and the thing with your dad, I guess it just knocked the dog beds right out of my head."

Justin walked into the middle of the garage and stood next to Pete. Together they looked around. Looked at the neatly stacked cardboard cartons, each sealed with tape and labeled with a marking pen so you could tell at a glance what they contained. And the way she had them stacked on wooden pallets so nothing would get ruined if the garage flooded a few inches in a heavy rain.

"I'm not sure what's weird about it," Justin said. "It's really neat."

"Right. That's exactly what I mean. When my dad throws stuff out in the garage he just . . . throws it out there. If it gets dusty or wet or moldy it just does. I guess the way he does it is weird and the way the doctor does it is right, but I've always only seen it his way, so this takes some getting used to."

"There are the dog beds," Justin said. "Right in that corner."

He pointed to a stack of cartons, each labeled with the words "dog beds." Actually, Pete had seen the stack already. But somehow he had not registered the words. His mind had been somewhere else entirely.

"I wish I could trade places with you," he said to Justin.

"I don't think I know what you mean."

"I guess I mean I wish they'd arrest my dad and let yours go. I'd like it if my dad was away for a long time and I got to stay at the doctor's and not go home. I know you don't like it. That's because you have a good dad. That's why I wish we could trade."

Justin did not reply. Neither said anything for an awkward length of time. So Pete moved off in the direction of the dog bed cartons and began to pull boxes down off the stack.

"These are all too small," he said to no one in particular as he plowed through the first box.

Pete realized he had no tape to reseal the boxes. And obviously the doctor liked her boxes stored just so.

"Justin, will you go inside and ask Dr. Lucy for some tape so I can tape these back up again?"

"Sure," Justin said, and ducked out of the garage.

Pete pulled down a second carton and immediately hit pay dirt. It was a padded bed a good five or six inches thick, and so big it had to be folded in half just to fit into the carton. In fact, it was apparently the only bed that would fit in the box, because it was in there alone. It had a zip-off cover in a dark hunter green, and the fabric felt soft like flannel.

"Oh, you're going to love this," he said out loud. Even though the wolf-dog was, of course, much too far away to hear.

—

Pete sat in the kennel run, the hard concrete of its floor hurting the scabs on his backside. He patted the bed he had placed by his right hip. Still Prince just stood, awkwardly, balanced on three legs and with his head down.

Pete sighed deeply.

He moved the bed farther away, as far as his arm would reach, and the wolf-dog hobbled over and sniffed it. He stepped onto it, circled twice, and carefully settled with his muzzle facing Pete. He kept his eyes open, watching. Aware.

"That's too bad," Pete said. "I wish you didn't feel that way. I thought we were better friends by now." Pete noted that tears were a possibility, and worked hard not to let them have their way. "I'm not sure why you liked me better when you were in the cage."

Justin's voice startled him.

"I taped up that first box and put it back on the stack."

"Thanks," Pete said.

Pete had his back to the yard, leaned up against the chain link. He didn't look around, but a moment later he felt Justin settle with his back to the fence on the other side. It felt almost as though he could feel the pressure of Justin's back against his own, but Pete figured it was probably just plain fence reacting to his friend's weight.

For a time no one spoke.

Then Justin said, "You going to sit with him all day?"

"No. I wish I could. But I have to go home."

He watched the wolf-dog's face as he spoke. Looked into his golden eyes. Pete felt his love for Prince like an empty space in his chest. An achy sensation, now that he was less sure his feelings were returned.

"Why? It's not very late."

"But yesterday my dad tried to get me to tell him where I've been going. And I wouldn't say. And for some reason he let it go by. But if I keep being gone all day, day after day, it'll come up again. I just know it will. I don't dare push my luck with him."

Another long silence. Pete realized he could feel Justin's breathing in a slight movement of the fence against his back. It felt comforting to him. Like the opposite of being in his life all alone.

Pete surprised himself by speaking. He hadn't felt any words coming.

"Remember when you said my dad was really tough? And I said I didn't think he was? That I thought he was just like everybody else's dad?"

"Yeah," Justin said. "I remember."

"Now I think you were right. I think he's really tough. I guess before that, he was the only dad I knew. Well, no. Not really. I know other dads but I didn't know how they were to live with. I guess I know Jack's dad best, and he's not so different from mine, except he's worse. In some ways, anyway. Because he changes into somebody else entirely when he gets drunk, and there's really no guessing what he's going to do. So I guess I thought that's just how all dads were. But now that I know your dad, I think I got a bum deal. And I think you're really lucky."

A long silence. Pete wondered if he'd said the wrong thing. God knows it wouldn't have been the first time.

"Not right now I'm not very lucky."

"No, right," Pete said. "I'm sorry. I didn't mean to act like I forgot about that or like it's not a big deal. But he'll be back. So in general you're lucky."

"Yeah, I guess. I do think I have a good dad. But other than that I wouldn't say I feel lucky most days."

"I'm sorry," Pete said, gently easing to his feet and dusting off the seat of his shorts. "I guess I can't say anything right today. I'll just go tell the doctor goodbye."

"Don't leave on my account."

"No. I'm not. I'm just having a bad day. I guess we all are. That thing with your dad, and Prince hardly seems to want to trust me, and I'm worried about what'll happen when I get home. I'm always worried about what'll happen when I get home."

"I guess I do feel a little lucky," Justin said. "I mean, compared to that."

—

Pete was less than a mile from home when Boomer Leggett caught up with him. He was just thinking how close he was to being done with the long walk, and how happy he'd be to get inside and sit down, and how maybe he should have taken the doctor up on her offer to drive him. But it was broad daylight, and he didn't want anybody knowing where he'd been going. He didn't want to get her into trouble.

Then Pete felt Boomer like a tingling at his back—actually felt him before the tow truck pulled level with Pete and stopped. And then when it did, and Pete saw it at the corner of his eye, he thought, *Oh, so that's what that weird feeling was.* He had never had an experience like that one, never known something before it was right and proper to know it, but he couldn't take much time to explore the strangeness of that moment because it all happened too fast.

Boomer was talking to him. And still Pete refused to look. And he refused to stop walking. So Boomer had to inch the truck along next to him.

"See, this is why you should always do what your daddy tells you to do," Boomer called out.

Pete had been vaguely aware of something brewing inside him. But he had only been half feeling the pressure of it, and had not yet been able to decipher what it was. But when he heard Boomer's voice it boiled up to the surface, and it was rage. Pure rage.

He stopped, and turned to face the truck, and Boomer stepped on the brake and dropped the smarmy grin completely when he saw the look on Pete's face.

"Did you always do what your daddy told you to do, Boomer?"

Pete wasn't sure why he had asked that question. It seemed like a digression from the more important matters at hand. But somehow Pete knew he was being given advice that Boomer probably never followed himself, and he wanted to start by getting the man to admit it.

"Well, no, not really," Boomer said, the irritating grin half returning. "But that's a little different, because my daddy was crazy as a loon."

Pete walked to the truck and stood at the open passenger-side window, feeling the rage. Pushing and playing at it to keep it just at the surface of things.

"Did you hurt Justin?" he asked, his voice strangely level.

"What's a Justin? I don't know nobody by that name."

"Well, unless you hurt a great big crowd of people in the last couple or three days, Boomer, it's still a pretty easy question."

"Oh. Right. The dark-as-night boy."

Boomer raised his right hand and pantomimed a bottle being brought down. It was strangely familiar, because it looked exactly the way it had looked when Justin had imitated the same gesture.

Which stood to reason, Pete realized, because they were both there when it happened.

"I heard his daddy got whomped on pretty good, too," Boomer added. "Seems that whole family's got a problem knowing where they do and don't belong."

If Boomer had been standing outside his truck, standing on the sidewalk with Pete, Pete would have assaulted him. He wouldn't have been able to stop himself. He would have flown at the older man, head crashing into gut, fists flailing. Despite the fact that he would lose. And probably get badly hurt. But he would have taken every good shot he could get before that inevitable end to things.

Instead Pete just stood there, feeling the heat and redness build up around the tops of his ears. Then, because his voice didn't seem to want to work, and because he knew no insults grave enough to suit the moment, he simply raised his middle finger and extended it in Boomer's direction. With a kind of fierce emphasis driven by his anger.

"Why, you little . . . ," Boomer began.

He trailed off without finishing the sentence, and then he was out of his truck, out on the street.

Pete took off running. Not so much out of fear, though he was afraid. But it was not his fear that caused him to retreat. He still would have liked a piece of the terrible man, and he could have chosen to stand his ground. But he didn't want to give Boomer the satisfaction of making Pete pay for what he had done. He wanted to win. He wanted Boomer to feel defeated.

Pete sprinted down the street, made a quick turn into a driveway, and sped up as he approached its six-foot chain-link fence. He jumped, grabbed, climbed. Swung one leg over the top. A jolt of pain ran through him as the deepest of the scabbed-over welts ripped open, but he didn't cry out loud. Just jumped down on the other side of the fence and turned to see how Boomer was doing.

Boomer was climbing the fence much more slowly and clumsily than Pete had done. He wildly swung one leg over, and his filthy work pants caught on top of the wires. As he struggled to untangle himself he lost his balance and fell backward, ripping the cuff of his pants and landing with a whump in the driveway.

"Got . . . damn it all to hell!" he shouted.

Pete gave him the finger again.

"Yeah, you see that, Boomer?" Pete howled, holding the finger in place. "I hope you broke your damn back. I hope everything bad that can possibly happen to a person happens to you. I hate you!"

Pete turned and trotted away.

He glanced once over his shoulder to make sure Boomer hadn't really broken his back. Truth be told, Pete didn't seriously want that and would have gone for help if help had been needed.

But Boomer was on his feet, cursing and hobbling back down the driveway toward his truck.

It struck Pete that Boomer knew exactly where he lived. And that Boomer would be able to drive there faster than Pete could walk.

In other words, now Pete couldn't go home.

He crossed the fenced yard and scaled the chain link on the other side, then slipped quickly through the empty space between the fences, where garages lined up back to back.

He reached around to feel, through his shorts, the spot he'd reinjured. His fingers came away bloody.

He decided if he couldn't go home he'd go to the lake. It would be the first time he'd given himself that little bit of pleasure all summer. Considering a sudden change of plan was needed, Pete figured there were far worse plans than a good hot-afternoon swim.

———

Pete stood on the muddy shore of the postage stamp–sized lake, enjoying the shade provided by the thick canopy of trees over his head. His sneakers left sucking prints in the slippery muck as he unbuttoned his shirt and removed it. The slight breeze felt good on his bare skin.

He pulled his feet out of his shoes without bothering to untie them, stepping on each heel with the opposite foot. He draped his shirt over a fallen branch and waded into the glorious water. It wasn't really cold.

It felt barely warm against his skin, but he knew the water would at least turn refreshingly cool deeper into the lake. So he dove forward and swam.

He stopped when the temperature was just right, just the way he liked it, and treaded water. All of his anger and fear and confusion felt as though they were leaving him at last. Washing away.

He turned his head and spun around in a full circle, enjoying his surroundings. But as he did, he could not help but notice a small trail of blood following him through the water.

And then the moment of bliss ended. Just like that. It had been there, he had reveled in it, then it was gone.

"Oh, hey, there you are, Petey! Where the hell you been?"

Pete knew the voice. He didn't see Jack, but he didn't need to. He knew who had discovered him.

"I been by your house half a dozen times," the disembodied Jack voice continued, "and you're never home, and I ask your dad where you been, and he always says he don't know. And I thought, well, that's just plum weird, because since when does Mr. Solomon not know where you are? So I asked him to have you come by soon as he saw you, but this morning I went by there again and he said you were home last night, but you never came by. So did he not tell you to come by, or are you staying away from me on purpose?"

By the middle of the last sentence, Pete had been able to follow the voice to the small figure of Jack hunched over the two fishing lines he was tending. Jack sat under that big gnarly tree, the one with the tangled roots that reached into the lake. Jack liked to fish there because trout hid in that labyrinth of twisted roots. Pete liked to avoid the spot because every time he hooked a fish there it managed to wrap the line around a root and break free.

"Both," Pete said. "He didn't tell me you came around asking after me. But even if he had, I'm staying away from you on purpose."

"What did I do so wrong?"

Pete swam a bit closer, though it was really more like treading water with some direction involved.

"I think you know."

"The damn dog, right? You're still mad about the damn dog."

"Right. I still am."

"Well, that's better than ditching your best friend altogether. Not just for one morning."

"Except I ditched you for a reason. Because I got a good look at who you really are, Jacky. Not just to be selfish."

On that note, Pete decided he'd had enough of the conversation. He turned and swam slowly away.

When he reached the other side of the tiny lake, the spot where he'd left his shirt and sneakers, he pulled to his feet and waded ashore, his feet slipping in the mossy ooze.

He shook the water out of his short hair and then straightened his head again. Just as he did, something smashed against the bone outside his left eye. He stumbled backward, then righted himself. He looked up to see that Jack had apparently run around the shore of the lake after him, and was now standing with his fist still cocked. Still ready to fight.

"What the hell was that for?" Pete yelled, rubbing his bruised eye socket.

"That's for thinking a dog is more important than me. And because now I know it's true what they're saying about you. I'm getting a good look at who you really are, too, Petey. You got a new friend, just like they say, and it's somebody you ought never to go anywhere near. You ought to know better. I kept saying no, Pete would never do something so stupid as that, but now I know. I never knew you at all, Pete. I'm glad you're not my friend anymore. You go be friends with that—"

But he never got to say the word he had lined up ready to go. Because Pete hit him full on in the gut with his lowered head and sent him flying. Jack hit the ground hard, and Pete landed on top of him and heard all the air fly out of Jack's lungs with a big "oof" sound.

Pete held an index finger in Jack's face as a warning.

"You don't talk about him! You never say a word about him or his father! You hear me? You got no right. You never met them, so just keep your mouth shut and stick to what you know something about."

Nothing happened. No words were returned, and Jack still seemed unable to breathe, so Pete got up off him and turned his back and put his shirt on and slipped into his shoes without even bothering to wash the mud off his feet.

He looked back to see Jack half sitting up in the mud, one hand to his chest. Barely breathing.

"I'm gonna forget I ever met you, Pete," Jack said in a strained whisper.

"Good," Pete said.

Then he walked home. Boomer Leggett or no.

———

There was no tow truck parked in front of his house. So Pete stepped inside.

He found his dad lying in bed, in pajamas, the covers pulled up to his waist. As if it weren't the middle of the damn afternoon.

"Well, well," his dad said, loosely indicating Pete's face with a motion of his hand. "Looks like you ran into something or somebody who's even madder at you than I am."

Pete had no idea whether Boomer had come by and ratted him out. So he wasn't sure how to play the situation.

"Jack's mad at me," Pete said.

"Seems you got a whole lot of people mad at you, boy. You seem to be developing a talent for ticking people off."

"Yes, sir," Pete said. "Seems that way to me, too."

"Where the hell you get off talking to Boomer like that? I was ashamed to hear some of the things you said."

"He probably made half of them up," Pete said.

He was feeling defiant and he couldn't hide it. Couldn't even bring himself to try.

"So you didn't give him the finger? Or tell him that you hoped his back was broke?"

"Oh. Well. Yes, sir. That was all true."

"Didn't I teach you to treat your elders with more respect than that?"

A fuse that had been lit in Pete earlier that day reached the powder, and there was no holding back the explosion.

"I'll *never* respect Boomer Leggett!" Pete shouted. "He's a horrible, horrible man. He broke a bottle over a poor helpless kid's head and cut his scalp so he could've bled to death, and he was laughing about it to me like it was funny. I don't care how old he is, I'll never respect a man like that, and nothing you can say to me will ever make me. You can punish me till the cows come home, but you can't ever make me respect somebody I don't."

Then Pete paused, ready to receive the blowback from what he had done.

His father's face, his eyes, looked troubled and dark but strangely calm.

"I see. We're feeling quite the big man today, aren't we? You got anything else you want to teach me about life, little man?"

"No, sir. But I do have a question for you. I want you to look right in my face and tell me you had nothing to do with what happened to Justin."

Pete realized as the words came out of his mouth that he was speaking to his father the way parents speak to their children. Or at least the way the person in control speaks to someone they're controlling. But it was too late to call the words back. So he just waited to see when and how—and how much—he would pay for what he had done.

"I shouldn't have to," his father said, still abnormally calm. "You can see I can't get around much these days."

"Not that you didn't do it with your own two hands. That you had *nothing to do with it.*"

A silence fell. It felt long, but it might only have been a single handful of seconds. It tingled, that silence. Pete could feel the tingle.

"I had nothing to do with it," his father said.

Pete didn't speak. He was busy feeling a huge amount of breath leave his body. He wondered how long he had been holding it.

"Now if you're done holding court, little man, you can go straight to your room. You will not get dinner tonight. And I'd best see a change in that attitude over the next couple of days, or you're going to be one mighty hungry boy."

Pete was hungry already. He had missed lunch. He had left the doctor's house before it was served, and had been walking and fighting at lunchtime instead of eating. He sighed at the news, but made sure the breath of his sigh was silent.

"Yes, sir," he said.

As he walked to his room it struck him that he'd still gotten off easy. Easier than he could possibly explain to himself in his poor exhausted brain.

—

Pete was lying facedown on his bed when he heard the soft knock on his bedroom door.

"What is it?" he asked, without much life in the words. Without much life in him.

The door opened partway, squeaking on its unoiled hinge.

"Just one more thing I wanted to say to you." His dad's voice sounded more the way Pete was used to hearing it. More in charge.

Not quite so calm. "Next time you come home to *my house* talking to me like I got to account to you for what I do, you're about to find all your clothes out on the front yard. And you can just get your room and board elsewhere. Do I make myself clear, boy?"

In a strange way it struck Pete as a relief. To have things back the way they had always been. Not so mysterious. A kind of bad he could easily understand.

"Yes, sir," Pete said.

Chapter Nineteen: Dr. Lucy

"How does it look?" Justin asked.

She had just peeled the old dressings away from his head wound and deposited them in the examining room trash can.

"I'm happy with it," she said. "It's healing well. But you need to keep it clean and dry for a few more days."

"Yes, ma'am. I was really careful when I took my bath. I didn't wash my head at all. I washed my face and my neck but not my head."

He sat on her examining table in a pajama top she had given him. It fit him like a dress, coming down to his knees. His bare lower legs dangled and swung, looking matchstick-thin and vulnerable. His hands remained invisible within the overlong sleeves. Dr. Lucy instinctively reached out for those sleeves and rolled them up until Justin's hands came back into view.

"That's good," she said. "I'll just put a fresh dressing on this and then we'll get you off to bed."

As she was working she noticed a cord around his neck, worn like a long necklace, but it disappeared under the pajama top in the front and she couldn't see what weighted it down.

"What's on the cord?" she asked, hoping it would be a house key. The boy needed his belongings from home.

"Oh, this." He grabbed at the cord and pulled it up and out. A shiny new-looking key emerged. "So I can get in and out of the house while my dad's at work."

"What would you say about loaning that to me for tonight? When it gets good and dark I'll go over to your house and get as many of your clothes as I can find."

"Yes, please. Thank you. And my toothbrush."

"Right. And your toothbrush. Your dad told me you're fastidious about your teeth."

"And . . . ," he began.

But he never finished the thought.

"And? Something else at home you need?"

"No, ma'am. Never mind. Doesn't matter at all."

———

She tucked him into bed in the guest room, in the bed nearest the window. She sat with him for a moment, unsure why. Unsure of what to say. It seemed a lot of words were resting uncomfortably between them, wanting to be spoken. Mostly—if not all—concerning Calvin.

But I'll be damned if I know what words they are, she thought.

Justin broke the silence.

"Dr. Lucy? Do you have kids?"

"I had a boy."

"*Had* a boy? Where did he go?"

So that's the difference between a grown-up and a child, she realized. The child has no idea what not to ask.

"Well. First there was the divorce. And he went to live with his father."

"Why? Why didn't he live with you?"

In the pause before she answered, she noticed that he was clutching the light blanket to his chest in a way that betrayed insecurity. It struck her that he might be asking questions because he was afraid of the moment she walked out and left him to sleep all alone.

"When my husband and I divorced, we gave him the choice of where he wanted to live. He picked his father."

Don't ask why, she thought. *Do not ask why.*

"Why?"

Dr. Lucy sighed. She briefly sorted through her options. A little white lie. The truth. Declining to answer the question.

"He thought I was too . . ." The word stuck in her throat. So she chose an easier one. "Remote."

"I don't know what that is."

"Distant. Hard to reach."

Cold.

"Oh. You don't seem that way to me at all."

"Well, I am. But not as much as I used to be, I suppose. People change. Situations change. At the time I was in my internship, and I was working long hours, and when I got home I was exhausted. He resented me for it. His father worked long hours, too. But fathers are allowed to. It's expected. I was supposed to be nurturing and always there. He was furious with me, and he chose his father."

"Didn't that make you feel terrible?"

She opened her mouth to dismiss him. To snap, even. To say, "I don't like to talk about the way I feel," the way she had when Pete asked a similar question.

Instead, to her surprise, she said, "It was devastating. It was the worst thing that's happened to me in my adult life. Well. Second worst."

"I'm sorry. Do you see him or talk to him? Can he live with you later?"

"No," she said.

Then they just sat that way for a long time, with Lucy saying nothing. While she said nothing, she scanned the inside of herself for emotion, but everything felt inert. Dead.

"While he was living with his dad . . . he went to bed one night with a really bad cold. Or what his dad thought was just a bad cold. But it was pneumonia. And he stopped breathing in his sleep. And I never forgave myself for that, because I'm a doctor, and if he'd been living with me, I would have known. I would have known it was more than just a cold. I would have been listening to his lungs. And he'd still be here. I let him go with his dad to indulge his little temper tantrum. I figured we'd put our relationship back together later. But there was no later for us, and I feel like it's my fault."

"That's really sad."

"It is. I know. And I'm sorry it's not a very good story to go to sleep on. But you asked."

Justin opened his mouth, probably to ask another question, but she interrupted him with a stop sign of a hand. Then, not wanting to seem harsh, she reduced the signal to one shushing finger.

"I understand what you're doing, Justin. You're feeling a little scared because your father is away, and I know you don't really want to go to sleep. And you don't want me to leave. But you need your sleep, and I need to walk out of here sooner or later. So how about we just take a deep breath and be brave about this?"

"Yes, ma'am," Justin said.

———

She looked both ways, up and down the dark street, for probably the tenth time since stepping out of her car. Then she took a deep breath and opened the door of Calvin's tiny rented house.

She stepped in and closed the door behind her too quickly. She wanted to pretend to herself that she was not afraid, but it wasn't working out well.

She pulled down the window shades on the street side, then turned on a lamp.

The home was clean and well tended. Decent, like the man who kept it. It was not fancy, and clearly it did not benefit from the money to buy nice things, but it fairly shouted of being lived in by someone determined to lead an organized life. It also struck her as fairly generic, a furnished rental that the new tenants hadn't had time to personalize. To make uniquely their own.

The exception was one huge, healthy potted plant that sat on a table by the window, injecting a surprising amount of life into the room.

There was only one bedroom. She walked to its doorway and looked in at the two twin beds, side by side in the tiny room, with just enough space in between for one person to navigate at a time.

She thought, *No wonder Justin is afraid to sleep alone.*

On one of the two beds lay a stuffed animal, ancient and too well used. Too often held. It was a rabbit, its ears flopping with age, its eyes long gone, just an *X* of black thread left on each side of its face. If it had been a color at one time, it was no longer.

Her mind flashed back to earlier in the evening when Justin had started to ask for one other thing from the house but refused to finish his thought.

She picked up the rabbit and put it in one of the bags she had brought.

The closet had no door, but it was neatly arranged with Calvin's clothes on the right, Justin's on the left. Shoes sat straight on the hardwood floor underneath the hanging shirts. Pants lay folded on a shelf above.

She reached for Justin's half a dozen shirts, then paused. Her hand moved to the right, and she pulled one of Calvin's denim work shirts to her face. She breathed deeply, hoping it would have retained some of Calvin. That scent of clean male skin and something unique to him. But it was freshly washed and smelled faintly of laundry soap and nothing more. Chastising herself, she tucked all of Justin's shirts, pants, and shoes into the bag. She found underwear and socks in the dresser drawer, and packed those up as well, careful to stay away from Calvin's side.

As she worked, her eyes fell on a photo. It was in a wooden frame, carefully carved and sanded. Possibly homemade. It was a photo of Calvin and a woman she could only imagine to be his late wife. She was slight and pretty, with skin almost a perfect match for his, wearing a light summer dress and looking up at him with adoration. Which he returned.

She placed the framed photo in the bag as well.

Then, in the kitchen, she rummaged through the cupboards for a large mixing bowl, filled it with water in the sink, and set the pot of the poor plant in it. To give it half a chance to live until Calvin came home.

Her hand was already resting on the front doorknob when she remembered the toothbrush.

She had no way of knowing which of the two toothbrushes dangling from a rack in the small bathroom was Justin's, so she took them both. She brought the toothpaste because he might like his own brand better.

She opened the front door and looked both ways. The dark street was still empty. She stepped out and locked the door behind her.

Halfway to the car the woman with the poodle appeared under the streetlight, fussing at her dog to "do potty" so she could go back inside. Dr. Lucy fairly ran the last few steps to her car before the woman could come close enough to recognize her. She needn't have bothered. The woman never once looked up from her little white dog to see what else might be taking place on her block in that warm summer night.

—

Dr. Lucy tiptoed into the guest room and began putting the clothes away by moonlight. She supposed it could have waited until morning. But she couldn't shake the image of the shirts becoming creased on top of one another in the bags after Calvin had obviously gone to the trouble to iron them so carefully.

She was placing underwear and socks in the top dresser drawer when Justin startled her by speaking.

"Thanks for doing that," he said.

"I didn't mean to wake you."

"You didn't wake me."

"You haven't been able to sleep at all?"

"No, ma'am. Sorry."

The "sorry" struck her as a tiny bit of tragedy. In fact, it reminded her of Pete. No wonder those two got along so well.

She walked to his bed and turned on the light and sat with him. Neither said anything for a time. They just blinked at the sudden brightness.

"I brought back two things you didn't ask me for," she said, finally.

"Really?"

He sat up straighter in anticipation.

She pulled the stuffed rabbit from the bag and held it out to him.

"I thought you might want this. It was on your bed. So I thought maybe you were used to having it at bedtime."

"Um. Not really, ma'am. I mean . . . I like him. But I don't *need* him. When I was little I couldn't go to sleep without him. But . . . you know. I'm eleven. I'm pretty big for that bunny stuff now."

He kept staring at the rabbit, but he still did not reach out to take it from her hands.

"Here's what I was thinking, though," she said. "I don't know about you, but sometimes when I get upset, I don't really want to be grown up. Not in that exact moment. It makes me feel younger when I've lost something, or I'm missing someone. So if you've outgrown that rabbit years ago, but you wanted to hang on to him while your dad is away, I just don't think that would be such a bad thing. I really don't think anybody would fault you for that."

"Pete might think I was a baby."

"I doubt it," she said. "But if it'll make you feel better, we'll keep it just between you and me."

Slowly, with his eyes wide, he reached out and took the rabbit out of her hands. Then he set it on his pillow. As though he couldn't imagine holding it with anyone watching.

"What's the other thing?" he asked, his voice barely over a whisper.

She reached into the bag and took out the only item left. The photograph.

"I thought you might like to have a photo of your dad while he's away," she said, holding it out for him to see.

"Oh, yes, ma'am. Thank you." He took it from her and stood it up on its easel back on the bedside table. Adjusted the angle until it was just so. "I think maybe I'll sleep better now. Thanks."

She rose to her feet. She'd been tempted to kiss him goodnight. A little peck on the forehead. But it seemed too personal a gesture, and she hadn't managed to follow the thought through.

"Goodnight," she said.

"I don't think you're remote, ma'am. Not at all."

She paused a moment, swaying slightly in the air. Then she ducked in and gave him that forehead kiss that had seemed so impossible.

"Goodnight," she said, reaching over him and turning off the light.

"Dr. Lucy?"

"Yes?"

"Do you love my dad?"

Her scalp tingled as she geared herself up to speak.

"Now why would you ask me a thing like that, Justin? I only met your dad last week."

"I know. But I was looking at this picture. I've looked at it a million times before, but I think this is the first time I've looked at it since I was here. Since my dad and I met you, unless maybe I looked at it since then but didn't really notice I was doing it. The way my dad and my mom are looking at each other in the picture, you and my dad look at each other like that. Maybe not *exactly* the same. But the same. If you know what I mean."

Dr. Lucy sank onto the bed again. She sat quiet for a moment, strangely aware of her breathing. She wondered, without actual words in her head, how one goes about answering a question like that.

She was glad to be having this talk in the dark.

"I know what you mean," she said, realizing she was heading for honesty. Which was good, she decided. She owed the boy honesty. Or life did, anyway, but she was the only one here with him. "And I'm not saying you're wrong about what you see. But love takes more time. I think maybe I *could* love your dad, if we had more time and we let ourselves get to know each other. But I'm afraid we never will. We don't dare, because . . ."

She wondered how best to finish that sentence. Or if she even needed to.

"I know," he said. "I know the because."

She placed one hand on the top of his head briefly, her thumb brushing the bandages. Then she took her hand back and rose to leave.

She felt surprisingly drained inside, as if she'd run a marathon without ever moving her feet.

"Dr. Lucy?" he asked as her hand touched the doorknob.

She sighed, but only inwardly. She didn't respond with words. Just stopped and waited.

"That was too many questions, wasn't it?"

"Don't worry about it," she said. "Just try to get some sleep."

She looked back at him, her eyes more adjusted to the dim room lit only by moonlight. The rabbit was no longer resting on the pillow. No longer separate from its boy.

———

In the middle of the night Dr. Lucy woke with a start, sitting up in bed. The dogs were barking and howling in their runs. It made her heart race. She hadn't heard a knock, but she knew there must have been one. That or a prowler. Something had the dogs on full alert, and nothing short of a sudden nighttime visitor had ever drawn such a reaction.

Winston the greyhound, who had come upstairs again because the wolf-dog was outdoors, tipped his head back and let loose a spooky, unsettling howl.

One hand to her chest and trying to steady her breathing, she reached out for the drawer in the bedside table and found the pistol by feel. It added to the discomfort of the situation. It did not alleviate it.

It's so easy to go out and buy a gun to feel secure. To feel you can handle what might come up. But in that moment the gravity of the situation felt far clearer. If you have a gun, and you're holding the gun, you might shoot somebody. And that's a real thing, with real consequences.

She almost left the pistol where it lay. But she thought about Justin in the next room, and she slid it out of the drawer and into the pocket of her pajama bottoms.

In the thin sliver of space under her bedroom door, she saw the light go on in his room across the hall.

"Stay where you are, Justin," she said out loud but under her breath. Too quietly for anybody but herself to hear.

She crossed to the window, which was already open for air.

"Who's there?" she asked, wanting her voice to sound steady and unafraid. It didn't.

"Are you the doctor?" an unfamiliar male voice called up.

There was only one figure on her front porch. Looking up at her in the dimness. One tall man. The dogs recommitted to their howling when they heard him speak.

"I'm *a* doctor," she said, still far more unsure than she used to be in these situations.

"I need a doctor," the man said.

"Then why don't you go to the county hospital like everybody else?"

"Well, see, that's the thing," he called up. Louder, if anything. "They ask too many questions. I knocked over that gas station out on the highway just north of town, and the night clerk had a gun. I don't want a doctor who's going to be asking how this happened."

Dr. Lucy swallowed hard, and the fear she'd wakened up to settled thickly around her ears and in her heart. This situation was not right, and she could feel it. Something was off here.

Why come to a place like this so you won't have to answer any questions if you're going to volunteer the very information you claim you're trying to hide?

She'd been in this situation maybe ten times over these past few years. And the men in question always played their cards close to their chests. What fool wouldn't?

"What makes you think I don't ask questions? Who told you I was even out here?"

Just for a moment she tried to calm herself. To convince herself that he was about to say Victor sent him. Maybe he was simply the dumbest criminal on the planet. That could happen. Somebody had to be.

"Well, you know," he said. "You hear things."

Her whole body buzzing with fear, she raised her voice and made it hard like steel.

"I'm calling the police right now," she said. "Get the hell off my property before they get here if you don't like answering questions."

The man didn't move. Just stood in the moonlight, leaning on her porch railing. Dr. Lucy wrapped her hand around the gun in her pocket.

A moment later the man jerked upright, shook his head, and turned away. He walked back down her pathway toward the road.

She collapsed onto the sill of the open window and watched him to be sure he kept moving. She worked hard at breathing normally until she heard a car start up and drive away. Then it was easier, and breathing happened more naturally.

Another knock made her jump so suddenly that she almost fell out the window.

"Dr. Lucy?"

She pulled a huge breath and realized it was only Justin at her bedroom door.

"You can come in, honey," she said, her voice audibly shaking.

The door opened slowly. Just a few inches. His silhouette appeared small and cowed, backlit by the lamp in the guest bedroom.

"What was that, Dr. Lucy? Did somebody come?"

"Yes, but it's okay. They're gone now."

He padded across the room to her, cutting a wide path around Winston. She pulled him close, and he sat next to her on the window-sill, clutching his stuffed rabbit.

"Who was it?"

"Just somebody who wanted a doctor. But I'm not the right doctor for him."

"What kind of doctor did he need?"

She opened her mouth to spare him with a lie, but the truth came out, almost on its own power.

"I don't think he needed a doctor at all."

"You said he did."

"Well, *he* said he did. He said he'd robbed a gas station and the night clerk had a gun. He said he was looking for a doctor who wouldn't ask a lot of questions."

"Hmm," Justin said. "That seems strange. If he already told you he robbed a place, then what did he not want you to ask about?"

Dr. Lucy smiled in spite of herself. She realized she had begun to calm some. Her heart and breathing felt nearly normal.

"You're a smart boy," she said. "That's what I was wondering, too. That's why I think he was lying."

"Why would he lie about that?"

Then she regretted getting this far into the truth with the boy. Because it was a scary truth. He'd be better off not knowing it. He would sleep better without it.

But she couldn't figure a way to back out of the situation again.

"I think maybe the police wanted to see if they could catch me doing something illegal. See, if I know that man robbed a gas station and I patch him up and don't report it to the police, that would make me an accessory to the crime. I'm sorry to have to tell you that, and maybe I'm wrong. Maybe the guy just wasn't a very good thinker. But either way, don't worry. They're not going to catch me doing anything I shouldn't."

"Of course not," Justin said. "You'd never do a thing like that. Why would they even think you would?"

The question raised two reactions in her troubled gut.

First, shame. That deep, sickening shame that sits in your heart and reminds you that no one will love you if they know the whole truth. If they find out who you really are. Second, it raised an answer to the question, one she had not considered. If they'd thought to set her up that way, they must have had a pretty good idea of what she'd been doing. *Why have they never attempted to prove it before?* she wondered. *Are they suddenly far more motivated to try?*

"I think we need to get some sleep," she said.

"I'll never get back to sleep after that."

"Maybe you will," she said. But she didn't fully believe it. And she knew sleep was out of the picture for her. "Tell you what. How about if I sleep in the other twin bed in the guest room? Would that make it easier for you?"

"Yes, ma'am. Much easier. Thank you."

Winston glared at her as she followed Justin to the door. *He needs me more than you do,* she thought, but did not say out loud. Winston set his chin down on his paws and sighed.

It struck her that she was going to have to find a new way to cover the animals' extra expenses. She had no idea what that might be. And now she had at least one new mouth to feed. Allowing for the ravenous and often-present Pete, really more like two.

And yet, both underneath and above those worries she felt a great lifting of pressure. The feeling could only be described as relief.

Chapter Twenty: Pete

Pete left his house in the pitch-dark. He made it to the highway while morning twilight was still so newly arrived that he could barely see two steps in front of his feet.

Only one car had raced past him so far.

He heard the second one coming, but it didn't race past. It slowed, then kept pace with him, creeping slowly by his side. He felt his belly turn to ice.

"I don't want any trouble," he whispered to himself. "No more trouble."

He refused to look over. As though not seeing who was there might be enough to prevent the trouble he didn't want.

"Pete," he heard a woman's voice say, and he knew immediately it was Dr. Lucy. "Get in."

Pete sighed out a big puff of breath intermixed with exiting fear, and turned to look. She was holding the passenger door open for him. He dove inside.

He settled with his knees on her passenger floor mat and his chest and head resting on the seat. Mostly to keep her safe by hiding, but it was more comfortable than having to sit. He silently cursed the fact that he had just been getting back to sitting again when he went and reinjured himself by tearing that scab.

He comforted himself with the reminder that he had been saved miles of walking.

"Did you come out here just to get me?" he asked her.

His head was turned in her direction, but all he really saw was one side of her blue skirt. He also saw her pull a pack of cigarettes from her skirt pocket. He didn't see her light it, but he heard it.

He knew before she answered that she hadn't driven out here just to get him. Because he'd given her no indication of when he planned to come back.

"No," she said, and he could hear the exhale—presumably of smoke—that came out with the word. "I had to go someplace this morning. Well. Maybe not *had to*. But I went."

"Where's Justin? Is he back at your house?"

"Yes. I wasn't gone long."

"Is he okay?"

"He is. He's healing well."

A silence.

Then Pete, who was wrestling with a surprising degree of curiosity, said, "I guess it's none of my business where you had to go. Or didn't have to go, but you went anyway."

A long silence during which she smoked but not much more. Pete assumed she never planned to tell him. Which he figured was her right.

"I had to go out to that gas station on the highway just north of town," she said.

"Oh. You needed gas?"

"No."

Another long silence. During it, Pete pondered what he thought of as his rights. For example, his right to ask something of an adult and expect an answer. He figured they were more or less nonexistent at his age.

"I had to see if they'd been robbed in the night," she said. "I know that sounds strange. There's a story behind it, but I'd rather not tell it right now if it's all the same to you."

"Oh. Were they? Robbed?"

"No."

"That's good, then. Right?"

"Not really."

"You wanted them to get robbed?"

"No. Of course not. Long story. It means someone didn't tell me the truth. And it means money is going to be really tight for a while. A long while, I guess. I had something I used to be able to do for a little extra money, but now I won't be able to. So it's going to be harder and I'm not sure what to do, especially with Justin eating three meals at my house for the next however many days, and you eating one or two."

"Right," Pete said.

He angled his head up to see her face. To see how worried she looked. They passed under a streetlight, and he saw her eyes and decided she mostly looked sad.

She looked back down at him.

"What happened to your eye?" she asked.

"Oh, I've just been ticking people off left and right."

"Your dad?"

"Nope. Not this time. My friend Jack. My ex-friend Jack. He's mad because I don't want to be his friend anymore. My dad didn't hit me this time. But he did make me go to bed without dinner. So it's too bad you're worried about how to feed us, because boy, am I hungry."

"Don't worry about it," she said, making a left-hand turn. Pete knew from experience that the turn put them on the doctor's street. "I'll figure it out."

"No, I *should* worry about it," Pete said. "You were fine before I came along. I'll get a summer job."

"Doing what?"

"I don't know. Delivering papers. Mowing lawns."

"Who can grow a lawn in the summer around here?"

"Right. Yeah. Well, I'll do something. Whatever somebody's willing to pay a kid to do. I just have to make sure it's something my dad won't find out about. Because he'd want most of the money if he found out. Dr. Lucy? How come you don't practice medicine anymore?"

"Oh. That." She slowed down and pulled into what Pete knew must be her driveway. "Not really my idea. I didn't quit the practice so much. It quit me. Turns out the people in this neighborhood didn't take very well to a woman doctor."

"And you didn't want to go someplace where they would?"

She stopped, shifted into park, and turned off the engine.

"I wanted to stay here because my father left me this house and land when he died. I'd never seen the place, and he'd never lived a day here because he bought it for his retirement, and he didn't live that long. But I moved here sight unseen because it's paid for. And then once I started collecting animals I couldn't very well move back to the city. And it didn't seem like such a bad deal at the time. Out in the middle of nowhere. Spending all my time with animals and none of it with people. You're just full of questions this morning, aren't you?"

"Sorry," Pete said.

"You don't have to be sorry. I've been answering questions for days and it hasn't killed me yet."

———

Pete was standing by the kennel runs saying good morning to his wolf-dog when Justin came out back to find him.

"Oh, hi," Pete said. "The doctor told me you're doing better. Healing."

"Yeah. What about you?"

Pete noticed that Justin was staring at the bruise by his eye. But he hadn't specifically asked about it, so Pete decided to see if he could skate around that issue.

"Oh, I went and messed up. Tore the scab on the really bad welt. It bled a lot. Now I can barely sit down." Pete let himself into Prince's kennel run. Then, just as he was about to close the gate behind himself, he stopped and held it open just a few inches. "Sorry," he said to Justin. "You want to come in, too?"

"No, thanks. He doesn't know me as well as he knows you."

And he doesn't know me as well as I figured he did, Pete thought.

He remembered Dr. Lucy telling him it would be dangerous to try to keep Prince. That he could hurt a neighbor or start killing cats or chickens. "He's not anybody's puppy dog." That's what she'd said.

Justin knocked Pete out of his thoughts by speaking.

"Well, at least you don't have much you're needing to do. You can kind of take it easy while it heals again."

Pete got down on his knees in the run. Prince hobbled over and sniffed his face. Pete held very still, hoping for a lick. Or even just a wag or two. But the wolf-dog turned and half walked, half hopped back to his bed, where he settled. He lay down mostly facing Pete, but at an angle. Pete figured that was going to have to do for progress.

"Not really," he said to Justin. "I wish I could just sit around. I told the doctor I'd go get a summer job. She's worried about money."

"Oh. Well, that was nice of you." Justin inched closer to the run. Intertwined his fingers in the chain link. Prince raised his head to look, then set it back down again. "What are you going to do?"

"Not sure. I haven't had much time to think about it. But I figure I'll go downtown. Go to the drugstore and the hardware store and the market. Maybe they need a stock boy or something."

"You'll have to get working papers."

"I will?"

"Yeah. You're under eighteen. So they'll ask for working papers."

"What do I have to do to get them?"

"I'm not sure."

Pete sighed, still on his knees, unable to figure out how to sit comfortably on the concrete floor.

"I guess I shouldn't bother trying to go downtown, then. I sure am tired of all this walking."

"Maybe the doctor will let you ride her bike."

"She has a bike?"

"Yeah. Didn't you see it? It was hanging on the wall in the garage."

"Hmm," Pete said. "Wonder how I managed to miss that."

———

They stood in the garage together, staring at it. As if it might be about to do something interesting. Pete still couldn't imagine how he had managed to miss it last time. It was hanging on the wall not three feet from the dog bed cartons. And he was interested in bikes in general, because he had always wanted one, but his dad had never felt they could afford it.

It was painted a deep fire engine red, with chrome fenders.

He must have looked right at it last time but with his mind a million miles away.

"I feel like I ask her for an awful lot of favors," Pete said.

"But you're going out to look for a job so she won't be worried about money."

"That's true."

"It's a girl's bike," Justin said. "Will you be embarrassed riding a girl's bike?"

"Yeah. A little. But I still think it's worth it so I don't have to walk. And the seat is nice and narrow. Looks like it might hit me in all the right spots and miss the wrong ones altogether." Pete thought about straddling the tree limb. How it had worked out better than expected. "And at least it's not pink," he added.

———

Pete found the doctor in the kitchen, hovering over a cup of hot coffee. Pete could see the waves of steam rising into her face. She was smoking a cigarette, leaning her forehead on the heel of one hand.

"I'm going out to look for some work now," Pete said.

She seemed to bring her attention around to him gradually. As if forcing herself awake.

"Are you sure about this? It's really my money problem. Not yours."

"That's not true. You'd have more money if you didn't have all these extra mouths to feed. And if you hadn't taken care of Prince for free. I'm sure, yeah. I just want to ask one favor. Can I borrow that bike that's in the garage? I sure am tired of walking."

"I can imagine you are," she said, seeming more awake now. "I'll have to show you where there's a can of oil. You'll want to oil the wheel hubs and the chain. And you'll have to walk it to a gas station and put air in the tires. It hasn't been ridden in years."

"I can do that, sure. Ma'am? What do you know about working papers?"

"Not too much. It shouldn't be too hard to find out, though."

"Do you know what I'd have to do to get them?"

"I think they'd probably want you to have a physical exam. I might be able to sign off on that. But I'm pretty sure you'd also need a parent's signature on the forms. Plus . . . I think you might be too young. I'm not sure what the cutoff is. Might be fourteen."

"Oh. Too bad. That's out, then. You just saved me a long ride downtown. I think maybe I'll go around to the farms and ranches on the edges of town. See if anybody needs a hand. Maybe they wouldn't be fancy enough businesses to want papers. Well. I'll see what I can get, anyway. Thanks for letting me use the bike."

"It's a girl's bike. Sure you want to be seen riding it?"

"Not positive, ma'am, no. But I sure am tired of walking."

"Oh," she said. And she stood. Carried her cigarette to the sink, ran water over it, and dropped it in the kitchen trash. "That's a good point. You've been doing too much walking. I'll put the bike in the back of my car and drive it to the gas station for air."

"That's very nice of you, ma'am. Thank you."

"You boys stay here where it's safe."

—

He found Justin out by Prince's kennel run, standing close to where the wolf-dog lay, and talking to him. But Pete couldn't hear the words.

Justin's head swung around when he heard Pete behind him.

"Oh. There you are. I was just talking to your wolf. And thinking. Did she say you could use the bike?"

"Yeah. She's taking it to the gas station to put air in the tires. What were you thinking? I mean, if you don't mind telling me."

"I was just wondering if I should try to get some work, too. I'll be eating here more than you will."

"No," Pete said. "You shouldn't. You should let me go do this. You should stay here and lay low and be safe."

Then he walked away, half wondering what Justin had been saying to the wolf-dog and half just plain feeling good. Feeling as though he could protect his friend by going off and earning the needed money so Justin could "lay low." Maybe that could even make up for Pete's failure to protect him in the past.

Anyway, he hoped so, and it was a start.

Chapter Twenty-One: Dr. Lucy

Two days later, at about six thirty in the afternoon, a knock on the door startled her and set her heart to pounding. She was in the kitchen, washing up the dinner dishes. Justin was out back feeding the horses and the dogs, and Pete was still gone on the third day of his job search.

Dr. Lucy thought about the police, but not as her protectors.

She thought about going upstairs to get the pistol, but didn't. However bad things already were, she figured it had the potential to make everything a lot worse.

"I'll be right there," she called toward the front door.

Then she ran out into the backyard and found Justin feeding kibble to two of the greyhounds. He looked up, and his face registered alarm when he looked into hers.

"Someone's at the door," she said in a taut whisper. "Stay out back where you can't be seen and don't come in until I tell you it's okay."

Justin nodded, mute and clearly afraid.

Dr. Lucy trotted back inside. She smoothed her skirt as she walked down the hallway. Then she peered through the small insets of window in the front door.

A man stood on her porch. Apparently not the police. He was a black man, maybe sixty years old or more, with a stoop to his shoulders, a creased face. Short hair shot through with gray.

She found herself breathing more easily.

She opened the door. He was dressed in blue jeans and a white sport shirt, holding a battered fedora in his hands.

"Yes? May I help you?"

"Dr. Lucille Armstrong?"

"Yes."

"My name's William Wilson. I have a message for you from Calvin Bell."

Oh, thank God, she thought. The not knowing had been straining her. Weighing her down. More than she'd realized. Until the moment it lifted.

"Please do come in," she said.

———

She sat him at her kitchen table and offered him a cup of coffee. Even though she was anxious to hear the message. She was grateful to him for making the long trip, and it seemed important to treat him as a valued guest.

"If it's no trouble," he said.

"I'll make a fresh pot. What's left over from lunch is too old. Is Calvin all right?"

"Seems he's okay, yeah. Please don't go to any trouble."

"Nonsense. It's a long walk out here and the least I can do is make you a decent cup of coffee. So what's the message? I'm sorry to be rude, but I'm anxious to hear."

"The judge sentenced him to sixty days."

Dr. Lucy stopped halfway to the coffeepot. She turned and walked back to the table. Sank down in a chair next to William.

"That seems like a lot. I take it the judge wouldn't believe Calvin didn't start the fight."

"That judge never let him so much as open his mouth, ma'am."

A long silence rang. After a few seconds of it, she got up and got back to the task of fresh coffee. She poured the old coffee down the sink and rinsed the pot.

Disjointed a thought as it may have been, she made a mental note to sneak over to Calvin's again and water the plant.

"He was pretty desperate to get a message to you," William said. "But he felt like he had to be careful, too. They wouldn't let him use the phone again. And if he'd written you a letter, well, the prison people read everything, coming and going. He doesn't want anyone to know where Justin is. I know you probably think that's being *too* careful . . ."

"No," she interjected into his pause. "Actually, I don't. I think it's just careful enough. Oh. I should go tell Justin it's okay if he wants to come in. I told him to stay out of sight."

"So you do get it, then."

"I'm afraid I do. The police—and just about everybody else in town, come to think of it—were taking way too much of an interest in me for a while there. Do you think anyone *does* know he's here?"

"Not so far as we can figure. Nobody's been coming around here for a few days, right?"

"No, thank God."

"I wouldn't think anybody's gonna guess a white lady is taking care of the boy. No, I think if they was to go looking for him it would be on the other side of town. Not literally so much, but . . . you know what I'm saying. Likely they don't care much about the boy. Likely they cared more about you and the grown man. But it's best to be safe."

"Yes. Good. So how did Calvin manage to get a message to you?"

"He didn't have to. I went by the county jail to see him. I work at the plant. I was there when it happened. I saw the police come take him away. I wanted to be sure he was okay."

"So you saw the fight?"

"Yes, ma'am. It wasn't so much a fight as they just jumped him. Two of the guys at the plant. Just ambushed him. They said a few things, but I'm not going to repeat them to you of all people. He tried to defend himself, but it was two against one, and Calvin's not the biggest guy in the world. And then the foreman came and broke it up. And the guys said it was Calvin started it, but that was nothing but a lie, ma'am. Just to save their own skins. I tried to say otherwise but the foreman called the police anyway."

"Was he hurt badly?"

"I wouldn't say badly. They banged him up pretty good. Nothing broken or anything. That was mostly why I went to see him, though. See if he needed some kind of medical help he wasn't getting. Not that I guess there was much I could've done about it, but I felt better going to see. The bruises'll heal on their own, I expect. There was a second part of the message, before I forget. He wanted me to tell you that he appreciates so much what you're doing, he'll spend the rest of his life trying to make it up to you. He loves that boy with all his heart. I'm sure you know that. If he couldn't count on the fact that Justin was safe here with you . . . Well, I don't even know how to finish that sentence. It's not something anybody really wants to think about."

"He doesn't owe me anything," she said quietly.

She moved around the kitchen in silence for a minute or two, setting up the coffee to percolate. She wondered if William knew there was something between Calvin and herself. She couldn't imagine Calvin would have told him straight out. Not after working with him for only a few days. But people know things at a number of different levels.

"I wish *I* could go visit him," she said.

She didn't realize until she heard the tone of her own words that if William hadn't known, he probably did now.

"I wouldn't recommend it, ma'am."

If he had other thoughts he kept them to himself.

She plugged in the pot and stood staring out the window for a moment. Then she broke herself out of the silence.

"I'll go get Justin," she said.

"That would be good," he said. "I've got a message for him, too."

———

"Justin, this is William," she said. "He works at the plant with your father."

"Worked," William said. "In the past. They won't let him come back now."

A silence, during which Dr. Lucy found herself gently holding Justin by the shoulders to keep him from backing up. She couldn't imagine he would find William threatening, and so had to assume that it was William's access to news that made Justin feel afraid.

"Your daddy says to tell you this, son. He said, 'Tell Justin we been through worse. And we'll get through this, too.' And he said to say you should keep your head down at the doctor's house. Try not to let anybody know you're here. And everything'll be okay again. He'll get back to you just as soon as he can."

"How long?" Justin asked, his voice scratchy and small.

"Sixty days," Dr. Lucy said.

"That's a long time," Justin said, his voice a little stronger.

"It'll go by, son," William said. "That's the thing about days. No matter what your opinion of days, they always go by."

———

"I don't know what to think about this world," she said.

They sat drinking their cups of coffee, together at the kitchen table. Justin had slipped back outside.

"I wouldn't be the one to help you with that, ma'am."

"I didn't really mean you should. Just thinking out loud, I suppose."

She pulled the pack of cigarettes out of her pocket, knowing as she did that she would quit them in the next sixty days. It would be hard, but she would do it. She hadn't cared enough to do it for herself. When she had heard the news of some link to cancer a couple of years earlier, she hadn't been able to find it in herself to care. But Calvin cared whether or not she got cancer. So she would quit them before he got back.

She held the pack out to William and he gratefully accepted one.

"I mean, I've known for a long while that people could be pretty awful sometimes," she said. "But now I see that I only had part of the picture."

"It's good that you see that," he said, accepting the lighter from her. "Not everybody sees that when it's right in front of their face. A lot of people only see the world the way they want it to be. They see what agrees with the thinking they've already got. The rest just falls away unnoticed."

They smoked in silence for a minute or two. Dr. Lucy was missing cigarettes already, even though she was smoking one as she nursed the thought.

"Did he tell you anything about me?" she surprised herself by asking.

She realized too late that she was doing a miserable job of playing her cards close to her chest.

"Not a lot. He said you were different."

"Different. Is that good?"

"Oh, yes, ma'am. That's very good."

Dr. Lucy sat back in her chair, nursing a buoyant feeling in her chest that had been missing exactly as long as Calvin had been away.

—

When he had finished his coffee and his cigarette she offered to drive him back. Save him the long walk.

"No, thanks," he said. "It's good of you to offer, but I'll walk and then take the bus, just like I did to get out here. You're in this deep enough as it is. Nobody wants any more trouble."

She thanked him for coming, but he didn't answer in words. Just tipped his hat to her on his way out the door.

—

Pete didn't get back until after seven.

"You're much later than I thought you'd be," she said as he walked the bike up onto the porch and leaned it against the house.

"That's because I got a job. I don't suppose you saved me any dinner."

"Of course I did. You have to eat."

"Nice of you to look at it that way, ma'am."

He followed her through the hall and toward the kitchen.

"Wait," he said.

She stopped. He held out his hand to her, offering whatever he was holding. She reached out her hand, and he dropped a dollar bill and two quarters into it.

"Oh. They put you to work right on the spot."

"Yes, ma'am. I worked three hours."

"Doing what?"

"Well, that's the great part, ma'am. They got me feeding horses and mucking out their stalls. They breed Quarter Horses. Their son used to do the work, but he's off backpacking around Europe because he graduated high school, and when he comes home in the fall he'll be going off to college. So my timing was really good, knocking on their door. They been trying to do all the work themselves, but they've got forty-two of them—horses, that is—and they're not as young as they used to be. The people, not the horses. So it's morning and afternoon, feed and clean. Seven days a week, because horses have to eat on the weekends, too. Fifty cents an hour, and they didn't ask about any working papers. So I could be making around three dollars a day. That's twenty-one a week."

She stared down at the money in her hand.

"That would help," she said. "But I feel guilty taking it from you."

"You shouldn't. That's why I earned it. Besides, you do a lot for me. You even saved me some dinner. And we need to get Justin a new pair of glasses. He can't go two months hardly able to see."

He stood there looking up into her face, waiting for some kind of reaction, his expression open and unguarded.

"You're such a nice boy," she said.

She couldn't quite read the look on his face. If she'd had to guess she'd say he either hadn't known she had that sort of overt, affectionate praise in her, or he didn't realize he was a nice boy. Or both. It seemed amazing to think he could not know that about himself. But nothing surprised her about human nature. Not anymore. Not even that.

PART TWO
SAY GOODBYE FOR NOW
August 1959—Two Months After

Calvin is Jailed

Chapter Twenty-Two: Pete

Pete jumped off the bike as it rolled up the gravel pathway to the doctor's front door. He walked it as quietly as possible to the porch, where he leaned it against the railing.

He slipped around the side of the house, surveyed the backyard, then crossed the grass to Prince's kennel run.

"Oh, crud," he said, standing a moment and watching the animal's ceaseless movements. "You're still pacing. That's too bad."

He let himself into the run and latched the gate behind. Then he dug into his back pocket and took out the piece of bacon he'd saved—at great personal sacrifice—from his own breakfast. As he unwrapped it from its double paper napkins the wolf-dog continued to pace.

There was something agitated about the pacing, and the agitation had been growing more extreme each day. That day it bordered on frantic. He held out the strip of bacon, but Prince just paced by without stopping.

"I saved this for you. It's *bacon*. How can you not want bacon?"

The wolf-dog stopped. Sniffed. He took the bacon gently from Pete's hand and, from the look of it, swallowed without chewing. Or at least without chewing much.

Pete reached out to pet Prince's head, but he wasn't fast enough. The wolf-dog had already resumed his pacing.

"Oh, there you are," Pete heard Justin's voice say. He looked up to see Justin standing on the other side of the chain link. "Dr. Lucy says she wants to talk to you. She said as soon as I see you I should tell you to find her."

"Okay," Pete said. But he noticed his voice betrayed the fact that it was not okay. He wondered if Justin noticed as well. "Where is she?"

"Upstairs, I think. What about yesterday? I gave you the same message yesterday. Didn't you ever find her?"

"Not really."

"Hmm," Justin said. "That seems strange."

Pete let himself out of the run and into the yard. He stood in front of Justin for a moment, not answering the indirect question. He thought about cutting around the side of the house again, but he didn't feel he could do so with an audience. What would Justin think?

"Okay," Pete said.

He let himself into the house through the back door. He slipped as silently as possible along the narrow carpet that ran through the hallway. Just as he was reaching out for the knob of the front door, he felt a hand close firmly on his shoulder.

He froze, but did not turn around.

"Well, if it isn't the elusive Pete," the doctor said. "I've been waiting to have a word with you for days. If I didn't know you better, I'd think you were trying to avoid me."

Pete kept his eyes trained on the door so she couldn't look into them and see the guilt.

"Why would I do that, ma'am?"

"Maybe because you know what I'm going to say and you don't want to hear it?"

"I don't know what you're going to say. How could I know that?"

Pete noticed that the hand remained firmly on his shoulder, holding him in place. She was smart enough not to lose him this time.

"Let's play a little game," she said. "Let's say, just for the sake of conversation, that there was a hundred-dollar reward for the right guess. There isn't, but let's just make believe. What would you *guess* I wanted to say?"

Pete turned to her in that moment, and lifted his gaze up to hers. And she let go of his shoulder. Because she knew she could now. All of his evasion was draining away. He couldn't fight this anymore, and they both knew it.

"That I need to let Prince go now."

She didn't answer. She didn't need to. It was obvious.

"Too bad that hundred dollars was just pretend," he said, trying to joke the emotion of the moment away.

Neither one of them laughed.

———

"I wanted just a little more time," Pete said.

They stood in front of the kennel run, all three of them, watching Prince pace. If anything, staring at the wolf-dog only made him pace more frantically. As if he knew when people were trying to make a decision. As if he couldn't bear to hold still to see what that decision would be.

No one answered, so Pete talked on.

"If I hadn't had to work a job all summer, I'd have had more time to tame him."

"Pete," Dr. Lucy said.

He didn't like the sound of his name in this case. It sounded like a plea for him to think about what he was saying. It also sounded like a complete sentence. As though she had no plans to say more.

He waited, but that impression seemed to bear out.

When he couldn't stand the waiting anymore he asked, "What?"

"You've spent an hour or two a day with him for the last couple of months."

"Yeah. Well. If I hadn't had a job I could have spent more."

"But a couple of hours a day for two months is a lot. It should have been enough. If he was tired of life on his own and wanted to cozy up to people, even a couple of hours once should have done it."

Pete shifted from foot to foot, unable to settle.

"He seemed so tame when he was in the little cage inside the house. He used to lick my fingers and try to lick my face. Remember that?"

"I do," she said. "When he was absolutely helpless he accepted having you close by. Now he's back on his feet and he's moving in the opposite direction. He wants to be independent again."

"Just a couple more days."

"Pete, if two months didn't do it, a couple more days isn't going to help. But I'm not going to force you on this. I'm going to let you make your own decision. You always had the best interests of this animal in your heart. If you didn't, he wouldn't be alive right now. So I'm going to trust you to make the right choice. You stand there and watch him pace, and you decide how long you're willing to keep him in these conditions."

Much to his humiliation, Pete began to cry openly. There was no holding it back. He didn't wipe the tears away with his sleeve, or turn his head in a more private direction. He just accepted it. Allowed the flow.

"Could you guys leave us alone for a few minutes?" he asked. "I want to say goodbye to him."

"Of course," Dr. Lucy said.

She placed her hands on Justin's shoulders and steered him inside. She stopped partway across the yard and looked back at Pete.

"He might not like it out there," she said. "He might not be able to hunt as well as he did before the accident. And if that's the case he knows where to find us. So just say goodbye for now."

Pete nodded, needing to wipe his nose but not doing it.

He opened the gate again and slipped inside with Prince. It was harder every time. Pete had been noticing that. The wolf-dog was looking for a chance at that open gate. Pete had to be fast.

"Please just stop pacing for a minute so I can say goodbye to you."

Prince did not stop.

"I promise I'll let you go as soon as I say a few things," he added, the tears still flowing.

No change in the wolf-dog's movements.

Pete flopped into a sitting position on the concrete floor.

"Okay, so you don't know what that means. Right. I get it. You don't understand any English. So you pace and I'll talk. I had a plan. But you didn't know about it. And I guess I can't force it on you. But I had this idea that you could stay with me and be my dog. I know Dr. Lucy said that's not safe, but I guess I sort of figured that could be a good thing. I could walk you on a leash except when I was in the house. And you could stand real close to me all the time. Just think. That day in June when I gave Boomer Leggett the finger. Boy, if you had been standing by my side, he would've stayed in that darn truck. Bet on it. And then out at the lake. I could've told Jack to leave me alone, and he wouldn't have run around the banks and socked me in the eye. Not with *you* there."

Pete paused for a breath and watched the wolf-dog pace. It was wearing Pete down. The sheer desperation of it was grating on him. As though he could feel Prince's discomfort in his own gut.

"And my dad. My dad would never raise a hand to me again. Who hits a kid with a big wolf standing right by his side? But that's not the only reason. It wasn't all selfish. I was getting to like you. Aw, hell. Who am I kidding? I liked you from that first day I met you. I thought we'd be good company for each other. And you could be my bodyguard."

Pete fell silent and admitted to himself—without words—that he had hoped this last conversation would get through to Prince somehow. That he could explain his intentions, and the emotion of his words would transcend the indecipherability of the words themselves. And that Prince would settle. Come to his side.

It wasn't working.

Pete leaned forward and reached up as far as he could, flipping the latch on the gate. He swung the gate open wide.

He had intended to say one more thing before moving his body away from the open gateway. Though he hadn't yet decided exactly what it should be. Some sort of more formal goodbye. Words he could remember in his head next time he missed his wolf-dog so much it snuck up on him and made him cry.

Prince lunged in his direction, as if planning to bowl Pete over and escape right through him. At the last moment, just as Pete braced for impact, the wolf-dog's feet lifted off the ground and he deftly sailed over Pete's head, landing on the other side of him. Then Prince froze, his head and shoulders out into freedom. He looked both ways, as though it might be some kind of trap.

Pete figured he might have been able to count to three in his head while Prince stood still.

Seconds later Pete was struggling to his feet, watching the animal lope a wide arc around the horse pasture—where the pig now lived as well—on his way to the woods. Prince still favored that rear leg. He ran with something of a limp. But his overall movements were fast and sure. He was back to one hundred percent power.

Pete took a few steps out into the yard.

"You can come back if you ever want to," he called after Prince.

Prince slowed to a trot, but kept going.

A moment later Justin and the doctor came to stand by his side.

"I'm sorry," Pete said. "I should've thought to ask if you wanted to say goodbye, too."

"I've been saying goodbye to him for days," Justin said. "Hey, look. He's coming back."

Pete looked up to see Prince trotting back in their direction around the whitewashed boards of the pasture fence. Pete took a handful of steps forward, and they met in the middle.

"You came back!" Pete said.

He instinctively reached his hand out. Prince touched Pete's palm with his muzzle, his nose wet and cold. He licked the hand three times.

"That's so wonderful," Pete said.

But he should have said that formal goodbye instead. Because Prince turned and loped off into the woods again.

Pete watched him go, willing him to turn back a second time. A minute or two after the animal disappeared into the woods, Pete sighed deeply and walked back to Justin and Dr. Lucy, still not trying to hide his tears.

"He didn't come back," Pete said. "I thought he was going to come back."

"But I liked the way he came back for a minute and said thank you to you," Justin said. "That was really great. He couldn't have said it any better if he could've opened his mouth and started speaking English."

"You did a good thing," Dr. Lucy said, rubbing the back of Pete's neck.

"Then why do I feel so bad?"

"You did the best thing *for him*. He's happy."

"What if he hates it out there?"

"Well, like I said . . . he knows where to find us."

—

Pete stayed at the doctor's house for lunch, but for the first time he could remember he wasn't hungry. He picked at the tuna sandwich. Asked permission to wrap it up to take home.

When he realized he could have fed it to Prince on any other day, he had to work not to cry again.

While the doctor gathered up the lunch dishes, Pete slipped out into the backyard and leaned on the top rail of the fence and stared at the woods. He was straining to see something, but in truth he didn't expect to.

But a moment later he was almost sure he saw two ears. He changed position for a better look, and saw what could have been a wolf-dog sitting between two trees, staring back at the house. At least, he thought so. But a second later he wondered if it was his imagination. It was so far away. It was frustratingly hard to tell.

He changed position again and bumped into Justin, who reacted with a kind of "oof" sound.

"Oh. Sorry. Justin, is that Prince?"

"Where?"

"Way off in the distance there. In the woods."

"Wait. I can't see much. My glasses are all smudged. Let me clean them off."

Pete waited, hiding his impatience, as Justin huffed steam onto each lens of his glasses, front and back, and wiped them on his shirt-tail. Pete was afraid Prince would lope off into the woods again. If indeed he really was sitting there in the first place. And then Pete would never know for sure if he had imagined the sighting or not. But he didn't say so, because he didn't want to be harsh with Justin or hurt his feelings.

"Hmm," Justin said, his glasses back in place on his head, peering off into the woods. "Oh. There, you mean?"

He pointed to the spot Pete had been watching.

"Yeah. That's him, isn't it?"

"Hard to say. It looks like some kind of big dog/wolf sort of animal. I can't figure out why any of them except Prince would be up there looking back at us. But it's so far away. It's hard to say for sure. And, you know . . . these glasses are pretty good but they're not as good as the ones you can get when you can go into the place yourself and have the eye test. But I still like them. I still appreciate how you guys got them."

"But it's definitely an animal."

"Yeah. Like a big dog."

"And, like you say, what other dog besides Prince would be up there staring at the house?"

He looked over at Justin, anxious to hear more thoughts that might verify his own thinking.

When he looked back to the woods, the animal was gone.

—

Pete rode his borrowed bike home soon after, because it felt too tragic to hang around at the doctor's house without Prince. At least, in that moment it was too much to bear.

He stashed the bike in the garage the way he always did.

He stuck his head inside the house.

His dad was up and walking around. Pete could hear the footsteps. He stuck his head into the kitchen, saw no one, then was startled by his father's voice just behind his left shoulder.

"Here's a question for you, Petey boy. You home for the day?"

"No, sir. I have to go out again."

"*Have to.* That's a strange couple of words for a kid on summer vacation. What exactly do you *have to* do? Summer is for play. You don't *have to* play. Am I right?"

Pete said nothing for a time, and while he wasn't answering his head swam. He couldn't believe this question was coming up now. He'd been working a schedule of two short shifts a day for nearly two months.

He'd figured he was home free after all that time. He'd figured if his father cared he would have asked a long time ago.

"The thing that feels strange about it to me is how rhythmic it all is," his dad added.

"Rhythmic, sir? I don't get that."

"You always seem to go out around the same times in the day."

"Why are you just asking me this now?"

"Because waiting for you to volunteer the information isn't working out, Petey boy. Summer'll be over in a couple or three weeks and you still haven't seen fit to tell me where you're going."

Pete turned around and looked up at his dad's face. Mostly to see how angry the older man looked.

He loomed over Pete, wearing his work pants and blue denim work shirt. Pete wondered if that was a sign of health—that he had gotten dressed again.

He couldn't read his father's face.

"Well, you know there was that dog. I been visiting him all summer."

"Was? Past tense?"

Pete didn't answer.

"And did he need you to visit on a set schedule?"

"No, sir. I don't suppose he could tell time."

"Well, I'm running out of patience with the honor system, boy. I'll give you a day or two to come clean on your own. But not much more, let me tell you."

Pete felt the words come up from his gut. Felt them in his mouth, waiting to be said. He tried to hold them back, because they might bring repercussions. It didn't work. He lost control of them immediately.

"And after a day or two? Then what?"

"Then I'll damn well find out what I need to know on my own."

"Yes, sir," Pete said. Because he had no idea what else to say.

—

After Pete's second shift at the ranch, and after a dinner so silent it almost killed his appetite, he took a bath and brushed his teeth and changed into pajama bottoms for bed.

He dropped his dirty work clothes into the hamper on the way to his room.

It wasn't even dark yet. More of a heavy dusk. It felt too early to go to bed, but Pete was exhausted and wanted the day to be over.

He stood looking out the window of his bedroom for a moment, over the backyard. The moon was rising, a few days off full, but Pete didn't know if it was headed for full or on its way back from it.

He saw the streetlights come on out front, even though he couldn't see the lights themselves. He could see the illumination they cast over the yard—the shadow of his house, and a spill of glow back toward the empty space that eventually turned into woods. But Pete couldn't see the woods.

But what he saw nearly stopped his heart for a split second: a pair of glowing eyes. The light reflected off two spooky-looking eyes, sitting up on the low hill behind his house.

Pete slipped out of his bedroom and through the mudroom, then barefoot out into the warm night. He stood still a moment, letting his eyes adjust. After a few seconds he was sure enough of who and what he was seeing to move in that direction.

"Hey, Prince," he said, keeping his voice steady and light. As if Prince sitting behind his house was no big deal. "You change your mind? How did you even know where I live?"

But even as he asked the question Pete knew the wolf-dog must have followed him home. Or followed his scent trail home. Unless he knew this town so well that he had known where everybody lived all along.

Pete was only steps away now, and he slowed down because he was afraid of chasing Prince away.

"It's good to see you, boy," he said, and reached his hand out. "This's a real happy surprise for me."

Prince sniffed the hand and licked it once, briefly.

"Come on in the house. I'll show you where I live."

He turned back to the house and motioned for Prince to follow. But the wolf-dog only backed up three steps.

Pete's heart fell. He could feel the crash of it.

"Oh. I guess that's a no, then."

He stepped in Prince's direction again, but the wolf-dog backed up farther and faster in response.

Pete decided he'd better leave well enough alone.

"Well, I'm glad you came by, anyway." He moved a few steps toward the house, so Prince would know Pete was not trying to catch him. "Come by and see me again, okay?"

As if satisfied by the visit, the wolf-dog turned on his haunches and trotted off toward the woods.

Chapter Twenty-Three: Dr. Lucy

It was about ten thirty in the morning when she heard Pete shouting to her from the front yard. It was a normal time for him to arrive, fresh from his morning feeding and cleaning at the Quarter Horse ranch. But it was not his usual entrance.

"Dr. Lucy!" he shouted. "Dr. Lucy! Come out here. You have to see this!"

Completely unsure whether it was a happy or a dreadful thing she had to see, she dried her hands on her apron and hurried to the front door. Swung it wide.

"Pete. What are you making so much noise about?"

"You have to see who's here! You'll never guess who's here!"

His face said she would be happy when she saw, or could guess.

She looked up toward the street to see Calvin turn onto her gravel walkway and move toward the house. He locked eyes with hers from that distance, and his face lit up. She didn't have to be any closer to see.

She ran to him.

As she did, it struck her that she reminded herself of one of those television commercials, the ones with the sweethearts running to each other in slow motion through a field of wildflowers. The only thing missing was the wildflowers. That and the perfectly homogenized whiteness of the actors' skin tones.

He threw his arms around her and she held him close for a moment or two, feeling his freshly shaved cheek against her own. Then she pulled back and examined his face to see if anything had changed.

His lower lip wore a line of scar she hadn't seen before. Other than that, he looked none the worse for wear.

She looked into his eyes and they drank each other in for a moment, and nothing more. Just the locked gaze was enough.

"I've never seen your face look like that before," he said.

"Like what?" she asked, already knowing it was a compliment.

"You're smiling from one ear to the other."

"I'm thrilled to see you. I thought it would be another three or four days."

Then, as if such a thing had never occurred to her before, she looked over his shoulder to the street to see if they were being observed. He caught the movement of her glance and turned. But there was nothing and nobody there.

"Well, that's rare," she said. "The town cut us a break for a change."

They turned toward the house and walked side by side, and he slipped her hand into his own and held it.

"So how did you get back early?"

"I got a few days off for good behavior."

"I had no idea they would offer you anything so generous."

"It wasn't generosity, believe me. They'd just gotten in a new crop of inmates. They needed the space."

A movement caught her eye, and she looked up to see Justin barreling in their direction.

"You're back!" he shouted, and leapt into his father's arms.

"Oof," Calvin said. "Did you get bigger? I can tell you're feeling better."

"All better. What about you?" He leaned back in his father's arms and surveyed his face the way Dr. Lucy had done. Touched the line on Calvin's lip. "You have a scar on your lip. But otherwise you look the same."

"Yes, well, it'll go away in time," Calvin said. "Scars usually do. And even if this one doesn't, life will go on, scar or no scar. And you got a new pair of glasses. How did you manage that?"

"Pete worked a job so the doctor would have a little more money. And she gave me an eye test here at her house, and then she went into town and got the glasses and fitted them to my head herself."

"You sure were in the right place, weren't you?"

"I'll say. Pete and I rode the horses! Not all of them. But a couple of them. I rode Smokey. And I stayed on!"

Calvin turned his face to her. "If you'll excuse me, Lucy, I'm going to take a few minutes to talk to my son. And then I'll be back to give you my full attention."

———

She was pouring them each a fresh cup of coffee in the kitchen when he came in and sat at the table.

She sat down next to him, and their hands extended between the coffee cups and came together. And held firmly.

She looked into his eyes, and he looked back. It was a look that came with an intensity and an emotion that almost burned her. It was not like her to do anything but recoil from being so thoroughly seen. But she resisted the temptation to look away.

"There's that smile again," he said. "It looks good on you."

"I had no idea how much I would miss you."

He offered a little smile in return, but it looked sad. Then he cut his eyes away. She registered that, and the effects of it inside her, but nothing more. She didn't try to define or explain it. She just waited for the moment to play out.

"Was Justin able to bring himself to admit to you that he still needs Bunny to sleep when he's upset?"

"Yes and no. Not exactly. But he ended up with Bunny."

"That's good to hear." He was still carefully avoiding her eyes. "Two things I need to say to you." His words felt heavy in her stomach and gut. "First of all, that was a wonderful thing you did. Taking my son into your home and caring for him as if he were your own."

"Nonsense," she said. "It's just what anyone would have done."

"No, you're wrong about that, Lucy. You're more unusual than you realize."

"What's the other thing?" she asked, knowing she would not like it nearly as well, and wanting to get it over with.

"I think you know what the next thing is I'm going to say."

She sat back in her chair, hearing and feeling the thump of her shoulder blades hitting the chair back. She instinctively let go of his hand. Pulled hers into her lap, where it would be safer from the truth of things.

It struck her, as it did several times a day, that a cigarette would be just the thing. But she hadn't smoked one for over a month, and she wouldn't this time, either.

"Funny," she said. "Pete and I had a similar conversation just yesterday."

"You do know. Right?"

"Yes. And so did he. You're leaving."

"I don't see that we have much choice. Do you?"

She sighed. Looked out the window at the boys, who stood inside the pasture fence fussing over the friendliest of the horses.

"I suppose you're right," she said. "Unfortunately. You're not safe here and neither is Justin."

"And *you're* not safe *while* we're here."

"I can take care of myself."

"Well, Lucy . . . if anyone can, I agree that you can. But sometimes we're just outnumbered in life."

A long silence fell. Unusually long. Several minutes. It wasn't so much a forced silence or a blockage of words. They just sat together for a time and did not speak. Calvin followed her gaze and watched the boys pet the horses. Watched Pete give Justin a leg up to straddle Smokey, the gray gelding, bareback. Watched the pig come close and stare up at them as if he couldn't bear not to be part of the thing.

"Will you go back to Philadelphia?" she asked after a time.

"Yes."

"But they didn't even give you a chance to work long enough to earn a paycheck."

"My cousin in Ohio is going to wire me a small loan."

"How long before you go?"

"We'll leave as soon as we can. It might take us two or three days to get our situation together."

She nodded a few times, lost in thought.

"We never did know each other all that well," she said. Almost as though talking to herself. "It's not like we knew how things would have turned out between us anyway. I mean, even without all the outside pressure. But, just out of curiosity . . . just so I have that to hold on to . . . what do you think we could have been?"

"Lucy," he said.

Then he stopped, and slid his hand across the table again. And waited. Waited and did not speak until she broke down and took his hand again and held it. Only then did he share his thinking.

"I think this: I think our lives aren't over yet, Lucy. Just because Justin and I are going to be in another city doesn't mean you and I stop knowing each other on the day we leave. There are telephones. There's the US mail. We still don't know the end to our story because it hasn't ended yet. I just need to get my son somewhere he'll be safe. But to answer your question, I think we could have been something wonderful. And I don't yet accept that we never will be."

He gave her hand a squeeze and she smiled again in spite of herself.

"Funny," she said, "but this is also similar to the conversation I had with Pete yesterday. He had to say goodbye to his wolf-dog, and I told him he didn't know whether Prince would stay away forever. I told him he should just say goodbye for now."

"Exactly," Calvin said. "This is just goodbye for now."

—

A few minutes after Calvin left for home with his son, Pete joined her in the kitchen. Almost as though he'd been waiting for what he deemed the more important matters to blow over. Waiting his turn.

"Nice that he's back, huh?" Pete said.

"Very."

"I hate it that they have to move. That's my best friend I'm about to lose."

"I know exactly how you feel," she said.

He sat down at the table with her. For a long time he didn't speak—which was unlike Pete—and neither did she.

"I never see you smoke anymore," he said after a time.

"I gave it up."

"Oh. That's good. What made you decide?"

She opened her mouth to give an explanation that glossed over the surface of things. Links between smoking and cancer. That sort of answer. What came out was more honest than she had intended.

"I wanted Calvin to be proud of me. And also . . . since I met him, I guess it started meaning more, the idea of being healthy and living a long time."

She expected Pete to ask questions. Dig into the bond between Calvin and herself. He didn't. Maybe it was more evident than all that. Maybe it went without saying.

"Prince was in my yard last night," he said.

"Really? That's interesting. Are you sure it was him?"

"Positive. I went right up to him. He wasn't in the yard *exactly*. Kind of out in the field behind the yard. We don't have a fence. But I went to him and he licked my hand. But he wouldn't come any closer to the house with me."

"He must have followed you home."

"That's what I was thinking. But why would he follow me home if he still wants to be wild?"

"Maybe he's keeping an eye on you to make sure you're okay."

"I thought of that. But then I figured it was one of those things you think, but really it's too good to be true. I mean, of course I *want* to think that . . ."

A long silence. Pete had something else on his mind. She could tell. But she didn't ask about it, out of respect for him. She let him offer it on his own timing.

"Dr. Lucy? If I didn't have my job anymore, or I couldn't give you the money from it anymore, would you be okay?"

"Of course. I'll get by."

"Even with all the animals to take care of?"

"I'll manage."

"Good. Because my dad wants to know where I've been going. And once I have to tell him I'm working a job, or if he finds it out for himself . . . that'll be it for the money."

"Don't worry about it," she said. "Just do what's right for you. Whatever makes you safe with him."

Pete squirmed uncomfortably in his chair.

"That's just the thing, though," he said. "I don't think there *is* such a thing as safe with him. He's been laying off me almost all summer, but I don't think that's going to last much longer. I don't know why he's been laying back on the punishment. But I have a really bad feeling about the way things are going. I can't even say exactly why I feel the way I do. But something about it doesn't seem right."

Dr. Lucy dug around in the pocket of her skirt and pulled out a small handful of change.

"Here," she said, separating out two dimes. "You know where I am if you need me."

"Two dimes, ma'am? Why two?"

"Oh, I don't know. Just in case it's a two-dime situation, I suppose."

Chapter Twenty-Four: Pete

Pete stashed the bike in the garage and let himself into the house. His dad was sitting in his chair with those half reading glasses on. Reading the morning paper. Which Pete vaguely registered as odd, because his dad didn't take the morning paper. He'd always said it was too expensive. So someone must have brought him this, or . . . would he have taken somebody else's?

He looked up at Pete. Right into his eyes. And though Pete had been unable to explain his dread to the doctor, and couldn't define the look on his father's face now, the older man's eyes were a road map of everything Pete feared. Everything that was souring and festering between them.

"Ticktock, Petey boy."

"Ticktock, sir?"

"It's a clock."

"Yeah, I got that much."

"Time is running out on your honesty problem."

Pete shifted from foot to foot and entwined his fingers in front of himself the way he might fold his hands on a school desk to show politeness and cooperation. Only a moment later did he realize he was also instinctively protecting his most vulnerable organs.

"Yes, sir. I know that. That's what I came back to talk to you about."

A silence. It felt eerie.

"So talk."

"I been working a job."

Pete watched his father and waited for him to respond, with a little of the energy of a wild horse who knows he's about to be quite literally broken. At first the only response was a visible working of his father's jaw. Those bulgy veins began to show in his temple, which was not a good sign.

"And the money went where?" His father was clearly struggling to keep his voice steady.

Pete had rehearsed his answer. It wasn't a hundred percent true. It wasn't the whole truth and nothing but the truth, as they said on those court TV shows, but it was true enough that Pete felt comfortable with it.

"I owed a lot for patching up that dog I found."

"So you worked a job all summer. And you gave the money to a stray mutt instead of me. Am I hearing that right?"

"Yes, sir. That's about the size of it."

Pete's father moved suddenly. Forward and partway into a standing position, as if about to come after Pete, who flew back a few steps. Then his dad froze. Half sitting and half standing.

"Did a stray mutt raise you and put a roof over your head and food in your mouth for twelve years?"

"No, sir."

"Then I would say your priorities leave a lot to be desired, boy."

"Yes, sir."

"You're gonna pay me back all that. Every dollar of it. All that money you stole from this family while I was down injured and you were young and strong and able to work and not even willing to help out in your own household."

Pete eyed his exits. Charted the path to both the front and back doors, ready to go for either if his dad blocked the other route to safety. His dad seemed to notice.

"I'm not sure how I'm supposed to do that, sir."

"We're gonna start by selling that nice bike you got stashed out in the garage. You think you got a right to pedal around in style like some kind of royalty while I struggle to put food on the table?"

Somewhere around the word "royalty" his dad lost a measure of control with his words. What began as a tightly modulated sentence ended in a roar of anger.

"I can't do that, sir. It's not even mine. I only borrowed it."

"Well, *I* can. And you can just owe a debt to whoever you're borrowing from, but you're not going to owe a debt to me. I won't have it. I'll get what's coming to me."

Pete sprinted for the back door, hoping his dad was still not well enough to catch him. But the old man was fast. He grabbed at the back of Pete's shirt as Pete stopped to turn the knob, but Pete pulled free and ran into the garage. He grabbed hold of the bike, turned it toward the door, then saw the doorway fill up with angry father.

Pete mounted the bike, pushed off, and attempted to ride right through his dad. It didn't work out at all. The older man simply grabbed the handlebars and wrenched the bike sideways. Pete had to lever one leg against the concrete garage floor for balance. Meanwhile his father attempted to wrestle the bike away from him. Worse yet, he was about to succeed.

Without any forethought, only knowing in his gut that he could not let such a disaster happen, Pete swung his fist. It connected smartly with his father's nose. The old man let go of the bike and teetered backward, bright blood running freely down his upper lip.

Pete righted the bike, stepped hard on the pedals, and squirted through the open door before his father could catch him.

As he stood pressing the pedals, desperately racing for the street, Pete had a flash of a memory. A conversation he'd had with Justin. It came into his head, all of a sudden, unbidden. Pete had claimed he'd never hit anyone and he never would. And now, if you counted head-butting Jack out by the lake, he had already broken his vow twice. If you went on to count what he would have done if Boomer hadn't been inside the truck when he said what he said, three times. Did life conspire to force you to do the very thing you said you would never do? And, if so, why?

"When I catch you, boy, you're gonna be sorry you were ever born!"

Pete looked over his shoulder to see his father doing a surprisingly good job of keeping up with the bike. When had he gotten so completely healed? Why was he suddenly so fast?

Pete pedaled harder and more desperately, and opened up a better lead. The shouting behind him continued. It deteriorated into plain cussing, and grew angrier and more desperate with every foot of lead Pete gained. He looked over as he raced by Justin's house, and saw his friend's face in the window. Justin must have come to see what all the yelling was about.

Pete sped up even more on sheer adrenaline, then shot around a corner. It was a good move. It presented him with a series of driveways. About six, from the look of it, in close succession.

He chose the fourth. Made a sharp turn. He prayed there would be no fence around the house he had chosen. Life was on his side for a change. There was no fence. Pete pedaled through the yard, jumped off the bike at the end of the garage, and hunkered down just behind it, invisible from the street in every direction.

There he crouched. And listened.

He listened to his dad yelling. Swearing. Insulting Pete. Threatening Pete. Verbally removing every last piece of worth from Pete's very existence. The voice reached him from slightly different directions as Pete listened. Clearly his dad was walking up and down the street trying to see where Pete had gone.

He could hear front doors opening as neighbors turned out to see what all the fuss was about. They must have been hearing all the terrible words flung at Pete as a weapon.

Still, he felt far more worthy than he would have if he'd returned to the doctor's house with a sad story instead of her bicycle.

———

Pete had no way of knowing how long he crouched behind the neighbor's garage with the precious bike. It felt like more than an hour, but time is a funny thing. It plays tricks, and Pete knew it.

When all had been silent for a staggering length of time, Pete looked carefully before dashing through open ground to the next garage, wheeling the bike beside him. Then the next garage. And the next. In just a matter of a minute or two he found his way to Justin's back door.

He knocked.

Mr. Bell answered.

"Pete," Mr. Bell said, his voice brimming with concern. "What was all that? We were worried about you."

"I think probably you were right to worry, sir. He pretty much wants to kill me. Can I come in?"

Mr. Bell stepped out of the doorway, and Pete walked the bike into the tiny living room and leaned it against the wall.

"Will you look after this for me? Until I can get it back safe to Dr. Lucy?"

Pete looked up and saw Justin standing in the bedroom doorway, his eyes brimming with fear, tears running down his face.

Before Pete could even ask what was so terribly wrong, Mr. Bell spoke.

"Pete, is that your father who was chasing you?"

"Yes, sir."

Pete watched Mr. Bell and Justin exchange looks, speaking with their eyes. It was a language Pete could not understand. But something grave was happening just beyond Pete's mental reach.

"What? Why?"

"Tell him, Justin," Mr. Bell said.

"Could you tell him, please?" Justin asked in his smallest voice.

"Pete is your friend, Justin. Tell him what you told me."

A long silence. Justin refused to meet Pete's eyes. He stared at the floor carefully. Thoroughly, as though studying a map on the wooden boards. Something that would help him find his way.

"That was one of the men."

At first Pete didn't get it. But in the silence that followed, he worried that he did.

"My dad? Was one of the men who beat you up?"

A nose wipe from Justin. Then a barely perceptible nod.

"What did he do? Did he actually hit you?"

"He was the one who broke that bottle on my head," Justin said.

Pete realized he wasn't breathing. Or was hardly breathing, anyway. He pulled a huge gasp of air and tried to steady his balance, which was suddenly less than assured.

"Justin, are you sure?"

"Positive. I'll never forget that face as long as I live."

Pete felt his way over to the couch and sat. He placed his head in his hands for a moment. Then he rubbed his face briskly. He looked up at Justin and Mr. Bell. If called upon to say what he had been thinking in that moment, he could not have guessed. It's possible that he was not thinking at all.

"Okay, I'm going to leave the bike here and go back and have it out with him."

"No, Pete," Mr. Bell said. "I don't think that's a good idea. You said yourself he wants to kill you."

"I didn't mean literally."

"I heard the things he was shouting at you. I don't think it's safe to go back there. I don't want you to go."

"You're right," Pete said. He sat in perfect stillness for a moment, knowing what he would do without even thinking it out in his head. "You're right," he said again, as though he had not just said it. "I'll go to Dr. Lucy's."

"Much better plan," Mr. Bell said.

"Hold on to the bike for now, please. Okay? I don't want to ride it over to her house until I know he's not out looking for me."

"Yes, of course. But we'll only be here another two days or so."

"Okay," Pete said. "That's okay. That's long enough." He walked to the door. Looked back at his two friends. "I sure will miss you when you go away," he said. "Both of you."

Then he walked out the door without waiting for a reply.

He turned in the direction of Dr. Lucy's house and jogged down the street. About three blocks later, when he knew he was well out of view of the Bells' house, he turned a corner and headed back toward home.

———

Pete swung the front door open so hard it slammed back against the living room wall. His father, who had been holding a handkerchief to his nose and looking out the window onto the street, jumped visibly.

"You've got some nerve coming back here without that bike, Petey boy." His voice was a nasally whine. At any other time Pete might have been tempted to laugh.

Pete said what he'd come to say, and his voice sounded strangely steady to his own ears.

"I asked you straight out if you had anything to do with what happened to my friend Justin. And you looked me right in the face and lied to me. And that was when your back was so bad you said you could hardly walk to the front stoop to get the mail. Did you lie to me about that, too?"

As he spoke, Pete watched his father's back straighten.

Pete's body surged with so much adrenaline that he had no way of knowing if he was scared or not. A kind of electric whiteness in his brain reminded him that he might be about to die, or something close to it. But he couldn't get in touch with how he felt about that. Nor did he want to.

"And I told you," his father said in a voice of gathering rage, "that if you ever came back into my house again talking like I got to answer to you for what I do, you could expect to find your clothes out on the front dirt. You're only my son as long as I say I want you to be."

"Fine," Pete said. "Put 'em out there. I don't want to be your son."

In a perfect silence, in a complete suspension of activity or intention, the moment stretched on. And where there should have been something akin to a world war in Pete's small world, there was nothing.

Then his father lunged at him. All at once and without warning.

Pete dodged away and avoided the tackle, and his father pitched forward and lost his balance, landing on his belly and chin with a bellowing grunt.

His father's body blocked the front door, so Pete ran out the back.

He was halfway across the backyard when his father caught him. He grabbed Pete by the back of the shirt, swung him around, and sank one enormous fist into Pete's belly.

Pete smacked down on his back in the rocky dirt, unable to breathe.

His father landed on him, straddling him, and punched him in the temple. Then he punched Pete again. And again. And again. And then again.

In that moment, in the disconnected land that was Pete's brain, a thought ran through. No, it didn't even run through, exactly. It just existed there. Just held perfectly still.

This is it for me.

He knew his father would just keep hitting him in the head until the older man was so exhausted he collapsed on his own. And Pete assumed, from the force of the blows, that he would not survive that long. And still it was a better option than not confronting his dad over what he'd done to Justin. For the first time in his short life, Pete had found a thing worth dying for.

Then, just that suddenly, the great wall of his father was gone. Light poured in where the curtain of man had been, and Pete saw a flurry of motion and heard a rush of sound he could not understand. At least, not for a moment. But there was snarling involved. And fur. A great deal of fur.

Pete sat halfway up, still struggling to breathe, and saw two strong paws placed in the dirt on either side of his hips. He was being straddled. By a wolf-dog.

"What the hell?" his father cried out, halfway to the house and backing up fast.

Prince dropped his head and showed his teeth. He let loose a rolling growl that shook even Pete to his core. And Pete knew the wolf-dog was on his side.

Pete pulled out from under the animal and staggered to his feet. He teetered behind the wolf-dog, keeping Prince between him and his father.

"What the hell!" his father said again. But, this time, more as though he knew. "You know this beast? You sicced this monster on me?"

He's my bodyguard, a voice in Pete's head said. Quite clearly. So clearly that he thought he had said it out loud, but in truth he was unable to speak. He placed one hand on the wolf-dog's shoulders, both out of pride and a need to secure his balance.

"Well, that's all I can take, boy. That's your line, right there. You just snapped this bond between us like a dry stick. You think you're such a big man? Fine. Go be a big man. On your own. You come back here one time and one time only. To get your things. They'll be out on the front stoop. That's it for us. I disown you."

And with that he backed into the house and closed the door behind him.

Pete dropped to his knees and wrapped his arms around Prince's neck, and held the animal for a time. Then he struggled to his feet and began to place one foot in front of the other.

He stumbled around the side yard of the house, down the street. In the direction of the liquor store. Just walking unsteadily. Not thinking.

Now and then he looked over his shoulder, careful not to lose his balance. Sometimes he saw Prince and other times he didn't. But when he didn't, if he looked again a minute later he would see the wolf-dog's eyes peering out at him from behind a fence or a hedge or a garage.

Cars passed him by, and the drivers slowed and stared at his face, which Pete figured must look a sight. Two older male drivers stopped to ask him if he was okay, or if he needed help. He shook his head and kept walking.

As the adrenaline drained from his body, Pete began to feel the pain of his injuries. And he could feel his knees shaking. And tears running down his face.

He crossed through light traffic at the liquor store parking lot. Prince waited and watched him from across the street as he made the call.

"Dr. Lucy?" he asked when she answered, not even trying to hide his sobs.

"Pete?"

"Can you come pick me up, please? I need you. It's kind of a two-dime situation."

Chapter Twenty-Five: Dr. Lucy

She opened her passenger side door for him. Pete climbed in and sat quietly. Didn't try to talk. Didn't look at her. Well, that would have been hard—to look at her. He didn't seem to be able to open his left eye, which was the one facing her. The side of his head had begun to swell and discolor.

She had expected something bad. She had known from his call that it would be bad. And in response to that knowing, she had shut herself off to inevitable reactions to bad news on her drive over. Sometimes doctors can do that. Sometimes they have to.

She waited, not driving away, but still he said nothing. He seemed to have retreated into himself in a way that made him cowed and small.

"Turn your face to me, honey," she said.

He didn't answer or comply so she gently held his chin in her fingers and turned it for him.

"Could you open that eye if you tried?"

"No, ma'am. It's swelled shut."

"Okay. Well. We'll take you home and I'll give you a neurological exam—"

The Pete she had known burst out of hiding. The talky one.

"You can't take me home! I can't go home!"

"Pete," she said, trying to sound calming. "*My* home."

"Oh. Your home. Yeah. Thanks. I want to go to your house. I always feel safe at your house."

That's because you always are, she thought but did not say.

"Did he do this to you with his fist, or some kind of object?"

"Fist," he said, staring straight through the windshield again.

"How many times did he hit you?"

"I'm not sure. I lost count. Four maybe, or five. Or six, I don't know."

"And then he stopped on his own, or you were able to defend yourself?"

"Pretty much neither, ma'am. He was never going to stop. I think he might've killed me. Prince stopped him. Prince broke up the fight."

Silence. Still she did not put the car into drive and pull away.

In time he turned his face to look at her, which wasn't easy. He had to crane his neck to see her with his right eye. When he did, his face fell with disappointment.

"You don't believe me."

"I don't for a moment think you're lying to me, Pete. I know you would never purposely do that. But if you hit somebody in the head hard enough and enough times, it's not unusual for them to see things that aren't . . ."

"He's right over there by that house," Pete said, pointing across the street. "You can see that, right?"

She followed the direction of his pointed finger, and was surprised to see that the wolf-dog was no hallucination. He was sitting on the pavement, crouched over from his shoulders as if imitating a vulture, peering out from behind a bush. His small golden eyes never left her car.

"I'll be damned," she said. She rolled down her window. "Good boy, Prince," she called. She opened her car door and stepped out into the street. Opened the back door and swung it wide. "You coming with us?" she called to the wolf-dog. "Come on, boy."

Prince rose and backed up two steps. Then he turned sharply, trotted away through a yard, and disappeared.

Dr. Lucy watched him go, then slammed the back door and sank into the driver's seat.

"He doesn't want to come with us," she said.

"No, ma'am. He never does. He was keeping an eye on me all right, just like you said. But he doesn't want to come in and be tame."

"That's a good friend you have in him."

"He's my bodyguard," Pete said, his voice small but proud.

She put the car in drive and pulled out of the parking lot.

"Thank you for coming for me," Pete added. "I don't know what I would've done if you hadn't given me those dimes. And if you weren't . . . you know. There. If you weren't you. I don't know where else I could've gone."

"You can never go back there with him again," she said as she drove. "You know that, right? I don't know how we'll manage that, but we'll have to find a way."

"Shouldn't be hard, ma'am. He disowned me. I don't know what that means *exactly*, but from everything he said around it I figure it means he never *wants* me back."

"Oh," she said. And then nursed her own surprise in silence for a moment. "I guess that simplifies things."

She turned the thing over in her mind for a few moments, but it still didn't make much sense. To simply pull the plug on parenthood. Then again, if the man had been properly plugged into parenthood it would have been safe to send Pete home.

"So. I have to ask you, ma'am . . . but I can't even bring myself to ask. But I guess I have to. Can I . . . Will you . . ."

Then he stalled. Ran out of words. Or courage.

"Yes," she said. "You can. I will."

"I didn't even finish the question yet."

"You can stay with me. And I'll take care of you."

"That's a big relief, ma'am."

She waited.

She had expected more. Though perhaps ignoble, she had anticipated some outpouring of gratitude. Instead the boy had gone silent. Disappeared inside himself again.

They were turning onto her street when he finally spoke up.

"But . . . how long?"

"How long what? How long will I take care of you?"

"Yes, ma'am. That."

"How about until you're old enough to take care of yourself?"

"That's a good deal, ma'am. Thanks. I owe you a debt. But, then again, I guess I already did."

He was smiling slightly when she pulled into her driveway.

They stepped out of the car and walked toward the back door. Pete was a little wobbly but she steadied him by the shoulders. He stopped suddenly and blocked her way. She assumed he was in some sort of distress. Until he threw his arms around her.

She stood awkwardly for a moment, knowing she should hug him back, but not doing so. She felt a wave of guilt, remembering she had overcome her physical distance with Justin. Managed a kiss on the forehead and a few other miscellaneous gestures of affection. But Justin was tiny and vulnerable and dear. Pete was hulking and big and shy, and made her feel shy.

She took a deep breath and held him in return. Pushed herself over that edge.

Satisfied, he let go and followed her inside.

"You know," he said, "before I let Prince go, I told him I wanted him to be my bodyguard. You think he understood me?"

"Do I think he understood the sentence? No. I'm sure he didn't. I wouldn't put it past him to understand by feel that you were scared and wanting help. But I think the even simpler explanation is that it's natural to want to protect the people who've been good to us. And it's not unique to humans. Now come into my examining room. We need to make sure you're okay. And you can tell me how all this started."

———

It was close to six p.m. when she looked out the living room window because the dogs had set up a racket. There she saw Calvin and Justin walking up her driveway. Calvin was wheeling her bicycle.

She opened the front door wide, feeling the smile bloom across her face. The one he kept noticing.

"You didn't have to do that," she said when he was close enough to hear. "I would have driven over to get it after dark tonight."

He stopped in front of her door, and Justin stopped, and she and Calvin just stood there smiling at each other. Meanwhile she couldn't help remembering that soon he would no longer be standing in front of her. And she couldn't help wondering if she would still smile then.

She noticed he was carrying a burlap sack with something not very large but seemingly heavy inside. But she didn't stop to think much about it, caught up as she was in the smiles.

"I figured you'd come around for it sooner or later," he said. "Thing is, when Pete dropped it by, I said we'd be in town for a couple of days. But now we're leaving in the morning."

"Oh." She took a moment to digest that news. "Still, your last night here. You must have packing to do. Or some sort of preparations. Something better than wheeling that darn thing all the way across town."

"We didn't wheel it. We rode it. I rode Justin on the handlebars. It was fun."

"It *was* fun," Justin said, his voice bright with emotion.

"Well, bring it in," she said. "Thanks." She stood out of their way to allow them by. "Truth of the matter is, it's not as important to me as Pete thinks it is. It's just a thing. It can be replaced. But now that he's practically gotten himself killed to get it back to me, the least I can do is act like I appreciate it."

She knew immediately from their faces that they hadn't known.

"What happened to Pete?" Justin asked, before his father could.

She motioned for them to follow her into her examining room, where Pete sat up on the edge of the table, holding an ice bag to the side of his head. His face fell when he saw them. He seemed to shrink into himself with shame.

"Go ahead and show them," Dr. Lucy said.

"Do I have to?"

"They're your friends."

Pete lowered the ice bag. His eye was so swollen now that the lashes had flipped inside and disappeared. And the color on that side of his face had turned a bright, deep purple.

A long silence fell.

Then Pete said, "I guess you figured out that I went home. I'm sorry, Mr. Bell. I know you told me not to, but I had to. And I knew if you couldn't talk me out of going home you'd feel guilty for whatever happened to me there. So that's why I didn't tell you. I figured you'd be happier if you didn't know."

"I'll get you some fresh ice for that," she said, and Pete handed her back the ice bag. "How's your pain level, honey? Do you need another pill?"

"No, ma'am, but thanks. The one you gave me is doing fine. Nobody ever gave me a pill to make me hurt less before. I like it."

Justin stayed with Pete while she and Calvin walked into the kitchen. He still had that burlap sack hanging from one hand, and she was growing more curious. But he didn't offer and she didn't pry.

Calvin spoke first.

"I don't think Pete made assumptions about how important your bicycle is to you. I think it's more about how important it is to Pete not to be the one to lose your bicycle when you trusted him with it."

"You're getting to know him pretty well."

"Tell me he didn't drag into his job today in spite of everything."

"He didn't. I didn't give him any choice. I called him in sick. The people he works for seem nice. They were concerned about him."

"Good. He deserves that. What are you going to do?"

"About what? Or . . . well, I guess I mean about *which*? I'm not suggesting there are no issues here that have to be dealt with. I'm just not sure which one you mean."

"I can't imagine sending him back there."

"Oddly, that part more or less resolved itself." She opened the freezer as she spoke. Cracked open a tray of ice cubes in the sink. "His dad threw him out."

"So where will he be?"

She didn't answer in words. Just pointed at the floor by her feet as a way of indicating "here."

"Really," he said, though not as a question. "That's quite generous of you."

"Don't sound so surprised." She swung her arms wide to encompass her surroundings. "Look around you. It's what I do. I take in the wounded ones. Nurse them back to health. And then if there are no better places for them to be, they stay here with me. I'm sorry, but I can't hold myself back from asking this another minute. What are you carrying around in that sack?"

"Oh, this." He set it down carefully on her kitchen table. "I hope you won't think it's silly."

He reached in and took out a potted plant. It looked healthy and strong, with round, scalloped dark-green leaves trailing down around all sides of its terra-cotta planter. It looked like the one she'd seen in his living room, only much smaller.

"It's something that's been in the family for a long time. It used to grow outside at my grandmother's house. When I got married, my wife really liked it, so my grandmother took some cuttings and rooted them and gave us a plant of our own. Rebecca planted it outside at our new house, and it got huge. Practically took over half the front yard. Of course it was a small yard. After she died Justin and I moved away from there, so I rooted a few new plants from cuttings and took them with me. It's just something that's been with me for so long. I wanted to leave part of it with you."

"I don't think that's silly at all," she said. "I think it's lovely. I just hope I can keep it growing."

"Please don't feel a sense of pressure, because I can always root you another one if it fails for some reason. Getting it to you would be the tricky bit. Still, I'm telling you, Lucy . . . this is not it for us. Mark my words."

"I so hope you're right," she said.

"I feel it in my bones."

"Let me just give this ice to poor Pete. And then come sit out back and talk to me. When it gets dark I'll drive you two home. But we have a little time left, anyway. And I want to enjoy it while I can."

———

They sat outside in lawn chairs in the dusky evening, respectfully apart. Even their hands managed to stay away from each other. Dr. Lucy wondered if it was a form of self-protection. Not wanting to come together just before coming apart.

Well, it was. For her. She only wondered if it might be mutually true.

"I guess it would be foolish," she said, "to start thinking about moving to Philadelphia. Especially since we're probably illegal there, too. And since you didn't invite me."

"Actually . . . there used to be laws all over. But some states have repealed them. I think Pennsylvania might not have that law anymore. But I'd have to check. When I lived there I had no cause to wonder."

During his last sentence she saw the dark shape of what she took to be Prince watching her from behind a post of the pasture fence. She saw his ears swivel, taking in sounds from every direction. But she was too caught up in the conversation to pay him much attention.

"That was really half an answer," she said, hoping she hadn't sounded confrontational.

"I would have invited you, Lucy. I wanted to. I thought about it a dozen times. But I just couldn't figure out where you could find an apartment in the city that would let you keep sixteen dogs, eleven horses, a pig, and an owl."

"Right," she said, still staring at the wolf-dog. "Interesting how I conveniently forgot that."

"You said it yourself. It's what you do. You can't go taking people away from what they do. And I would just feel too guilty," he added, "if something went wrong for us. It would be a hard life for us, even in Philadelphia. It could get ugly at any time. And if it did, I'd have to feel that it was your idea to come up there. I couldn't live with myself if something terrible happened because I talked you into coming."

A brief silence fell, during which she continued to watch the wolf-dog. Possibly because of a need to extricate herself from the conversation.

"Hey, Prince," she called, raising her voice. "You want to come down here?"

The wolf-dog stared at her in the gathering dusk—or at least, his head remained tilted in her direction—but he did not move closer.

"Where do you see Prince?"

"Right over there." She pointed. "On the other side of that fence post. He has a way of disappearing behind things."

"I wonder why he came back."

"He wants to know Pete is okay."

"How would he know anything bad happened to Pete?"

"Because he was there. He's been hanging around near Pete's house. Keeping an eye on things. Apparently he's what stopped that fight today from becoming even more disastrous than it was."

"Well, I'll be damned."

"I have to go get Pete. Wait here a minute."

She made her way through the darkened yard and back into the house, where the indoor lights nearly blinded her for a few moments. She found Pete and Justin sitting cross-legged on the examining room floor, their heads leaned together. Both boys were in the process of wrapping elastic bandages around their right thumbs.

"Somebody out there wants to see that you're all right," she said.

"Oh," Pete said. "Okay."

But she could tell by his tone that he didn't get it. She helped him to his feet and guided him by the shoulders toward the back door.

"Who's out there?" Justin asked, following along behind.

"A friend of Pete's."

They stepped out into the night.

It was fully dark now, or seemed so because her eyes had not adjusted. She hated that it was dark, because it meant Calvin would need that ride home soon.

It took her a moment to identify the correct fence post, and when she did she saw nothing behind it. But a second later a movement closer to the house told her that the wolf-dog was already on his way down.

"Prince!" Pete said.

Prince trotted up to Pete and sniffed his battered face thoroughly.

"Tell him you're okay," Dr. Lucy said. "He came all the way back here to see with his own eyes that you're okay."

"I'm okay, boy," Pete said, and wrapped his arms around the wolf-dog's neck. He said a few more words, but the animal's fur swallowed them up. Which was okay, she decided, because the words were for Prince, not her.

Pete let go and the wolf-dog sidled away toward the dark woods.

She felt Calvin's hand on her shoulder.

"I know this is not what you want to hear me say, Lucy, but Justin and I had best get home and finish packing. And besides, I don't know about you, but I hate that moment when you know goodbye is right around the corner."

"I hate it, too," she said. "I'll just go get my keys."

———

"The other thing I hate," she said as she shifted into park in front of their little brick house, "is knowing you're about to say some parting words to someone. And then all of a sudden those words have to be good. They have to sum up just about everything. And then the pressure's on and you can't think of anything to say at all."

"It's not going to be like that, Lucy, because as soon as we get to Philadelphia I'm going to call you and tell you we got in okay. I won't be able to afford to talk long, but I'm damn well going to call. And then no more than two or three days later I'll be writing you my first letter. And you'll be getting them no more than a week or so apart after that. And I can only assume you'll be writing me back. So all you have to say right now is 'Talk to you soon, Calvin.'"

She pulled a deep breath and let it pour out again. It felt tragic. Everything did.

"Talk to you soon, Calvin."

"Talk to you soon, Lucy."

He kissed her on the cheek and climbed out of the car. She sat a moment, watching him—them—go. Part of her wanted to pretend it was only that polite thing you do to be sure someone gets inside safely.

In reality it was more about knowing she was fresh out of chances to watch him do anything.

She was still staring at the house when the lights clicked on inside.

"You okay, ma'am?" Pete asked from the backseat.

"Oh. Yes. I'm fine. We'll go home now."

She shifted into gear and drove, thinking it felt interesting and strange to refer to her house as home for both of them. But not disturbing or wrong.

"Okay, now tell me the truth," she said as they drove. "Why would you and Justin both have a hurt thumb at exactly the same time?"

He didn't answer for a long moment. Long enough that she knew he didn't want to tell the truth, and also that he wasn't about to lie.

"You might be mad if I tell you."

"Try me."

"We did blood brothers."

"Oh. Blood brothers. Okay. And you drew blood with what?"

"My little penknife."

"The one you use to scrape mud off your shoes and cut fishing bait? *That* penknife?"

"I cleaned it up with some of your alcohol, ma'am."

She figured he'd have to stop calling her "ma'am" pretty soon, but she hadn't yet decided what he should call her instead.

"That's good. I guess I'm starting to rub off on you a little."

"Yes, ma'am," Pete said. "I kind of think you are."

PART THREE
NEARLY EIGHT YEARS GO BY, SO FAST
September 1959–June 1967

SEPTEMBER 1959
ONE MONTH AFTER THE BELLS
MOVED AWAY

Chapter Twenty-Six: Dr. Lucy

She heard Pete's bike wheels on the gravel of her driveway at a few minutes after five thirty p.m. It was a little later than she had expected him, but not much. He had his shift at the ranch after school. She'd known that. So it was not late enough to stop her already delicate heartbeat.

A minute later he stuck his head through the kitchen door.

"Anything to eat?" he asked, sounding almost guilty.

Guilty for what, she wasn't sure. His constant hunger, maybe? His very existence?

"I'm making a casserole for dinner, but it won't be ready for half an hour."

"Anything I can eat between now and then?"

"There are some cookies in the breadbox."

She watched him wash his hands carefully in the sink. Then he took down one of the everyday Melmac dishes and loaded it up with ten cookies. She had trained him to fix snacks for himself on a plate, and with a paper napkin.

He tried to slink off toward the stairs.

"I'd rather you eat those at the table," she said.

He stopped. Froze. Did not speak.

"Crumbs," she added.

This was not an entirely true statement. Yes, cookies had crumbs. But mostly she wanted him to sit at the kitchen table so they could talk.

"Please," she said at last.

Pete sat.

Dr. Lucy sat next to him, marveling at the amount of dirt he'd managed to grind into his shirt that day. She hoped he'd picked up all of the soil at his job and none of it fighting at school.

"How was your first day back?" She asked it as calmly as she could. She tried to keep her voice light, as if it were not a loaded and potentially tragic question. She only partially succeeded.

Pete shrugged.

"Well, I hate to say it, Pete, but that's not enough information. Did anybody give you a hard time?"

He seemed to struggle to swallow a mouthful of cookie. As if his throat had grown more constricted.

"Depends on what you mean by a hard time, I guess."

There was a line to walk in this situation, and she knew it. She had known it for some time, but hadn't managed to figure out how to walk that line in advance. She'd felt as though she had to see it, experience it first. Now she would have to figure it out as she spoke.

"Did anybody lay their hands on you?"

His eyes seemed to widen. Or maybe that was her imagination.

"Why would anybody do that?"

"I meant in a violent way. Did anybody try to physically hurt you?"

"No, ma'am."

"You don't have to call me 'ma'am' anymore."

"Yes, ma'am."

He shoved the second-to-last cookie into his mouth whole.

She almost asked him if anybody had said anything cruel. She opened her mouth to ask. But that, she decided suddenly, was on the wrong side of the line. There was no way she could control what people said to Pete, and she knew it would cause him pain to repeat any such comments to her. So she closed her mouth and left it alone. That might have been a right move or it might not have been, but it's what she did.

Pete shoved the last cookie into his mouth and chewed it, working diligently to keep his lips closed around it. He swallowed hard. Then he spoke. Voluntarily.

"Did they give you any trouble in the principal's office when you went to sign me up?" he asked.

For a moment she didn't answer. She'd been worried about the moment when she went down to register him for school at a new address, because she was not his legal guardian. She'd thought it might cause all kinds of trouble. Instead they'd just changed the address on his records and life had gone on. The feeling she'd gotten was that no one at the school seemed to care. But she might have been wrong. They might have been so happy to see him in a safer home that they chose to ask no questions about the situation. Or maybe they were not even required to ask.

Her own son had not lived long enough to be registered for school, she thought with an inward wince. So how was she to know?

Meanwhile, she was not answering, so he added, "I mean, I know it worked. Because my name was in the roll call and all. I just wondered if it was hard."

"Strangely, no," she said.

"Okay. Good."

He ran his plate over to the sink, clearly ready to head for a part of the house not filled with such difficult questions.

"Before you go upstairs," she said, "did you see that letter from Justin I left on your bed this morning?"

"Yes, ma'am," he said, heading toward the stairs again.

"Is he doing okay?"

"Yes, ma'am."

Pete stopped on the second stair, and turned to face her. Looked right into her eyes, which was unusual.

"You get letters from Mr. Bell, too. Right?"

"Yes. I do. All the time. But I haven't asked how Justin was the last couple of times I wrote. And also I just wondered . . ."

Pete waited. But in the end, he waited for nothing. There was nothing she could say out loud that would tell her what she wanted to know. Or at least, nothing she *should* say.

"What did you wonder?"

"Never mind," she said. "It's nothing. Go on."

Pete trotted up the stairs and disappeared from her view.

She sat still at the table for a moment, wishing she still smoked. It was a sensation that arose in her now and again, without warning. Part of her knew it might pay to note what she'd been thinking at those times.

She wanted to know if Calvin was seeing anyone new in Philadelphia. Which was probably silly, because it had only been a month. But if he was, she worried he would not mention it in his letters for fear of hurting her. At least, she assumed he would avoid mentioning it until he knew whether or not it was a serious relationship worth mentioning.

Just for a moment she had almost asked Pete if Justin had revealed any information on the matter. Fortunately she'd stopped herself in time.

Ruffled now to the point of agitation, she walked to the hall closet and took down the shoebox in which she'd been keeping Calvin's letters. There were only five so far, but she knew there would be more, so she'd stored them in a box with plenty of room for expansion.

Besides, she had been keeping copies of her letters to him as well. She had been typing her letters, rather than handwriting them as he did, so she could make carbons. She passed it off to him as a solution to her miserable doctor's handwriting, but that was less than half the truth. She would never have admitted the carbon copies to Calvin or anyone else, because it seemed so compulsive. But, lying in bed at night, she would go over in her mind not only what he had written to her but what she had written back to him. Both sides of the dialogue seemed to demand at least the option of rechecking.

She sat in the wing chair across from Archimedes and found the third letter from Calvin. The one he'd written in response to her using the word *love* for the first time—not just as a simple closing to her letter, but drawing direct and honest attention to the way she meant it.

She turned on the reading light beside the chair and read his response again.

August 29th, 1959
Dear Lucy,

Love. Yes. I'll happily own up to love.

Funny how you used the word love and then immediately noted that it was too soon for all that. Maybe it's too soon to know what we might be in the long run. But if two people meet and fall in love, and try to make a life together, and fail, does that mean they were wrong and there was no love? Or does it only mean that they didn't manage to carve out a space for each other?

I don't have a crystal ball, Lucy, and I know you don't either. I can't predict the future. But yes, here in the present, I agree that there is love.

Also with us in the present is reality. And the reality is that you might meet someone who can be a part of your life right now. And if that happens, I'm not going to be so selfish as to suggest you should pass up the opportunity and wait for me. Because, frankly, I'm not entirely sure what it is we'd be waiting for.

I think in time the world may change some. It already has, to some degree. My great-grandfather was subject to being sold and owned and I am not, so no point saying nothing ever changes. Whether or not another sea change will come about in our lifetime is beyond me to know.

In the meantime I do love you, and for all the right reasons.

All my love,
Calvin

She looked over her shoulder toward the kitchen, as if to assure herself that she was not being observed, before unfolding the carbon copy of her response to him. She really didn't need to read it again, as she almost could have recited it by heart. She had reread it two or three times as often as any of her other letters. But she reread it all the same.

September 9, 1959
Dearest Calvin,

I know I don't usually take so long to respond, and I hope you weren't worried about what I was thinking. But the truth is, you proposed a scenario and I didn't want to respond to it off the top of my head.

My initial response was to sit down at my type-writer and immediately write back and say, "No, of course not. I won't meet anyone else. I won't love any-one else."

But it made me remember times when I was younger and I would do such things thoughtlessly, with absolute youthful assurance that I would never feel even the slightest bit different from the way I felt in that moment. And then time would prove to me that everything changes.

Though nothing can be said with certainty, if over the years some space is created for us to be together (probably up north, maybe when Pete is old enough to live alone here with the animals, and if he is willing?), it's highly unlikely that I would already be with someone else when that window opened.

First of all, if we don't count Pete I'm by myself here. And considering my current options, I like it that way. The rest of the people who live around here seem satisfied with the arrangement as well. I really don't have a big array of new people parading through my world. It was quite an unusual moment when life brought you to my door.

But let's say for a moment that another strange turn of events brought a new man this way. My eyes have been opened to some situations. I guess it might be fair to say I woke up, which will be a difficult situation for this fictional new man to accommodate. If I were to tell him about what happened to Justin and to you, his reaction would have to be an almost perfect match for my own. Even if he were the sort of man who would never commit such overt violence, if he just had a casual and slightly callous attitude toward the thing, I would have to put him off my land.

Based on what I know about this place I've called home for a handful of years now, I'd say a reaction such as "Oh, that's a shame, but now that they're back with their own it'll be no problem" is about as good as I would get. And that's not nearly good enough.

As a result, it's a pretty sure bet that I'll be alone.

Another subject which feels tough is the fact that you are far more likely than me to meet someone, living in a big city as you are. Were this to happen, I can't say I would not be hurt. But I have thought it over carefully and decided I would not be selfish, and I would bear you no ill will. If you really love someone you want them to be happy, with you or without you if it comes right down to that. Anything less can't be real love because it's too much about self-interest.

Here's hoping for change in our lifetime, because the above would be a hard thing for me to bear. I won't give in to my nature, which tells me to act tough and invulnerable and pretend otherwise.

I'd also like to back up slightly and note that the moment when life brought you to my door might not have been entirely random and accidental. I suppose it depends on your thoughts about life. In certain moments I suspect life knows exactly what it's doing.

All my love to you,

Lucy

She refolded the letter and placed it in careful order back in the shoebox. Just as she was replacing the lid, she heard Pete's voice.

"Ma'am?"

He was leaning his shoulder against the wood trim of the living room doorway, looking bigger than he'd been when she met him. Even though it had only been three months.

"'Dr. Lucy' is better than 'ma'am.'"

"Yes, ma'am."

"What is it, honey?"

"I ran into my dad in town today."

She felt crystals of ice appear fully formed, from nowhere, coating all of her internal organs at once.

One of her deepest worries was that Pete's father would have a change of heart and want him back. In fact, she had expected it to happen by now. But there had been nothing but radio silence on that channel.

"What did he say to you?"

"Nothing. He didn't say a word to me. He was coming out of the hardware store. I had to go into town to the hardware store to do an errand for my work. And just as I'm going in, there he is coming out. And he didn't say a word. He turned his head away and acted like I wasn't even there. Or like I was just any other stranger you'd look at and then look away. But I could see . . . something. I don't know how to say in words what I saw. Kind of a jolt, I guess. A jump. Like if you touch an electric fence. We both got that jolt. But then he just acted like I wasn't even there."

She watched his face for a moment, waiting in case there was more he wanted to say. She couldn't quite read his expression. His face looked the way it always did. The way it always had, as long as she had known him. Maybe his sadness over these new events was no bigger or more powerful than the sadness he had brought with him to her door on that first day.

"Are you okay?" she asked him after a time.

"Yes, ma'am."

"You want to sit with me and talk about it?"

"Well, that's really all there is to say, I guess. I just thought I should tell you."

"Thank you. I'm glad you did."

"Except . . . I just don't get it is all."

"How he could do that."

"Yes, ma'am."

"I don't really get it, either," she said. But she knew he needed more. So she dredged up more. "I think he's probably feeling hurt. I think about it sometimes. I wonder if when your father threw you out he thought you'd be back in forty-five minutes with your hat in your hands."

"I don't have a hat, ma'am."

She almost laughed, but she stopped herself, because he might not understand the reaction. She wished again he would come sit with her, but he clearly didn't care to. He was restless, and probably wanting to remain just at the periphery of this discussion, with plenty of room to retreat.

"It's just an expression," she said. "He probably figured you had no other options for where to live. He might have been trying to teach you how much you needed that miserable home. If so, it really blew up in his face, and maybe he's hurt by the fact that you're getting along just fine without him."

"So, you're saying he loves me? Because I thought he hated me."

"I guess I'm saying it must be really hard to love someone and hate them at the same time."

She heard him breathe, even at that distance. Heard him expel air he must have been holding on to for a while.

"Yes, ma'am. I can tell you for a fact that it is."

Then, because he did not seem inclined to come to her, she stood, left the box of letters on the seat of the chair, and walked to him. He did not retreat. She put her arms around him, which was still a fairly new experience for them both.

"Thank you, ma'am," he said into her shoulder.

He broke away and ran upstairs.

She put the letters away in the closet, then sat down at the typewriter to write a new one. She had to tell Calvin about Pete's first day at school, and how she had signed him up at the new address without incident, and how Pete had run into his father in front of the hardware store.

She would not ask Calvin if he was seeing anyone new. Partly because he would not want to feel compelled to say until he was ready. Partly because she didn't want to know.

NOVEMBER 1962
THREE YEARS AND THREE
MONTHS AFTER THE BELLS
MOVED AWAY

Chapter Twenty-Seven: Pete

At the end of his school day, and after work, Pete slipped into the house, silently looking around for Dr. Lucy so he could ask her a question. He looked in the kitchen, but didn't find her. But then, through the kitchen windows, he saw her out in the backyard feeding the horses.

He trotted to the back door and threw it wide.

"Hey!" he shouted. "What're you doing that for? That's *my* job!"

She looked up. Smiled in a way that looked oddly content. At least, for Dr. Lucy.

"You come home from work so tired, though."

He jogged across the yard and ducked through the boards of the fence. It was harder than it used to be. He'd grown a lot in the three years he'd lived here with her, and he had to position his body just so to squeeze through what had gradually become a tight space.

"Doesn't matter," he said, gently removing the grain bucket from her hands. The five horses who had not yet been fed milled around him, tossing their heads and bumping him with their noses. "It's still my job."

He looked into her eyes for a moment, and she into his. And he almost asked her. But then he didn't. Couldn't, really.

"I'll get started on dinner," she said, and reached up high to give his shoulder a pat.

He watched her go and wondered why these tough moments of communication looked so easily done by other people, and why they felt so desperately hard to him.

———

In the morning, at the breakfast table, he asked.

He accomplished this partly by gearing himself up for the task before coming downstairs, partly by being careful to look away from her face as he did.

"Dr. Lucy? Did you read the paper yesterday?"

She looked up from her coffee with obvious curiosity, but he was careful to keep his gaze trained down at the table.

"Did I read the paper? That's an interesting question. I *get* the paper, as you must have figured out by now. I sit here with the paper on the table with me while I eat. I read the weather and the funny pages because the news breaks my heart. Sometimes I think I should stop taking it altogether, but then I think, 'What will I use to line the bottom of Archimedes's cage?' Why? Was there something special in the paper yesterday?"

"Maybe," he said, carefully staring at a jar of jam on the table.

A long silence fell. Pete couldn't tell if she felt inclined to fill it, because he didn't dare look at her face. Not even in his peripheral vision.

"Pete," she said after a time. It was that quiet, patient voice indicating he was being foolish. "Isn't this the part where you tell me what it might have been?"

"Oh. That. Yeah. I suppose so." His throat felt tight, but he pushed on. "Couple kids at school yesterday . . . and one teacher . . . they said my dad might've been in an accident. Well . . . I guess accident is the wrong word. More like a . . . fight, I guess. They said it was in the paper.

There was some kind of brawl at that bar in town, and a couple people got stabbed. And I guess my dad was one of them."

He braved his first look at her face, but it was too late. She had turned away sharply and risen from the table. He watched her hurry out into the living room.

Pete sat frozen for a moment, wondering what had just happened. What did it mean when you told someone a thing like that and they ran away? And what did it mean you should do next?

A moment later she reappeared, holding a section of newspaper in her hands. Pete breathed for what felt like the first time in a long while. And understood. The older newspapers were stacked on top of Archimedes's cage.

His heart beat faster as he watched her flip the pages.

"Oh," she said. And stopped flipping.

"Found it?"

"Yes."

She read in silence for a moment as his heart pounded—possibly hard enough to kill him from the feel of it.

"They told me he was alive," Pete said when he couldn't stand the silence any longer. Even though it might only have been four or five seconds.

"That's what it says here. Want me to read it to you?"

"No, ma'am," he said firmly. It surprised him to hear himself say it, and it seemed to surprise her as well. "Um. Yeah, that sounded strange, I guess. But I'm not sure my heart could take it. You know. Every little thing they wrote in there. Maybe just give me the gist of the thing."

"Okay." She tried to look into his eyes, but he didn't allow it. Her voice came out soft. Gentle, as if trying to deliver cutting truths in such a way as to leave Pete uncut. "There was a drunken brawl down at the Welcome Inn. Somebody pulled a knife. Must have been somebody who doesn't live around here, because the police don't know who it was, and nobody's been arrested. But your dad got stabbed nine times, and the bartender got stabbed once trying to pull the guy off him. He's at the county hospital in serious but stable condition. Your dad, not the bartender. The bartender wasn't seriously hurt."

"Is that good or bad?"

"Getting stabbed nine times? I think most people would agree that's bad."

"No. Not that. I know that. That condition thing at the end."

"Oh. Serious but stable. I'd have to say it's a little of each. I'll make you some cereal to save time and then I'll drive you down there if you like."

His gaze came up and bored right into hers. And he saw the pity there. The hurt on his behalf. Which, he suddenly realized, was just what he'd been trying to avoid all along.

"Ma'am?"

"What's the confusing part, Pete? I'll take you down there if you want to go."

"I can't do that, ma'am. I have work. And school."

"I think this is important enough that you could be excused."

"But I can't, ma'am."

"You can miss an hour of school. I'll write you a note."

"That's not what I mean. I can't go see my dad. It's *my dad*. I can't go near him. He won't want me to."

He looked away from her again. To avoid all that hurt on his behalf. Another long, drawn-out silence fell.

"I'm sorry if it was thoughtless of me to suggest it," she said after a time. "I thought maybe this was one of those circumstances that cancels out everything else. But that's a call you have to be the one to make."

"Yes, ma'am," he said.

She offered him bacon and eggs, since they were in no hurry now. But he chose the cereal instead, because he'd lost his appetite. Which hadn't happened in as long as he could remember. Even when he was upset he usually ate like a horse. But not that morning. That morning he forced down a bowl of cornflakes because he knew he would need the energy. But it tasted like cardboard, and he really only ate it out of need.

———

He was on his bike, pedaling from work to school, when he decided. Though, in truth, it didn't feel much like a decision. It felt as though the handlebars of the bike turned on their own. As if they chose for him.

———

He rode up to the front doors of the county hospital and glanced down at the watch Dr. Lucy had given him for his fifteenth birthday. It was twenty after nine. That brought up a panicky feeling, because he had been due at school twenty minutes earlier. He had never been late to school. It seemed unthinkable.

But it was no longer a fixable problem. It was done.

He locked his bike to a power pole out front and forced himself to walk inside. He'd always been afraid of hospitals, ever since he was four and his mom had had that operation for her appendix. Though it was nothing he could have put into words, hospitals smelled like death to him, and wore a pall of grief and loss that seemed to penetrate his skin and infect him.

He walked up to the front desk at the far end of an impossibly long lobby. It took the woman behind the counter a long time to look up. He cleared his throat lightly.

"Can I help you?" she asked. Her voice was hard like metal, her accent thicker than most in these parts.

"Bernard Solomon?" It sounded too squeaky, but anyway he had gotten it out.

"Are you family?"

"Yes, ma'am. I'm his son."

Before he averted his eyes so he would not see it, her face turned into a mask of the same pity he'd seen on Dr. Lucy that morning. He felt tears behind his eyes, but he fought them.

"Room 104," she said.

———

Pete stuck his head through the door, leaving his body in the relative safety of the hallway.

His father lay in a hospital bed with his eyes closed, a sheet pulled up to his armpits. He looked small. And old. It seemed impossible that a man could age so completely in only three years. And could his dad have gotten smaller? It didn't seem like a possible thing. Pete must have been remembering wrong.

He took four steps into the room.

Pete stood staring down at the figure in the bed, wondering why he didn't feel afraid. He had expected to feel terror in seeing his father again. Instead he only wondered how it was possible that this frail older man had ever inspired fear.

Then his father's eyes opened, and he looked right into Pete's face. And Pete did feel a jolt of fear. Old habit, maybe.

"What?" his father asked calmly.

Pete realized—from the look on his father's face, from the tone of his voice—that the old man had no idea who he was talking to. He hadn't recognized Pete yet. Granted, there had been a great deal of growing involved, but still it seemed strange.

Maybe they had him on a lot of drugs.

"It's me," Pete said.

The silence that followed felt electric. Dangerous. Dark. Pete watched his father's eyes change, and knew in some deep place in his gut that his father would be physically assaulting him in that moment if his condition had allowed.

"You've got some nerve coming here, Petey boy!" The sentence started as a low growl in his chest and ended as a full-throated shout.

"Okay. Never mind. I'll go."

"Damn right you'll go!"

The old man looked past Pete, and Pete turned to see a nurse run into the room to see what all the shouting was about.

"You get him out of here!" his father said to the nurse. "This . . . *person* is no family to me. I want him gone!"

Pete didn't wait for the nurse to take sides. He just ran.

———

Pete woke from a strange stupor to feel his bicycle wheels bumping over the gravel of his driveway. Only then did he realize he had ridden home instead of to school—not thinking, not aware of his surroundings. Just pedaling and crying.

Dr. Lucy met him at the door. She looked into his face for a long time.

"Well, that explains a lot," she said softly when it was clear he did not intend to speak.

"What does it explain?" he asked, his voice muddled by the crying.

"Your school called and said you were absent. I knew it wasn't like you to cut classes. To put it mildly. So I figured you must have gone to see your dad."

"Yes, ma'am."

"And it didn't go well."

"No, ma'am."

She stepped back from the doorway to allow him through. She held her arms out to him, but he only hurried past and ran for his room.

"Can I fix you something to eat?" she called out as he trotted up the stairs.

"No, thank you. I'm not hungry."

She didn't comment on what a huge development that was. Pete, not hungry. She didn't have to. It was a thing that spoke for itself.

———

She left him alone for a time. It might have been an hour. It could even have been two. Pete had been sitting on the edge of the bed, staring out the window at the horses. Not bothering to look at his watch.

He'd been nursing a feeling of longing. Of *missing*. But it was not his father he was missing. It was his blood brother. It was Justin. He could have talked to Justin about this. He could write to him about it, and he would. But in that moment it didn't feel the same. It didn't feel like enough.

She knocked softly.

"You can come in, Dr. Lucy," he called.

Truthfully, he'd gotten his fill of being alone. If asked, he would still claim—in simpler words—that he wanted no one's attention to his suffering. But it would no longer be a full truth.

She sat on the bed with him, her hip a few inches from his own. She did not try to touch him in any way. She also didn't speak. He found himself grateful to her for that.

The silence lasted for a minute or two.

"I always thought he'd change his mind," Pete said. "You know. Wish he could have me back."

"Yes," she said. "I thought so, too."

"Not that I wanted to go back with him. It's much better here with you. It's just . . ." For a long time, Pete didn't say what it just was. And she didn't push. "Why doesn't he want me, Dr. Lucy? What's wrong with me?"

Pete's tears began to run freely again, but nothing else changed. They both just sat there, watching the horses graze.

"There is absolutely nothing wrong with you, Pete. Not one damn thing. There's something wrong with him. I don't know him, so I can't tell you exactly what his problem is, but I think he's one of those people who can't stand to be surpassed." Then, before he could even ask, she added, "That means bested. I think he was able to be a better dad for you when you were just a little guy, and he was the big, strong one. Sometimes I think he just couldn't handle your growing up into a young man with your own opinions and a better sense of honor than his. And a big, powerful young man at that. And if I'm right about that theory, there was nowhere that situation could possibly go except wrong. Then other times I'm just glad I *don't* know the workings of that man's brain. But the problem is him, Pete. The problem was never you."

She patted him on the knee and let herself out. Left him to sort things through.

Alone with his thoughts, Pete was surprised to find that he tended to believe her. Yes, there was still a small place in his chest that would always feel empty. That would always tell him he was never enough. But that day he began to believe that emptiness a little less and believe Dr. Lucy a little more.

—

When he came downstairs for dinner she was sitting at the typewriter. Pete could hear the familiar clacking of the keys.

"Writing a letter to Mr. Bell?"

"Yes," she said, still clacking.

"Telling him about what happened with my dad?"

She stopped typing. Turned to look at him over her shoulder.

"I was. But maybe I should have asked you if that was okay."

Pete let that situation turn in his brain a couple of times.

"Yeah. It's okay. If it was anybody else it wouldn't be. But it's Mr. Bell. So it's okay."

MARCH 1966
SIX YEARS AND SEVEN MONTHS
AFTER THE BELLS MOVED AWAY

Chapter Twenty-Eight: Dr. Lucy

Dr. Lucy sat at the breakfast table, drinking coffee and catching up on a week's backlog of morning papers. Or perhaps it would be more accurate to say she was flipping through the papers. Looking for an article of interest but not finding it. Yet.

Then her eyes landed on just what she was looking for. But after reading the first paragraph, her brow furrowed with disappointment.

She stopped reading. Sighed. Looked up.

Pete was staring into her face. He had actually paused in the process of shoveling scrambled eggs into his mouth, which evidenced a surprising amount of concern.

"Thought you never read the paper," he said.

She wondered if it was possible that he really hadn't noticed her change of habit in that department in the last couple of years, since she and Calvin had started following the case together.

She wasn't answering, so he added, "I thought you just read the funny papers and the weather and then used it to line Archimedes's cage."

The skin on his face looked red and a little raw from his recent shave, and his long, slightly shaggy hair had been slicked back, wet looking, to appear presentable at his latest full-time job. It was a Saturday, but he still worked a morning shift.

"I didn't use to," she said. "But Calvin and I are following a legal case together. *Loving versus Virginia.* Have you heard anything about it?"

"No, ma'am. Not as I know of. But I know it must be worth following if you and Mr. Bell find it so interesting. So tell me about it, so I know."

"Okay. Well. Let me see how I can compress this. There's a couple. A married couple. The husband is white and the wife is Negro and Indian. They're from Virginia, but they left the state and traveled to the District of Columbia to get married, because it's illegal in Virginia. Just like it is here in Texas. Then they went home and promptly got arrested. This was something like 1958, I think. They've been forced to live outside the state all these years. But they want to go home. They have family there. So they've gotten the American Civil Liberties Union to take up their case. That's a group that defends people's rights. Calvin and I have been a bit hopeful about it. Well. Guardedly hopeful, I suppose. Sometimes I feel like I'm just setting myself up for a fall, and that nothing will ever really change. This morning, for example. This morning is one of those times."

She gestured toward the article.

"What does it say?" Pete asked, his brow imitating her own.

She dropped her eyes to the article again and scanned quickly.

"It's disappointing, but it's not *all* bad. The Virginia Supreme Court of Appeals upheld the state's antimiscegenation laws. That's the bad part. The good news is that the court also set aside the original conviction. Of the couple, I mean. It said a sentence requiring the defendants to leave the state is 'unreasonable.'"

"But you were hoping they would make it legal."

"Yes."

"But we don't live in Virginia."

"I know. But sometimes case law is like dominoes. One law falls in one state and other people in other states can cite that decision to challenge the remaining laws. I'm not saying it'll happen anytime soon, or even that it will happen at all. Just that Calvin and I have been following it."

Letting ourselves hope, she almost added. She recalled a time when not letting herself hope had been something of a specialty of hers. But that seemed so long ago now.

"Know what I like best about that case?" Pete asked, sounding upbeat again. Or at least as though he was trying to be. "The name. *Loving versus Virginia.* Usually those cases have these legal names that don't really mean anything and you can't even remember them. But this one . . . this one is so . . . honest. Like they're just flat-out admitting that it's loving that Virginia is trying to fight against."

Dr. Lucy smiled. To herself, and a little sadly.

"Actually, that's the couple's name. Mildred and Richard Loving."

"Really? So it's just a coincidence?"

"Yes, but I agree with you. The name of the case is one of the best parts of the whole thing, coincidence or not."

"Is it all over now? And they lost?"

"Probably not. It'll probably go all the way to the Supreme Court. Which doesn't mean they'll hear it. Or decide it well. But anyway, Pete. It's after eight. You'd better get going."

His eyes flickered to the clock, and he quickly slurped the last of his coffee.

"Oops," he said, and darted away from the table.

Dr. Lucy returned her gaze to the paper and began to read the article word by word from the beginning. Maybe there was some other scrap of positive news she had missed.

"Dr. Lucy?"

She looked up to see Pete's groomed-for-work head peering at her around the kitchen doorway.

"Yes, Pete?"

"If they do decide that case right, and the laws change, would you and Mr. Bell get married?"

She sighed. She wondered, as she gathered herself to answer, if her face looked red to him. It felt a little flushed to her.

"I don't know, Pete. I don't know if that's what he still wants. It's been so long. Things can change. People can change. He might have met somebody new by now."

"Wouldn't he have told you?"

"That's a hard thing to tell somebody."

"Couldn't you just ask him?"

"Yes," she said. "I suppose I could."

All the times she'd almost asked him slipped through her mind, an unintentional loop of memories. The letters she had typed—carbon copies and all—then balled up and thrown in the trash. The sentences begun on the phone and never finished.

"Problem is," she added, "then I'd find out."

—

Once Pete was safely out the door to work, she took down the shoeboxes of Calvin's letters, and found the very first one. It wasn't hard, because she had continued to keep them in order. She knew the letter had to do with faith in the world—that ever-tenuous subject—and so allowed herself to believe it would help her that morning.

She sat in the wing chair, brushing aside the jungle of tendrils of the overgrown "Calvin Plant," and removed the letter from its envelope. The paper had yellowed with age and the creases had grown fragile from folding and unfolding.

August 4th, 1959

Dear Lucy,

It was such a delight to speak with you on the phone today, even if it was only a quick call to let you know we'd gotten in safely. I wish I were a rich man. I'd call and talk for hours. If I can find work and when Justin and I are no longer staying with family, maybe a short call is a luxury I'll be able to afford once a week or so. I hope I'm right about that.

I thought about you a lot on the bus. I was watching people. Watching the world. I made a set of observations that kept bringing me back to you. I wasn't doing it on purpose, but I couldn't help watching the masses of humanity in public bus stations, and on the buses themselves, and noticing how people automatically divide themselves up. Or maybe it's not automatic, I don't know. Maybe it's something we learn at a young age without even realizing it. And I don't only mean dividing into black and white, though certainly that's a big part of it. But it seems even more basic at its core. Public accommodations divide people into money and no money. And unfortunately black and white follow a fairly predictable pattern within.

I try to take the world as it comes, Lucy. I wonder if you've noticed that about me. But I have to say it's a face I put to the world that, while certainly not phony or false, is not without its cracks.

I began to get discouraged on the bus. I began to lose faith in what kind of world we live in. I wanted it to be a place where I could stay in Texas with you, harm no one, and live my life. But it's not. It's a world in which my son was beaten for doing nothing more heinous than being a friend. But then I thought, it's also a world where a pretty woman doctor sewed him back up and tended to him lovingly and didn't even want money in return.

That's a lot to do for someone, Lucy. You rescued my faith in the world.

I guess the world will always be like this. I suppose we're built with complete free will, and as much as we're capable of depravity, to the same degree we are wired for greatness. Everyone gets to choose, I think. And my challenge is to decide where I'll place the bulk of my attention. What I'll most believe in.

I mostly believe in the lovely lady doctor who saved my faith in people.

Please write soon.

Love,

Calvin

She refolded the letter and put it away, noting that it hadn't helped much. It had only filled her with still more doubts as to whether the emotion they'd shared could survive so many years of crushing distance.

———

She arrived home from the market at two thirty that afternoon.

Pete came trotting down the stairs when he heard her come through the door.

"Mr. Bell called," he said.

She found her insides torn between disappointment at missing the call and fear that something was wrong. He didn't call often, because it was hard to afford it. For both of them.

"Did he say why?"

"Yeah. He said his father died. He just wanted to talk to you."

"Thank you," she said. "I'll call him right now."

She dialed the number by heart and listened to nine rings, each echoing in an empty pit of her belly—a soft spot that hurt right along with Calvin.

No one answered.

No matter how many times she tried the number again over the weekend, it always turned out the same.

She thought several times of getting in the car and driving to Philadelphia, though it would have taken a solid two days at the least. But she felt unable to make such a move without first knowing for sure she was wanted there. Her thoughts on the matter kept taking her around in a circle and leaving her nowhere.

Another part of her life that always turned out the same.

———

His letter arrived several days later.

March 12th, 1966

Dear Lucy,

This has been a heartbreaking week for our family. I'm sure Pete gave you the message. I'm sorry if I missed your return call, but there were so many arrangements to be made.

It was very sudden. He had a heart attack when no one even knew he was having trouble with his heart. If he'd been feeling poorly he never said.

Justin is deeply grieved. He looked up to his grandpa. Just about everybody who knew him well did. He wasn't a perfect man. He was a little rigid sometimes in his thinking and didn't always express affection easily. But he was a deeply principled man with a great sense of integrity. I know you would have loved him, because I modeled myself after him in many ways. You would have seen a lot of me in him and the other way around.

That leads me to my deepest regret in all of this: You will never meet him.

Sometimes when justice is not close at hand, people are quick to tell you that you will simply have to wait—that until the people standing on your neck feel more comfortable standing elsewhere, you have no choice but to be patient. They talk of this like it shouldn't be all that much of an inconvenience for you. But how do you hand a person back the time that was taken from him?

Very real losses are happening while people wait.

Sorry to end on a down note, but it's hard to sound cheerful in the wake of your father's death.

I love you, and that's a bright point in all of this.

Calvin

She held the letter in her hands for several minutes.

He loves me, she thought.

Not that he didn't say so often. Not that she hadn't known. It was more that she had begun to lose track of *how* he loved her. Of course they had been through a lot together. And of course there was love. But they no longer talked about making a space for that love, or whether the love had a future in a world that continued to begrudge them the space.

—

She would call him several more times in the two days that followed, and eventually reach him. But when real losses are happening, and there's nothing you can do to restore them, it's hard to know what to say.

DECEMBER 1966
SEVEN YEARS AND FOUR MONTHS AFTER THE BELLS MOVED AWAY

Chapter Twenty-Nine: Pete

It was a Sunday morning, early, and colder than most for this part of the world. Even for December. Pete was preparing to give the horses their morning feeding. If nothing had distracted him, he soon would have moved on to letting the dogs out for a good run.

But something did distract him.

The door of the shed was open again. Not wide open, but distinctly ajar. It was the fourth morning in a row he had found it that way. The last three times he had assumed the fault was his own—that he had failed to properly latch it closed the night before. This time he knew he had been careful.

He walked over warily, hearing the dogs whining and hitting the wire fencing behind him. He pushed the door wide and looked in. Just like the previous three mornings, there was nothing out of the ordinary inside the shed.

He quickly fed the horses and opened all the run gates to let the dogs out. Then he stuck his head into the kitchen to see if Dr. Lucy was awake. She was, and she looked up from an empty skillet she had just set on the stove. Smiled at him.

"Dr. Lucy? Have you been going into that shed for any reason?"

"No, I let that be your territory these days. Why do you ask?"

"Because every night I make sure it's closed. And every morning I find it open. For the last four days this's been happening."

"Hmm," she said. "That seems strange."

It struck Pete that she sounded a little like Justin in the way she said it, and that she might have picked up the expression from him.

She followed Pete out into the yard. The dogs milled around them, and jumped up, hoping to involve the humans in their play.

"I do think I might have left it open the first night," he said. "But after that I was real careful."

"That latch hasn't been very good for as long as I can remember. It's not lined up quite right anymore. I think a good push would be all it takes, no matter how carefully you think you closed it."

They both stuck their heads inside the shed. There was one small, high window that let in a slant of early morning light. Pete could see their breaths blow out as clouds of moisture in that beam of sun.

Dr. Lucy walked inside and over to a stack of folded drop cloths on the concrete floor. She ran her hand over the top of the stack, then looked closely at her palm in the slanted light.

"Some kind of animal fur," she said. "Something's been sleeping in here."

"Something wild, you think?"

"I don't know. Could be. Stray dog, maybe? You said it's been happening for the last four days. And that's when this cold snap started."

"Wouldn't the dogs bark, though? If some strange animal came around? They can see the shed from their runs."

"Hmm," she said. She pulled to her feet and dusted off her hand against her apron. "That does make it a bit of a mystery."

But she didn't stay around to help him solve it. She walked back into the kitchen to resume the making of breakfast. Pete was hungry, as usual, so he didn't argue or complain.

"I could put a hook and eye on that door," he said. Then he shoveled another oversized bite of pancakes into his mouth while he waited to hear her thoughts.

"I hate to see you do that. Seems like we're here to help animals, not keep them out in the cold."

"I was thinking that, too," he said, his mouth still mostly full. It was a habit he tried to avoid in her presence, but some things needed saying right away. "Depends on what it is, though. If it's a wild animal . . . you know, one that was dangerous to the horses, I'd want it out of here. Especially with Smokey being so old and now lame. Just what he doesn't need is a coyote or something that thinks it lives here."

"Coyotes are pack animals. And the dogs would have a fit if one got near. I don't know. I leave it up to you, Pete. You're a humane boy. Or . . . man. I'm sorry. Of course you're a grown man now. You do what you think is best."

—

Pete sat up on the edge of his bed, looking out the window into the dark yard. Waiting. It was nearly ten o'clock. Pete knew he had to be up early to get his chores done before work, and on any other night he would have been asleep. His eyes drooped, but he refused to give in.

The moon was fairly strong, almost directly overhead and a little better than half full. If an animal came along, he'd at least be able to see the size and shape of it. He'd at least know if it was an animal to lock out or take in.

A few minutes later he saw a movement near the woods. Something was walking down. A dog. Dr. Lucy had been right. It was a stray dog. Big, and with enough of a coat that Pete wondered why it couldn't keep warm on its own. But it was heading toward the shed, walking gingerly, as if stiff or sore.

The dogs and horses had no reaction. Pete could see the horses were still asleep, standing with their heads down, or resting on each other's backs, and the dogs were silent enough that Pete could believe they never had wakened.

When the new animal reached the carefully latched shed, it reared up and hit the door with its front paws and the weight of its upper body. The door swung open a few inches.

Pete jumped up and pulled on his heavy boots and his coat with the hood. He found a flashlight in the kitchen pantry and turned it on, following its beam through the cold yard.

Be careful, he told himself silently. *Desperate animals can be dangerous.* Dr. Lucy had taught him that, and taught him well, so he could live here safely.

He stood at the open door of the shed and wrapped his hand around the knob, prepared to pull it closed and hold it closed if he felt threatened. He shone the flashlight inside. On the stack of folded drop cloths curled an animal that was anything but unfamiliar or new.

"Prince," he breathed out loud.

Only then did Pete realize that part of him had already known. Or at least, known it was a possibility. But it was a thought Pete had kept from himself until he saw for a fact it was true.

Prince winced into the light and thumped his tail audibly against the cloths. Pete turned off the flashlight and waited a few moments to give his eyes a chance to adjust. Then he stepped inside, watching for any signs of the wolf-dog's defensiveness. But Prince only thumped.

Pete sat down in the corner, a foot or two away, and wrapped his arms around his knees.

"Prince, what are you doing here? We haven't seen you in ages."

Prince thumped, but—of course—did not otherwise explain.

"I asked Dr. Lucy a million times why you never come around. When I was thirteen she told me she figured you must know I was okay now. That you watched out for me when you knew I was scared and in trouble, but then when you knew I was fine you went off to live alone."

Pete could see the steam of the wolf-dog's breath, and just enough of the animal's eyes to make him ache. It was all so familiar. He reached out one hand, carefully, and let the wolf-dog sniff it. Then he stroked the rough fur of Prince's head. It was a gamble, and he knew it. If Dr. Lucy had been there, she would have warned him to go slowly. But the shed door was still standing half open, and Pete could not—would not—believe that Prince would do anything worse than to retreat. Prince did not retreat. He held still and breathed steam and allowed Pete to run his hands over his neck and back and sides.

"You're too thin," Pete said, shocked by the prominence of the ribs under the wolf-dog's thick fur. "You must not be getting enough to eat out there. You want something to eat?"

Pete rose and turned on the flashlight. Then he made his way through the cold yard and back into the kitchen, where he opened two cans of dog food and spooned them into a mixing bowl. He carried the meal out to the shed.

His plan had been to set it down and back away, but he immediately thought better of it.

"No," he said out loud. The wolf-dog cocked his head, listening to Pete's voice. "You need to come into the house. It's still too cold out here. I'm going to get your old bed out of the garage and put it down in the examining room. That's a place you ought to know well enough. And you're going to follow this food inside. That's just the way it's going to be. You hear me?"

Pete prepared himself for a nightlong struggle as he spoke those words. Prepared to tempt Prince along one inch at a time, possibly without success. Instead the wolf-dog simply pulled stiffly to his feet and followed the meal into the house.

By the time Pete had found Prince's old bed in the garage and carried it in, Prince was done eating and had settled, sphinxlike, on the linoleum floor, licking his chops.

Pete didn't wake Dr. Lucy. He felt bad asking her to miss sleep, and maybe scaring her. Besides, it wasn't really an emergency. Prince was fed, and warm, and wasn't going anywhere until morning.

Pete laid the big dog bed down on the floor and stretched out on one side of it, prepared to sleep. A few minutes before he drifted off, he felt Prince circle three or four times before settling on the pad beside him.

———

"Well, I'll be damned," he heard Dr. Lucy say.

Pete opened his eyes, blinking into the light, not awake enough to speak.

"I wondered why your alarm was just ringing and ringing and you weren't turning it off."

Pete sat half up, and Prince raised his head and looked at Dr. Lucy but did not tense or retreat.

"Guess who's been sleeping in the shed?" Pete asked, his words softened by sleepiness.

"It crossed my mind who it might be. But I hated to get your hopes up, just in case I was wrong."

Pete shook off sleep as best he could and looked carefully at the wolf-dog in the strong morning light.

"He must be sick," he said. "He doesn't look good."

"He looks okay to me."

"But his fur is all dull. And his face looks . . . I don't know how to say it."

"Old?"

Pete didn't answer, because he was busy trying to sort out his impressions.

"He's old, honey. I'll give him a complete exam if you like, but I had him figured at four or five when you first brought him here. So he must be something like twelve by now. At least. And that's old for a dog."

"But he's too thin. You can feel his ribs sticking out."

"Maybe he doesn't hunt as well as he used to. You have to be fast to catch game in the wild."

"Please give him the exam and make sure he's okay, Dr. Lucy. I'm not sure he's okay."

"Fine. I will. I'll make up a bowl of breakfast for him with some tranquilizers in it, and then we'll see what's what."

———

"He seems fine to me, honey," Dr. Lucy said.

She had Prince stretched out on his side on the table, barely conscious. Every now and then Pete could see the wolf-dog's eyes flicker slightly.

"This reminds me of the first day I came here," Pete said.

"I was just thinking the same thing. I'm going to draw some blood while we have him out. But his temperature is normal, and his heart sounds great, and his eyes are clear and good for a guy his age. We might want to test him for parasites if we can get hold of some of his stool. But mostly he's just older, and his joints are inflamed. So he's probably not hunting as well as he used to, and the joint inflammation makes him want to stay warm, and the lack of calories makes that harder . . ."

"What's joint inflammation? Why does he have that?"

"Just a fancy way of saying arthritis, honey. We'll all have that to one degree or another if we're lucky enough to live so long."

He watched her prepare a syringe for a blood draw, but then looked away as she pushed the needle through the skin of the wolf-dog's front leg.

"So should I just keep him in?"

She looked up and met Pete's eyes. The idea he'd proposed must have seemed nonsensical to her, based on the curiosity in her face.

"He has to go out sometime."

"Why? It's good and warm in here."

"He has to go to the bathroom, to phrase it gently. He has to get whatever exercise he can."

"Oh. Right. But maybe he'll just go again and not come back."

Pete waited, but she said nothing. At least, not for a time.

"That's another one of those areas where I won't advise you," she said at last. "You're a grown man. Nearly twenty. You have the best interests of this animal at heart, and you always have. I've done my part, the medical part. I'm going to leave the rest of it up to you."

———

Pete stuck his head into the examining room on his way out the door to work.

Prince was lying on his side on the dog bed. When he saw Pete he promptly sat up and looked deeply into Pete's eyes.

"Oh, you're awake. Come with me."

Pete walked to the back door and opened it. The morning had turned nicely warm, but with a crisp feel. Pete looked back, but Prince had not followed.

"Dr. Lucy?" he called upstairs. "I'm leaving the back door open for Prince. I figure he's eaten here twice, so he knows where to get a meal and a warm bed if he wants them."

"Good call," he heard her say.

Then he patted his wolf-dog on the head and went off to work.

———

It was nearly six before Pete got home.

He ran into Dr. Lucy in the hallway—almost literally—as he barreled through the door.

"What happened? Did he go?"

"Yes, he let himself out sometime in the morning."

"Oh," Pete said, trying to hide his disappointment.

——

Barely half an hour later, as he was feeding the dogs in their runs, Pete turned to see Prince standing behind him, nostrils working the air for the smells of food.

"Good to see you, boy," Pete said, blinking back surprising tears. "I'll make you up a bowl. Come on into the house. You'll eat in Dr. Lucy's examining room from now on."

——

Pete sat cross-legged on the floor watching Prince bolt down the food, and felt his chest fill with something unfamiliar. A sensation he could not recall. It felt like a confidence in things. The normally empty chest space seemed to surge with the sudden notion that losses can be restored—at least some of the time. That things can turn out, long after you had accepted that they never would.

He wanted to share the sensation with Dr. Lucy, who seemed to need a feeling like this one, but he didn't think he could. Partly because he could never have wrapped words around the feeling, but also because Dr. Lucy had been disappointed by the world a lot.

If Pete was wrong, and her losses were never restored, he didn't want to be the one to blame for foolishly raising her hopes too high.

JUNE 1967

SEVEN YEARS AND TEN MONTHS

AFTER THE BELLS MOVED AWAY

Chapter Thirty: Dr. Lucy

Dr. Lucy sat drinking coffee and staring at the morning paper folded on the kitchen table. She could feel herself purposely postponing getting up and washing the breakfast dishes, which Pete had dutifully rinsed and left in the sink before trotting upstairs to get ready for work. Not for any special reason was she stalling. She just couldn't muster much energy, and inertia was having its way.

She rose, poured a fresh cup of coffee, and unfolded the paper. There on the front page, above the fold, was a photograph of Richard Loving with his arm around his wife, Mildred. Around her neck. Her eyes went first to the photo, then to the first line of the article.

With little stabs like cold needles in her belly, she began to read.

"The US Supreme Court has unanimously ruled that Virginia's antimiscegenation statutes violate the Constitution's Fourteenth Amendment. The decision effectively overturns the bans on interracial marriage in sixteen states."

Unanimously.

That word echoed in her cloudy head before she could read on.

"Chief Justice Earl Warren's opinion for the unanimous court held that: 'Marriage is one of the "basic civil rights of man," fundamental to our very existence and survival . . . To deny this fundamental freedom on so unsupportable a basis as the racial classifications embodied in these statutes . . .'"

Dr. Lucy stopped reading and dropped the paper.

"Loving won," she said out loud.

The energy that had previously evaded her coursed through her body and her brain like electricity. She grabbed up the newspaper again and ran upstairs calling Pete's name.

"Pete!" she shouted for the fourth time as he stepped out of the bathroom doorway.

"What? What's wrong?"

He towered over her, as always, his face mostly covered in shaving cream, a safety razor clutched in his right hand.

"Nothing. Nothing's wrong. Everything's wonderful. Look!"

She handed him the paper. He took it with his left hand and moved his lips as he read. Then a smile broke onto his face.

"What's 'unanimous' mean?"

"It means every single Supreme Court justice agreed."

They stared at each other for a moment, smiling. Then she ducked in for an embrace.

"Don't get shaving cream on yourself!" he said. But he needn't have bothered. Because her head only came up to his collarbone. "Aw," he said, the hand still holding the paper wrapped around her back. "I knew they'd decide it right. Didn't you?"

She stepped back. Looked up into his face.

"No," she said.

"Really?"

"Yes. Really. I'm so used to the world breaking my heart, I guess I just expected it to keep on as usual. Oh! I have to call Calvin!"

She trotted down the stairs to the kitchen and dialed his number by heart. But the phone only rang. Seven rings, then eight. Then nine. She glanced at the clock over the stove. Five minutes after seven. He should have been home. It was an hour later there, and he didn't leave for work until 8:45. But a tenth and then an eleventh ring went by, each dropping lower into her gut, mirroring the high of the news with corresponding deep lows.

What was a moment like this without Calvin to share it with her?

She hung up the phone.

A moment later Pete appeared at the bottom of the stairs, clean and shaven and combed and ready to leave for the day.

"What did he say?"

"Nothing. He's not home."

"Oh. Well, you'll talk to him when he gets home from work."

"Yes," she said. "That's true."

With much effort, she reset her internal clock for five thirty and prepared to hold on to her elation in solitude until then.

———

Five thirty came and went. Then six. Then seven thirty. And nine p.m. And still the phone only rang.

"Still not getting him?" Pete asked before going to bed.

"No. And I'm starting to get worried."

"About what?"

And that was a very good question. One she did not feel prepared to answer off the top of her head. Any answer she could imagine contained information she might not have been willing to share with Pete at all, over any time frame.

"Nothing could have happened to him," Pete added when she didn't answer.

"What makes you say that?"

"Because Justin would have let us know."

But something could have happened to both of them, she thought.

And yes, she knew, that was possible. But it was not the most likely scenario. A deep, sickening feeling in her gut had identified the most logical cause of his sudden absence. He had heard the news, too. Of course he had. It was on the front pages, on the television news. He knew. Wherever he was, he knew.

He must not have wanted to celebrate with her.

Maybe he didn't want to talk about what was next for them. Maybe he didn't want that anymore.

Maybe he was even with someone else after all this time.

"You really look worried," Pete said. "Relax. Something came up that he had to do or something. You'll get him in the morning, and then he'll tell you where he's been."

"Yes," she said. "Of course. You're right."

—

But Pete was not right.

In the morning, the phone still just rang. Neither Calvin nor Justin was there to tell her where they had been. To still the voices in her belly.

The ones that were so used to having their hearts broken by the world.

—

"Oh, you're home," she said.

She had walked into the kitchen to find Pete standing in front of the refrigerator eating a leftover chicken drumstick. That part was not a surprise. He always came home from work famished, and he always raided the refrigerator for a snack to tide him over until dinner.

She just hadn't heard him come in.

She couldn't shake the sense that he had been slipping around quietly that day. Almost the way he did when he was avoiding her. Or avoiding *something*.

"Yes, ma'am," he said, not meeting her eyes.

She had not been able to train him to call her anything but "ma'am." She had given up the fight years ago.

"Have you tried to reach Justin?"

"Justin?"

"Yes. Justin. I think you remember who that is."

"Oh yes, ma'am. I remember him all right."

"Have you talked to him?"

"Talked to him?"

"Something's not going quite right with this conversation, Pete. I've been asking you for the better part of two days if you've talked to Justin or if you know anything about where he is, or where his father is. At first you didn't seem to know any more than I do, but now you're being more than a little . . . vague."

Pete grabbed a paper napkin from the holder on the kitchen counter, then laid it down flat and set his drumstick on it.

"I'm not sure what the word 'vague' means," he said.

He began to wash his hands in the sink, which conveniently turned his back to her.

"Hazy. Not definite. Shouldn't you wash your hands *before* you start to eat?"

"Yes, ma'am. And I did. But then when we were talking I looked down at my fingernails and decided I could do better."

She walked to his side, leaned over the sink, and purposely stared directly into his face, which involved quite a bit of looking up. He cut his eyes away.

"If you know something, I'd appreciate hearing about it, Pete. I'm worried about them."

"Oh, you shouldn't worry," he said, sounding far too definite.

"Aha! So you do know something!"

"No, ma'am," he said, drying his hands on a dish towel. Still avoiding her eyes. "I don't know anything. You ought to know that about me by now. I'm always the last to know. Just . . . don't worry."

"I'm about to get a crowbar and pry this out of you, kid."

"Oh, please don't, ma'am. You know how hard stuff like this is for me."

He grabbed up his chicken and hurried out of the room.

A moment later he stuck just his head back in. His hair was shaggy and long, so different from the way he'd worn it in the '50s under his father's thumb. Everything about him seemed to have naturally relaxed.

"Here's what I was thinking, though," he said. "If you're worried, you know what might help? Fix yourself up a little. You know. Do your hair up nice and make up your face. Just . . . you know. To feel better."

Then he disappeared again. And Dr. Lucy smiled, alone in the kitchen. And stopped worrying.

Mostly.

———

It was about a quarter after seven that evening when she heard the knock on the door, and knew.

Pete ran breathless down the stairs.

"I wonder who that could be?" he asked. Unconvincingly. Comically so.

"Give it up, kid," she said. "You'll never be an actor."

She walked to the door, painfully managing her expectations. If she was wrong in what she was thinking, it would be a long fall.

She opened the door.

"I wasn't wrong," she said out loud.

He was almost eight years older. Well, of course he was. So was she. But on him it came as more of a surprise, because she saw herself every day. His closely cropped hair had gone to gray at the temples, and she couldn't decide if it was premature or not. Probably not. She had to remind herself that he was getting on closer to fifty than to forty and so was she.

The line of scar was gone from his lip. The skin around his eyes showed additional creases, a reflection of how much more he had seen.

One step behind him stood Justin as a young man. He was as tall as his father, and broomstick thin, with a calm, knowing face.

She was unable to contain her smile. Then again, she didn't try.

"Loving won," Calvin said.

"So I heard."

"Did we manage to pull off the surprise?"

She glanced over her shoulder at Pete, who looked noticeably relieved. Even more relieved than thrilled.

"I knew he was holding on to something. But I never quite got it out of him."

She stepped back from the doorway, and Calvin came in. She instinctively stepped forward to embrace him. But before she could, he dropped to one knee.

Tears sprang to her eyes immediately.

"Oh my." The two simple words came out a hoarse whisper.

She looked past him to Justin, who was still standing on her welcome mat, smiling. When she looked down again, Calvin had opened a small black-velvet ring box and was holding it up for her to see. But the tears blurred her vision.

"Lucille Armstrong," he said, "I've come here to ask you to accept this simple ring and enter into an engagement to marry me. I know that may sound like a strange way to phrase a question, but here's my thinking: Under normal circumstances two people spend a great deal of time together and then decide they're each the right person for the other to marry. But we had that time stolen from us. So I'm asking you to begin an engagement in which we'll take that time back. And the end goal, of course, will be to marry. Which, by the way, is legal in this state!"

She laughed out loud, and her reaction cracked his demeanor into a smile.

"And all the others," she added.

"I don't know where we'll marry or where we'll live, because it's not the sort of thing I'd even begin to work out without hearing your thoughts. In fact, I don't know much more than I did all along, except that it's time to ask this. But before you answer, before you say anything, I just have to say one thing. You know it, but I have to say it all the same. Changing the laws of a country is not the same as changing its hearts and minds. This might not be much easier than it would have been all along. It might even be danger—"

He never managed to finish the word. Before he could add the final syllable, she placed her hand firmly across his mouth.

"Calvin," she said, pressing tightly. "Dear, sweet Calvin. Will you please stop talking for a split second so I can say yes?"

—

She wandered downstairs around bedtime and sat next to Calvin's legs on the couch. She did not turn on the light. She half expected to have to gently wake him. Either that or settle in and wait.

But apparently he hadn't fallen asleep yet, either.

"Everything all right?" he asked quietly.

He reached a hand out and she took it and held it.

"I need to tell you something," she said.

"Okay."

"It's something of a confession."

"I'm listening."

"I have to tell you this, and then you'll tell me if you still want to marry me."

He braced his other hand behind his head to prop himself up slightly. As if to better see her face. But it was dark. She was glad of that.

"I'd bet money there's nothing you can tell me that will make me not want to marry you, but if you think you've got something that bad, then go ahead and give it a try."

"Before I knew you . . . I needed money to take care of all these animals. There were more of them back then. Some of the wild ones had been able to go back into the wild before you met me, and some of the domestic ones I found homes for. At the height of the thing it was much more than my alimony would cover."

"Right. I remember you said you had to get creative to cover those costs."

"Yes, that. So . . . what I used to do was . . . I'd get these referrals. The desperate kind. I'd put guys back together without asking any questions about how they'd ended up apart in the first place. In other words, I knew they'd done something against the law. But I didn't say anything. It was partly for the money. Well. Mostly. Ninety percent. But also I was mad at this town and all the people in it for being so closed-minded about a lady doctor. I guess I felt like I didn't owe them much. And I was still furious at the world for taking my son away."

A brief silence. But she wasn't afraid. Because she was holding his hand. Nothing had changed. She could feel that it hadn't.

"I can relate to being mad at this town," he said. "And being furious at the world. Why did you stop?"

"I was more or less forced to stop. It really wasn't because I came to my senses or anything. Well, I did. I did come to my senses. But with help."

"And how did you feel when you were forced to stop?"

"A little scared about money. And also incredibly relieved."

"There," he said. "See? That's a nice healthy conscience at work. Is that really all you've got?"

"That's the worst of me, yes."

"Well, then I'm sorry. You'll need to do better than that if you want to get out of marrying me. Now try to get some sleep."

"There's another thing," she said. "But it's not a confession. More of a worry."

"I'm open to hear whatever you've got."

"When I first took Pete in, he asked how long I'd take care of him. I said until he was old enough to take care of himself. At the time I was thinking along the lines of eighteen. But eighteen came and went, and I still don't really think of him as old enough to take care of himself. I'm not slighting his abilities. If he wanted to be on his own I'd support him a hundred percent. But he's making no move to leave. And I never pushed, because I'd miss his company. He works a full-time job, so I'm not suggesting he's refused to step up to the responsibilities of adulthood. Then again, you know Pete. He never met a responsibility he didn't like. But living alone is another matter. I never told you this, because it's the kind of thing you keep to yourself until you know how it's going to play out, but I had a plan that when Pete was eighteen I'd ask him to live alone here and care for the animals so I could come to Philadelphia. That is, assuming you still wanted me there. But I couldn't bring myself to do it. I just can't picture Pete living alone out here in the middle of nowhere. I think he'd be miserable. I planned it again for nineteen, but long before the birthday came around I knew I didn't have the heart to do it."

She paused. Stalled, really. Waited to see what he had on his mind.

"Then we'll stay here," he said.

"It'll be hard here."

"It'll be hard everywhere. We'll work it out."

"Yes," she said. Followed by a little smile that felt sad. "I suppose we will."

She didn't move. Or speak, at least for a time. Then she said, "I'm not sure why you're down here and I'm up there."

"Because we have plenty of time. The rest of our lives."

"Yes," she said. "I suppose that's true."

She walked to the stairs. Stopped. Looked back at Calvin.

Then she walked back upstairs and did not sleep.

Chapter Thirty-One: Pete

Pete sat on the edge of the bed, staring out the window at the woods, and the moon over the trees, and the horses sleeping peacefully on their feet in the pasture. He listened to Justin rattling around in the bathroom getting ready for bed.

A moment later the light went dark in the bathroom, and Justin came in and sat on the edge of the bed with Pete, and bumped him with his shoulder.

"Nothing ever changes," Justin said.

"You mean like you brushing your teeth for six minutes?"

"No, I mean that." He pointed out at the moon hovering over the backyard and its calm herd. "That plant got huge," he said.

Pete knew Justin was referring to the plant in the living room. The one Mr. Bell had brought Dr. Lucy as a cutting before he'd gone back up north. It had more than filled a corner of the living room in eight years, and Dr. Lucy never seemed to have the heart to prune it back.

"Yeah. She fusses over it a lot. Waters it just so. Gives it plant food. Lately I've been saying, 'Hey, Dr. Lucy, you sure that plant needs food?

Seems like it wants to take over the house as it is.' She just says the bigger it gets the happier she'll be."

They sat in silence a moment, staring out at the yard. Not needing to speak.

Then Justin said, suddenly, "Oh. Wait. Where's Smokey?"

Pete squeezed his eyes closed, and his mind filled with a clear image of the gray Thoroughbred gelding. The one they had ridden most often.

"I was afraid you were going to ask that. He died a couple months back."

"Oh no. Of what?"

"Old age. He was twenty-six when we used to ride him. Thirty-four when he died. Turns out that's why he was the best one to ride. He was already old. I should have told you. I thought about it every time I wrote you a letter since then. But I was kind of broken up about it and I didn't want to be the one to have to tell you."

A long silence fell. Pete felt compelled to break it.

"Your voice got really deep. Somehow I wasn't expecting that. I knew you got bigger and taller and grew your hair out because I saw pictures. But I forgot your voice would change. I hope you know why I never tried to talk to you on the phone when Dr. Lucy called your dad or he called her. I hope you know it's not that I wouldn't have liked to talk to you."

"I figured you wanted to save the time for them."

"Right. It was really important to her. Anyway, I guess I'm talking a lot, probably because I have this thing on my mind and I'm halfway trying to avoid it. But I can't avoid it forever. They shouldn't get married here, and they shouldn't try to live here. They should go back up north."

"Probably so," Justin said, clearly not knowing where Pete was heading with this.

"So I have to stay here alone and take care of the animals so they can be happy. So they can go where they need to go. I don't want to. It's scary to think of living here all alone. But she deserves this. So I'm just going to do it anyway."

"That's a nice thing," Justin said.

"It's just what has to be. After all she's done for me."

Justin patted him on the shoulder and then got up and walked around to his own bed. His bed for the night was a twin-sized mattress on the floor, which Pete had hauled up from the garage. As soon as the guest room had become Pete's room, nearly eight years earlier, the second bed had only gotten in the way.

"Oh," Justin said. "That's interesting."

Pete looked around to see that Prince had settled his old bones on one corner of Justin's mattress while they were looking the other way.

"Prince," Pete said. "You have to go back to your own bed, boy."

"No, not really," Justin said. "I mean, not if he's willing to share."

Pete watched as Justin arranged himself into bed without disturbing the wolf-dog, who had one eye half open, watching to see if he was about to be ejected. When it was clear he could stay, he closed the eye again and sighed.

"It'll be like a wedding present for them," Justin said.

"What will?"

"What you just said you would do."

"Oh. That. Right."

It hurt a spot in Pete's stomach to think about it again. But he couldn't put it out of his head. In fact, it made it impossible to sleep for what felt like most of the night.

He lay awake thinking of all the times he'd heard Dr. Lucy say her time with Calvin had been stolen from her, and absorbing that he felt a little bit the same way about Justin. Here Justin was grown, and—other than a couple hundred letters, which hadn't felt good enough—Pete had missed eight years of his brother/friend's life.

And in a couple of days Justin would go away again.

Everybody would.

———

"Pete," Justin whispered. "Are you awake?"

Pete was pretty sure he hadn't been. But he was unused to sleeping with anyone in the room with him, so the quiet voice startled him awake.

"Um. Yeah. I think so. What?"

"What if you weren't alone here?"

"Who else would be here with me?"

"Maybe . . . me?"

Pete sat up in bed. The moon was down, the room dark, and it took his eyes a moment to adjust. When they did, he could see that Prince was still curled tightly in one corner of Justin's mattress.

"You?"

"Yeah. Why not? I'm nineteen. I can go off on my own. I've been looking for work. Why not look for work here?"

"But you're afraid of it here."

"Yeah. I was just lying here thinking about that. About how when I was a kid if something scared me I wanted to stay as far away from it as possible. But now I'm not a kid. And I want to be braver."

"So you'd live here? And help me take care of the animals?"

"Yeah. What do you think? Is it a stupid idea?"

"No, it's a great idea!"

"Good. We'll tell them in the morning. It'll be like a wedding present from both of us at once. But you have to tell Dr. Lucy you were going to do it anyway, even if you were going to be here all by yourself. If you don't tell her, I will. Because that's the best present of all right there."

Chapter Thirty-Two: Dr. Lucy

Before getting on the train, Dr. Lucy hugged Pete twice, then Justin for an extra-long time while Calvin hugged Pete, then Pete again while Calvin hugged his son a second time.

"You better get on the train, ma'am," Pete said. "It's about to go."

"Call me if you have trouble with anything."

"Like what?"

"Like anything you find yourself trying to do."

"Everything I'm about to do I've been doing since I was twelve, ma'am."

"I was thinking about things like paying the light bill or turning off the gas in a storm or maintaining the car or . . ."

But then she couldn't think what else.

"Fine," he said. "I'll call. Now you need to get on the train and stop worrying and go be happy."

"We won't be away forever," Calvin said. "Give it some time. We'll see."

Pete kissed Dr. Lucy on the cheek.

Then she felt a slight tug at her hand as Calvin gently pulled her toward the boarding stairs.

They stepped up onto the train still holding hands. It was a radical act, and she knew it. But she didn't feel cowed and she didn't consider letting go. They moved along the aisle to the next, less crowded, car, Calvin slightly behind her to accommodate the narrow space.

She watched the faces of the people they passed. Each person looked first at Calvin and then at her, or the other way around, then at their linked hands, then away.

One older man with an angry face and a buzz cut did not finish by looking away. Instead he looked back into Calvin's face, his emotions forming a brick wall that he seemed to challenge them to break through.

They quietly cut around him and kept walking, and no further challenge was issued.

She looked to her right to see Justin and Pete moving down the platform with them, waving through the windows. She waved back.

They found two seats together in the next car, and sat, she in the window seat, Calvin on the aisle. Still holding hands. She blew the boys a kiss as the train began to move.

"Did we raise them right or did we raise them right?" she asked Calvin quietly.

He laughed lightly.

"Is that funny?"

"Not exactly. I agree. I just liked the way you said it."

"I shouldn't take credit for Pete, though. He was a great kid the first day he turned up on my welcome mat."

"You helped him stay that way, though."

"Am I worrying too much?"

"I have no idea, Lucy. I don't even know how much *I* should worry. I would never try to draw that line for somebody else. But they're just as suited to make their way in the world as anybody else's boys. I think they'll be okay."

—

They sat in the dining car, finishing up their dinner with coffee and watching the sun set behind a rolling and changing horizon.

Now and then she stared at the ring on her finger.

"I'd have bought you a fancier one if I could have," he said.

"It's perfect. Don't even say that again." She placed the left hand with the ring lightly on top of his hand, and continued to stare at it. "What I can't figure out is how you even had time for ring shopping. You got here so fast after the news."

"Oh, I bought that ring months before the Supreme Court decision. I would have asked anyway at some point."

They sipped in silence for a moment. The buildings of a small city rose to block her view of the setting sun. But what city, she didn't know.

"I've been thinking about everything you told me when you walked through the door," she said. "There's only one part I take exception to. I know there's a lot of trial by fire that two people have to go through. But I think the years we were forced apart showed us a lot about how we'll do under pressure, and so I just don't know what we would be waiting for. I think we should get married more or less when we get off the train."

"Then that's what we'll do," he said.

"That was easy."

"The engagement idea was more for you. I wondered if maybe a woman needs more time to familiarize herself with the physical presence of a man."

"Which is why you slept on the couch last night."

"Yes."

"That won't be a problem for me."

They enjoyed their coffee in a satisfied silence for a time.

"The boys will feel bad they missed the wedding," she said. "That's the only thing."

"How about this: We have a small civil ceremony at the courthouse when we get to Pennsylvania. Then when we decide to try going back to Texas we'll have a reception or renew our vows, and they can be there. They'll understand."

"I think that works."

She looked up to see an older woman, dining alone, staring at them. Not looking or glancing. Rudely staring. She had white hair all done up in beauty-parlor style, and a high collar that made her whole being appear starched. Dr. Lucy stared back, and the woman cut her eyes away. Calvin glanced over his shoulder to see what the trouble might be. But there was nothing left to see.

"Maybe I'll go back to practicing medicine," she said.

"If that's something you'd enjoy, I'm all for it."

She looked up at the woman again. She was, again, staring.

"Would you excuse me, please?" she asked Calvin.

She marched over to where the woman was sitting and flopped into the seat on the other side of her table. Then she rested her chin on the heels of both hands and stared directly into the woman's face.

"What on earth are you doing?" the woman asked. She had the voice Dr. Lucy might have expected. High. Tight. Artificial.

"I'm doing exactly what you were doing, so you tell me."

The older woman rose, huffed audibly, and flounced out of the dining car, leaving the rest of her dinner uneaten.

Dr. Lucy walked back to her own table and sat down across from Calvin again.

"It might pay not to get too upset every time," he said. "If you can help it. You know. Save your energy."

"Upset? Who's upset? That was the most fun I've had in years."

—

The rocking of the train car soothed her, but did not put her to sleep. She sat staring out the window into darkness, listening to the rhythmic clack of wheels on rails. She didn't know if Calvin was asleep or not, but his eyes were closed, one arm hooked through hers.

A strange feeling sat, twisting slightly, in her stomach.

It took her a few minutes to realize she was afraid.

She couldn't shake the feeling of the train hurtling into darkness, speeding her to a place entirely unknown and impossible even to see. Everything in life would be new. Everything familiar lay behind her. And still she was utterly committed to go there. Wherever "there" was.

She nursed the feeling for two minutes, or twenty. It was hard to tell.

Then Calvin spoke quietly.

"Penny for your thoughts," he said.

"I was just thinking how scary it is to leave everything behind and head out for a completely new life and not know anything about how it's going to be. I wasn't really thinking about it so much as feeling it. I was just sitting here feeling it."

He cleared his throat lightly. Moved his hand down to enclose hers.

"How much of a problem does it seem to be?"

"Oh, it's not a problem," she said. "Not at all. I've been hiding from the world for too long as it is. Not everything that scares me is a problem."

He squeezed her hand and smiled. And, in time, let his eyes drift closed again.

She stayed awake, feeling herself hurled into the unknown. And breathing deeply. And allowing it.

BOOK CLUB QUESTIONS FOR

SAY GOODBYE FOR NOW BY

CATHERINE RYAN HYDE

1. By choice, Dr. Lucy closed her medical practice and moved to an isolated Texas ranch far away from people and places that remind her of the past she left behind. How does her isolation from society affect her interaction with the other characters? How do her relationships with the other characters change the person she becomes?

2. Dr. Lucy spends her days rescuing and caring for abandoned and injured animals and doctoring criminals on the run to help pay for her sanctuary. Do the ends in this situation justify the means? Is breaking the law ever a sanctified act?

3. Pete finds an injured wolf-dog at the side of the road. Despite the apparent danger and hardships involved, he manages to get the dog to Dr. Lucy for care. What does this say about Pete's character? How would you have

handled this situation at his age? What might you have done differently?

4. After Pete and Justin become friends, the whole town, including Pete's father, turns violently against the interracial friendship. But the boys continue despite the threats. Do you agree with the choice they made? Would the violence against Justin have happened regardless of the decision they made?

5. While Justin is recovering, Calvin spends the weekend at Dr. Lucy's, and to both of their surprise, despite the dangerous circumstances, they form an easy and comfortable connection. Why do you think these two people from such diverse backgrounds were drawn to each other? How does the topic of marriage drive the plot of the story?

6. After his son is beaten, Calvin is framed for a fight and thrown in jail by the local police. How much do you think racism has changed since the 1960s in this country? Do you think the criminal justice system truly sees no color, or is race still a defining factor?

7. Pete forms a strong bond with the wolf-dog. After Prince recovers, Pete must make the decision whether or not to release him back to the wild. Dr. Lucy and Calvin form a strong bond and must decide whether to stay together or let go of the relationship in hopes that it can continue at a later date. How does love play a part in letting go in both relationships?

8. At the end of the book, Calvin and Dr. Lucy are reunited after the Supreme Court ruling regarding the *Loving v. Virginia* case. Why do you think the author based the story around a true court case? How did it impact your reading of the story?

9.   After Prince returns in his old age, Pete thinks, "It felt like a confidence in things. The normally empty chest space seemed to surge with the sudden notion that losses can be restored—at least some of the time. That things can turn out, long after you had accepted that they never would." What emotion is Pete trying to describe here? How does that emotion become an underlying theme for the main relationships in the book?

ABOUT THE AUTHOR

Catherine Ryan Hyde is the author of thirty published and forthcoming books. Her bestselling 1999 novel *Pay It Forward*, adapted into a major Warner Bros. motion picture starring Kevin Spacey and Helen Hunt, made the American Library Association's Best Books for Young Adults list and was translated into more than two dozen languages for distribution in more than thirty countries. Her novels *Becoming Chloe* and *Jumpstart the World* were included on the ALA's Rainbow List; *Jumpstart the World* was also a finalist for two Lambda Literary Awards and won Rainbow Awards in two categories. More than fifty of her short stories have been published in many journals, including the *Antioch Review*, *Michigan Quarterly Review*, the *Virginia Quarterly Review*, *Ploughshares*, *Glimmer Train*, and the *Sun*, and in the anthologies *Santa Barbara Stories* and *California Shorts* and the bestselling anthology *Dog Is My Co-Pilot*. Her short fiction received honorable mention in the Raymond Carver Short

Story Contest, a second-place win for the Tobias Wolff Award, and nominations for *Best American Short Stories*, the O. Henry Award, and the Pushcart Prize. Three have also been cited in *Best American Short Stories*.

Ryan Hyde is the founder and former president of the Pay It Forward Foundation. As a professional public speaker, she has addressed the National Conference on Education, twice spoken at Cornell University, met with AmeriCorps members at the White House, and shared a dais with Bill Clinton.